PSION
OMEGA

OTHER WORKS BY JACOB GOWANS

Psion Series:

Psion Beta (2010)
Psion Gamma (2011)
Psion Delta (2012)
Psion Alpha (2013)

A Tale of Light and Shadow:

A Tale of Light and Shadow (2014)
Secrets of Neverak (2015)

PSION OMEGA

By

Jacob Gowans

For Kat,

and Lily,

and Jake,

and Asher,

and Cal-L,

and Mom and Dad,

and Shannon, Becky, Rosalee, and Adam.

And for you.

They went with songs to the battle, they were young,
Straight of limb, true of eye, steady and aglow.
They were staunch to the end against odds uncounted;
They fell with their faces to the foe.

They shall grow not old, as we that are left grow old:
Age shall not weary them, nor the years condemn.
At the going down of the sun and in the morning,
We will remember them.

They mingle not with their laughing comrades again;
They sit no more at familiar tables of home;
They have no lot in our labour of the day-time;
They sleep beyond England's foam.

–"For the Fallen" by Laurence Binyon

PSION
OMEGA

Tuesday, November 11, 2087

A BITTER STENCH emanated off Sammy and Jeffie's clothes and hair. Scents that would never wash off. Mingled with the smells of death—blood and urine and other things, worse things—it was all unbearable. On Sammy's left, a dying Hybrid moaned, the sound of its last breath rattling in its throat. Jeffie put a bullet in his head, and the sound stopped. Then she limped to Sammy and squeezed his gloved hand tightly, and Sammy returned the gesture.

They sat on the floor of a room that had once been as white as a blank sheet of paper. Now the stains of blood, brain, and other bits of human that were supposed to stay inside the body covered the walls, floor, and their zero suits. Sammy wished he could enjoy the quiet a little longer, but he knew what was coming—who was coming.

"What do you think is happening out there?" Jeffie asked with a tremor in her voice that told Sammy she was fighting back tears. "I hope it's working. I don't—don't want it to be for nothing."

Sammy glanced at the time on his com and licked his lips, but his tongue was too dry to offer any moisture. "Are you ready?"

Jeffie took a breath that seemed to stretch on for minutes. She was tired to the core. Sammy could feel it too, deep in his bones. But they weren't done yet. The time was almost ripe.

"No, not really," she answered. "But I can't say that, can I?"

So much depends on us.

Jeffie rested her head on his shoulder. Sammy stroked her hair and kissed her forehead. "I'm sorry," she said. "I'm fine … I promise."

"I know you are."

"I'm ready—really, I'm ready." She wiped her eyes and nose. "How much time do we have?"

"Twenty minutes."

"How are you so calm?"

Sammy wasn't calm. He was exhausted, yet some reservoir of restless energy made him twitchy. He dreaded what was to come, but deep down sensed his own resolve… and acceptance. He pulled her closer and savored her. *How many of these moments do I have left?* Perhaps none. With his mouth close to her ear, he whispered, "I'm terrified."

Jeffie hugged him fiercely and began to shake again. "I don't want—"

"Shh," Sammy told her. "I know. It's okay. You can go back. You don't have—"

"I do!" she shouted. "I'm not letting you do this alone."

"I can do it by myself. If I just use it—"

"We can't risk failure. Two of us increases the odds by—"

Sammy let her go. "I know all that. I'm just saying …"

"Then stop saying." Jeffie regained her composure quickly. "I'm all right."

"Okay."

"Are you, though? Remember your promise, Sammy."

A flash of rage passed through Sammy, but he suppressed it and let it go. Releasing the rage was like watching a train pass by and observing the faces inside, frightening, monstrous, and alluring all at the same time. He was getting better at doing it. *Makes no difference now, does it?*

Not true. It makes a difference to her. "I remember."

Sammy checked his watch again. *Nineteen minutes.* Then they would finish it. Finish it all.

And at the end, if everyone did everything correctly, Jeffie's fears would be realized. They would die.

1 | History

Thursday, March 13, 2053

"I PLEDGE MY loyalty to the flag of the New World Government. And to the welfare and advancement of mankind, for which it stands, one world, united and indivisible, with freedom and justice for all."

"Take your seats," said Mrs. Hepworth in her strained, croaking voice, "and set your desk screens to lecture mode. I won't tolerate any messaging during class today. Understand, Katie?"

Katie Carpenter blushed as her classmates glanced at her, some with glee, others with condolence. Just yesterday she had been written up for messaging her friends during Mrs. Hepworth's lecture on the Industrial Revolution. Immediately her desk screen lit up with messages from her four best friends.

Priyanka Patel: Heppy hates you more than she hates her anti-wrinkle cream.

Vivian Wu: Why does she single you out?

Courtney Marzban: What a stupid [censored] [censored]!

Rachel Linn: Can't stand that moled cow.

Katie winced at the names they'd called her teacher, but then hurried to clear the messages before Mrs. Hepworth caught her and froze her desk. Unfortunately, she wasn't quick enough. She tried to swipe them away, but nothing moved. Katie grimaced as she slowly brought her gaze up from the screen to her teacher's face. Mrs. Hepworth's wrinkled, sagging cheeks turned red as she glared at Katie. The redness highlighted her moles like big black ants on a red picnic blanket.

"You," Mrs. Hepworth's voice sounded more strained than ever as she stared Katie down. "And you, Miss Patel, and you, Misses Marzban, Wu, and Linn … all of you will serve detention today and tomorrow with me."

Katie rolled her eyes and looked out the window. *This place is a prison.* She hadn't done anything wrong. It was her friends who had sent the messages. *Except Mrs. Hepworth is too bitter to see it.*

Courtney's auburn hair practically glowed from the sunlight streaming in through the window behind her. The gleam caught Katie's eye.

"Sorry," Courtney mouthed to her.

Katie didn't respond. Behind Courtney, a flock of geese flew above the tree line. They went wherever they wanted. No one stopped them. No one put them in detention. *I am less than a goose.*

She yawned and rubbed her eyes, then rested her head and arms on top of her desk while Mrs. Hepworth droned on about how royalty in England affected the Industrial Revolution. Katie's eyelids felt heavy. She hadn't slept well lately. Dark nightmares haunted her. She wanted to talk to someone about them, but couldn't. The school counselor would tell her parents. Her parents would make her see a therapist. Her friends would think she was a freak. And if people thought she was a freak, her chances of winning Prom Queen for the third year in a row were over.

Last night's dream had been the worst yet. Katie had taken a bath in blood, human blood. She knew it was human from all the bodies lying around the basin—faceless corpses that looked like crash test dummies. Then she'd been transported to a forest in the dead of night. She walked a few steps forward, wet leaves squishing underneath her bare feet, sinking between her toes, the soles of her feet uncomfortably cold.

You can be free, a voice said in her dream.

Katie paused and looked around until she saw a shadow, so faint and thin she almost didn't notice it. The shadow belonged to her, but it didn't behave as shadows should. It had a three-dimensional form and the closer it drew the more detail she observed. The shadow stood next to her, walked alongside her. Every time she moved, it followed. She tried to run away, but the shadow stayed with her step for step. Finally Katie had no more breath to run. Gasping with her hands on her knees the shadow stepped in front of her.

Don't run from your destiny.

"What is my destiny?" she asked breathlessly.

To be the greatest. The Queen of All.

"What do you mean?"

You were born to be free, not in chains. Free yourself in the cave.

Katie took her hands off her knees and stood up straight. The shadow was exactly her height, looked exactly like her, but all in black. When it smiled with its black teeth and black eyes, Katie screamed and woke.

When her history class ended, Katie grabbed her bag and walked up the aisle to her teacher's desk. Mrs. Hepworth pretended not to notice her until the other students had left the room. "What can I do for you, Miss Carpenter?" she asked without looking up.

"I don't deserve detention."

"Oh, you don't?"

"No. I didn't write those things. I tried to erase them. I can't control the actions of my friends."

"You can't?"

Katie found Hepworth's answer-questions annoying. "Are you serious? Of course I can't."

"You are the reigning prom queen, Miss Carpenter. You started a film club. You are on the varsity basketball squad. You organize the pep rallies. You have more friends and admirers than some B-list celebrities. You know that. Everyone knows that. That makes you a leader. You influence other girls. The way they talk, think, act ... all of it stems from you."

"I didn't tell them to say those things!" Katie protested.

Mrs. Hepworth finally looked at her with an expression of utter loathing. "Was I born yesterday? Miss Carpenter, I became a teacher because of people like you. People who think they're superior and special simply because they have a gift for athletics, a clear complexion, straight teeth, the right clothes, or a symmetrical face. It's bad enough to watch you diminish girls your own age, but to put me down … in my own classroom … *I think not.*"

"You're right," Katie responded. Her frankness made Mrs. Hepworth pause. "The things my friends wrote were rude. But I didn't write them. I don't say those things about you. And I don't treat other girls badly."

Katie's last two statements weren't entirely true. She *had* said rude things about Mrs. Hepworth to her friends. In fact, she'd said nasty things about all her teachers at one time or another, even the ones she liked. But those comments stemmed from frustration, not malice. As for the other girls in her class, she only despised the girls who despised her. She hadn't started any gossip wars; she ended them in brutal fashion.

"Katie, you rule this school like a queen whether you see it or not. You will serve detention. You will take responsibility for your influence over your friends."

"What if I can get my friends to do something good?"

"Like what?" Hepworth fixed Katie with a skeptical look.

"I don't know. I haven't thought of anything yet."

"If you want out of detention, you'd better impress me."

Katie nodded. She glanced at her teacher, then quickly looked away. Seeing all those moles on her teacher's face up close made her sick.

"By the end of the school day," Hepworth added.

Katie hurried to find her friends. They had to come up with something good. Anyone who received five days of detention or more was ineligible for prom queen, and Katie had already served two. The two detentions Hepworth had just assigned would put Katie dangerously close to five.

Her next class, Home Tech, was her favorite: sewing, cooking, woodworking, and repairing small appliances. Her parents had suggested she take it to learn valuable "life skills." Katie instead signed up for Intro to Nursing, but got squeamish when told they'd have to volunteer at a nursing home and change elderly people's diapers. Her Home Tech teacher, Mr. Cooley, caught her and her friend, Priyanka, at the door two minutes before the bell.

"Did you bring the knife?" he asked.

Katie nodded and dug in her backpack. "My mom will kill me if she finds out I borrowed it. She won't even tell me how much it cost."

"That's because they're so expensive." Mr. Cooley gasped dramatically when she showed it to him. "Look at this elegant grip. Balanced shank and cutting point. Perfectly tuned cutting ability. Pulsing‧wavelengths render the laser incapable of cutting human flesh, but slices through any fabric … like butter."

He turned the device over in his hand, groaning and admiring it the same way Katie and her friends would a particularly handsome celebrity. Priyanka glanced at Katie with wide eyes and mouthed, "What a freak!"

"I'm going to test this out," Mr. Cooley continued, "show it to my department head and see if I can fit one into our budget for next semester." He lowered his voice. "You'll pick it up after school, right? And even though it's not a weapon, do not show it around. You could—maybe, potentially, possibly, and *probably*—get in trouble."

Suddenly Katie was pushed from behind. A massive figure walked by holding a hat above his head. "Bobby John loves you!" he called out as he waddled down the hall, laughing hysterically.

Mr. Cooley leaned past Katie and Priyanka through the doorway so he could yell, "Watch where you're going, Bobby John! You almost hurt somebody!"

"Ew," Priyanka griped, "Bobby John touched me. He's so gross!"

Several other kids around Katie and Priyanka laughed, but this gave Katie an idea. She knew exactly how she could get out of detention.

* * * * *

Saturday, April 26, 2087

In the conference room of the fox's penthouse, the holographic images of several men and women appeared around a large table. At the head sat the Queen, glowering at them. They represented some of the most powerful individuals in the CAG, each deeply ensconced in government, media, or business. For over three decades, the fox had collected them, a group known only as the Council.

The Queen wore a zero suit as she sat in the middle of a hologram projected around her body. The zero suit prevented her body from interacting with the hologram, letting her move freely and undetected so long as she didn't break the holographic cylinder the projector cast around her. To all cameras trained on her, she looked like the fox. The microphone she used transformed her voice into the fox's by using sound wave manipulation. She'd now performed this ruse successfully for over three months.

"You forget an important point," said Julia Navarre in her typical terse tone. She served as Chief of Staff to President Newberry, leader of the CAG. Her focus was on the Chief Operating Officer of CAG's largest media group, America Media Network, who had argued that the public was tiring of war coverage. "Your time spent advocating the cause is far more effective than anything the President's administration can do alone. It has to be together with the three-pronged effort we have long advocated."

"Polls show our goals are currently not within reach," a CFO of a giant banking corporation stated. "Public opinion—"

"Polls are no reason to waiver in our commitment," the Chief of Staff responded. "They rise and fall like the tide. Ignore them."

"Ironic, those words coming from a politician," said another media mogul down the table.

"Yes, we knew the war would be unpopular," the COO of America Media said in a drawling, almost bored voice, "but this data is detrimental. Despite our efforts, the public believes the war shows no sign of ending. We need to consider other options in case public support continues to plummet. Perhaps we could give the enemy a face."

"That is an intriguing idea," the Queen agreed. "People want a villain to hate. Is there someone we could turn over to the media?"

"It won't matter," said the man at the other end of the table. "It certainly won't stem our dropping support."

"Such a pessimistic view," the Queen said in the fox's voice. Using her incredible memory, she mimicked the fox's tones and mannerisms to perfection. The holograph surrounding her duplicated her movements. "I do not think the war is likely to last longer than a few months. Since the attack in San Francisco, we've increased clone production, fortified our factories against insurgent attacks, and have crippling offensive strikes planned by the end of next month. The war could be over by the end of May, I think."

"The NWG forces have shown more resiliency than you initially believed, fox," the CFO stated flatly. "What makes you think you're not underestimating the enemy yet again?"

"Let me remind you," the Queen responded coldly, "that *our* plans were not built on guesses. You know better. What some of you are experiencing, I think, is unfounded buyer's remorse. We will win this war if we stay the course. Once we win, the public will be forgiving as we usher in an era of peace, stability, and prosperity unlike anything they have ever seen. Newberry will be re-elected for life, if we wish it. Businesses loyal to our cause will prosper while the rest fall by the wayside."

Around the table several nodded their heads in agreement. The Queen noted the few who did not. "Meeting adjourned," she announced.

Despite all her experience with the fox, she had no idea he spent so much time in meetings: meetings with the Council, meetings with the CEO of N Corp, meetings with so many puppets and yes-men that some days they never seemed to end. The fox had transformed himself into nothing more than a shadow, but everyone who knew him was a string attached to his fingers.

Even I was a string.

The Queen deactivated the hologram and stripped from her zero suit. Naked, she left the room and crossed the penthouse. She paused at a mirror to examine her reflection. Her eyes found no wrinkles, no noticeable sag anywhere. Despite her fifty years in age, she looked like a woman in her twenties. More importantly, she felt like a woman in her twenties. She stared closer, making sure her beauty wasn't a trick of the light.

Turning her back on the mirror, the Queen went to the smallest of the three bedrooms. Voice, thumb, and eye verifications were required to enter. Once it opened, she heard the beeps coming from monitors surrounding a hospital bed. Confined to the bed was a man, talking to himself again, mumbling something she couldn't quite hear. All she caught was the word *parameters*.

"Do I need to remove your vocal box too?" she asked in a sweet voice. "It would be a pity. I do so enjoy our conversations."

The fox's thighs ended abruptly in short fleshy stubs. Instead of arms, he had a few centimeters of lumpy, pink masses that ended five centimeters beyond the shoulders. The Queen had performed the amputations herself. He had been awake while she did it. He had been given no anesthesia. The surgery had been a glorious event. Liberating and beautiful.

Years ago, he had been her savior, her mentor, her lover. She had adored him with a reverence she'd shown no one else. He'd treated her like a treasure. While all the other Thirteens and Aegis had been made to drink the *solution*, the Queen had not. He'd given her a unique freedom, and she'd soared like the phoenix she always imagined herself to be. Then she made a single mistake, and he took her freedom away. He made her drink the bitter cup. That act had been unforgivable. She stepped next to the bed and surveyed his pitiful body while his eyes rested on her face, cold in fury, but impotent.

"The meeting went well," she told him. "A few have doubts, but I set them straight. The war will not end as soon as they hope, but it will not last as long as they fear, either."

The fox smiled. "Doubts will undermine you, Katie."

Before he could say another word, the Queen grabbed a scalpel off the bedside table and held it to his face. "Call me Katie again and I'll do so much carving that you'll make Diego look handsome."

"My apologies, but I stand by my statement. Doubts are diseases. You must eradicate them with swift and extreme prejudice."

"I have taken care of it. The Council is strong."

"Not without me leading it."

The Queen laughed. "You *are* leading it."

"How long?" the fox asked after a notable pause. Pain filled his eyes. "How much longer will you keep me like this? You don't wish to kill me, I think, yet you don't trust me. What options remain?"

The Queen's laughter turned into rage. She bared her teeth at him. "Until you learn what it means to be imprisoned. You have no idea what you did to me by making me drink the solution." She grabbed his nose and twisted it until it nearly broke. "Don't you get it?"

"Then end it. You'll never have to worry about me again." He took a deep breath and sighed as though even living was a chore. "Take the scalpel and draw it across my neck. Do it now."

The Queen already had a scalpel in hand when she noted his use of voice inflection. Crippled, grotesque, and unable to move anything but his head, the fox could still be persuasive. "You taught me too well to recognize the subtleties of your talent," she said as she set down the blade.

"It must be torture for you," the fox continued. "The Anomaly Eleven is different for everyone. For some it makes them mathematical or literary geniuses. Others tactical. For me … it lets me read people and manipulate them to near perfection, I think. But what about you? What does it do for you?"

The Queen did not answer.

"Has Anomaly Eleven restored your ability to feel emotions? If so, what has it been like to feel revulsion, remorse, fear, and joy again for the first time?"

A tear threatened to fall from the Queen's eye, but she pretended as though she had an itch there, and scratched it away. When the fox noticed this, the corners of his mouth twitched. "Don't be ashamed of your emotions. They make you stronger. The pain, the fear, the regret …"

"Shut up," she whispered.

"Embrace the remorse," the fox said softly. "Listen to your conscience or it will torture you. I have begun to do the same. I've realized now that I was drunk with power. Thinking that I could change and save humanity. Let's end this mad—"

Laughter burst from the Queen's gut. She hadn't laughed so hard in weeks. It felt good. She laughed hysterically at the fox and his foolishness. *How did I ever think you were anything but a fool?*

"You mentioned torture … I can only imagine what torture you're experiencing," she told the fox. "Your quality of life is forever diminished. It must be maddening. And to think that it all could have been prevented by simply asking for my forgiveness. Such a thought must be like a splinter in your mind."

"The cave." The fox said the two words very simply, but they jarred the Queen's mind and spirit. Her head jerked back to look at him.

"What cave?"

The fox's eyes told the Queen that he knew she was lying. Every few nights she dreamed the same dream. She stood at the bottom of a cave at a door made of stiff, rotting flesh. She beat on it, tore at it, but nothing would make it open. No matter how much she or the young girl on the other side of it screamed and shoved, it would never budge.

"You cry out in your sleep," the fox stated in a perfectly even tone. "Have you been experiencing bad dreams?"

"Are you experiencing phantom pain in your missing limbs?"

"Not at the moment. But I do. Sometimes it becomes so intense that I shiver and tremble because all my mind wants to do is itch and rub the spots, and it can't. And sometimes, more often than you would think, I forget that I can't move at all."

The Queen shivered as she experienced a distant, faint version of what the fox described. A trickle of hot discomfort ran up her spine to her neck. She pulled at her collar. The fox observed this passively.

The pains are getting worse. They had started the day she removed the fox's arms and legs, a mild but real aching in her own limbs each time she cut and he screamed.

"What is going on in your head?" the fox asked her. "Tell me. What harm can I do?" He laughed weakly. "I certainly can't walk away or plug my ears."

Again he inflected his voice. He did it so masterfully that the Queen wanted to confide in him. Yet he had to know she was aware of this. *What game are you playing?* He was no stranger to her innermost thoughts, but she recognized the danger of letting him have influence over her. *I'll give him a small amount of information just to see how he uses it.*

"I have begun to feel pain again. My body is growing accustomed to it, however."

"I told you before of the great irony associated with the Anomaly Thirteen. The Thirteens think their resistance to pain and most emotions is a strength, but now you see that is not the case. Your mind must also learn to cope with fear that comes from a realization of mortality."

"I have no fear," the Queen responded.

"Perhaps you never will. Who am I to say? I have never been a Thirteen."

The Queen had heard enough from the fox. She left the room and turned off the light. As she closed the door behind her, she stared at the fox, a lump of wasted flesh. A small stitch of pain grew in her chest. She slammed the door shut to the fox's room. *Not again. Go away!* Even with her eyes squeezed tightly shut, she saw the faces again in the dark recesses of her mind. Dozens of faces. Thanks to her Anomaly Eleven, she recalled each face perfectly.

She recalled them because she had killed each one. She could even match the faces to the methods of execution she had employed: guns, bombs, knives, acid, drowning, strangulation, electrocution … If she focused on one person too much, the sensations returned.

Yes, her body, her mind, something inside her wanted her to feel this remorse, this empathy, this primitive, pathetic emotion, but she would not. Instead she smiled and pictured herself killing them, reveling in their blood and death.

I am stronger than you think, fox. The Queen gritted her teeth and walked onward. *Ignore anything long enough and it will go away.*

Work needed to be done. She still had to find Sammy and the resistance before they caused any more problems. Even as she walked away, her thoughts went to the fox; to his wretched body. His mutilated form. The pain started to blossom again. Before it could gain any traction, the Queen found a tube of cream that she kept in a drawer in her bedside table. The tube had only one word printed on it: *Fire.*

She squeezed some of it onto a gloved hand and applied it to her thighs and calves. Her breaths turned ragged as the warmth crept into her skin, growing in intensity like an electric stovetop. As her legs burned, the emotional torment dissipated. In the height of the agony, she got up and stumbled out of the room. It was time to get back to work. She could not waste precious moments on petty feelings. The fire would purge them from her.

It was almost two hours before the effects of the cream fully wore off, but the Queen's sense of clarity returned. *Sammy.* He was the goal. She needed everything on him. Every scrap of data, video, idea, theory, or thought the fox had ever collected on the boy. Nothing could go undetected or overlooked. Where the fox had failed, she would succeed. The amount of data collected on him was impressive.

Know thine enemy.

Hours into the research, her attention went to Sammy's days in Rio, particularly the days he'd spent in custody, and under the care of the man Sammy had called Stripe. She watched the recordings, paying careful attention to the things he muttered and moaned during his most agonizing moments. Then she viewed them a second time. During one of the pain sessions, there was an interruption. A second Aegis barged into the room talking about how another prisoner was ready for extraction.

Extraction. What does that mean? Why have I never heard it before?

After hours of searching through video and transportation files, she discovered that orders for extraction from Diego were always followed by a delivery to Mexico City. Not to the Mexico City Thirteen cell like she expected, but to a different building.

What are you hiding there, fox? What happened to the prisoners— the anomalies—who were extracted? Was it the fox's fancy term for death? Did he take their DNA? She tried to shift her focus back to Sammy, ·but the problem gnawed at her brain. She dug deeper, examined the data closer, but the answers still eluded her.

* * * * *

Thursday, March 13, 2053

Mrs. Hepworth studied Katie with disdain as Katie returned to her classroom after school. Katie tried her best to ignore it and slid into the chair nearest to Mrs. Hepworth's desk. Hepworth tapped her fingers on the wooden surface in front of her, her lips twisted as though she'd sucked on a lemon.

"So?" she asked with her eyebrows tickling her widow's peak. "What brilliant plan did you come up with to save your bid for prom queen?"

Katie took a deep breath and began. "Okay, so I wanted to do something that would be meaningful and make a difference to people. You know, like something to change lives, but I didn't know what to do until I saw Bobby John."

"Mmm hmm … " Katie noted the mixture of disbelief and curiosity in her teacher's tone.

Bobby John was one of the eight kids at school with special needs. Everyone knew Bobby John because of his old, tattered, red Razorbacks cap that he lifted off his head every time he passed a girl in the hall. Sometimes, between classes, he walked to and from class with his hat hovering above his head the whole time, a large smile on his face as he nodded to each girl.

"Bobby John loves you," he'd say to every girl with whom he made eye contact.

"I asked Bobby John to be my date to prom," Katie said.

"Ah—" Mrs. Hepworth didn't finish what she planned to say. Clearly she hadn't expected this. Her mouth hung open and her eyes wandered over Katie's face as though they'd never met.

Katie took this as an invitation to continue. "And I asked my friends to invite the other special students. I've seen those kids get bullied and teased. Hopefully that won't happen anymore if they're seen with, you know, my friends. Plus … everyone deserves to go dancing for one night, right?" She flashed Mrs. Hepworth a hopeful smile.

Mrs. Hepworth cleared her throat and turned her face away from Katie and wiped her eyes.

"Are you okay, Mrs. Hepworth?"

"Fine," the older woman croaked. She cleared her throat a second time and then faced Katie with a smile. "You know why I hated school so much, Katie?"

"Um, homework?"

"No, I actually liked homework. Try again."

Katie grew braver and ventured the answer she believed to be true. "Your moles?"

Mrs. Hepworth actually laughed. "They didn't develop until I was in my thirties. It was Marybeth. My little sister. She suffered from Trisomy 21. A very mild case, and she was one of the last to have it before doctors found a cure. But the other students, girls and boys, were so mean to her. So cruel. I could tell you stories, but I won't. It broke my heart to see my sister smile even while people called her names. That was all she knew to do … smile back. She wouldn't cry until after we were in bed. She didn't want our parents to know. And you know what I did, Katie?"

Katie shook her head. No teacher had ever been so personal with her before; she wasn't sure what to do or say.

"I watched. I stored it all away. And I promised that I'd never let anyone bully or tease one of my students."

"Okay," Katie finally said. "So my idea was good or bad?"

"No, Katie," Mrs. Hepworth responded, dabbing her eyes again. "It's a wonderful idea. If someone had done that for Marybeth … it might have changed everything."

That night at dinner, Katie's mom grabbed Katie's hand, beaming. "Rachel's mom told me what you and your friends are planning to do for prom," her mom said. "I think it's incredible."

Katie grinned sheepishly. "Thanks."

"What gave you the idea?" her dad asked.

Katie's response was a shrug. The truth, however, was much darker. Five nights ago she'd had a dream where she'd slapped Bobby John and stuffed his hat into his mouth while he screamed, "Bobby John loves you." The dream had stuck with her, and she still cringed each time she thought of it. The pain and terror in Bobby John's eyes made her stomach ache, and seeing him in the hall reminded her of it.

"Won't it hurt your chances of becoming prom queen?" her dad teased.

"I don't know. Maybe."

"What about Mark?" Katie's mom asked.

"He doesn't mind." Mark Newcomer, Katie's boyfriend, had even agreed to take Meagan Horn, another one of the kids with special needs, although he was less than enthusiastic about the idea.

"All four years," her dad continued, "that was your goal."

"It still is. I can take Bobby John to the prom and still win prom queen."

"Is it safe?" his mother asked. "I mean, is he safe?"

"Gosh, mom." Katie rolled her eyes. "He's like the sweetest guy I know. Everything's already worked out with his parents."

Katie's dad put his hand on hers. "I'm speechless, Queen. I really am. I can't believe you came up with this all on your own."

"Okay … thanks." She looked to her mom, not understanding why her dad was making such a big deal out of it. Her mom's only response was to keep smiling.

"It's days like this I wish we could have had more kids," her father said.

Katie got up and began clearing the table. *Don't take the comment as an insult*, she told herself. *He means it as a compliment.*

She turned the water on as hot as she could stand it as she soaked the dishes. Her father's occasional comments didn't feel like compliments. They felt like accusations. Like she wasn't enough for them.

Her father took her hand out of the water and drew her attention to his face. Cupping her chin, he kissed her nose. "Queen, I'm proud of you. You're great. You're special. Someday you're gonna change the world."

Katie forced herself to smile. "Okay."

She hurried to finish her chores and then ran upstairs. A message waited for her on her watchphone. The text hovered in the air just above the device. It was from Courtney Marzban:

```
Priyanka thinks you're trying to make her look bad
because she has a THING about special needs kids creeping
her out. She's pissed and on a warpath. WATCH OUT.
```

2 | Birds

Sunday, April 27, 2087

"TEAM EAGLE IS in place," Anna Lukic reported over the com radio from level 65 of the Joswang Finance Tower in downtown Detroit. "Are we clear to place the eggs?"

"Copy that," Sammy said from his perch in a nearby tower. "Stand by for approval. Albatross, what do you see?"

"No sign of any trouble, Mother Hen," Brickert responded, wiping his hands on his pants for the third time. *Why, palms? Why do you betray me? I don't need you to be sweaty right now.*

He sat inside the security booth on the ground floor of the building with Natalia, Strawberry, and Hefani. Meanwhile, six other teams worked inside the building placing explosives. Brickert had wanted to be on Anna's team taking orders, not leading the group tasked with guarding the security center.

"I'm not a leader," he'd told Sammy, but his best friend wouldn't hear it. "I'll mess everything up. And I don't want Strawberry on my team."

"You being her leader was the only way she would go. I need you watching out for the others. Your friends. And it's time you started to lead. You're ready."

"I'm not the kind of guy people want to listen to ... or follow."

Sammy folded his arms. "What kind of person is that?"

When he couldn't answer, Brickert threw his arms in the air. "Look at you. Tall, smart, eloquent."

"I'm eloquent?" Sammy laughed. "Tell Jeffie that."

Brickert had not been able to convince Sammy that the decision was wrong, so now he sat in the security room with his sister and two fellow Betas watching security footage. Around them the guards lay on the floor, tied up and unconscious.

"What do you see on the footage, Brick?" Sammy asked. "No sign of anyone else in the building?"

Brickert glanced around the room. He had a thumbs up from the rest of his team. "Copy that. We are good to go."

Via security cameras throughout the building, Brickert watched teams, comprised of Psions, Tensais, Ultras, Elite, and civilian resistance fighters, converge on strategic targets on the upper levels of the building. The targets were the cloning labs: several floors dedicated to the research and development of Hybrid clones of Sammy. The resistance believed towers had been chosen as cloning sites because they were harder to infiltrate and destroy without mass casualties. Seeing dozens of copies of Sammy in glass tanks gave Brickert the heebie-jeebies.

"Mother Hen, Team Eagle is en route to deliver the egg," Anna said as her team spread out across the floor to place remote-detonated explosives.

"Team Hawk," Sammy said, "check in."

"Team Hawk is ready to rock," Al announced. Brickert thought he sounded a little more cheerful than normal, a sign that perhaps things were improving between him and Marie. "Are we clear to leave the egg, Mother Hen?"

"They're clear, Mother Hen," Brickert stated. "All teams are clear to proceed to deliver the eggs."

"All teams clear. Hawk, Eagle, Goose, Turkey, Falcon, Owl. All teams deliver your eggs and report."

At Sammy's word, the six teams moved in on their target locations. Brickert watched with pride as the teams worked as cohesive units, placing explosives in predetermined locations to inflict maximum damage on the cloning equipment and growing subjects, yet not damage the infrastructure of the building. They had already hit the Kadaber Tower in San Francisco. Zero casualties other than the clones themselves.

"One minute until the next security check, Albatross," Natalia reported.

"You ready to put in the code, Hefani?"

Hefani gave a thumbs up. "Roger, roger."

To ensure that the security center was manned and alert, the Joswang Tower's building systems ran a check every fifteen minutes. Guards had one minute to enter a four-digit code given to them the day before, which they were required to memorize and destroy. Fortunately, the codes were generated and stored months ahead of time in the data banks at the Hive, which Sammy, Nikotai, and Jeffie had hacked four months earlier.

Hefani typed in the code of the day—4801—and clapped his hands. "Good for another fifteen minutes."

Everyone's attention returned to the myriad monitors mounted throughout the room. Brickert, Hefani, and Natalia studied the levels the other teams were on while Strawberry watched the cameras aimed at the lobby to ensure no one snuck up on the security center. From a neighboring skyscraper, Sammy and his team had eyes on the building for any signs of intrusion from the street.

So far the operation was going as smoothly as the San Francisco mission.

Anna, Al, Justice, and the other team leaders moved their teams about the labs with surgical precision. Each bomb was armed, tested, and checked off a list which Jeffie kept in the neighboring skyscraper with Sammy and his team. If they missed anything, she reported it to Sammy, who reported it to the team leader. So far, nothing had been missed.

Another fifteen minutes passed. Natalia warned the team again that it was time to input the code. Brickert didn't think twice about it until Hefani held up a warning hand instead of a thumbs up.

"I—I screwed up the code," he said. "Let me put it in again." He retyped it and hit SEND.

Everyone watched him.

"It says 'Error.' What am I doing wrong?"

"I don't know," Brickert said, licking his lips, "but one more incorrect entry and we're gonna have some problems, I'll tell you."

"What did you put in?" Natalia asked.

"Same as always. 4810."

"It's 48*01*," Strawberry and Brickert said simultaneously.

Hefani winced. "Sorry, guys, I've put that code in so many times that my mind is messing with me."

Everyone's eyes left the monitors and watched Hefani to make sure he put the code in correctly. He did it slowly, saying each number aloud as he pressed it. When he finished, the computer screen told him he had completed a successful entry. Everyone let out a breath of relief and turned their attentions back to their monitors.

Next to Brickert, Strawberry stood and peered closely at one of the video feeds on her monitors. "What is that?"

"Where?" Brickert asked his sister.

"Right out—"

The door to the security center blew open. Gas containers flew into the room. Brickert held his breath and shot blasts in the direction of the canisters. Thirteens crowded into the room wearing gas masks and wielding guns. The sound of the bullets was deafening in close quarters. The four Psions put up shields, but the telltale signs of coughing told Brickert the battle might already be lost. The coughs came from Hefani, deep booming, gagging hacks.

Hold it together, Hefani, Brickert thought. He didn't dare say the words aloud for fear of breathing in the gas. Already his eyes burned and watered. In their gas masks, the Thirteens weren't able to communicate well, their attack less coordinated. But in the confines of the small security center, a room about four by five meters, they didn't need much coordination.

Sammy mentioned something about white noise coming through the coms, but Brickert still couldn't speak without inhaling the noxious fumes. Under the hailstorm of bullets, the screens and equipment around him shattered, popped, and sprayed debris everywhere. Strawberry and Natalia drew close to Brickert, still shielding. Hefani fell to his knees as booming coughs exploded from his lungs. His eyes were large and watery, but he kept his arms straight in front of him, still protecting his front.

We have to get out of here!

Brickert had no idea how long he'd been holding his breath, but it felt like an hour. In reality, it had only been fifty or sixty seconds. His heart beat faster the longer he denied himself of air.

I told Sammy I wasn't a leader.

Two Thirteens dashed forward, perhaps unable to restrain themselves any longer. Brickert dropped down to one knee and fired several blasts up at their heads. One of them flew back, flipping over in the air. Bullets from his own comrades tore into his body. The other's mask shot back, exposing his face. He immediately gagged and coughed.

Have to fix this somehow …

Brickert counted six more Thirteens in masks. If he and his team were to have any chance, they had to get out of the room so they could breathe and call for help.

Brickert mustered the last of the air in his lungs and bellowed to his team, "CHARGE THEM!"

The outburst prompted questions from the other team leaders over the com—questions Brickert couldn't answer—as he, Natalia, Strawberry, and Hefani pushed forward in unison. They pushed back the Thirteens until Hefani went to his knees again, now coughing so violently that flecks of blood came up with each breath. The Thirteens identified him as the weakest link and focused fire. Hefani kept one hand up to shield, the other down to break his fall.

Natalia sidestepped closer to him so her shields would provide him cover. Strawberry moved over to Brickert. Neither Hefani nor Strawberry had been involved in combat before. Brickert didn't want to think about what thoughts were going through their minds. He had to focus on what he could do to survive.

I'm not the right man for this job. I'm not a leader!

Gas continued to cloud the room in a yellowish haze. Their efforts to drive the Thirteens back succeeded in part. Brickert blasted at the enemy but his lungs were close to bursting. How could he concentrate with the need to breathe so persistent?

Don't break. Don't do it, he urged himself. *Stay strong.*

He tried to push forward again, but his lungs betrayed him, sucking down both sweet air and noxious gas. The reaction came at once. A burning in his chest coupled with the need to retch. Eyes watering so badly that he couldn't breathe. Then came the irrepressible cough. It was a deep, barking boom that immediately led to another one and another one.

"Help us!" Brickert wheezed into his com. "Attack ... on the ... security center!"

"Each leader send half your team downstairs now!" Sammy ordered. "I'm coming in, too. You four hold tight and keep your shields up."

"Gas," Brickert coughed. "They've got gas."

The words came with great difficulty. Brickert's world burned. His eyes, his mouth and nose, his lungs. Even his guts were aflame. The Thirteens continued to fire shots from just inside the doorway, unwilling to spread out around the room. *They have the upper hand. Do they not want to press it?*

It was easy for Brickert to shield himself while on his knees. His body became a smaller target. The Thirteens could shoot forever and hit nothing. Pretty soon, however, Hefani's coughing turned to gagging. Then, without warning, he leaned over and threw up. The stench mixed with the gas was nauseating. Both his hands hit the carpet to brace his body. Bullets flew. Blood spattered the carpet, mixing in with the pool of vomit, and Hefani hit the ground, dead. Strawberry screamed and then began to cough.

The Thirteens chose her as their next target.

No! Brickert jerked his body to the side to cover his sister. *Gotta get back to my feet. Gotta be a leader.*

The same moment he tried to get up, a tremendous cough racked his body, so strong that it nearly knocked him over. The Thirteens turned their guns back on him. Brickert kept one hand up, but it wasn't enough. A bullet pierced his shinbone. The fire in his abdomen was nothing compared to the searing heat in his leg.

Seeing Brickert get shot seemed to rob Natalia of her sense of reason. Rather than moving in to shield for him, she charged the Thirteens with a powerful blast, unholstered her weapon, and fired. Her efforts forced them back; she clipped one Thirteen in the neck, causing him to bleed out. In the process she opened herself up to the Thirteens' attack. They took advantage, fired back at her, and hit her in the stomach.

"No!" Brickert screamed, finding his voice amidst the flames in his throat. "Get back! Get back!"

Natalia stumbled back, dropped her gun, and clenched her stomach while shielding herself as she hit a table with a *CRASH*. The table broke and collapsed around her. With Hefani and Natalia immobilized and Brickert injured, the Thirteens moved in boldly for Strawberry. She fired blasts at them, coughing and shouting for help. Brickert scurried to help her. He saw the Thirteens' guns move away from Natalia's direction and back toward him, but he didn't care. Only Strawberry mattered. Only his little sister.

Brickert fired blasts from both feet and shot himself into the Thirteens, bouldering into them with his body. He knocked two over but two others grabbed him and seized his arms. Fresh pain blossomed in his shoulder and he cried out from the agony. Shrieks came from all directions, muffled by gas masks and clouded by the hissing from the canisters spewing out their contents into the air. Brickert struggled and fought, but the Thirteens wouldn't let go. Two more came forward and took hold of his ankles. Brickert fired blasts at the enemy to no effect.

He heard his sister scream his name as they carried him out of the room.

"Save Natalia!" he yelled back.

Brickert knew he was dead. He waited for one of them to put a bullet in his skull, but it didn't happen. Once they reached the lobby, the Thirteens hustled Brickert to the elevators.

Where are they taking me?

Two more Thirteens joined the group, each with a gun trained on Brickert's head. Their dark red eyes told Brickert they were exercising great restraint by not killing him. These beasts would jump on any excuse to splatter his brains across the wall. The elevator arrived quickly. Two sets of doors opened side by side: one elevator for the Thirteens and Brickert, the other full of Psions.

The Psions poured from the lift. Al and Brickert's eyes met, but it was too late. When the doors closed, Brickert heard pounding on the sliding doors. One of the Thirteens pressed his thumb to a scanner above the columns of floor buttons. The panel of buttons popped open and revealed another, smaller panel set into the elevator wall. Brickert only saw two buttons on this new panel: one black and one red. The Thirteen pushed the red one.

The elevator car descended deep into the earth. The Thirteens held Brickert in such a way that they rendered his blasting useless. *Why don't they kill me?* The Thirteens weren't known for taking prisoners. Two guns jammed against his head, one on each side. They could turn him into pulp on a whim.

They need me, he realized. *But for what?*

The elevator ride lasted longer than he expected. When the lift came to a stop and the doors opened, the Thirteens pushed him forward. The air wafting in from the floor smelled like contaminated meat. The walls were covered in stains of brown, red, and black. The carpet, tattered and burned, was worse than the walls. Even the ceiling was dirty with splatterings of varying sizes and shapes.

Lining the hallway on both sides were small rooms. The smells coming from them were worse than the scent in the hallway. The squalor inside them made the hallway look somewhat tidy. A combined common room and kitchen was at the end of the hall. Several pieces of torn and abused furniture decorated it.

The Thirteens threw Brickert to the ground as more of them came into the room. Several guns pointed at him now while the Thirteens spoke to each other in shrieks. A couple of them left in a hurry. The others eyed Brickert hungrily. Their blood red eyes shone in the dim light. None of them wore gas masks now. Their scarred, tattooed, and pitted faces were on full display. A couple of them jerked rapidly, communicating to each other in silence. Brickert tried to figure out what they were saying, but even Sammy hadn't learned their form of speaking. He wanted to appear brave, but didn't dare meet their gazes. His head began to tremble, the hairs on the back of his neck stood up straight, and his cheeks burned as hot as irons. The horrible silence gave time for dread to settle into Brickert's bones.

The Thirteens had taken him into their den; it didn't seem likely he'd find his way out. In their eyes he saw his death. How long could he last against so many? A minute? Two?

What are they waiting for?

Two Thirteens who had left in a hurry returned with a camera. They trained it on Brickert, a red light blinking at the front, the lens trained on their prisoner. The Thirteens conversed in low, animalistic growls for several seconds while still staring at Brickert. The way they watched him made his stomach churn. One of them licked her sharpened teeth with a forked tongue. Another made claws with his fingers and scratched up his own chest until it bled.

Then, all at once, they pounced.

Brickert tried to blast them away, but their fists and feet were everywhere. Dozens of limbs kicking, punching, beating, breaking.

Merciless. Pain erupted everywhere: ribs, face, arms, legs, groin. He couldn't keep up with the blows. Too many. Too fast.

His nose broke with a loud crack. His teeth shattered, newly regrown after being broken by the Thirteen in Colorado Springs. *God … please … save me or let me die now.*

When his cheekbone cracked, it felt dull and far away, but fire blossomed when the toe of a boot met the top of his skull. His vision blurred. He heard them shrieking to each other in low tones, urging one another on. His ribs protested every puff of air, so he could only take small, shallow breaths.

Someone … help me, Brickert begged. *They're killing me. Sammy. Someone.*

The beating went on until they stopped at the sound of a single shriek. Brickert couldn't move. His universe was agony. Pain was everywhere and in everything. The Thirteens dragged him to a chair by his arms, lifted him up, and dropped him in it. He was wet with blood or sweat or both. Through the wetness covering his face, Brickert saw one of the Thirteens place a sheet of white paper against Brickert's chest. Then, using Brickert's own blood, the Thirteen painted words on the paper while another stuck the sheet to Brickert's chest using a staple gun.

Brickert screamed as the staples pierced his flesh.

The camera turned on him again, surrounding him in light. Brickert's com was ripped from his ear and plugged into the camera. *They're going to broadcast this.* His chin hit his chest as he was unable to support his head any longer. Through his blurred vision, he read the sign, even as his own blood continued to drip down his face onto the paper like dark red raindrops. Ice flooded his veins when he read the words:

```
Remove the bombs or he dies.
```

Brickert was a dead man. His team would never remove the bombs. They would never negotiate with these animals.

3 | Fallen

Sunday, April 27, 2087

INSIDE A LARGE executive office on the top floor of the First Continental American Bank tower in Detroit, Sammy stood at a large window, a pair of binoculars pressed to his eyes. The view of the city was gorgeous, so were the plush decorations of sleek, modern design. The skyscraper neighbored the Joswang Tower. He let the binoculars hang around his neck and checked the time in the upper corner of his com's holo-screen.

0238

His eyes grew blurrier the longer he stared, and it took several seconds of rubbing to make the blurriness go away. Then he yawned and rubbed his head. His hair had grown long in the last few months, now reaching past his ears. Jeffie seemed to like it that way, so he didn't cut it. Sammy brought his night-vision binoculars back to his eyes. *So far, so good.*

Rain poured down from the skies, splattering the large windows which he, Kawai, Li, Jeffie, and Nikotai stared through as they observed the street around the Joswang Tower. Part of Sammy wished he could be with the teams planting the bombs. It felt odd being away from the danger. He didn't like leaving his friends to do the dirty work, but they wanted him in control of the mission, ready to move in only if needed.

They were too protective over him, even insisting that he wear their best armor despite being out of the action. It was the same flexible, woven bulletproof mesh Psion Alphas wore in combat. Only two other suits had been salvaged from Capitol Island. Anna wore one, and Al the other.

Brickert was doing an excellent job of coordinating between Sammy and the teams. *I told him he'd make a good team leader,* Sammy thought. Lorenzo Winters, one of the resistance men who'd accompanied Sammy to the Hive, had led Albatross Team in San Francisco, but had broken his foot a week before the trip to Detroit. Sammy had tapped Brickert to replace him.

If this mission goes well, maybe Brickert will lead Albatross Team in Dallas. Dallas was the site of the third cloning facility they planned to bomb.

Using his binoculars, Sammy checked the street around the lobby entrances to make sure his team had no unwanted visitors. When the explosives detonated in the upper floors, they wanted to keep casualties to zero. Though they had made every effort to limit damage to only the floors where the Hybrids were grown, nothing was certain when dealing with bombs and buildings.

After the all-clear came for the three teams to plant the explosives, Sammy waited for the next update. Some strange sounds came from the coms of Brickert's team followed by hissing like static.

"Albatross, check your com. Everything okay? I'm getting some white noise."

There was no answer except the strange crackling sounds.

"Albatross," Sammy said to Brickert again, "I'm picking up some interference from your coms. Please respond."

No answer. Jeffie cast Sammy a nervous glance.

"What do you want to do, Sammy?" Li asked. "Send someone to check on them?"

Sammy's mind flew through his options. It would be almost impossible for someone to catch Brickert's team unaware. No reason Brickert couldn't warn Sammy if a problem occurred. *Then what's causing the static? And why isn't Brickert responding?*

"CHAR—!" Brickert's voice yelled over the com.

"Albatross?" Sammy asked. "Report to me now!"

The only answer Sammy heard was a muffled booming sound like a cough or a distant drum. He heard other sounds, too, but couldn't tell what they were.

"Sammy?" Li asked. "What are your orders?"

"Go," Sammy finally said. "You, too, Kawai."

Without another word the two Psions ran for the elevator. Nikotai and Jeffie went back to watching the street. Sammy eyed the zipline guns stowed in the pack in the corner of the office. Back in

February, when they had started training for these urban missions, Sammy and his team practiced using the guns for speedy escapes from the office towers.

"Albatross," Sammy said, "if you can hear me, Li and Kawai are coming over to check on you. If your com starts working, report in as soon as—"

"Help us!" Brickert said in a wheezing voice. "Attack … on the … security center!"

"Each leader send half your team to Albatross Team's position now!" Sammy ordered. "I'm coming in, too. You four hold tight and keep your shields up."

"Gas," Brickert's voice cut through his own coughs and gags. "They've got gas."

Sammy looked at Jeffie and Nikotai. "You two stay put. I need you to be my eyes in the sky. Nikotai, snipe any enemy who tries to enter from the street. Keep me informed. You're in charge."

"Be careful," Nikotai told him.

Jeffie gave Sammy a nod. With his hands spread apart, Sammy blasted the large glass window multiple times in rapid succession until it wobbled and then shattered into thousands of pieces. The difference in the air pressure sucked the glass out into the night where the pieces fell like tiny twinkling stars. He wasted no time in setting up the zipline gun, anchoring it into the wall and floor at three points. Then he aimed the zipline and fired it into the roof of the neighboring building. He tugged firmly on the line, testing its strength and elasticity. Satisfied he wouldn't plunge to his death between the towers, Sammy grabbed the handles and triggered the release. Pressurized air shot him forward until he dangled across downtown Detroit at speeds nearing sixty kilometers per hour.

Once he knew his momentum would carry him to the rooftop of the Joswang building, Sammy released his hold of the zipline and flew onto the roof. Loose gravel awaited him below. He used his Anomaly Fourteen to fire several blasts from his feet, powerful pushes of energy that slowed his fall and allowed him to set foot on the rocky floor at a run. Across the way was a door to the rooftop. He sprinted to it, fired three shots at the lock, and kicked it open. A deafening *BANG* assaulted his ears as the door crashed into the wall.

"Sammy, they've taken Brickert in elevator 13," Al reported. "We barely missed it."

"Was he alive?" Sammy asked. There was a catch in his voice as he spoke the words. The thought of Brickert dying….

"Yes, but wounded."

"If they took him to the elevator, it must mean they're going down."

"How do you know?" Al asked.

"Because that's where they took me." Flashes of his own elevator ride with Stripe and other Aegis flashed before Sammy's eyes. "Are there any Thirteens left on the main floor? Are the others okay?"

"I don't know."

"Find out! If you see a Thirteen, kill it and cut off its finger. I'm going to need it."

"We have to be out of the building, Sammy. The explosives are in place. Nine minutes to detonation. We agreed on this."

"Get everyone out. You're honcho inside the building. Nikotai is now mission leader. As far as everyone else is concerned, I'm on a solo rescue mission. Contact Rosmir and have him bring the ambulance around to the lobby doors. Got it?"

"Be careful."

Sammy reached the top floor of the Joswang building. It wasn't a penthouse suite like the fox's N Tower in Orlando. It was a fitness center with a large pool, racquetball and basketball courts, and a dozen other amenities. Sammy sprinted across it and came to the stairs next to the elevators. The stair door wasn't locked. He pushed it open and hurled himself over the railing.

Down he fell. Every few floors he used foot blasts against the walls of the stairs to slow himself to a manageable speed. With his Anomaly Eleven, Sammy's brain calculated everything, from his speed and acceleration to the amount of blast energy he needed to control his fall.

"Sammy," Nikotai reported, "the Thirteens are broadcasting a feed using Brickert's com. They've got him. He looks really—"

"Patch it through to mine," Sammy ordered.

The holo-screen on Sammy's com came alive, displaying the live feed from Brickert's com. When Sammy saw his best friend slumped over on a chair with a sign stuck to his chest—copious amounts of blood dripping from his nose and mouth, a dull, lifeless expression on his face—he wondered if his friend was already dead.

Not Brickert. I can't lose Brickert.

He read the sign. Saw Brickert stir, the faint rise and fall of his chest.

You chose the wrong hostage.

Sammy ground his teeth together so hard they squeaked. His jaw began to ache as his pulse quickened, his blood roaring through his veins. *I will kill you all.* The rage inside threatened to transform him into something darker, baser, and deadlier.

When he reached the ground floor of the Joswang building, he left the stairwell and ran for the security center. "Al!" he shouted. "I need that finger now!"

Al came out of the security center. His clothes were covered in blood and he cradled something in his hands. "It's not good, Sammy," he said. "Hefani is … Natalia's unresponsive. Strawberry's in shock."

"Just give me the finger!" Sammy screamed in a primal, rage-filled tone.

"Here! Here! Go."

Sammy took it and ran to elevator 13. He jammed the button repeatedly until the door dinged. Once he was inside, he pressed the digit against the scanner and watched as the panel opened. Two choices: black and red. In the elevator in Rio, there had been a third choice: white.

I've seen black. Black is where they keep the anomalies for questioning.

He watched the feed coming in live from their location. The Thirteen couldn't seem to hold the camera very steady. Sammy noted the furniture, torn and shredded.

He's in their living quarters. Like at the Hive. He saw them again as clearly as he saw his own reflection in the elevator doors. Their eyes, their clothes, their lust for blood.

Sammy mashed the red button with the severed finger, and the elevator began its descent. Images filled his mind as he sank deeper into the earth. He saw himself destroying them. It would be a massacre. He wanted to smell their blood. Every blow they had landed on his friend would be paid for with a life.

No, no. That's not me.

On the com screen, Brickert muttered something. His words came out thick and wet. Slick red liquid trickled from his mouth. Then he coughed. It sounded like he was choking. Sammy watched closely as his friend spat out something long and white.

His front tooth.

Rage so strong and violent passed through Sammy that he shook—crackling with a lively, dark energy that needed to be expended. A brief vision passed before his eyes of himself tearing apart thylacines in the jungles of the Amazon. He remembered the guilt after seeing what he'd done, after losing control over his mind and body. He had let the anomaly take over. The Thirteen.

Sammy closed his eyes. Letting it out would make him nearly invincible. Keeping it reined in could mean his death. But each dance he had with the darkness inside—the Anomaly Thirteen—the darkness grew stronger, louder, harder to ignore. He thought of Trapper, how he had changed from being Commander Byron's best friend to something twisted and unrecognizable.

A whimper came through his com's earpiece. He opened his eyes and saw a Thirteen holding a knife to Brickert's face.

"Please ..." Brickert moaned.

They're going to carve his face.

"DON'T TOUCH HIM!" Sammy roared into his com.

The elevator came to a stop. The Thirteen on screen paused at the sound of Sammy's voice coming through Brickert's com. The doors opened with a soft ping. Sammy walked out of the elevator with his arms held high above his head. The stench of the floor assaulted his nose. Two Thirteens appeared down the length of the corridor, in the doorway of the large common room where Brickert was held, weapons aimed at Sammy's chest.

Fully automatic assault rifles. One hundred twenty rounds per magazine. Nine hundred RPM.

The red-melt-to-black uniforms met him halfway down the hall, their guns still trained on his heart. "You better be here to give us the detonators," one said. "Or you are never gonna see the sun again. And your fellow Fourteen … he hasn't even begun to know pain yet."

"Burn in hell." As they reached out to pat him down, Sammy attacked first, blasting them in the chest with his most powerful hand blasts. As the Thirteens flew backward, they opened fire.

Sammy used his right hand to shield while performing a small blast jump. With his left hand, he used a strong push blast to support his body while running along the right wall, his body now parallel to the floor. The Thirteens adjusted their shots, but Sammy anticipated this and jumped again, turning his body another 90 degrees until he was running on the ceiling. The Thirteens followed him with their bullets. Sammy turned again, switched hands, and continued running along the left wall. All the while his computer-like brain kept count of the number of bullets each gun had fired.

One hundred five … one hundred twelve, one hundred twenty.

Sammy dropped down to the floor and used his left hand to shield the bullets coming from the Thirteen who'd been more conservative with his ammo. With his right, he pulled his syshée from its holster and fired five bullets into the other Thirteen. The Thirteen had just finished reloading when the barbs hit him in the chest and gut. He hit his knees and sprayed his clip wildly around the hall. Sammy fired again, this time making a headshot.

The other Thirteen didn't have time to watch his comrade die. He backed away, still firing at Sammy, who used his shields as he pursued.

It's like taking candy from a baby, a dark voice sang in Sammy's head.

Sammy hummed as he fired a shot into the Thirteen's kneecap. The Thirteen staggered, but stayed standing. Sammy aimed again and shot, this time hitting the other knee. The Thirteen's weight nearly brought him down to his knees, but the remarkable ability of the anomaly allowed him to stand, his face in a twisted grimace of effort and fury. Sammy crossed the distance between them, easily blasting away the last of the Thirteens bullets.

"You're out," he told the Thirteen.

The Thirteen shrieked and hissed at him. His face was so screwed up with hate that his scars looked like wrinkles. He lunged as soon as Sammy drew near enough, but Sammy caught his head and twisted hard until he felt a snap. As the Thirteen slumped to the floor with a twitch, the door ahead to the common room closed and locked.

Sammy checked the time. *Six minutes until the bombs go off.*

Urgently, Sammy tried the door handle and found it would not give. His holo-screen showed him the feed from the camera on the other side of the door, and he watched as the Thirteens lined up around the room, their guns aimed and waiting for him to enter.

Using super-heated blasts from his left thumb, Sammy melted the three hinges on the door. The stench of liquid steel and burnt flesh smelled like melted sugar and vanilla. He looked at his thumb and noted the raw, peeling flesh, but the pain was not as severe as he'd expected.

Third degree burns. May need a skin graft. The thought hardly bothered him.

He knocked on the door with his syshée. One of the Thirteens on the other side stepped close. "Who is it?" she asked in a sweet, girlish voice.

"I'm here to negotiate the release of the prisoner in exchange for the bomb codes. I have the detonator. I will give it to you with the code to deactivate the weapons."

Through the door and over the screen, he heard and watched them communicate in their bizarre language of body jerks and shrieks. After about thirty seconds, she returned. "Slide the detonator under the door."

"Release the prisoner first."

"Slide it under the door or he gets a bullet in the skull."

Via the holo-screen on his com, Sammy saw a Thirteen put a gun to Brickert's head. Brickert made no sign that he felt the nuzzle press against his temple. Sammy set the detonator on the floor and eased it slowly under the door with his foot. The girlish Thirteen bent down by the door to pick it up.

Sammy watched her over the camera. Just before she stood, he blasted the door with both hands using maximum power. The door, no longer held in place by its hinges, flew inward, crushed the

Thirteen, and slammed into three more behind her. As he walked in the room, Sammy glanced at his com.

Five minutes.

Bullets greeted him like flies to a cut of meat. For the moment, Brickert was forgotten by the animals. They all wanted the new guy. One of the Thirteens screeched to the others, and in all the noise, Sammy heard one say, "Berhane! Berhane!"

He smiled at the idea that they were aware of who he was, that word had spread about him. He felt powerful and larger than himself.

At a glance, he counted ten Thirteens in the room with him. Four had been knocked down by the door, but besides the girl nearest to it no permanent damage had been done. He chose the angle that would give him maximum shielding ability from as many enemies as possible. In his left hand, he held the syshée with twenty-two rounds left in the magazine. Even with his weapons—his Anomaly Fourteen and Eleven—he could not beat so many enemies. Not without help.

Release me. Use me. Then you can put me away again and forget about me.

Sammy had no choice. He exhaled and embraced the darkness, the rage, the cold. Energy surged into his limbs. The pain in his thumbs vanished. His fear melted.

His first shot found its mark in the forehead of one of the Thirteens who'd been hit by the door. The second missed. The Thirteens fanned out at once, quickly attempting to surround him. Sammy didn't care this time. He only wanted their attention on him and away from Brickert. He let them move around the room, his body tensed, coiled, ready to spring when the time was right. Though the camera had been set down, it was still on, broadcasting the events in the room. Sammy positioned his body so that he could see behind himself by watching the camera feed on his com screen. Without moving, he could see around himself in almost 360 degrees.

For a brief moment, everything stopped. Sammy stayed completely still, and the Thirteens froze, waiting to see if he would make a move. Sammy, however, was content to be patient. He saw a Thirteen's fingers twitch and knew this would be the first one to fire. Sammy shifted his weight ever so slightly, turning his body as he did to put himself in between two Thirteens.

The moment the trigger finger twitched again, Sammy blast jumped up to the ceiling. The bullets flew under him harmlessly, striking the Thirteen behind Sammy twice in the chest. Now using hand blasts, Sammy pushed hard off the ceiling at an angle and landed directly in between two more Thirteens. He paused only long enough to allow them to fire at each other before blasting again. As he shot forward toward the wall to his left at an upward angle, the bullets passed through the space where he'd stood. One Thirteen took a bullet to the shoulder, the other dodged, receiving only a graze across his cheek.

Sammy hit the wall and bounced off. He jetted around so quickly the Thirteens couldn't keep up. To protect himself, he kept his shields placed at angles providing the most coverage. He sent his body toward a Thirteen, who thought she had a good shot at hitting him. Sammy dropped his shields at the last instant and slammed his fist into her neck, crushing it. The sensation of breaking bones and cartilage under his blow was glorious. As she crumpled, he blasted away again.

Midair, Sammy saw in the holo-screen that a Thirteen had a gun trained on his back. Two upward blasts pushed Sammy back down to the floor, where he slid, shielding himself and shooting the syshée's deadly barbs into another Thirteen. The sounds of firing guns and shrieking enemies assaulted his ears like an orchestra turned up too loud.

Less than three minutes left.

Die. All of you.

It was a game. The whole battle was a game, and Sammy held the best cards: speed, energy, superiority, strength, and intelligence. With all three of his anomalies, plus his precise training and formidable physique, how could he not? The Thirteens were always a step too late. The bullets always just missed him. The combination of his three anomalies made him better, uncatchable. It let him do things he normally couldn't have done, bend himself, twist himself, throw himself, and break his own bones on their bodies without consequence.

A small voice inside his mind whispered, *Stop this. There are consequences ...*

Sammy ignored the voice like he would a bee buzzing in his ear. The Thirteens did not go down without a struggle. Despite taking numerous shots to the chest or abdomen, they fought on. In some perverse way, Sammy found this admirable. But it didn't stop him from killing them.

One minute left.

Sammy wasn't going to make it in time. He had to just keep fighting and hope for the best. If his calculations were correct, the Joswang Tower would be fine.

Keep fighting to save Brickert. To win the war.

Wrong. You're doing it because you enjoy it.

His heart rejoiced each time he saw the lights go out in their eyes, and he reveled in the way their fluids splashed across walls, ceiling, and floor as the syshée did its deadly work. At some point during the middle of the battle, his five minutes ran out and the bombs detonated. Sammy was so far below the earth that he heard no detonation. But he knew something had gone wrong when he felt the tremors in the building. If the bombs had been placed correctly, no tremors should have been felt this low in the structure. All the damage was supposed to be contained to the upper floors.

Sammy cursed. *This building can't come down. I didn't plan it this way.*

Six Thirteens still remained of the original ten. Two of them were badly injured, one of which had absolutely no chance at surviving the next twenty minutes without immediate medical attention. Sammy had eight rounds left in his last magazine.

One of the Thirteens paused to reload. As fast as he was, Sammy was faster and put a bullet in his throat. The Thirteen died as he finished reloading and fired one last bullet into the ceiling as he stumbled backward into the table where the camera sat. His body crashed and sent the camera to the floor and his gun clattered at Brickert's blood speckled shoes. By then Sammy was already five meters away attacking two more Thirteens. Another tremor ran through the walls and floor. Sammy cursed again.

Can't you wait until I'm finished?

He focused his energies on the two weakest Thirteens. The game was becoming easier now with so few players remaining. Boring almost. They gave up trying to surround Sammy, instead trying to shoot him with sporadic and chaotic movements and angles, using helter-skelter tactics in attempt to confuse him. But it didn't work. They bounced off the walls, dove, jumped, and threw things at him. Sammy countered by keeping them off balance, never staying in place for more than a second or two.

One by one the remaining five fell. The first of them threw half of a broken dining table at Sammy. Sammy blasted it back, impaling the Thirteen on the metal leg, and finishing him off with a bullet to the head. Two other Thirteens became so enraged that they emptied their clips at Sammy from opposite sides while a third took careful aim at Sammy's head, and the fourth tried to get back to his feet despite massive blood loss.

Sammy shielded the two on his left and right flank and waited until the last moment to jerk aside and avoid the bullets from the third Thirteen—something he could never have done without using the Anomaly Thirteen. The forward Thirteen adjusted and fired again while the other two reloaded. Sammy shot multiple blasts at the Thirteen, hitting him and shoving him backward into the wall. As Sammy got closer, the strength of his blasts increased. The blasts crushed the Thirteen's body while behind Sammy the two Thirteens finished reloading and fired at his unprotected back. Again he surprised the Thirteens by jumping out of the way and leaving a crushed, defenseless enemy to receive the full fury of his brothers.

Three left, a gloating voice reminded him. *Finish them.*

Stop using the anomaly!

Sammy shielded with only his left hand now, the other held his syshée. *Seven bullets.* He fired at one Thirteen while blasting at the other. Both missed. He jumped with a medium blast and turned midair, firing the syshée twice at the one behind him, while shielding in the direction of the one he'd missed. One bullet struck the Thirteen's shoulder while the other hit his lower abdomen.

"And then there was one," Sammy said.

The Thirteen snarled at him. He was one of the more normal-looking Thirteens Sammy had seen. For some reason, this made Sammy hate him even more. Sammy flicked the safety of his syshée to the "on" position and dropped the gun. The Thirteen must have found this insulting because he roared with rage and shot at Sammy. Sammy taunted him with his blasts, mixing up shields and strikes to push around the Thirteen like a toy.

"Sa—y, hurry," Al urged, his com signal distorted by the depth of the tower's sublevels. "The b—ding is c—mpr—ised—! Get Bric— and get—!"

"Don't tell me what to do," Sammy growled through gritted teeth. He continued to screw around with the Thirteen, keeping him off balance with blasts to his legs and chest.

Two veins bulged in the Thirteen's forehead, another in his neck. His deep red eyes fixed murderously on Sammy's throat, but he was powerless. Finally he charged, a stupid and reckless decision. Sammy stepped forward and clotheslined the Thirteen at the neck. Before the Thirteen could recover, Sammy sat on his chest, pinning him to the ground. The Thirteen bucked and tried to kick Sammy off, but Sammy punched him in the mouth.

Listen to Al. Get a grip on yourself.

Hitting the Thirteen sent a wave of bliss through Sammy. Nothing else mattered. He had no sense of self. No responsibility.

No worries. Nothing. Just the euphoria of the violence. He hit the Thirteen a second time.

And a third.

And a fourth.

Someone moaned Sammy's name, but he ignored the sound. His fists flew into the Thirteen's jaw and skull, feeling bones break and shatter. Some of them might have been his. It didn't matter. Blood flew and splattered with each blow Sammy delivered. The Thirteen had stopped struggling, but this didn't matter either.

Someone groaned Sammy's name again, but he didn't let it stop him. All the hatred and rage locked inside of him—in the darker side—poured out through his arms. It turned him into a machine, cold and powerful, capable of perpetual motion. He would go on forever, so long as he had something to strike, a target for his darkness.

A gun fired. It struck the Thirteen, but startled Sammy enough that he jerked back and looked around to find the source of the disturbance. Whoever did it would die. All he saw was Brickert slumped over on his knees in front of the chair. His face was unrecognizable from the swelling and bleeding. His chest rising and falling in rapid, shallow gasps. A gun dangled from his hand. Sammy charged his friend, ready to kill. He grabbed Brickert by the shirt, cocked his fist back, and let it fly. A bone broke beneath the blow. Then he punched again. He pulled back to do it a final time, to mash the face into a pulp.

DO IT! a voice told him. *KILL!*

Brickert's eyes fluttered, but only one could open. The eye was unfocused, roving around the room until it finally fixed itself on Sammy.

"H—h—h—" Brickert struggled to speak. Each breath brought with it a wheezing sound, hollow and light. "Who ... are ... you?"

Sammy nearly dropped his best friend. The fog of darkness lifted from his mind. As the haze diminished, the pain grew. His hands, legs, ribs, and arms ached. His thumbs throbbed and seared with pain.

He tried to pick up Brickert, but his arm didn't work properly. Blood soaked his shirt. He touched the center of it carefully. Pain radiated outward. Horrible pain. His mesh armor was in tatters. *I was shot and didn't even notice.* Regardless of how Sammy felt, it was nothing compared to how Brickert looked. Large purple and black bruises colored whatever wasn't covered in blood. His left arm hung at a weird angle. Sammy had never seen anyone so beaten.

"Come on, Brick," he said as he knelt down to lift his friend. "We can do this."

The shooting agony brought tears to Sammy's eyes as he pulled his friend up and over his shoulder. He breathed through his nose in sharp, forceful draws. His first three steps were staggers as he stumbled toward the doorway. When he reached the hall, the building shook again. Needles stabbed his legs with each step he took toward the elevator. Sammy's eyes stayed locked on his target, allowing himself to see nothing else.

Another quake under his feet nearly sent him to his knees.

"Leave me," Brickert whispered behind him. "You can't ... save ... us both."

"Yes, I can," Sammy grunted back. "Now shut up and don't die."

Bracing himself on the filthy walls, Sammy lurched step after step until he slammed against the elevator doors. Holding Brickert with one hand, he reached out and pressed the call button to go up.

"Hold on," he whispered. "Just … hold on … buddy."

He counted the seconds silently until the elevator arrived. When he reached nine, he heard a soft *ping*.

Thank you.

The doors closed behind Sammy, and the elevator began its ascent to the lobby. Sammy eased Brickert off his shoulder and lowered him to the floor. "You still with me?" he asked Brickert.

Brickert gave no response.

"Brickert?" Sammy gave him a gentle shake, but still Brickert didn't answer. Sammy checked Brickert's wrist and found no pulse. His trembling hands moved to Brickert's neck. *Please, please, please.*

The elevator stopped. They hadn't reached the ground floor. Sammy jammed the button again, but the elevator didn't budge. He slammed his fist against the panel. A robotic operator's voice came over the intercom: "Due to building instability, elevator use is suspended until further notice. Please use the stairs. Please do not attack or damage the elevator as it will not improve your situation."

Sammy spoke into his com. "Al, can you hear me?"

"Barely. Where are you?"

"I'm stuck in the elevator! I need help."

"You're cutting in and out. What do you need?"

"HELP! I need your help!"

"Okay. What can I do?"

"Are you still in the building?"

"No one's in the building, Sammy. It's coming down soon. You have to get out!"

"*I'm trying to get out!*" Sammy screamed. "I need you to open the elevator doors on the ground floor. Can you do that?"

"Open the ground door?"

Sammy repeated his request, barely keeping his cool.

"Yes—yes, I can do that, but you have to hurry."

Sammy blasted open the top escape hatch of the elevator car. It was too dark to see how far up the doors were. *Doesn't matter. I have to make this right.* Sammy grabbed Brickert and lifted him up high.

He yelled at the top of his lungs as stabs of pain ripped through his arm and burned thumb. He shot blasts from his feet until he was high enough off the ground that he could push Brickert up through the hatch. Fresh tears blinded him, but he continued to heft his friend's weight until Brickert rested on top of the elevator. Then Sammy climbed out, sat next to Brickert, and wiped his eyes with his better arm.

"Hold on, buddy." He placed his hand on Brickert's head. "I'm going to take care of you. Just hold on."

"Sammy, I'm in the building," Al reported. "It's bad. We gotta be fast. Be ready to move as soon as I pop open these doors."

"Copy that."

Sammy used the elevator cables to pull himself back to a standing position, ignoring his body's protests. Then he picked Brickert up again and trained his eyes on the darkness above him. In those few seconds, he noticed how it never ended, the blackness. It was limitless and consuming.

"Don't die, Brickert." His words tasted hot and bitter, filled with guilt.

A shaft of light appeared almost thirty meters above them. After turning on his own com light, Sammy wasted no time jump blasting toward it. Carrying Brickert severely reduced the height of his blast jumps, forcing Sammy to adjust in midair. He bounced from wall to wall, gradually scaling the distance to the elevator doors on the ground floor. The space between the doors widened, and more light filled the shaft. The better Sammy could see, the more confident he felt in his blasts.

"Hurry!" Al shouted from above.

Sammy could not go any faster. The tremors in the building grew worse. The pain in Sammy's limbs grew worse. The quaking in his arms grew worse. At one point, Sammy's body nearly gave up and he barely hung onto Brickert. It was too much. He could hardly summon the strength to blast. He thought of everyone who had helped him, sacrificed for him, enabled him to be where he was. He called on their strength and reached the elevator doors.

Al was there to help him. The moment Al reached Brickert to take him from Sammy, a ghastly haunted noise rang through the walls, reverberating so powerfully that it deafened Sammy. The sound surrounded and filled him with its high-pitched groans as steel folded on steel and the structure collapsed on itself.

Debris fell from above as Sammy, still carrying his best friend, ran behind Al toward the doors. Before they could reach them, a massive chunk of the ceiling crashed onto the floor, blocking their path.

"This way!" Al yelled.

Sammy huffed and stumbled after his friend. He tried to ask Al to take Brickert for him, but couldn't find the breath to speak. A tremendous roar came from the building followed by a monstrous tremor that did not stop. Al sprinted toward the nearest bay window and shot at it several times until the glass shattered. With his blasts, he blew away any remaining shards. "Go, Sammy! GO!"

Sammy hurried forward and jumped through the window. Al followed behind. They didn't stop once they hit the street, but kept running until they reached the stealth cruisers parked in the road. Behind them, the Joswang Tower began to crumble.

Ice filled Sammy's gut. *How many people did we estimate could be in the building during these hours?* "God help us," he said. "What have I done?"

4 | Hyding

Friday, May 9, 2087

SAMMY SAT NEXT to Brickert's bed with a book balanced by the cast on his left arm. His friend lay still on his left side with his eyes closed; a breathing tube snaked down his mouth and throat while I.V. catheters went into his arms. Other than Sammy's voice, the only other sounds were the reports from the monitors connected to Brickert, speaking in their monotonous, repetitive language of beeps.

"'There was something strange in my sensations, something indescribably new and, from its very novelty, incredibly sweet. I felt younger, lighter, happier in body; within I was conscious of a heady recklessness, a current of—'"

Sammy sighed and paused to set the book down on his cast so he could rub his eyes with his good hand. Somehow this made his vision worse and everything in the room was a blur. So he rubbed harder, his skin making a wet sucking sound. Fortunately his burned thumb was almost completely healed and only dully ached. The effort left him so exhausted that he had to rest a moment before going back to the book.

He hadn't slept well before Detroit, but since returning sleep had become impossible. Every time he closed his eyes he saw Brickert beaten, bloody, bruised, and barely clinging to life. Half the time, in his dreams, Sammy tried unsuccessfully to resuscitate his best friend. The other half, he wrapped his own bleeding hands around Brickert's neck and choked the life out of him.

Not a night had passed that he didn't wake up crying, sweating, aching, or apologizing. *I'm sorry, Brick*, he thought now as he looked at his friend.

"Hmmnn," Brickert moaned.

Sammy leaned toward his friend, his book fell to the floor. "Brickert? Hey can you hear me?" He reached over and pressed the call button next to Brickert's bed. "Brick? You awake?"

It had been twelve days since the disastrous attack on the Joswang building in Detroit. Brickert had been unconscious all dozen of them. Sammy, Strawberry, Jeffie, and others had taken turns sitting with him for two or three hours at a time, mostly reading aloud in hopes that he could hear. After going through several books, Sammy was now reading *The Strange Case of Dr. Jekyll and Mr. Hyde*.

A minute after he pressed the button, Dr. Maad Rosmir entered with an assistant. "What happened? Is he awake?"

"He moaned."

Dr. Rosmir pried open Brickert's eyes and examined them. "That's good news." He shook Brickert gently. "Brickert, this is Dr. Rosmir. Can you hear me?" After getting no response, the doctor began manipulating various points on Brickert's body, checking reflexes and automated responses with great care.

Sammy looked over his friend. Heavy bruising was still evident on Brickert's face and arms from trauma and the subsequent surgeries to repair the damage done by the Thirteens. Seventeen broken bones fixed (eight ribs), five teeth implanted for regeneration, and repair of both punctured lungs.

"You saved him, Sammy," Rosmir had told him after the tower fell.

I all but killed him, Sammy had wanted to reply.

As for the rest of Brickert's team, Strawberry had been treated for minor injuries, while Natalia's wounds had been far more serious. It was Strawberry who saved Natalia. After the Thirteens dragged Brickert from the room, Strawberry fought the one who remained and killed him, then rushed to unbury Natalia and staunched her bleeding.

Strawberry had cried in her room for days, unable to get past having killed another human being. Sammy wanted to tell her that Thirteens were hardly even human, but knew it wouldn't help. He had spoken to her briefly in Brickert's room at the infirmary, but neither he nor she had kind words for each other. Yet their brief conversation still stuck with Sammy.

"After this is all over," she had said, "I'm done being a Psion."

Sammy didn't believe her. "What would you do, Strawberry? Walk away from your fellow Psions?"

"Fashion. I was given a scholarship, you know. A school in Lyon. I'm going to call them and see if I can still accept their offer. I just—I'm done."

"Fashion." He'd spat the word back out at her. "Why would you give up such an important life for something so shallow and fleeting?"

Strawberry's eyes turned cold and her expression stony. "Ask Hefani."

Hefani's body now rested in a graveyard outside Glasgow, a crude tombstone marked the spot. Hefani's death had hit Sammy hard, mostly because despite being acquainted with him for almost a year, Sammy had never actually taken the time to really get to know Hefani.

Strawberry had known him best. They'd arrived at Beta headquarters at the same time. During his funeral ceremony, she spoke about how he had liked quiet and solitude and that he preferred to keep things about himself private, much like Sammy. From her description, Sammy decided he would have liked Hefani if he'd made the effort to talk to him. Now it was too late.

Dr. Rosmir finished his examination of Brickert. "His condition is improving. I'm going to have Janna take him in for testing. Have you met Janna? She'll be here in a—"

The faint sounds of two people yelling came through the wall: one male voice and one female.

"She'll be here in a minute or two." Dr. Rosmir acted as though he didn't hear the shouting, but his eyes glanced at the wall through which the sound came.

When one of the voices grew louder, Sammy asked, "Is that Janna?"

"It's not our business," Rosmir said.

No, Sammy realized. *It's Al and Marie.*

The noise continued until Sammy was certain he was right. Then a door slammed shut and the voices stopped. A moment later a pancake thin nurse entered wearing a strained smile, her face red and sweaty. The small bump in her midsection told Sammy that she was likely expecting.

Dr. Rosmir saw her and asked, "Is everything all right?"

The nurse glanced at Sammy and nodded. "Hi, Sammy. I'm Janna Scoble." She tried to give him a better smile, and was mildly successful.

"Janna's a nurse. Recently joined us from … where was it?"

"Star Valley." Her smile turned sad.

"Yes," Rosmir said, "wherever that is. You hungry, Sammy?"

Again Sammy shook his head even though his stomach gurgled in protest. His thoughts were on Al and Marie. He knew their marriage had been struggling since Marie had revealed her pregnancy to her husband. He knew Al felt betrayed that she'd intentionally let herself conceive to prevent them from being selected to go on missions. But what he'd just overheard was a major row. Marie was due soon to deliver their baby, and apparently its impending birth hadn't fixed their problems.

"Okay," Dr. Rosmir said. "Well, Commander Byron's been looking for you. He wants you to meet him in the cafeteria. Or do you plan to continue avoiding him?"

"I haven't been avoiding him," Sammy lied.

"He said you pretended to be asleep every time he visited you in the infirmary."

Sammy couldn't hide his reddening face. "I—I didn't feel like talking to him."

Dr. Rosmir put a hand on Sammy's shoulder. "When have you known him to have anything but your best interest—"

"I know he does. I also know what he wants to talk to me about, and I don't need to hear it. Between the leadership committee and Brickert and—and … everything else, I have a lot on my mind. Getting lectured isn't a priority at the moment."

"From what I hear you can't even be bothered to go to your committee meetings."

Sammy fixed Rosmir with a cold stare. "The commander should worry more about Al and Marie than me."

"I'm just asking, Sammy. Just asking."

Sammy had no response for Rosmir. He knew Commander Byron wanted to discuss how Sammy had managed to save Brickert. He knew Byron had suspicions … and rightfully so. After a long pause, he sighed and gave Dr. Rosmir half a smile.

"Whatever. I'll go find him."

"I'll let you know what Brickert's tests show soon. Okay?"

"Yeah. Sure." Sammy stood up slowly and limped toward the door.

"And Sammy?"

Sammy paused but did not look back. "What?"

"You need to rest. You look like—well, like nothing good."

Biting back a rude retort, Sammy left the infirmary. His com beeped, informing him that he had a message from Jeffie. That made a total of twenty-two she had sent him, all of which remained unread. He turned off his com in case she tried to call again. In his mind it was easier to justify ignoring her calls if he never heard the com ring.

Everybody on the Detroit mission had seen what Sammy did in the Thirteen den to the enemy. It'd been broadcast to every com on the network. They'd seen his brutality and efficiency. Fortunately the camera had been bumped before Sammy turned on Brickert, or they would have seen that too.

Since returning to Glasgow, he'd ignored the resistance's leadership committee members and their summons, he ignored his friends, and he ignored Commander Byron. Sammy woke up, spent time with Brickert, and went home. Most of his friends and colleagues had given up trying to talk to him when he was at the infirmary. And when they did, Sammy refused to respond.

I'm a killer. A murderer of hundreds. And they all know it.

During the first week after Detroit, Sammy had locked himself in his room and studied the mission plans and detonation schematics until he figured out what went wrong. The part involving Brickert's team was easy enough to unravel. Hefani had messed up the code, and Strawberry took her eyes off the screens watching the lobby at the same moment the Thirteens chose to strike the security offices. A dumb decision combined with bad luck.

As for the errant destruction of the Joswang Tower, that was a different matter entirely. Sammy and fellow Tensai, Justice Juraschek, along with three resistance members with experience in demolition, had planned the placement of the explosive devices using building schematics stolen from the Hive five months ago.

Sammy, being one of the highest ranking members of the leadership committee, had overruled Justice, Lorenzo Winters, and Dave Hudec's advice regarding placement of the bombs. Sammy and Duncan, Dave's brother, had both believed a more aggressive strategy was well within the realm of safety.

It was Sammy's error that had caused the tower to fall. *My mistake. My pride.*

Even now, as he drove through the underground tunnels that connected the buildings of the resistance, Sammy couldn't shake the thought. It was a stake driven deep into his brain, ever present. He'd once fantasized of being thought of as a hero, someone who history would look favorably upon for his role in the Silent War. Instead he had become a villain. A mass murderer.

When Sammy reached the old high school, he parked his car and went inside. Since the destruction of Psion Beta and Alpha headquarters and the start of the war, Sammy and his friends had lived in Glasgow. Eight months. It felt like eight years. Over those eight months, constant renovations had turned the decrepit school into something resembling a bustling community center. It now boasted a functional exercise facility, dozens of classrooms, and a large mess hall—all of which made it a place for the community to gather.

Holo-visions in the mess hall blared the news, which the resistance had been watching non-stop since the Joswang Tower toppled. Even now, whenever they showed the footage of the building collapsing, Sammy couldn't look away. Every night came the same nightmare of the building, steel screaming like a dying animal.

And when the dust cleared, Sammy stood alone, bodies piled around him. All of them bore the same face.

Brickert's.

My idea, my strategy, my team. My fault. My mistake. My pride.

Each time he saw the footage of the tower crumbling, a heavy, lumpy sickness filled his stomach and his heart turned into lead.

"… breaking news coming in as we speak," one news reporter said to a politician being interviewed, "Two weeks since the catastrophic attack in Detroit, and we finally have a name to the man behind the attacks. Reports show that the mastermind is Samuel Harris Berhane Jr., a NWG terrorist encamped with a group of insurgents calling themselves only 'the resistance.'"

An image of Sammy showed on the screen. It had been enhanced to make him appear about ten years older. It also gave him long dirty facial hair and a buzzed haircut. *But it's me.* Sammy gripped his stomach and looked for the nearest garbage can. He spotted one next to a water fountain. As he vomited, tears leaked from his eyes. Head in his hands, he sat on the floor and listened to the reporter continue.

"Joining me now is President Newberry's Chief of Staff, Julia Navarre. Ms. Navarre, how are terrorists like this allowed to roam free? How are NWG terrorists arming and aiding insurgents?"

"You are right to demand answers to those questions," the Chief of Staff answered. "What America needs to remember is that the President and his staff are doing everything in their power to win the war, minimize casualties, and keep America safe. These are the kind of horrific events that we went to war to stop. The President never said these attacks would end immediately, he only—"

"But this is a targeted attack on civilians. Tens of millions of dollars in damage to the downtown area. Hundreds of lives lost. People are asking themselves, 'How safe are we?' How does President Newberry answer that?"

"We press harder on the throats of the NWG and any domestic rebels like this Samuel Berhane. We squeeze until they give up."

"So that's it? You squeeze? You get more aggressive?"

"No, no, no. Our strategies are more detailed, but I can't discuss them."

"For obvious reasons," the reporter added in a plain, matter-of-fact tone.

"Of course. But we will respond with aggression, be sure. Our focus and intent has never been greater. We aim to win this war decisively, to not only provide the American people with freedom from fear, but also to liberate the territories of the NWG who wish to join our union."

"What message do you have—or does the president have—for the American people? If he could speak to them right now, what would he say?"

"Have hope. Put your trust in us. We will take care of you. We care about your safety. And a message, if I may, for Samuel Berhane and those insurgents who committed this despicable act. You will answer for your crimes. We will hunt you down and exact justice. You have the blood of hundreds of lives on your hands. That spilled blood will never be forgotten."

Sammy's heart boomed in his chest when he finally turned away from the screen as the reporter thanked the politician for her time. Then he threw up again. When the first reports had come out regarding the death toll of the bombing, he hadn't believed them. He thought surely the CAG was sensationalizing the story. But a resistance member who'd performed search and rescue at the scene had confirmed that the reports were true. Between the building itself and the collateral damage of the collapse, over six hundred people had died.

As the leader of the failed mission, Sammy offered his resignation to Thomas and Lara Byron with the explanation that he was not fit to be in command. When they refused to accept his resignation, he stated that he did not want it anymore. He was stepping down to let someone more capable lead the teams.

"There are better people," he'd insisted. "Your son, your grandson, Anna Lukic, Justice Juraschek, Nikotai … all of them have more experience."

Thomas still wouldn't hear it. "We knew when we planned these missions that the collapse of a building was a real possibility. You and everyone else did everything you could to prevent it."

"The casualties—"

"Are a part of war, Sammy," Thomas said.

"I can't accept that!"

"Neither can we," Lara said. "Which is why we trust you'll figure out what went wrong, and improve." She smiled tenderly at him before pulling him into a hug. "I—I have wept for my part in those deaths, Sammy. I know you have, too. So has Thomas. And while I wept, I reaffirmed my commitment to freedom so that those deaths will not have been in vain."

"'How can I forget that stillness prevailing over the city of three hundred thousand?'" Thomas's eyes had that faraway look they got whenever he quoted poetry. "'Amidst that calm, how can I forget the entreaties of the departed wife and child through their orbs of eyes cutting through our minds and souls?'"

"I appreciate your advice and sympathy," Sammy told them, "but I've made up my mind. I won't lead another mission."

That conversation took place a week ago, and Sammy's mind hadn't budged. He wondered if this was what Commander Byron wanted to speak to him about. Behind him, Jeffie, Natalia, and Strawberry came into the cafeteria for lunch. As Sammy had spent a great deal of energy avoiding his friends, his first instinct was to move away quickly before they spotted him. He hunched his shoulders, ducked his head, and headed for the nearest door. Unfortunately Commander Byron was entering through that door at the same moment.

They nearly bumped into each other. "Whoa, Samuel," Byron said. "I was looking for you. Nice of you to come to me instead."

"Commander, I was just heading to a meeting," Sammy lied.

"Oh, is that right?" The commander's tone told Sammy that he didn't believe him. "May I walk with you? I have been wanting to have a word."

"Yeah … I know."

The commander's bright blue eyes shined even as Byron smiled sadly at Sammy. "Samuel, you need to face the facts of what happened in Detroit."

"I have faced them," Sammy said, still heading toward the stairs to the tunnels, pretending as though he had a meeting. "That's why I told your parents I'm done leading teams. I'm done with the leadership council."

"Then what meetings could you possibly have if you are quitting all those things? Have you joined the janitorial crew?"

"Don't make fun of me!" Sammy shouted.

The expression on Byron's face told Sammy he regretted making a joke. "Sorry." The commander put an arm around Sammy's shoulders and steered him into an old, non-renovated classroom where dozens of old desks had been stacked in piles. Byron used his sleeve to wipe away the dust off the large teacher's desk so they could sit on it.

Sammy slumped down, his elbows resting on his thighs, and his face in his hands. The commander sat next to him. "Six hundred seventeen," he said, "that is the latest count I heard. I bet you can imagine them. I have no doubt the growing number has been on your mind for the last twelve days. You know how I know?"

Sammy made no effort to respond.

"Because I have also killed innocent people."

5 | **Blame**

Friday, May 9, 2087

"OCTOBER 31ˢᵗ, 2065," said Commander Byron. His brow furrowed and his gaze grew distant. "Do you know what happened that day?"

"The Battle of Quebec."

It did not surprise him that Samuel remembered his history lessons well. He remembered everything well.

"Every account I've read of that battle said only the Elite were involved."

The commander nodded, even more impressed now. "Officially the Psion Corps was not involved in that battle. On the books it was Elite only. However, unofficially, it was all Psions in Elite uniforms. Militant rebel forces had captured several government buildings with hundreds of captives, some high-ranking. Reports at the time were unclear if it was a military operation or a civilian coup."

Byron and his father had fought over this very point a month later and not spoken to each other again for almost twenty years.

"Everything about the situation was messy with public support in Quebec already wavering for the NWG. Most of the former country of Canada had already seceded and joined the CAG. We were sent to figure out what was going on and help in any non-combative way we could. Orders were clear to avoid engaging in combat unless authorized by the president.

"General Wu ordered me and Emily to go in first for reconnaissance. It was one of the first missions using stealth cruisers—not nearly as good as the ones we have now. Our team arrived in the dead of night. We entered the main government building through the roof. Black clothes, skin and hair painted black, black goggles over our eyes. We spent three days in the ventilation systems, in the walls, in the crevices of the buildings. Took pictures and video, planted over a dozen mics and cameras to provide the NWG with constant surveillance.

"Emily hated it. After only a few hours, we knew it was a hostage situation, but no word came down from Wu to take action. She wanted to forget orders and call in reinforcements. But Emily was never one to disobey her commanding officer."

"You were her commanding—?" Samuel asked.

Byron nodded. Emily's face floated in his mind, and it made his heart ache. With everything going on these days with Albert and Marie, their constant arguments, Albert's recent turn to drinking for solace, Samuel's difficulties ... *I could use her smiles. Her laughter. Her soothing embrace.*

"For some reason being on the same squad worked well for me and Emily. I would not recommend it for most couples, but we loved it. It seems to work for you and Gefjon too. We had each other's back, and preferred it that way. Maybe it was from all those hours we spent in the flight simulators together." Byron's eyes met Samuel's, and he nodded, certain that his memories were still fresh in Samuel's mind. "Days went by, but still no orders, no contact. Our team continued to search for solutions to present to Command. We sent a recommendation to have snipers take out key targets. We advised an advanced clandestine operation to sneak out the hostages. We must have given them a dozen different plans.

"Despite all our communications, we got no answers and no orders. After a week in Quebec and no contact from anyone on Capitol Island, things grew tense. Everyone knew something was going on back home with the higher-ups, but we were all in the dark. The government trains us to be tough, you know that. But something about that mission ... we broke down mentally faster than we should have. We were all young and inexperienced. Almost all the jobs they had sent us on up to that point lasted two or three days. Now we were well over a week in enemy territory, tight dark places, no contact from Command, no warning that there would be loss of communication.

"We had seven Psions there: me, Emily, and Victor, of course. And Blake Weymouth, Muhammad Zahn, Annalise Havelbert, and Jason Ling. Called ourselves the Lucky Sevens. *Unlucky* would have been more apt. Only Annalise and I are still alive.

"On day ten with still nothing from Command, the team asked me to override our orders and formulate a plan of action. Even Emily advised me to disobey orders."

"Your wife told you to ignore Command?" Samuel asked in a skeptical tone.

"At first, I made the call to wait. No engaging the enemy, only surveillance. But the situation with the hostages got worse. The CAG agents' treatment of them ... It started with beating, starving, then turned into rape and torture. The things they made the hostages do—my conscience forced me to disobey orders."

A throbbing phantom pain started in the commander's legs, long past the joints where his bionic limbs attached to the stumps of his thighs. The pain wasn't so constant now as it had been months ago when he'd first been injured. He tapped his feet and rubbed the metal legs together until the sensation passed.

"It was Quebec where we met the Thirteens for the first time. They already had the red eyes. We assumed it was something contagious or a side-effect of something they were using— some chemical or drug. No one imagined they had done it intentionally.

"We planned an attack, executed it, and were beaten. Nothing prepared us for the Thirteens' ruthlessness in combat. Even now, twenty years later, I do not know how we all survived. Victor nearly died. Emily saved him and Havelbert. Jason Ling lost two fingers on his left hand. Bitten off. Cameras caught us fleeing, and after we left, the Thirteens massacred everyone in the buildings. Hundreds of people, Samuel."

Commander Byron put a hand to his mouth to regain control over his emotions, always so close to the surface these days. *Part of growing old*, he figured. But the emotions were so strong, so fresh. Guilt he hadn't felt in a long time.

"You would think that people would remember the carnage, but no. They remembered us surrendering, essentially, running from the scene. That was what news footage showed. Officially, the CAG disavowed the actions of the assailants, but almost all the targets were government officials blocking the secession of Quebec to the CAG. They announced their intent to withdraw from the NWG while our reinforcements were en route from Capitol Island."

Samuel's face mirrored the remorse Commander Byron felt deep in his bones. "You blame yourself for this, Commander? For the secession of Quebec?"

"The CAG was waiting for us to intervene, Samuel. They knew we were coming and blocked our communications when we got there. It was an elaborate trap designed to make the NWG look weak while also removing the last barriers of Quebec's withdrawal. And I gave the order to send us into their snare. Wu removed me from command of the Psion Corps. It is one of the reasons I was in charge of Beta for so long."

"I thought it was because you liked teaching us, sir."

"I do. But they would have promoted me long before you were recruited were it not for that black stain on my record."

"Why are you telling me this?" Samuel asked with a tone of obstinacy.

Commander Byron sighed. "I guess I like talking to you. Most of my conversations these days with Albert end in him shouting and leaving the room."

Samuel looked away and nodded. For some reason this made Byron feel even older. *Emily, it should have been me who died, not you. You always knew what to say.*

"I rarely talk about my regrets, my mistakes. But with you, it comes easily. I know what happened in Detroit weighs heavily on you. You think I cannot imagine—"

"No, you can't."

"I can," Byron said sharply. "When Quebec seceded, I did not understand the ramifications at the time. I was a soldier—one with responsibility, yes—but still a soldier. Over the years that followed, the Silent War years, I realized that losing Quebec was a massive blow to the NWG. We lost important footholds in CAG territory. If I had not blown that mission, Quebec might not have seceded. If Quebec had not seceded, neither would have the other remaining NWG territories in North and South America. You see, Samuel, my actions—my decision—profoundly impacted the NWG in a terrible way."

Samuel shook his head. "It's not the same. You were doing your best in a messed up situation."

"So are you."

"I—I messed up. His face—their faces, I see them in my dreams. I watch the tower fall over and over and over every night. The metal twisting, the glass shattering ... I see it all, Commander. And their blood stains me. Who else is to blame?"

There was an edge in Samuel's voice that the commander didn't like. *And he said "his face."*

"Why does there have to be blame?" Byron asked.

"Because I messed up!"

"Every Psion who has died in the last three decades has been a friend or a student of mine. With each death I wonder what I might have done better as a teacher and mentor to prevent that death. In your nightmares you see nameless faces, I see men and women I knew and taught and recruited to a shortened life. And those who live? What kind of life have I brought them?"

"So then why did you keep doing it? You would recruit again tomorrow if you could. Wouldn't you?"

"I would."

"Why?" Samuel almost shouted the word. His eyes flashed either rage or confusion, the commander couldn't tell which.

"'War is an ugly thing, but not the ugliest of things.' John Stuart Mill."

Samuel sighed. "So then what?"

"Learn from it. Try not to repeat it."

In the silence that followed, Samuel's face lit up and his eyes stared through the commander as though he were a ghost. "No ..." He whispered. "No, we *have* to repeat it. Excuse me, sir. I need—I need ..." He got up, his eyes still unfocused.

"We have the leadership committee in twenty minutes. Are you going to be there this time?"

"I know ..."

"But—" Before Commander Byron could argue, Samuel was gone. "At least you didn't shout at me like Albert," he muttered to no one.

A half hour later, the commander sat next to his father in the old air traffic control tower in Saint Marie, the neighboring city to Glasgow. These two towns formed the two halves of the resistance's headquarters. The air tower had long been the meeting place of the leadership committee.

To the commander and many others' surprise, Samuel arrived shortly after the meeting started and took his place at the table without fanfare in between Anna Lukic and Justice Juraschek. Across the table from Byron sat Albert, his eyes red and his face drooped. *Hungover again*, he thought with a sigh.

"Let's give the floor to Commander Byron," his mother, Lara, said, "for a report on the NWG efforts."

The commander had been serving as the NWG-resistance liaison for almost four months now. Part of his duties included speaking at each meeting, briefing the resistance as to what the NWG advised or wanted the resistance to consider. In return, he provided the NWG information about the resistance's plans. At least twice a week, the commander communicated with either General Annalise Havelbert or Ivan Drovovic, the NWG's first Tensai. In the wake of General Wu's death during the initial attacks on Capitol Island, Havelbert had been appointed by President William Marnyo as Director of Military Operations, and Drovovic as Deputy Director.

"NWG leaders anticipate a new push ... another offensive strike from the CAG in the coming weeks," Commander Byron informed the committee. "They are making preparations to defend against these assaults and minimize casualties. If losses are kept to a minimum, they plan to respond with an offensive strike of their own. They are asking us to consider a joint strike and request that we submit several ideas to them by the end of next week."

Samuel raised his finger and caught Lara's eye. She recognized him and gave him the floor. "According to my calculations," he began, "we have the firepower to hit nine major towers that hold Hybrid cloning facilities—"

Justice shook his head. "No … we have far more than that. Twenty to twenty-two was my latest count."

"Yes," Samuel agreed, "*if* our plan is to continue our assaults with the same conservative approach we've been doing, then we can hit twenty or more towers. But let's think bigger for a moment. Let's envision something so big that we grab the world's attention. So bold that every last citizen of the CAG wants out of the war in an instant. Gloves off. Total warfare.

"We could simultaneously hit a maximum of nine towers if we orchestrate a multi-faceted strike so big the CAG will be crippled. Massive damage in urban areas followed by a precipitous drop in support for the war on the side of the CAG. Clone production would be cut nearly in half."

The commander felt light-headed as his eyes met Samuel's. For a moment he thought he must be misunderstanding Samuel's proposition. But when he realized he hadn't misunderstood anything, he paled and stared at the young man. His head shook very slightly from left to right. *Why would you suggest such a thing?*

Justice muttered to himself, his eyes sweeping side to side as though searching for the answer. Then they widened when he too realized the breadth of the idea proposed. "Whoa. That's wild, Sammy. That's … a little too wild."

Lorenzo Winters raised a hand. "Are you suggesting we obliterate ten city towers? Kill tens of thousands of people?"

All eyes were on Samuel, and his expression changed from one of confidence to someone swimming in shark-infested waters. "I'm saying we need to consider the ramifications of doing something drastic to tip the scales in our favor. All we've done so far is cling on, scrape by, and pray for miracles. Our sabotages of the clone production centers haven't had the desired effect. They have too many of them. But after Detroit … the public is waking up. Multiply that effect by nine, combine it with a similarly brutal strike from the NWG targeting more urban areas, and the war may come to an end. Isn't that what we want? To win the war?"

"With what cost attached?" Lorenzo asked. The shock on his face made Samuel wither. "Thousands of lives? Innocent people?"

"It's the bigger picture I am thinking about," Samuel said.

"Tens of thousands of victims is a pretty big picture," the commander's father countered.

"Casualties are a part of war," Samuel told Thomas, feeding him his own words. "*'How can I forget that stillness prevailing over the city of three hundred thousand?'*"

"Enough," Thomas said firmly.

Lara stared at Samuel aghast, a hand over her mouth.

"I'm offering a suggestion, that's all," Sammy finally explained. "It should at least be considered since it *will* work. Does anyone else have ideas?"

"I agree with Sammy." The words came from Albert, but a couple others nodded. "If we can end the war, we should."

Commander Byron didn't have time to react to his son's statement before Duncan Hudec spoke up.

"Who's to say it won't escalate things?" Duncan said. "We bomb cities with our ordnance, they pull out a nuke. Pretty soon, ain't no one left standing."

"Nuclear weapons have been disarmed and banned since the Scourge," Anna argued.

"Don't be so naïve, miss," Duncan shot back. "You really think countries really got rid of all their best toys? Ask ol' Byron here if the NWG fully disarmed."

All eyes turned on the commander.

"Escalation is a possibility. The NWG does have a small number of nuclear warheads at its disposal, as does the CAG. Nowhere near the numbers of, say, a hundred years ago, but enough. The course of action Samuel has suggested could drive the CAG to consider their use." Commander Byron turned his attention to Samuel, "But in light of our conversation less than an hour ago, I am stunned you would suggest such a thing."

"It's my job to suggest something if it has the possibility to achieve our goal. Am I wrong in assuming that our goal is still to win the war?"

"You people can't really think the CAG will respond with nukes, can you?" Albert asked. "You aren't that stupid."

Commander Byron winced at the way Albert slurred his *s* sounds. *Have you already started drinking today?*

"Let's just blow the world to hell!" Duncan Hudec hollered from where he sat at the corner of the table with his brother. "That'll end all wars."

Several people laughed uneasily. Thomas Byron and the commander both put up a hand to ask everyone to quiet down.

"Grow up, Duncan," Samuel responded. "I'm not proposing mass destruction. Not even city-wide destruction. Nine buildings in nine cities. Nine buildings that produce the clones we're fighting and hold Thirteen cells. The collateral damage will be high, yes, but not catastrophic."

He may as well have called everyone in the room *morons* with his tone.

"The CAG has consolidated power by orchestrating terrorist acts and blaming the NWG," Lorenzo reminded the committee. "If we go and commit more terrorist acts, we're undermining our entire argument."

"I suggest we turn our focus to more practical solutions," Commander Byron said, keeping his voice light and even, "and not on something that could prove to be a *catastrophic* mistake."

"Yes," Samuel answered, "if anyone knows about making catastrophic mistakes, it'd be you, sir."

While no one else in the room knew what the comment meant, Commander Byron stared at Samuel with a gaping jaw. For a moment, he couldn't even breathe. Even Samuel seemed shocked at what had come out of his mouth.

"Excuse me," Byron said as he stood slowly. "I believe Samuel and I need to speak in private while this meeting continues without us."

Samuel glanced around the room. All eyes were on him. Byron got up first and left the air traffic control tower's main room. Samuel followed at a much slower pace, his gaze on the floor. Byron waited right outside, his arms folded and his face stone. His blue eyes searched the younger man's. He spoke in a whisper. "What is going on?"

"I—I—I—" Samuel rubbed his hair with both hands and shook his head. "I'm sorry, sir."

"Sorry?" The commander raised his eyebrows as his eyes continued to bore into Samuel's. "No. I told you something private. *Extremely* private. Fifteen minutes later you throw it in my face. Now you say 'sorry?'"

"Sir, I don't know what—"

"*Sammy* ..." The commander paused as he tried to find the words to express all his jumbled up thoughts. "An hour ago I was trying to console you because I thought you were burdened by what happened in Detroit. Now you want to blow up nine more buildings. Help me understand what is going on because I am lost."

"Well, so am I!" Samuel shouted. In the blink of an eye he transformed from someone sorrowful to enraged. "I don't know what's what anymore! Now that I've seen how we can win, it doesn't make a difference to me if one person or a million people die, so long as we win."

"Why? Where is this coming from?"

"I don't know!"

The commander had his suspicions, knew what he had to do, but didn't like it. He grabbed Samuel hard on the shoulders and shook him. "Do not lie to me! You know something. What is going on?"

Then he saw what he was looking for in Samuel's eyes. *Rage.* Samuel wanted to kill him, kill everyone. He saw a need to spill blood and revel in it. When their eyes locked, Byron took a step back, afraid of what he saw.

"When—when did you let it out? Why?"

The fury that a moment ago had emanated from Samuel's very being now dissipated like a popped balloon. The younger Psion's frame slackened and bent. He regarded the commander now with an expression of deep remorse that seemed to reach his bones. He didn't answer, didn't speak. Commander Byron put a hand on his shoulder.

"I understand now, but you need to talk to me. When did—"

"When do you think? *Why do you think?* I didn't have a choice."

Commander Byron had seen the footage of Samuel fighting the Thirteens in the basement of the Joswang Tower in Detroit, but he hadn't believed Samuel had used the Anomaly Thirteen. Surely Samuel had shown restraint and good judgment. His obvious prowess and speed in battle, that had all been the rush of adrenaline and Samuel's other natural gifts. That was what he had told himself.

I was wrong.

"There is always a choice, Samuel," Byron finally said.

"It helped me. I couldn't have gotten Brickert out of there without it."

"You do not know that."

"I *do* know!" Samuel clenched his fists tightly that his knuckles whitened. "I know what I'm capable of."

"I told you to keep your emotions in check. You cannot use the anomaly. Not even a step down that path!"

"It's too late. Okay? And I'm not sorry because I saved my best friend's life."

"There is no good excuse. There is not one excuse good enough for that. How many times do I have to tell you that you are—"

"The most important asset in the war?"

"Yes! You are too valuable to lose."

"I'm fully aware that Command licks their chops at the prospect of having me for a lifetime of service … provided we win this war, of course." His voice dripped sarcasm.

"Valuable to me is what I meant." Byron's grip on Sammy's shoulder tightened. "As far as I am concerned, you are my son. Have I not told you that?"

"More than once, sir," he whispered.

Byron let go of Samuel's shoulder and grasped him behind the neck. Before Byron knew it, Samuel had wrapped his arms around him.

"I'm sorry, sir. But I couldn't just let him die. I had to do everything I could."

"I know, but the darkest deeds are often done by desperate people who mean well. Promise me. Never again."

"I can't."

Byron released Samuel so he could look into his eyes. "You have to. I want your word. You will never again use the anomaly."

"I can't give you my word, sir. I can't promise I'll never do it again."

"Samuel … *Sammy* …"

"No. Because I don't know what the future holds or if someday I'll have to break that oath."

"Nothing is worth—"

"Some things are. Brickert's life. Jeffie's life. Yours. I refuse to accept someone's death when I can do more to save him."

"Sammy—"

"I'm done talking about this, sir. Tell the committee I'm not feeling well, and I withdraw the idea I submitted to them. And—and give them my apologies." Then Samuel left before the commander could respond.

* * * * *

Back at his house, Sammy threw himself on his bed. His room carried the faint smell of sweat and old laundry. Dirty clothes littered the floor. Across the hall, in Brickert's room, things were tidy, almost pristine. Nothing in there had been touched for days. But in Sammy's world everything was a mess.

And my fault.

A noise came from the kitchen, distracting him from his misery.

"Who is it?" he called out.

"Hiya stranger," came Jeffie's voice.

Sammy dropped his head back to his pillow. "What do you want?"

"To see my boyfriend." She appeared at the door to his bedroom, smiling like it was Christmas morning.

Sammy groaned in response. He knew it was rude, but didn't care at the moment. Jeffie frowned and sat by him on the bed. Her fingers combed through his hair; he closed his eyes and savored the sensation. In a world as screwed up as his, it was nice to have one thing to provide a little comfort.

"Can we spend some time together this weekend, Sammy?" Jeffie asked. "Just us? Doing something fun?"

"I don't know," Sammy said. "I'm really busy."

"Yeah, you've been busy since Detroit."

The idea of being alone with Jeffie, having to talk about feelings and pretending to be happy so she could be happy, did not appeal to him. A big pile of fake happiness between them. But if he wasn't with Jeffie, he'd be by himself. And he didn't want that either. Neither did he want to be around other people. Truthfully, the only person he wanted to talk to was Brickert. He wanted to know his friend would be all right. Wanted to tell him sorry for everything, that punching him had been a mistake, and that he'd never regretted anything so much in his entire life.

"Sammy? Are you even in the room with me?"

"What kind of question is that?" Sammy asked.

"The question that's been on my mind for weeks. You're AWOL. I call. You don't answer. I send you messages. You don't respond." She snatched his com from him and pulled up his screen. "You're not even opening them!"

Sammy grabbed it back from her, his face red and hot.

Jeffie seemed to swallow her anger as she pressed on. "Even when we're together, you're somewhere else. Like now. You've been distant ever since Detroit, Sammy. Distant and different."

"I'm not—what does—I don't have time for this, Jeffie."

Jeffie gestured to his bed. "Sorry, didn't realize you were so busy laying there and all. Should I leave so you can get back to that?"

"That's not what I meant." Sammy turned over onto his side so all she could see was his back.

"Please talk to me," Jeffie pleaded. "You're a fighter. You always have been. Look at all you've accomplished—"

Sammy laughed harshly. "No thanks."

Jeffie grabbed him and twisted him around. "Stop. This isn't healthy. Whatever it is that's causing this, we can talk about it. We can get through it."

Sammy shook his head. "You don't even know what's going on. Why do you think you can fix my problems?"

"Because I love you."

The words were not what Sammy had expected to hear. And judging by the shocked look on Jeffie's face, she hadn't expected to say them.

"Take that back, Jeffie. Take it back now and say it was an accident."

"Why?"

"Because you don't mean it."

Jeffie's gaze focused on something far away. She was looking past Sammy, or perhaps through him. Her hand slipped into his, and though her touch warmed and comforted him, he wanted her to let go. She sensed this and tightened her grip. And when she looked at him again, she smiled. "Actually, I think I do mean it."

It was wrong. It was all wrong. Not because she loved him but because of what he was, what he'd done. The only reason she could think she loved him was because she didn't know him. Not really. She couldn't see the ugly reality behind the person everyone thought was a hero.

"I'm a monster." He thought he'd said the words in his head, but he'd spoken them aloud. Jeffie stared back at him with confusion. Sammy crawled off the bed, putting distance between himself and Jeffie. "Stay away from me. This is over. It has to be."

Just as he'd run away from Byron, Sammy walked as fast as he dared, closed the door behind him, and then fled while Jeffie shouted his name.

6 | Extraction

Wednesday, March 26, 2053

KATIE JERKED AWAKE. Her heart punched the inside of her ribs with each beat. Sweat soaked her clothes and bed sheets, cooling rapidly as the night air hit them. She fumbled in the dark until she found the switch to her lamp and flipped it on. Her eyes went straight to her hands, but there was no red on them. They were clean.

"A dream," she whispered as her head hit her cold pillow. But even still, she had to examine her palms and fingers again. Once satisfied, she dropped her hands to her sheets and felt the wetness there. Katie sniffed her hands. It wasn't sweat.

"Oh no."

She worked in silence; ripped the bedding off her mattress, changed out of her soiled clothes, and threw it all in the washer. Her parents couldn't know, which meant she had to stay up until they had dried so she could put the sheets back on the bed.

Once she had the machine running, she slumped onto the couch in her robe and tried to read the book she'd been assigned for her Literature course: *The Strange Case of Dr. Jekyll and Mr. Hyde*. After a few paragraphs, she set her tablet down. It was no use. All she could think about was the dream. Priyanka had been voted prom queen, Katie the princess. Priyanka taunted Katie as she passed her on the dais to receive the queen's crown. Katie tackled Priyanka and smashed her face in with the crown until Priyanka's blood covered her hands and face.

Then the dream had changed. Katie walked barefoot in the cold forest. The smell of the earth and the leaves filled her nose. The shadow version of herself joined her again. Katie stared at the shadow for a long time, realizing that it was not as scary as it seemed the first time. It was her, only without color.

You can be free, Shadow-Katie said. *Do you want that?*

"Free from what?"

Katie caught a glint in Shadow-Katie's black eyes. The shadow grinned as though filled with pure euphoria. *Everything.*

"How?"

Shadow-Katie raised a hand, and Katie knew that it was an invitation for her to touch the hand with her own. Hand slightly trembling, she raised her limb and placed it against the shadow's hand. And then woke.

"What's wrong with me?" Katie said as she rubbed her head. "Stupid dreams … go away."

A beep from her tablet alerted her to a new message:

Someones up late … What are you doing?

It was Mark, her boyfriend. If she didn't answer soon, he'd start talking dirty. So she quickly replied:

Homework. Just finished. U?

Mark answered.

You dont wanna no. It aint homework. You really doing homework? Or "homework?"

Katie made a grossed out face and wrote:

REAL homework, perv. I'm so beat. Lit is gonna kick my butt. See you tomorrow. xoxo

She rolled her eyes at the lameness of her own message, but it was what all the girls did when they signed off with their boyfriends. Mark buzzed her again before she could end their chat:

Hey wait. Heard Pri's gonna ramp things up tomorrow. Gettin ugly.

Katie had no choice but to respond.

What's she doing?

Mark's answer came quickly:

Posting pictures of you at a slumber party with stuff all over your face. Just stupid stuff but it makes you look dum. Says something like "prom queen or court jester?" I dunno. Damien was telling me about it. Sorry babe.

Katie laughed as she finished their conversation:

Wow. If that's all she's got, I'm not really worried. Night.

The next day, when Katie saw the pictures, she wished she'd taken Mark's warning more seriously. Someone put them up during first period, and they were everywhere when she left her class.

The pictures were horrific. She recognized them from a slumber party she'd gone to at Courtney's house. Katie had been the first girl to fall asleep, so her friends had taken a bunch of shots of her in weird poses. Now, with several undressed men doctored in, the photos made Katie look like a slut.

"PROM QUEEN OR *PORN* QUEEN?" they read.

Crowds of students gathered around the photos, gawking at them. When Katie saw the first one, she tore it down, but there were dozens of them plastered all over the building. Students jeered and whistled at her when they saw her, calling her filthy names and wagging their tongues.

Katie burned with rage. She pulled down every poster she saw, screaming as she did so. Several students filmed her with their phones and watches, but she didn't care. Her cries reached the ears of a few teachers, who came out of their classrooms to investigate. When they saw the cause for her alarm, they helped her take down the pictures. It took them the better part of an hour to locate them all, but by the time they finished the damage was done. The images were so vulgar, so obscene—she looked like she'd been caught making a smutty film.

How could Priyanka do this?

Before Katie made it to her next class, the principal, Mrs. Simpson, approached her in the hall and put her hands on Katie's shoulders. "Come to my office, Miss Carpenter." Without realizing it, Katie was gripping the pictures so tightly in her hands they left small paper cuts. Mrs. Simpson gently pulled them from her grasp and led her away. Katie hadn't taken five steps when she broke down in tears. Her life was over.

* * * * *

Saturday, May 10, 2087

Diego sat in the center of the Hive watching his screens. *My friends.* They glittered and sparkled at him like diamonds, feeding him information and connecting him to the world. He was Superman observing the world from his Fortress of Solitude. He was an angel on top of the world. Nothing could touch him. Nothing could harm him. He was a secret, powerful and unseen. Everywhere and nowhere. Godlike. It was a nice way to live: no distractions, no interruptions, no people.

At least that was how it used to be until a few months ago, when visitors came, including Samuel Berhane, Jr., The World's Most Arrogant Boy. Sammy had almost ruined everything. While removing evidence of the boy's visit, Diego had thought of many colorful nicknames for Sammy. *Pubescent petulant pissant.* That one was his favorite.

It had taken him days to clean up the mess: tossing weighted bodies of Thirteens into Lake Coari for the piranhas to devour, removing lines of code from the databases and servers where Sammy's team had hacked the systems, deleting system alerts that Sammy's team had set off entering the Hive. Diego had wanted to tell the fox everything that had happened, to raise all the alarms, but someone had stopped him.

Trapper.

I should have activated the fail-safes of the Hive the instant I knew he was here. Instead, he'd let Sammy speak, and the very mention of Trapper's name, had woken Trapper, a man long since beaten. Now Trapper had renewed purpose and strength, gathered from years of isolation. He decided he wanted a voice and refused to be ignored. And his primary mission was to stop Diego from communicating to the fox. At every turn he was there blocking Diego with threats of murder.

Suicide, Trapper reminded Diego. Even Trapper's voice inside Diego's head had that maddening lisp.

"I am not you!" Diego had screamed more than once at the intruder. "I have nothing to do with you!"

He knew Trapper's threats were real. Trapper would do it. He would kill Diego. Diego had woken up from the gas, even had his finger on the alert button, but Trapper had put a gun to Diego's head. A long talk followed, ending in a compromise. Diego would allow the Hive infiltration to be covered up, and Trapper would let Diego continue his daily duties serving the fox.

Most of Diego's screens showed CAG and NWG news stations' coverage of the war—the hottest story for the last nine months. Both sides spun the story in their favor, yet neither side gave very accurate details. The truth (as only a few knew) was that the war wasn't going well for either side. The devastating attack on Detroit had demoralized the northern and eastern CAG territories. Clone production couldn't meet demands, and the product was still severely flawed and underdeveloped. Meanwhile the NWG still didn't have the strength or manufacturing power to mount an effective offensive strike. The data didn't lie.

A beep from one of his screens called his attention. Diego turned to see a purple animated fox staring back at him. He instinctively sat a little straighter in his chair and waited to be addressed to show his respect for the greatest man he'd ever known.

"The Queen will visit you shortly. She is already en route. Provide her with all the information she requests. I need you to brief her on confidential matters."

Diego raised what remained of his left eyebrow. The Queen had never visited the inner sanctum of the Hive. And the fox had never called her the Queen. Something was amiss. "Have you seen the news recently?"

"I haven't. Is there some matter of which I need to be made aware?"

"No—no … I was—never mind."

The graphic of the fox disappeared, replaced with satellite images of areas designated as important to watch.

It's not him, Trapper said.

"I am aware of that!" Diego snapped.

Years ago, the fox and Diego had made an arrangement that if Diego ever suspected the fox was acting under duress, he would ask the fox if he had read the news. The fox, in return, would state, "The news is never new if you knew what I know." And the fox had not said those words.

A hologram? Trapper suggested.

"Or a test?" Diego countered.

Shoot her down. The fox won't blame you. Tell him you were acting in his best interest.

"Don't be foolish. I can't just shoot down the Queen!"

Sure you can. Wait until she appears on the radar and give the command.

Diego's eye socket and broken, scarred lips twitched violently as he tried to decide what to do. When the Queen appeared on his display, he kept his eye fixed on her cruiser but made no attempt to kill her.

Do it. Do it. Do it, Trapper whispered incessantly.

She landed on the small island and entered through the main doors. Diego watched her on camera as she ascended the stairs to the top floor. He sensed an air about her that disturbed him, though he couldn't pinpoint exactly why.

The door opened and she strode in very much like a queen, took the empty chair, crossed her legs, and smirked at him. "Diego … Feels like I haven't seen you in years. Ugly as ever, I see. Why is it so quiet here? Where are our brothers?"

"On assignment," Diego answered in a growl. "What is so urgent that the fox has sent you to interrupt me?"

"The fox is busy too. I haven't seen him in days. But I got the call, and I go where I'm asked to go. Send your questions his way."

"I don't answer to you!" Diego screamed and jumped at the Queen.

An invisible force slammed into him, and before he knew it, his butt was back in his chair, sliding until he banged into a panel. "You—how—you—you can't blast!"

"Times are changing, Diego."

"The fox hasn't alerted me of this. Why hasn't—Does he know? How long has it been since you last saw him?"

The Queen waved the questions away like they were flies. "I don't keep a calendar. Nor do I impose information about myself upon the fox without his invitation. His mind is absorbed in the war."

"Then what's your purpose here?"

"The extraction program."

Diego suppressed a smile. All this time he'd thought she knew about the program, but she didn't have a clue. "What about it?"

"Everything. He wants me to know everything about it."

"I wonder why he didn't just send you to the extraction site ..." Diego kept his voice neutral so she wouldn't hear his suspicion. "Seems much easier."

"I don't question him."

Something was wrong. The fox didn't operate like this. Was someone impersonating him? Did the Queen know about it or was she also being fooled by the imposter? Diego's lips twitched again before he spoke. "I don't know *everything* about it. Perhaps you should have gone there instead of wasting my time."

"I don't know where the extraction site is."

Diego narrowed his eyes on the Queen, watching her closely. "So the fox sent you to me to tell you its location. And that doesn't strike you as odd?"

The Queen's eyes flashed dangerously. "Either tell me or don't, but you can take up whatever concerns you have regarding the fox's behavior with him."

"You want to go there today?"

"Now." She sniffed the air with disgust. "This place stinks like a cripple."

Diego couldn't help but note her beauty. He hated looking at her face because it served as a constant reminder of his own hideousness. Every scar and disfigurement burned in the presence of her magnificence, and suddenly he hated Emerald with the heat of a blitzer.

Focus, Trapper said. *Stop thinking about the girl who gave us the scars.*

Diego snarled and then remembered the Queen. He had to give her information.

You don't have to give her anything! The fox probably didn't even endorse this.

But the idea of ignoring Trapper's advice made Diego grin inside.

"The extraction program ..." He searched his memory for everything he could tell her. "It was created side-by-side with the citizen surveillance initiative: the fox's brainchild. Round up as many anomalies as possible by encouraging CAG citizens to be on the lookout for suspicious behavior. The theory was to get on-the-ground, real-time feedback, and identify anomalies faster than the NWG. The idea worked. People were willing to comply. They still are. Identified individuals go to cells for triage, and those chosen for extraction go to ... the extraction site."

"Get to the point, Diego. Where is it?"

"What was the first major catastrophe the fox orchestrated to implicate the NWG in terrorist acts against the CAG?"

"The Mexico City bombing."

Diego tapped what was left of his nose to tell her she was right. "That wasn't chosen randomly. The contract to rebuild the site into a memorial was given to Murrolems Construction Group, a subsidiary of N Corp. An underground facility exists there called the Extraction/Implantation Project."

The Queen snorted and rolled her eyes. "Sounds like a dental clinic."

"Every anomaly under the age of eighteen is sent there for extraction and implantation."

"And those eighteen and over?"

"Incinerators."

The Queen's lips formed a tight grin. Diego wished he could read her better. Before another word was said, she stood up and paced around the room, running her hand over the consoles and operating boards as she moved. Diego watched her closely.

"What do they do there?" was her next question.

"I don't know. It was never within my scope of oversight."

She laughed and paused, her hands gripped the edge of one console, her face turned toward him. He still could not read her perfect face. "If I go to this site today, will they let me in or does the fox need to grant me access?"

"The fox will need to call ahead and let them know you are coming," Diego lied. The truth was that both Diego and the fox could authorize visits to the site.

The Queen didn't respond. "I'll ask him to take care of it." Then she left, and Diego sat in his chair, stewing over what had just taken place.

Someone is impersonating the fox, Trapper said.

"And the Queen ..." Diego mused. "Something strange about her too."

She can blast now. How did that happen?

"I have no idea."

Perhaps it is all connected. But what can you do? You are on an island.

Diego had no answer for Trapper. It was wrong. Wrong. All wrong! He paced the room, scratching at his head, rubbing the face that Emerald had mangled years ago. "Why do people have to mess things up? Why can't I just be left alone?"

You mean why can't we *be left alone?*

"SHUT UP!" Diego had no one to go to for help. No one who understood. For years it had been only he and the fox. When he needed assistance, when rare bouts of loneliness hit him, or when he saw something that worried him, he called the fox.

Sammy, Trapper suggested. *You need Sammy.*

Diego laughed. It was a garbled, hoarse thing that reminded him of a toilet not flushing properly. He'd always liked its sound. But the laugh died when something caught his eye. A bump. A protrusion where there shouldn't be. An aberration. He got down on his hands and knees and crawled across the floor, staring at it. His eye twitched the closer he drew.

When he stopped crawling, his nose and eye were nearly pressed up against the underside of his console where a small flat device stuck magnetically to the metal. Instinctively, he reached out to grab it, but his hand froze less than a centimeter away when Trapper yelled, *Don't! You don't know what it is.*

"She planted it," Diego told the pest.

Exactly. To spy on us.

"To spy on me."

If it has an accelerometer, she'll know you moved it.

Gently, slowly, carefully, and more gently, Diego slid it until the magnet had nothing left to hold. It took him an hour to take the device apart, but when he finished he knew exactly what the thing could do.

"She'll know everything I do," he told Trapper. "Every call, every keystroke."

The fox will, too, if she's working with him.

"The fox trusts me." Diego licked his four lips with a dry tongue. "This is your fault! Yours! You wouldn't let me call him. You made me hide the evidence. What if they found out about Sammy and the girl and—"

Something has happened. You need to contact Sammy. He's the only way we can get out of this mess.

Diego shook his head, but what if Trapper was right? "I don't even know how."

You're smart. You'll figure it out.

* * * * *

"Welcome to the Extraction/Implantation Project," a pretty woman in her early thirties said to the Queen as she met her at the door. She had bleach-blonde hair and walked with short, tight steps. "I only learned of your impending arrival ten minutes ago. My name is Judy. The Project Director has asked me to show you around and answer all your questions. He said you are to be given full access and security clearance."

"Thank you," said the Queen smugly. Her ability to impersonate the fox gave her access to any door she wanted open. "I want to know everything, so don't stop talking unless I tell you to or interrupt you with a question."

They were in an underground world of pristine chrome and glass. Ultra-security to get in and out. A place so perfectly quiet that it was obvious something horribly imperfect was happening. A sickly thrill ran down the Queen's body, starting at the muscles on the back of her skull and stopping at the very base of her spine.

How could the fox have kept this place a secret from me?

Judy led the Queen to her office. A chrome door with the words `Project Director - Assistant` carved into the metal paneling with a laser. The door shut behind them with a hiss. The office was not very homey. Spartan, modern furnishings decorated it: a simple desk, three chairs, and a computer. No pictures, plants, or personal items proudly displayed. Nothing to give the Queen any idea regarding Judy's interests, background, hobbies, or home life. Judy must have noticed the Queen's curiosity because she smiled plainly and said, "I'm married to my work. I can assure you, we all are here. That's why we were chosen. Depressing, huh?"

She wore a lab coat, and underneath it a fitted gray sweater and stylish khaki-colored pants. Her long blonde hair was pulled back, a black barrette held it all in place. Her legs were crossed, right over left. At least once every five minutes, the holo-screen on her com turned on and displayed an alert, only to disappear seconds later. From what the Queen could tell, Judy read and processed each message.

"The Project has been in existence for twelve years. The same year the Safety Laws were passed by Congress. Budgetary earmarks to the Safety Laws have kept the project well-funded ever since. All candidates for the training come from Aegis interrogation units based independently in the Thirteen cells. Over the last twelve years, our protocol has evolved. Each subject endures two rigorous programs. If they fail the first, they do not proceed to the second. We have a 75% failure rate in the first program, but that's quite an improvement from our earlier years. It used to be as high as 90%. Fortunately our success rate in the second program is 100%."

"Tell me more about these programs."

"I'll show them to you. The first program is called H.A.M.M.E.R. Habitual Acquiescence, Memory Modification, Education Reconstruction. The name is self-explanatory. Success in this program is vital to the second. All the subjects in H.A.M.M.E.R. are kept in the main facility."

"Both programs are located here?" the Queen asked. "The building doesn't seem that large."

"The second program is located much deeper underground. They all want to reach the second level, I assure you. It's one of the first things we condition into them."

"Which anomalies go through this training?"

"Eleven, Fourteen, and Fifteen. Not Thirteen. Training for Thirteens and Aegis takes place in individual Thirteen cells. Once an Eleven, Fourteen, or Fifteen completes H.A.M.M.E.R., he or she is sent to S.H.I.E.L.D.

"S.H.I.E.L.D. stands for: Skill Honing, Intelligence Enhancement, Learning Development. Our aim is to create operative teams that exceed what the Alpha program of the NWG has produced. I think we are on the verge of success. We hope to do test deployments in real battle situations in the next four to six weeks."

"What happens to those who fail H.A.M.M.E.R.?"

Judy smiled and re-crossed her legs, her eyes staring off to the side. "They are released from the program as efficiently as possible. We have a release scheduled today. Possibly two." Judy's smile grew and she wasted no time getting to her feet. "Let's begin the tour."

First Judy showed the Queen the offices of the project directors, staff psychiatrists, nutritionists, and other laborers. These offices were separated from the H.A.M.M.E.R. facility via a metal door nearly a meter thick.

"This type of impenetrable reinforcement surrounds the entire complex," Judy noted proudly. "An amalgam of seven different metals. It's impossible for Anomaly Fourteens to even dent. A couple even had the chance to try. It was … interesting." She ran her fingers along the metal with a lover's touch. "The stories I could tell you …"

Once through the door, they came to a room with Aegis guards watching a host of monitors. To their right stood a stack of weapons, including the new mini-blitzers that the Queen had heard about. The small surveillance room had four doors placed symmetrically around the room: the one Judy had brought the Queen through, one directly ahead, and ones to the left and right. The letters H.A.M.M.E.R. were scored into the floor with a massive mallet emblazoned in the background.

"Cells to the right, testing rooms straight ahead, and to the left … classrooms. Which would you like to see first? All are fascinating, I assure you."

The Queen chose the cells, knowing they would be the most boring. She was wrong. Only half of the two hundred cells were occupied. "How long does the H.A.M.M.E.R. program take to complete?" she asked Judy.

"It all depends on the candidate. Some have completed it in less than a year, others take several. After the age of twenty-one, the chance that a candidate will succeed drops precipitously. To conserve our efforts on more worthy investments, we consider those candidates hopeless, and we release them."

"Efficiently," the Queen added.

"Assuredly."

The Queen observed a few dozen cells. All the ones she peered into had occupants. They had metal walls, carpeted floors, beds attached to the walls. Some had more luxuries and comforts, others were bare.

"We have full control over the rooms. Candidates who behave badly see their privileges removed. The bed will lock into the wall so they have to sleep on the carpet, which can retract into the floor. Sometimes we soak the carpet in ammonia-scented water to make them miserable and cold. The walls can expand or shrink to disorient them or make them feel claustrophobic. Dozens of discomforts and rewards are at our disposal to modify or encourage certain behaviors. All tailored to the individual. That's why our psych team is so important."

"They keep the candidates from killing themselves?"

Judy smiled. "That rarely happens. Normally they breakdown— and very rapidly, be assured." She pointed down the hall to one door in particular.

The Queen looked inside and saw it was empty, but the walls were covered in filth, brown and red.

"That candidate turned into an animal. Chewing on his fingers till they bled. Playing in his feces. Once they get to that point, they're hopeless for moving to the next level. He was immediately released."

Memories of her solitary prison cell in the Wyoming Ultramax Facility awoke in the Queen's brain, followed by revulsion and anger. She had nearly gone mad, imagining herself to be a goddess—a phoenix—until the fox rescued her. For a moment, so strong was her indignation at the torment these children were experiencing, her fingers began to ache and throb as though she had chewed on them. She wanted to tear down the H.A.M.M.E.R. facility piece by piece. Hate twisted her stomach like a wrench.

The Queen yearned for her creams to help her control the pain and emotion.

"I've seen enough," she said in a strained voice. "Take me to the other areas."

The next area was the testing center. The Queen asked, "What sort of tests are they given?"

"Obedience," Judy answered. "Obedience is key. To graduate from H.A.M.M.E.R. means we are absolutely sure the candidate will follow orders and be loyal to the CAG. We have a graduation test today for one of our most promising candidates. Would you care to observe it?"

"I would."

"Very good." Judy nodded and adjusted her barrette as they entered another hallway. "In the meantime, let me walk you through and familiarize you with the testing process in general. We use a mix of several schools of psychology to mentally and behaviorally condition our candidates. Some methods are hundreds of years old, others are far more recent, fine-tuned by some of the brightest minds in psychology today. For example, here, look …"

The women peered through a window to see a small room of five youth, none older than fifteen, standing behind desks. Each desk had several objects on it placed in different locations. A teacher stood at the front of the room, a whistle in his mouth. He blew it once, no one moved except one girl, who barely flinched. The teacher walked up to her and touched her with a black stick. A blue spark shot from the stick, and the girl jumped. Then the teacher returned to his original position and again blew the whistle once. This time the girl did not move.

The whistle blew twice, signaling a flurry of action. Each of the students assembled the pieces with extraordinary precision. It was like watching an Aegis assemble a firearm from its various parts. One boy's hand slipped as he moved to finish his assembly. The plastic piece dropped from his desk onto the floor, clattering loudly. None of the other students turned at the incident. They finished the assembly without mistakes. The teacher calmly walked up to the boy and administered a shock, much longer than the one the girl received. The boy's body twitched for almost five seconds. The Queen's hand traveled up to her neck as she observed, remembering perfectly her own shocks delivered via a collar. A strong electric tingle ran up and down her spine causing the hairs on her neck to rise and her skin to crawl uncomfortably.

"A simple test," Judy explained. "All beginners. Let's look at a more advanced trial … we should have two going on down the hall. I believe one is a desensitizing—yes, here we go. Observe this one."

This group was larger and composed of older trainees than the previous one, most candidates were fifteen or sixteen years old. About ten students stood behind similar desks, scalpels in hand as they worked. Each wore a white apron and a face shield. On each desk was a clear glass bowl filled with water, empty otherwise. Next to the bowl were dissection trays, all with large goldfish laying on them. The fish were in various stages of dissection, some still twitching even as their organs were removed.

"The goldfish have been in the cells with them for the past two weeks. The candidates have fed and cared for them as a reward for good behavior. So far the test looks promising."

No sooner had she said these words then one of the girls in the room dropped her scalpel and sobbed into the crook of her arm. The teacher moved quickly, injecting a syringe into the girl. Five seconds later, she vomited into a waste bucket. Just as in the other room, none of the other kids were distracted by the punishment of one.

"They learn quickly to ignore the punishment of others," Judy stated as if she read the Queen's thoughts. "It's one of the very first lessons we teach."

Judy led the Queen around the facility for over two hours, talking most of the time. After touring most of S.H.I.E.L.D., the holo-screen on her com popped out. "Oh, look at that. It's nearly time for a graduation test. We all have high hopes that this will be a pass. Shall we go back up and watch?"

The Queen motioned for Judy to lead the way. After taking an elevator, they stopped at the very end of a long hall where a closed black door waited. Judy took them through a side door to a small observation room. Several other doctors and teachers joined them in silence. Beyond the one-way glass that separated the observation and testing rooms, a young man with jet-black hair sat in a chair with his head down, arms folded. Without seeing his face, the Queen couldn't be certain how old he was … perhaps in his late teens? Next to him was a small table, very similar to a nightstand, with a gun resting on its side. Under the gun was a slip of paper.

The Queen watched the young man for only a couple of minutes when the black door opened and two Aegis brought in a girl who couldn't be eighteen—couldn't even be sixteen. Once the Aegis seated her, they left. The girl wore a plain white outfit, a tight shirt and leggings which put every curve and detail of her body on intimate display. Judy leaned in and spoke so softly the Queen strained to hear her.

"Fifteen-year-old female with Anomaly Fifteen … aka Ultra. Has responded well to all treatments and tests despite recruitment at age thirteen. The male is a seventeen-year-old facing expulsion from the H.A.M.M.E.R. program due to notable lack of progression of releasing memories of family and childhood. The two have copulated over a dozen times in the last sixty days as part of their positive reinforcement regimen. Our behavioral psychologists noticed displays of affection beyond standard copulation techniques. I assure you, this will be an fascinating test—something you wouldn't want to miss."

One of the male teachers in the room with the Queen and Judy pushed a button on a console adjacent to the window through which the Queen and everyone else observed the test. "State your name for the record," he said into a microphone.

"13F712072-Jane," said the teenager.

"The alphanumeric sequence is unique," Judy informed the Queen. "Thirteen-year-old female when she arrived. Then month, day, and year of birth. The names are recycled. The next female candidate will be given the name *Jane* if this one fails. Her birth name was Vitoria. They called her 'Vivi.' How humiliating."

"The test will commence," the male teacher said. "Pick up the paper and follow your orders."

Jane—or Vivi—stepped forward, ignoring the young man in the chair. She slid the paper out from under the weapon without disturbing it. With steady hands, she unfolded the slip, read its contents, and set it back down on the table. Then she picked up the gun, checked the magazine, and fired it. The first bullet hit the young man in the head, the second in the chest, and the third in the navel. When she finished, she placed the gun to her temple and pulled the trigger. Instead of a *bang* there was only a click. The girl blinked twice, then placed the gun back where she'd gotten it and put her hands behind her. Applause and murmurs of satisfaction and congratulation came from the teachers and doctors. The girl couldn't hear them. She simply stood in her spot, her white clothes spattered with the blood of the boy she'd killed.

Judy turned to the Queen, a smile of jubilance plastered on her face. The Queen, however, felt the beginnings of a sharp headache coming on, accompanied by an even sharper pain in her sternum.

"I'm glad you were here to see that," Judy stated. "Would you like to return downstairs and visit S.H.I.E.L.D. again or might I interest you in some refreshment?"

* * * * *

"I didn't put up those pictures!" Priyanka shouted in the principal's office. "I didn't do anything!"

Mrs. Simpson's eyes were fixed on Priyanka Patel, who did not blink or look away. Katie had to admit, despite loathing her, Priyanka was an amazing liar. She always had been. Watching her friend get away with what she'd done made Katie want to shriek. She clutched her tablet stylus in her hand, imagining herself plunging a dagger into Priyanka's eyes. The images were so realistic that it made her break into a sweat.

"Mrs. Simpson, I got a message last night from Mark—"

"Your boyfriend," Priyanka cut in to say.

"—that she was going to do this. I can prove it! The messages are on my tablet. Then the next day it happens. You can't believe this was a coincidence."

"You're just mad that you can't walk your way to prom queen!" Priyanka shouted. "So I was angry at you. Big deal! So I said I was going to do some stuff. But—but that is disgusting! I would never …" Shaking her head furiously, Priyanka's voice broke and she dissolved into a teary mess.

Oh I will make you cry, Priyanka. I will make you wail.

Mrs. Simpson put up her hands and kept her attention on Priyanka. "I've heard enough. What happened to Katie today was beyond vulgar or obscene. I've never seen anything like it, and I hope I never see anything like it again. What happened today is also illegal, Miss Patel. And you had better believe that I will do everything in my power to ensure that it never happens again. *Never.* As soon as you leave this office, I will be contacting authorities, parents, and the administration to catch whoever did this. Expulsion is more than a possibility. Even criminal charges."

Priyanka crossed her arms. "I'm not worried because I didn't do it!"

"I hope so. But someone did. Do you know who it was?"

"I don't."

Liar. Katie shook so hard that she needed to act, pounce, do something, but Mrs. Simpson turned her attention to her.

"Miss Carpenter, I know you're furious. I know you're hurting. And I will help you, but you need to remember that retribution … retaliation … any negative response to this will hurt your cause. Try to brush it off."

"Brush it—"

Simpson's hand went up again. Four rings adorned her fingers. One of them caught the light and blinded Katie. "I know it sounds impossible. I hurt for you, and am going to do everything I can. So work with me. Help me. Don't be stupid. I'll be in touch with both your parents about the matter. Priyanka, go back to class. Katie, would you rather go home for the day?"

"No," she answered right away. "It'll just make me look worse."

Mrs. Simpson smiled as though to say she was proud of Katie's decision. Both girls left. When they reached the hallway, Katie turned to Priyanka and grabbed her by the shirt. Priyanka smacked her hands away. "Don't touch me, slut."

"They're gonna catch you, Pri. I'll be waving goodbye when you're expelled."

Priyanka's smirk unnerved Katie. "They'll never pin it on me. My mom paid a pro to make and print those posters. You tried to make me go to my junior prom with a *retard*. You've lost your mind."

"I'll make sure they get you. I don't care what I have to do."

Priyanka giggled. "Oh sweetie, you're so used to being on top, you can't stand the view from the bottom." She stopped giggling and stared Katie down. "Your reign is over. Mess with me and I will burn you."

7 | Alone

Friday, June 13, 2087

SAMMY LAY IN bed with the sheets pulled over his head to block out the bad dreams. Rapid gunfire coming from the left flank. *In the trees. They're in the trees.* The forest was dark, too dark to see far. He repeated his orders to the Psions on that area of the battlefield to shield, but gunfire still got through, peppering holes in the Ultras and Elite. Dozens of men and women—soldiers all of them—fell to the earth, but the gunfire continued. The faces of the Thirteens could be seen from afar, red eyes glowing. All of them looked like him. All the fallen were Brickert.

"Sammy!" a voice called out—Jeffie's—urgent and desperate. "Sammy, can you hear me? Answer me!"

He searched the forest floor for her face among the wet leaves and dirt, but didn't see her. *Is she one of the fallen?* A horrible emptiness filled his stomach. The pounding gunfire grew louder, more rapid. *Artillery.* He ordered his soldiers to take cover, full shields. Explosions came from far away, growing closer too rapidly.

"Sammy!" Jeffie cried again. "Open the door."

Everyone else faded until Sammy was the only one in the forest. It was unnaturally dark and the air raised goosebumps on his arms. From a distance he saw a black shadow facing him, along with the distinct impression it was watching him. *Shadows can't watch things. They're just shadows.* But before he could get a closer look it faded into oblivion with a haze of color and a melting of sound. His sheets were soaked with sweat. But the sweat reeked of ... Sammy sniffed, realized what the wetness really was, and cursed.

His nightmares had started after Detroit, growing worse each week. *And now I'm wetting the bed?*

"Sammy!" Jeffie yelled again.

"Just a second," he called out to her.

"Hurry up."

Sammy tore off his shirt and pants, and changed into dry clothes before answering. Jeffie frowned at him when he finally opened the bedroom door. "What took you so long?"

Frowning at her and hoping she didn't notice the smell of urine, he said, "What do you want?"

"The baby. Marie gave birth."

A smile appeared on Sammy's face—a rare thing of late. "You serious?"

"Yes. And I thought you would want to know right away. I'll take you there if you don't mind my company."

"You know I—"

"I don't want to get into it, Sammy." She sighed and played with the doorknob, glancing at him as she did so. "Do you want to come now? I have your car already running in the tunnels."

Sammy pulled at his shirt, noticing for the first time that it was a dirty one. "I need to—"

"I know. Put on some cologne, too. It smells terrible in here. Is that because of Al?"

Sammy hesitated, then nodded. Al had moved in with Sammy three weeks ago following a fight with Marie that got so bad Commander Byron forcibly ejected him from the house. Since Brickert was still in serious condition the decision was made to put Al with Sammy for the time being.

"I wouldn't have hurt her," Al had told Sammy a hundred times, both sober and drunk. "Never."

Al drank every night until he fell asleep, and the house often carried the scent of vomit and booze.

After changing his clothes and splashing on some cologne, Sammy followed Jeffie out the door. They hadn't been alone together in over a month—not since he'd left after she told him she loved him. When they ate together or hung out, it was always in a group, usually with Kawai, Li, Natalia, and Strawberry.

While Sammy and Jeffie hadn't officially broken up, they weren't a couple either. Sammy didn't know what they were. Sometimes they held hands around their friends, sometimes they didn't. They spoke cordially to each other. They hugged occasionally. But it wasn't the same as it'd been. It was as though an unspoken agreement existed that Jeffie would give him his space for now, but when they were around others, they could still act like a couple and catch up.

It worked for Sammy. He still liked Jeffie, and thought she was as beautiful as the first day he saw her. In fact, she was more beautiful, her curves more feminine after two years of aging and developing. Her green eyes still brightened when she found his face in a room or when he made a comment that only she would find funny. Holding her hand still gave him a feeling of pride in his chest.

The problem wasn't with Jeffie. It was him, and he knew it. *Why did I freak out when she told me she loved me?* Sammy wondered while Jeffie tried to restart the car. Even now, a month later, the question still bothered him.

The car gave a whine instead of whirring to life.

"I hate your stupid car."

"Lemon?" he asked her. "Why are you picking on Lemon?" Sammy patted the dash. "She doesn't mean that."

"You're the most important person here, and they assign you the worst car. Tell me how that makes sense."

"You're the best, Lemon. Don't listen to Jeffie. She's jealous she doesn't have a car of her own."

"Seriously, why do you get this piece of junk?"

Sammy shrugged. "Thomas said I'm a teenager, so I get the teenager car."

Natalia had named the car Lemon because of its bright yellow color and because it usually took more than one try to get it started.

"It was supposed to get fixed last week, but the mechanics are still repairing the cruisers. Are you going to be a gentlewoman and push or do I have to get out and do it?"

Jeffie glared at Sammy.

Sammy got out, mildly annoyed, and flashed Jeffie a mocking grin that stretched his cheeks. The tunnels were cold, even in the summer, and he shivered. The only way to be sure the car would start was by giving it a push. After using a strong hand blast on the car's bumper to shove it forward, the car started and Sammy climbed back in the passenger seat. He rolled his window down so the air would blow on his face and help dilute his stench. Despite the cold, his skin was clammy from the night sweats.

"You okay?" Jeffie asked.

"Yeah. Fine. You?"

"Good."

"Good."

"I heard you saw Croz the other day for something," Jeffie mentioned, her voice only louder than a whisper. "Is that true?"

Sammy stirred in his seat. "That's not your business."

Two weeks ago, Commander Byron and Dr. Rosmir had approached Sammy and suggested he visit Croz, the resistance's chief psychologist, about getting a better handle on his Anomaly Thirteen. Sammy insisted that he already had a handle on it, but went anyway. The visit had been short, polite, and interesting, but Sammy hadn't felt the need to set up another session, despite Croz's multiple invitations.

Jeffie drove in silence for two or three minutes, but Sammy knew her too well. She wanted to talk, and was figuring out a way to bring up her desired subject without offending him. The only way to prevent this was by starting a new conversation before she did and keep the topic away from what she wanted to address.

"So—"

"When did you hear about the baby?" Sammy asked, barely voicing his question in time to cut her off. "Who told you?"

Jeffie gave him an annoyed side-glance that told him she knew exactly what he was doing. "Twenty minutes ago. Natalia's been assisting in the infirmary to keep an eye on Brickert. Rosmir told her and she told me right after."

"Is Natalia the one who told you about my appointment with Croz?"

Jeffie's lack of response confirmed Sammy's suspicion. "It slipped. Her mind's been on Brickert, not worrying about you."

"Has Brickert been awake more lately?" The last time Sammy visited his friend, three days ago, all Brickert did was sleep and mumble.

"He's awake a little more every day. That's all I know. Are you going to keep asking questions so that I have no time to bring up a different subject?"

"That was my plan."

Jeffie snorted a laugh, but there was no mirth in her eyes. "It's been a month."

"So?"

"I want to go back to the way things were. How much longer are you going to punish me?"

Sammy watched the lights of another car pass them as they drove slowly through the tunnel to the infirmary parking area. He should have known better than to think he could have ducked the conversation. "I haven't been punishing you."

"It feels like it."

"I'm busy." When he heard her sigh, he added, "Really, I am. I get home from meetings and I still have to read over reports from other subcommittees and analyze data to plan our strategies. You think I like doing it?"

"You don't have to be as busy as you make yourself. Why can't you talk to me about what happened? We were getting better about talking things through, now you act like I'm diseased—"

"No, I don't."

"You do!" She fixed her eyes on him, and he could feel her trying to get him to look back at her. But he didn't give in. "Geez, Sammy, I said I love you. I didn't ask you to marry me or something."

"Stop saying that!" he shouted so loudly that she flinched.

"It's true!"

"It's insane. We're sixteen and in the middle of a war. We're screwed up."

"Do not tell me what I feel!"

"I'm not."

"Kawai and Li are planning to get married when the war's over. People can still fall in love and plan for the future."

Sammy hissed a short, cruel laugh. "Kawai is what? Barely seventeen? She's gonna marry Li at eighteen? That's ridiculous."

"She's eighteen, and she'll be nineteen. What's really going on in your head?"

"I'm fine."

"You're not."

A spark of rage turned into a roaring flame, and Sammy kicked the dash, cracking the plastic in three places. Jeffie shot him an angry, disapproving look.

He closed his eyes, breathed, and leaned back in his chair. "Fine. I have problems, but I don't want to talk—"

"You have ducked everything and everyone lately. Your responsibilities to the leadership committee. Your friends. Showering too, apparently. And you've been like this since Detroit."

"I'm sorry to give you another thing to worry about."

Jeffie ran her fingers through her hair. "You know what? Yeah, I worry about the war, about my family, about Brickert, but I *like* worrying about you. If I had nothing to do but worry about you, that'd be the best life I could hope for. And I'm never going to stop because—"

Sammy couldn't listen to her anymore. He couldn't sit in the car and hear her say affectionate words while he only wanted to say or do hurtful things back to her. He opened the door, jumped out, and used his blasts to prevent an injury. Jeffie slammed on the brakes. "WHAT IS WRONG WITH YOU?"

"I don't know," he lied as he picked himself up and dusted off his pants.

"You've been saying that for weeks."

"Because it's true."

"Liar!" Jeffie smashed her palm into the steering wheel. "You think I didn't see what you did in Detroit to those Thirteens? Or that I don't know everyone's suspicions? Or that I possibly made a connection between that and you meeting with Croz? I'm not stupid, and I want to help."

Sammy couldn't answer. He wanted to tell Jeffie everything, about the spurts of rage he was feeling ever since Detroit, the dreams, the bedwetting. But he *needed* her to leave him alone. When he didn't answer her, she said, "When you're ready, okay?" Then she stepped on the accelerator and left him behind.

He was both glad and annoyed to be by himself. *How am I supposed to think with her around?* The war had to be his focus. He needed to *see* the end, needed a new idea. Something the committee would agree on.

Think about the war. That's what matters.

Why'd she have to go and tell me she loves me?

Sammy tried to put the last question out of his mind, but it wouldn't go. It kept snapping back like a rubber band. His pace quickened until he ran at full speed to the tunnel entrance to the infirmary. Cologne or no, his body odor was ripe by the time he reached Marie's room.

Lara Byron sat on one side of the bed flanked by Al, Thomas, and Commander Byron. Jeffie sat on Marie's other side and tried to smile when she saw Sammy. Dr. Rosmir was at the foot of the bed with his tablet, checking off diagnostic boxes while his nurse, Janna Scoble, fussed with Marie's monitors.

When Sammy came in, everyone stared. Dr. Rosmir reached him first and offered a hand to shake, in his other he held a small device that blinked the words ANALYZING DATA. Both Lara and Thomas hugged Sammy; they didn't seem to care that he smelled like a giant latrine. Marie cradled her little baby who slept, a peaceful expression adorned its face. All eyes flickered between the baby and the device Dr. Rosmir held.

"Boy or girl?" Sammy asked.

"A girl," Lara whispered. "She's so beautiful!"

"Congrats," Sammy told Al, who looked as shabby as ever, but a genuine smile hung on his face as he watched Marie hold his daughter.

"Any name yet?"

Al shook his head. "We're talking about that."

Sammy nodded and looked around the room, but avoided Jeffie's gaze.

Commander Byron's face glowed. "I am a grandfather. Forty-eight years old and a grandfather. Still has not quite sunk in though, the reality of it all."

Thomas patted his son on the shoulder. "I'm a great-grandfather. Wait until you get to my age. I feel like I should have more wrinkles."

Lara rubbed Thomas's arm with a loving grin. "You have plenty, old man."

The device Rosmir held gave a beep, and everyone froze, eyes on him. He looked at it, grinned, and said to Al and Marie, "Congrats. You just created the first third generation Anomaly Fourteen."

Cheers and hugs erupted. Sammy's hand was shaken five times, even though he hadn't done anything. Al and Marie embraced, and Al kissed her forehead. While everyone celebrated, Sammy took Dr. Rosmir aside.

"How's Brickert doing?"

"He was awake for almost two hours this morning. I'm upgrading his prognosis to a full recovery."

An incredible weight lifted off Sammy. Brickert was going to be all right. Hours spent by his side, reading to him, praying over him, talking to him … all worth it. "Does he remember much?" was Sammy's second question. *God, please don't let Brickert remember. I'll lose my best friend if he does.*

"Don't know yet. But I doubt he will."

"He asked about you," Janna, the nurse, mentioned.

Sammy's mouth went dry and a lump the size of an egg grew in his throat. "What—what did he say?"

Janna shrugged. "Just asked where you were."

Jeffie watched him closely. However, when their eyes met she immediately looked away. Rosmir glanced at the clock, then said to the Byron family, "I need to check on a few more patients. You have ten or fifteen more minutes before I kick you out so Marie and baby can get some rest."

"You want to go see him?" Jeffie asked Sammy. "Kawai, Strawberry, and Natalia are all there."

"Sure."

They walked side by side to Brickert's room. Sammy was so used to taking Jeffie's hand that he almost did so. When his hand brushed hers, he mumbled, "Sorry."

Jeffie rolled her eyes and opened the door.

Almost instantly Strawberry wrapped her arms around Sammy. "How have you been?" she asked him when she let him go. "Seems like I haven't talked to you in weeks."

"Probably because you haven't," Jeffie said dryly.

"I'm well," Sammy said. "Busy. With everything going on it's hard to find time to socialize."

Just then, Janna Scoble came in to check on Brickert. When Sammy glanced at her, he caught Jeffie giving Strawberry the tiniest shake of the head. Sammy wondered what they were silently communicating about. Him? What had Jeffie been telling his friends? Strawberry looked back at Sammy and gave him a sisterly smile. "Try not to be a stranger. We miss you."

"You'll miss me even more when you're going to school in Lyon."

Strawberry blushed and dropped her head. Sammy realized that he was the only person she'd told about that.

"What school?" Kawai asked.

"Nothing," Sammy said, smiling, "just a joke between us."

Jeffie's face told Sammy she knew he was lying, but she said nothing. Janna finished her check on Brickert and announced, "Everything looks good. Natalia, don't forget you're due for a check up this afternoon. Or we could do it now, if you'd rather get it over with."

Natalia, who'd been shot and severely wounded in Detroit, still spent ample time in the infirmary with Rosmir and the nurses. She stood and said, "I'll go now."

Once they were gone, Kawai turned to Sammy. "Is it starting to get to you? Is that why you're MIA all the time?"

"Is what getting to me?" Sammy asked.

"All of this."

"If it were going to get to me, wouldn't it have gotten to me in Rio? Or Omaha? Or a dozen other times after that?"

"Is that how it works?"

"I don't know. Is it getting to *you*?" Sammy asked Kawai. "Or you, Jeffie?" He didn't ask Berry because he already knew how she felt.

Neither girl answered.

Finally Kawai said, "You're asked to carry more than we are."

Brickert moaned and turned. All eyes in the room fixed on him to see if he would wake. Then he snored softly, grinned, and his breathing deepened again. Sammy let out a deep breath. "Have any of you seen the baby yet?"

"Yeah," Strawberry said, "we looked in on her just before Jeffie left to get you."

"She's beautiful," Kawai added. "Looks like Marie more than Al."

"Does Al seem happier lately?" Strawberry asked.

Sammy shook his head. "We don't talk much. He comes home and passes out on the couch. It doesn't take very much to get him wasted."

"Still can't believe he moved out of the house," Jeffie said glumly. "Marie makes it sound like they're getting divorced."

Sammy shook his head.

"Crazy, huh?" Strawberry said.

"Everyone has a breaking point," Kawai repeated.

"I haven't hit any point yet," Sammy told her. "I can't afford to let it get to me, and neither can any of you." He directed his last words at Jeffie. "The war isn't over."

"Doesn't mean we can't relax," Strawberry said. "How about a party to celebrate Brickert waking up?"

Sammy's com beeped as a message came through from Thomas.

We need to go to the tower NOW. Apparently there's HUGE
NEWS.

"I have to go," he told them as he hurried for the door. Jeffie
looked to her friends for help.

"Wait," Strawberry said. "Does that mean no party?"

"I don't know if I can do it. Why not wait until Brickert can
come?"

"Sammy." Her tone was stern, "You can't do this to yourself.
You need to take a break and let yourself be a kid."

Sammy paused at the door before facing his friends again. "You
guys really think we're still kids? You're *kidding* yourselves."

In under half an hour, Sammy, Thomas, Lara, and the
commander arrived at the air control tower in Saint Marie. Most of
the leadership committee was present along with some new faces,
most of whom Sammy vaguely recognized from his days spent in the
data center sifting through information stolen from CAG data
servers. In the center of the meeting table, a holo-tablet projected its
information high into the air.

"Sammy!" Justice said when he entered. "Come have a look at
this."

A few people moved aside to let Sammy through. All he saw in
the hologram was computer code, and as smart as he was, he had
never learned the languages of computers. Two of the experts spoke
in technical jargon as they pulled out and highlighted bits of text
from the hologram. They both stopped when they saw Sammy.

"Hello, Samuel," one of the experts said as she offered her hand
to him. She wore a drab lab coat and a rather odd hairdo that made

her look like a peacock. Sammy remembered her as one of the Tensais who'd flown in from Capitol Island with Commander Byron. "My name is Doctor Khani Nguyen. Call me Khani, though. I dislike the title of Doctor. Too many—"

"Khani, why don't you rewind a bit and show us all what you've found?" Lara interrupted with an overly pleasant tone.

Khani gazed at Lara with a look of mild offense. "Certainly. Last night my team of experts stumbled across a code which we believe is linked to a possible kill switch in the CAG systems. We're running searches for similarly worded coding to find more information."

"A kill switch for what?" Sammy asked.

"Possibly their entire army," Justice said.

Khani rolled her eyes. "There's no proof of that."

"Wait … what?" Sammy asked. "How would that work?"

"There certainly is proof," Commander Byron argued. "We have seen Thirteens explode after capture. Not all, but some."

Khani straightened her glasses with pursed lips. "Your theory is nonsense."

"Yet the time stamp on this part of the code shows it was executed less than a minute before Victor Wrobel detonated during his interrogation."

Khani snorted with derision.

"I was in the room, Khani," the commander insisted. "I witnessed it."

"It's not your eyes I doubt, Commander. It's your brain. Why would the CAG leave something this important in their databases? It should be erased. Scrubbed out of existence. They would never commit such an oversight if it was so important."

"As you of all people should know, sometimes even the most impenetrable systems have errors."

Another one of the data analysts spoke, though he seemed nervous about saying anything to upset Khani. "It could be we're misinterpreting the data—"

"No," Khani snapped. "I did not misinterpret it. That's classic kill switch coding."

The computer experts began arguing amongst themselves until Thomas clapped his hands together loud enough that it made Sammy's ears hurt. "Let's settle down, folks." Thomas looked mainly at Khani and her team. "We need time to be sure we're acting on good information. How long will that take?"

"Anywhere from an hour to an infinite amount of time," Khani responded. "If there's no more information to be mined in the data, all we have is a teaser."

A thought struck Sammy. "What if I go straight to the source?"

"What source?" Thomas asked.

"The Hive. What if I go back?"

"Absolutely not," Lara and Commander Byron both said.

"I'm not talking about another hike through the jungle," Sammy clarified. "I'm saying I fly in and meet Diego."

"He will shoot you down," Byron said.

"He'd shoot *you* down, not me. He and I have a deeper understanding. A connection. Let me take a stealth cruiser tonight. I'll be back by morning."

The committee spent the better part of an hour arguing over Sammy's request. Only Anna agreed that he should go. The rest obstinately refused, especially those who had accompanied Sammy to the Hive: Lorenzo Winters, Duncan Hudec, Duncan's brother, Dave, and Nikotai. The meeting ended with him soundly losing the battle.

Sammy went home, skipping dinner. With Brickert still in the infirmary and Marie with the newborn, Sammy hoped he had the place to himself. Unfortunately Al was already on the couch, snoring loudly in his sleep. On the table near his head was a half empty bottle, its scent made the air musky and heavy. Sammy sighed.

Now what? he wondered. He could go back to the infirmary and hold the new baby. Or perhaps Brickert might be awake. Or he could wake up Al and try to talk some sense into him.

Most nights Sammy poured over maps or read through data reports for hours. He could scan those very quickly, but he often read them more than once, looking for something to give the NWG and the resistance an advantage in the war. After making preparations for the next day's committee meetings, if he still wasn't tired, Sammy read books—novels mostly—anything to keep from wallowing in his own thoughts.

Before leaving the meeting, he'd asked Khani Nguyen for a copy of the code for study. He wanted to try and make some sense of it, but she laughed at him. When he told her he wasn't joking, she stared at him and then walked away without a response.

Sammy went to his bookshelf and scanned the titles written on the spines, most of them crusty and faded from years of sitting unread. He'd finished almost all of them—some to himself, others to Brickert. The ones he hadn't read did not interest him.

For a brief instant, he thought about finding his friends and hanging out with them, but he could hear their comments in his head.

"The Great Sammy condescends to visit us lowly plebes," Kawai or Li might say.

Or Jeffie might cozy up to him, interpreting his presence as a sign that things between them were improving. She might tell him again that she loved him.

He couldn't tolerate hearing those words again. The idea that she, someone so perfect despite her flaws, could think she was in love with him … *It's not right.*

Nothing's right.

Sammy wanted to grab the half empty bottle of booze and smash it over Al's face. Then he would scream at him, throw him out the door, and tell him to pull his head out of his butt, to quit screwing up his life. What did Al know about pain or problems or anything? Al didn't have the Anomaly Thirteen. He had a beautiful wife and a new daughter; a family that loved him despite his stupidity.

Anger gathered in him like a storm, gradually building up in his chest and gut. *Go away*, he told the rage. *Leave me alone.* But it didn't. It only grew until the bottle looked ever more inviting. He wouldn't just smash it over Al's head, he'd use its jagged edges to cut out his heart.

No!

Sammy went to the kitchen and splashed water on his face. He saw his reflection in the polished chrome, hideously distorted in the curved metal. *Like me.* For weeks he'd pushed everyone away. Now he wanted someone around, a friend, a group of friends. Anyone. But Sammy knew if someone were to show up, he'd just ask them to leave.

"What's wrong with you?" he asked his reflection.

On the kitchen counter near the sink was a knife stand. Sammy removed one of the knives and held it, then turned it over to let the light catch the metal. He wished he could cut it out of him, the Anomaly Thirteen. Everything would be all right. With two hands on the grip, he held it, blade pointed at his gut.

No one will miss you.

That's not true. Byron told me he thinks of me as a son. Jeffie said she loves me.

A month ago. She doesn't feel that way now, not after the way you treated her.

Sammy rested the tip of the blade on his navel and pressed until he felt the pressure. A creak came from the corner on the other side of his small home, and he looked up. There was nothing there but an old phonograph Thomas Byron had given him weeks ago. The resistance had only two and the other was in Thomas and Lara's house. Thomas had loaned Sammy over a dozen vinyl records. Classics, he called them. Sammy had let both the records and the machine gather dust.

"Listen to them and tell me what you think," Thomas had told him. "Find the ones you like, and I'll give you more. Music will keep you sane."

Sammy hadn't listened to any of them. The idea was stupid, but he found himself carrying the phonograph and records into his bedroom, then thumbing through them one by one. They were old and dusty and smelled like they'd come from a thrift store, their sleeves stiff and fraying at the corners. He stopped on one that bore the face of a man with a large nose and a dark mustache. A crack ran across the paper, traveling through his eyes, but the man's smile was so large and genuine that Sammy slid the vinyl out of its sleeve without another thought.

He stared at the record for a long time wondering why people needed things like these to play music so long ago. Thomas had never shown Sammy how to operate the machine, but he worked it out on his own after a couple minutes of fiddling. When he placed the stylus on the record and the music began to play, something happened to Sammy. His breath caught in his throat, and the soft sounds of guitars strumming stirred his soul, a ripple of waves in time with the music.

A man's rich voice sang loud and clear, *I'd save every day like a treasure and then again, I would spend them with you.*

Jeffie, Brickert, Kawai, Natalia, and all of Sammy's other friends floated in his mind, their faces happy and free. He remembered his carefree days as a Beta, training in the Arena, learning to blast, playing at a water park, arguing over things that didn't matter. In a way, it was as if those memories didn't belong to him, but someone else. And Sammy had only borrowed them.

But there never seems to be enough time, the voice sang, *to do the things you wanna do once you find them.*

When the music stopped, Sammy played the song again. He huddled on his bed and listened to it all the way through. Another person's life appeared in his mind, the images a stream flowing along pleasantly. This person was a boy with parents who took him fishing on lakes, played football in parks, made ice cream on his birthday, and kissed him on the cheek at bedtime.

The song ended once more, so he played it a third time and a fourth and fifth. He didn't even remember getting up and moving the stylus. Tears flooded his face as he rocked himself, his chest tight as he sobbed.

I've looked around enough to know that you're the one I want to go through time with …

After listening to the song countless times and feeling lighter than he'd been in weeks, Sammy picked himself off the floor and went to the infirmary. The drive took him longer than usual. Lemon took two attempts before she would start up. Sammy had to have one foot on the ground and one on the accelerator. Then, with his foot out the door, he used strong angled foot blasts to push.

The infirmary lights were dimmed. The only sound in the building was a movie playing from the attending nurse's holo-tablet. She looked up from the hologram until she saw Sammy's face in the glow of the lights above her desk. They exchanged a nod, nothing more, their usual gesture to each other when Sammy came in the middle of the night to read to his friend.

Brickert's room was dark except for the thin strip of light above his bed which gave just enough illumination to see his face, nothing more. Sammy took the chair to his friend's right and rested his hand on Brickert's. Part of him hoped Brickert would wake. Part of him didn't.

"I blew it, Brick." When Sammy saw that Brickert did not respond to the sound of his voice, he continued, "I went down there to save you, but instead I almost killed you. I wanted to control the anomaly—to use it. Instead I nearly … " Sammy licked his lips and tasted tears. "I punched you over and over until you spoke. You—you asked me, 'Who are you?'"

Sammy squeezed Brickert's hand, mirroring the tightness in his chest.

"You didn't even recognize me … your brother. I'm sorry."

Someone moved in the darkness. At first Sammy thought it was Brickert, but it was another person, a figure in the shadows. For a moment Sammy feared it might be the shadow person from his nightmare, but it wasn't. Brickert's door cracked open, and Sammy caught a wisp of blonde hair in the dim light.

"Jeffie!" he called out, getting to his feet. "Jeffie, wait!"

She did not stop. When Sammy called after her he was hushed by the attending nurse. He ignored her and called again, but Jeffie hurried away. In order to catch her, Sammy had to sprint, and by the time he did, he was nearly out of breath. The moment he touched her arm, Jeffie whirled around and pushed Sammy against the wall of the stairs leading down to the tunnels.

"Now you want to talk to me? Now?" There was venom in her eyes.

"Yes," he stated firmly, "now I'm ready to talk."

His response caught Jeffie by surprise. "Well … that's too bad because I don't want to listen."

Enraged, Sammy spun, pressed Jeffie to the wall with a hard knock, and held her tightly. He instantly regretted it. For the first time ever, Jeffie looked at him with fear in her eyes. "You say you love me, well this is me! You know I'm a Thirteen! You know I'm one of them! Can you not love that part of me?"

"Don't give me that. Everyone has things that should be kept buried—that should never be let out. You don't get to make excuses."

Sammy's anger deflated and he stepped away from her. Jeffie caught him and pulled him into a tight hug.

"Are you done?" she asked.

Sammy knew what she meant. She wasn't asking if he was done sulking or feeling sorry for himself, but was he done with using *it*. "I don't know."

Jeffie looked at him in the eye. "Promise me."

"No. I can't."

"Why not?" she shouted.

"Because I don't want to break a promise."

"Then promise me and keep it."

Sammy shook his head. "If it comes down to watching you die or using the Anomaly Thirteen, I will choose the anomaly. The choice won't even be difficult."

"I don't want to be saved by a Thirteen."

"It's not—"

Jeffie frowned. "I just heard you tell Brickert that you beat on him—"

"Yeah, I lost control for a minute, but then I was fine. He snapped me out of it."

"What if I can't snap you out of it? What if you save me and then kill me?" She kept talking before Sammy could answer. "You are stronger without it. You are *better* without it."

"I'm not. I know my limits. If I have to use it to save you, I will. And that's all I can say."

Jeffie smiled sadly. "I want to hit you right now. You know that?"

"Do it. Trust me. I could use a good slap."

"And we're not done talking about this!"

"I'm just glad we're talking. It's been—it's been hard for me since Detroit." Sammy's voice cracked. "Dreams … guilt … mistakes." His chest grew tight, but he was determined not to cry in front of her. "I killed so many people, Jeffie. Now my name is all over the news like I'm—like I'm a mass murderer."

"I know," she whispered. "It's not right."

"And I wet the bed this morning," he admitted.

This statement was met with silence. Sammy suddenly felt terribly stupid and wished he hadn't said anything. Then Jeffie giggled. She crooked a finger under her nose as it turned into a full laugh.

Sammy started chuckling too. "It's not—" He jostled her. "Stop it, it's not—"

The harder she laughed, the harder he did. Finally they were both holding their stomachs, barely able to breathe. When they stopped, Sammy had to wipe the tears of mirth from his eyes.

Their eyes met. Jeffie's gaze turned fierce. "I do love you, Samuel Berhane."

"You still want to hit me?"

"Yeah." She smiled and leaned toward him. Sammy's stomach did a flop and his heartbeat quickened. His arms went numb and tingly, and the rest of his body was jittery and trembling.

Rather than hitting him, Jeffie kissed him. They hadn't kissed in weeks, and Sammy responded to it by wrapping his arms around her and lifting her up until she could wrap her legs around his waist. Her mouth opened wider, so did his. Their breath mingled hot and tangy in the cold tunnel air. All of Sammy's worries about Jeffie, Brickert, his anomaly, and Detroit vanished for a few moments. Jeffie's affection and tenderness wrapped him in a warm blanket, comforting his soul and mind. He wasn't in an underground tunnel; he wasn't in Glasgow. He was home.

When they stopped to breathe, Jeffie grinned, her lips red and raw. "Dang. I've needed that for about a month."

Then she kissed him again.

8 | Caller

Monday, June 30, 2087

YOU HAVE TO *make a choice, Sammy*, said the voice of the shadow. *You can't walk the fence forever.*

Sammy studied the shadow. Whenever he held up a hand, the shadow mirrored him. If he stepped closer, so did the shadow. The closer Sammy came to the shadow, the more the energy of it pulsed and pulled. "What will happen if I touch you?"

What will happen if you touch me?

Sammy punched at the shadow, stopping millimeters away from the shadow's copying fist. Then Sammy opened his fingers and let his palm show. Like invisible rubber bands connecting them, the shadow pulled at Sammy in time with Sammy's heartbeat. Bored of going through the same thing night after night and curious to see what would happen if he gave into the pull, Sammy finally connected their palms and fingers. The shadow brightened and shrunk until it disappeared, and Sammy was left with nothing but a key in hand.

Sammy woke gripping the wooden rail on the side of his bed. He'd wet himself again. Cursing, he got up and stripped the bed of its sheets and his body of his clothes. *I'm sixteen years old … not six … stupid dreams.*

By the time he finished cleaning up, it was a little after 0400. Sammy couldn't go back to sleep so he dug up his holo-tablet and resumed his efforts to teach himself programming code.

For the last two weeks he had tried to convince the leadership committee that he should go to the Hive and talk to Trapper, but no one else consented. Even Anna no longer supported him, mostly because she was annoyed that he kept asking. Without any support, Sammy turned his attention to the kill switch code. With all future bombings of cloning sites put on hold, it was the only trail of crumbs the resistance had to follow for the time being. Sammy's hope was that by teaching himself coding languages, he could figure out some way to exploit the code Khani Nguyen had discovered in the data stolen from the Hive.

Through the wall of his house, he heard a news report. Al often fell asleep watching CBN and left the holo-vision on all night.

"The White House announced yesterday evening," said the news reporter for CBN, "that four major military operations were conducted successfully during the past week, all targeting NWG military sites and terrorist centers. The first target was an atmospheric cruiser construction site in the deep African desert outside of Agadez. The second at coastal shipyards in Quanzhou. A new terrorist training facility had been built in Norilsk, Krasnoyarsk

Krai. According to reports this attack led to the most casualties for the NWG at well over two hundred, though very few were civilians. And finally, CAG forces destroyed an arms manufacturing plant in Nagercoil near the Tamil Nadu coast. Minimal CAG forces were lost in these strikes, and many experts are calling this the opening act to the close of the war. To bring us more details on these operations, we've brought in our special wartime correspon—"

Sammy chuckled as he left his bed, turned off the holo-vision, and returned to his bedroom. Commander Havelbert, Director of Military Operations for the NWG, had already informed Byron of the assaults. Only one of the attacks had been unforeseen: Quanzhou, and it was the only real blow to the war effort. The new training facility in Norilsk was a fake. New Beta trainees were being sent to Geneva, and there certainly weren't two hundred of them yet. Fortunately, the false information had led to the discovery of a mole in the upper circles of the NWG ranks.

The cruiser construction site in Agadez had been abandoned a month earlier as part of their plans to rotate sites every eight weeks. And Nagercoil was one of three recently converted small arms manufacturing plants, and fortunately the smallest of them. From the way Commander Byron made it sound—or perhaps the way Havelbert made it sound—the CAG had taken such severe casualties at Norilsk and Agadez that the NWG was the real victor of this round.

Deet! Deet! Deet!

Sammy glanced at his com laying across the room on the table. The holo-screen said UNKNOWN CALLER. Sammy frowned at this. *Who would be unknown?* By the time he reached the com and answered with a harried, "Hello?" the line was dead.

Sammy ate breakfast with his friends. Brickert would soon be released from the infirmary, so planning a party for him was the topic of the meal. Not far from them sat Marie, baby bundled up in a sling against her breast. Al had stopped taking his meals in the cafeteria weeks ago. Sammy watched Marie sadly, wondering if he should say something or if he could do anything for her. Natalia must have taken note of the expression on his face because she put a hand on his.

"Don't," she said, "there's nothing you can do. Rosa told me Al and Marie are done. Al told her last week."

Jeffie shook her head. "All because Marie got herself pregnant without his permission. Al makes me sick."

"He wanted kids," Li said with half of a banana in his mouth. "I heard him talking about it to Martin and some other Betas about three or four years ago."

"You remember something Al said three years ago?" Kawai asked.

Li shrugged. "I'd remember any conversation where a man says he wants seven kids. And that was Al."

"He hardly talks to his dad, either," Sammy said. "Not outside of the committee. Comes home, turns on the holo-vision, and drinks."

"Intoxication isn't allowed," Natalia said.

"That's why he does it on our couch," Sammy said. "I'm not gonna tell on him."

"Does Byron know?" Li asked. "Thomas and Lara?"

Kawai arched an eyebrow. "It's not Sammy's business to snitch. You know Al's upbringing as well as I do. The Byron family— they're all—"

"It's my business as his friend," Sammy said. "I know I should talk to him about it, but I don't know what to say."

Li put up a hand. "Nah, when you were going through your thing, we let you have your space until you were ready to deal. Al needs his space, not you reminding him of his beliefs about drinking."

Underneath the table, Jeffie squeezed Sammy's thigh and smirked at him. He put his hand on hers, and they locked fingers. "How's your oatmeal?" she asked.

"Oaty," he answered.

"Are you sleeping better?"

"Like a baby." *Not a total lie. Babies wet themselves at night.* Though Sammy had told Jeffie about peeing himself that first night, he hadn't mentioned that it was now a recurring event. Nor had he said anything about his shadow dreams. After seeing the fear in her eyes when he'd almost hit her, the last thing he wanted to do was scare her.

Meetings were scheduled after breakfast. When the leadership committee convened, Sammy told himself more than once that he wouldn't bring up his request again. But as the meeting wore on with more debates about ill-conceived ideas and plots that would ultimately amount to nothing, Sammy couldn't stop himself.

He raised his hand. Lara saw it and sighed, but changed topics instead of calling on him. Each time Lara glanced at him, Sammy met her with a pleasant smile. After five minutes of this, she sighed again. After ten, Sammy's raised hand was all anyone could think about, wondering when or if Lara would recognize him to speak. When she finally did, his arm dropped to the table, aching and tingling from lack of blood. He'd held his hand high for fifteen minutes.

"All right, Sammy, the chair recognizes that you wish to speak … even though we all know what it is you want to talk about."

"Thank you," he said. "I've been put in charge of all operations, right? Which means if there's an operation to be done, I get the final say."

Commander Byron cocked an eyebrow at his father and mother, silently asking them for their opinion. Thomas Byron shook his head.

"You are in charge of the subcommittee of operations, yes," Lara admitted, "under the supervision of the leadership committee. And no one on the committee thinks your idea is wise."

"I agree," Thomas said.

"We have nothing else to go on," Sammy argued. "We've been stalled since Detroit. Six weeks of nothing but talking. I know you hate this inaction, Thomas. So do I. Let's do something."

"It is too risky," Commander Byron stated as though it was the final word.

"Everything we do is risky. I'll go alone."

"Like hell you will," Anna said. "You take a stealth cruiser to the Hive and chances are you don't come back. Now maybe you don't consider a stealth cruiser a luxury, but the rest of us do. I can't pull them out of my butt. Can you? Because if you can, take the one from your butt, and leave the other one for us to use because your cruiser is gonna get blown to smithereens."

"Look, we have a kill code or part of one on our hands," Sammy said. "Doesn't anyone think this might be the answer—"

"We're not sure what it is until we use it and actually kill someone!"

"What else could it be?" Sammy yelled. He was suddenly so angry that his hands shook, and he wanted to hurt Anna. "I watched our CAG prisoners blow up with my own eyes after we captured them! They imploded from the inside. Remember Akureyri, Anna? Al saw it too."

Al looked up from where he'd been sitting or sleeping. It was hard to tell which because his eyes were so blurry and bloodshot. "Huh? Oh yeah. I saw it too."

For about ten seconds no one in the room said anything. Then Khani stood up and said, "Technically an implosion is an external force causing an object to collapse inward on itself due to a difference in external and internal pressures. What you described, Sammy, sounds more like a textbook *explosion*." Then she straightened her glasses and sat back down.

"Let's break into subcommittees," Lara announced abruptly.

As Sammy left the air control tower, he noted a faint stench of something stale and sour. He turned around to see Al, his eyes half open, his face pale and sporting pressure marks on it.

"Didn't get much sleep again?" Sammy asked with a half-hearted chuckle.

"Hey Sammy," Al mumbled in a hoarse voice. "No, haven't been sleeping well."

"I finally got to hold your baby," Sammy said. "It's a, uh, cute little thing. You have a name picked out yet?"

Al shook his head. The rumor was every time Al and Marie tried to settle on a name, they ended up screaming at each other. Despite having heard them through the walls, Sammy couldn't imagine it. They were two of the most agreeable people he knew. And now they hated each other.

"You want to do something tonight, Al?" Sammy asked him. "Play a game? Blastketball? I'm bored and Jeffie's got a late shift at the data center."

"Nah, I'm not feeling great, Sammy. Raincheck, okay?"

"Sure. Yeah."

"In fact, I'm going to skip the subcommittee meeting. Tell the others I'll try and make it tomorrow … if I'm feeling better."

Sammy had the distinct impression that Al would not be feeling better tomorrow. His thoughts wandered during the subcommittee session from Jeffie to Al to the new baby to how long it had been since he'd eaten pizza. Nothing new was discussed, and when the meetings finally ended, Sammy felt more tired than he did after his regular exercise sessions with the other Psions.

Instead of heading home as he normally did, Sammy went to the cafeteria and made a pizza. He had to call in a few favors with the men and women in charge of the kitchens to do it, but when it was done it smelled just right. The cooks put it in a box and he drove it back to his house. Sammy knocked before letting himself inside. He found Al sitting in boxer shorts and an old t-shirt with four green aliens on it. One of the aliens was eating a slice of pizza. Sammy smiled at that.

Al's face was redder and puffier than before. His eyes were watery with a tinge of red. He was either drunk or crying. Or both. It wasn't until he spoke that Sammy knew.

"Hey," he slurred, "how was the meeting?"

"I brought pizza."

Al stared at the box for a long time. "I just wanna be alone, man."

"Well, I don't really want to go away. And, frankly, it's my house. You can't make me. But you *can* eat half of this pizza ..."

Al's teeth clenched together so hard they squeaked, and his hands balled into fists. Sammy thought things might get a little rowdy until Al's hands relaxed. His whole body sagged. "I don't want you seeing me like this, man. Can't you just ..." His voice cracked. "Can't you go away?"

"I could. I probably should. But I keep thinking about when your dad made me honcho for the first time in the Arena. You remember that?"

"Not really," Al mumbled.

Al's answer deflated Sammy's spirits. "Really? It was a first-to-three-victory match. I was against Marie and Kobe ... you accused me of having a crush on Marie."

Al snorted, then belched. "Oh, yeah, I do remember that."

"You helped me get myself together."

"So now you're gonna do that for me?"

Sammy shook his head. "No, bro, I'm just here to eat some pizza with you. I made it myself."

Al cleared three empty bottles of liquor off the coffee table to make room for the food. The longer they ate, the more the signs of

Al's drunken state wore off. It sometimes surprised Sammy that there was such a difference in their age. Al was almost twenty-one, but looked older. His face was getting puffy, his skin pale with a grayish tint, and the faintest of crow's feet were creeping in at the corners of his eyes.

"I have a name for you to consider," Sammy said.

Al raised an eyebrow. "For my daughter?"

Sammy nodded. "Mallory."

Al snorted into his pizza. "I thought you were going to say *Samantha*."

"Mallory is a portmanteau. A cross between Al and Marie."

"That's actually kind of clever. What does it mean?"

"I think it's a type of duck."

Al wagged a finger. "Mallard." Then he grinned. "Not often that I know something you don't."

Sammy asked his com to look up the name Mallory. "On second thought, that's not such a good idea. It means 'misfortune or bad luck.'"

Al rolled his eyes. "Surprise, surprise. That's my relationship with Marie to a T."

"Are things really that bad?"

"I don't wanna talk about it, Sammy."

"You gotta talk to somebody. You know I won't judge you. I like Marie. I like you. I have no horse in this race."

"Bet you'd like to see me off your couch, though, right?"

Sammy laughed because it was true. "I think you're fine until Brickert comes home. But I was wondering if you could give me some advice. What would you do differently if you could go back?"

Al stared at the wall blankly, his pizza hanging limply in his hand. "Marie, she—you know how you—I mean ..." Al shook his head. "I don't know what I'd do different. Maybe nothing ... I don't know, Sammy." This statement made him laugh joylessly. "There's your answer, man. I don't know. I don't know anything. I'm just a stupid waste of flesh. I mean, what am I good for?"

"That's not true, Al. You're my friend. I look up to you."

"Please don't. Please don't be anything like me."

Sammy frowned. "You gave me faith, Al. I didn't believe in anything until I met you. I don't know what I believe in, but I think there's something out there ... or someone. When all this is over, I want to pursue that belief and see where it leads me."

"Me? I feel dead inside. Alone. Rotten. Lost. I don't know where all this started, but I wish I could go back to where I didn't feel like the whole world is on a roller coaster to hell and I'm sitting in the front car."

They ate in silence after that. When the pizza was gone, Al leaned back into the couch and patted his stomach with heavy eyelids. "That hit the spot," he said, yawning widely. "Thanks, Marie."

Sammy raised an eyebrow, but Al was already dozing. "You're welcome." He stared at Al for a long time, wondering what on earth was going on in his friend's mind. *What switch flipped? Why can Jeffie and I fix things, but not him and Marie?*

Once Al began to snore, Sammy left, taking the pizza box with him, the pieces of crust rattling around as he walked. The evening was quickly turning to night, but Sammy wasn't tired. He considered grabbing his friends for a visit to the infirmary, but his com rang. For the second time his holo-screen said UNKNOWN CALLER. That wasn't normal. The only people who knew his number were part of the resistance.

"Hello?" he answered. "Hello? Who is this?"

The line went dead. The scenario reminded Sammy too much of the time the fox had called him at Psion Beta headquarters on the night of his graduation. He told his com to patch him to the operator.

"Operator," was the response.

"Hey, this is Samuel Berhane. I've gotten a couple of strange calls from an unknown number, I was wondering—" Another call beeped in, again from UNKNOWN CALLER. "Yeah, wait, they're calling me again. Should I answer it?"

"Uh, I don't know. Let me check with one of our techs." The operator put Sammy on hold for two minutes. During that time, the connection from the unknown caller ended. "Sammy, I've got Harv, the lead communications officer, on the other line."

"Put him through."

"Hi Sammy, Harv here," a man with a soft, high voice said. "I'm running diagnostics on your call and I can't trace the source, okay? So that shouldn't happen in our closed system. I would advise you not to answer the call."

"What do you want me to do?"

"Ignore the calls. I'll monitor your line in case it comes through again. See what I can come up with. So it could be someone has mistakenly linked into our network, but that's highly *highly* unlikely."

"Any chance it's CAG?"

"Maybe. I'll alert Thomas and Lara, and keep you updated."

Sammy went to his room, wishing that Jeffie wasn't on the late shift. He could have found Kawai, but she was likely with Li. Hanging out with them would be about as much fun as watching Brickert and Natalia make out. Those two managed to make kissing look like two dogs trying to lick each other's faces off. When he walked in the door, his com rang again.

UNKNOWN CALLER

Sammy ignored it and found his holo-tablet. Khani had sent several reports for him to read in preparation for meetings later that week. Glancing at his clock and seeing that it was not as late as he'd hoped, Sammy sighed and opened the files. He hadn't been working for thirty minutes when the com rang again.

UNKNOWN CALLER

"Who are you?" Sammy asked the words on the screen.

It didn't ring again for another hour. Sammy had fallen asleep on his bed reading a report on amphibious codes in complex systems. He hadn't even stayed awake long enough to learn how a code could be amphibious. The ring of the com woke him with a start.

UNKNOWN CALLER

Without thinking, he answered it. "Hello," he mumbled.

"Sammy …" The voice made Sammy sit straight up. A jolt of adrenaline flooded his body. The lisp in the *S* of Sammy was unmistakable.

"Trapper."

9 | Repentance

Tuesday, July 1, 2087

THEY LEFT UNDER the cover of night, hours after sundown, the cruiser protected by stealth technology. Sammy yawned. Jeffie's gaze remained fixed on the window. "The leadership committee didn't seem happy about letting you go. Why's that?"

"Lots of reasons," Sammy answered from his seat in the pilot chair. He smiled smugly as he remembered the looks of resigned disappointment on the faces of most members of the committee when he told them he had spoken to Trapper on his com. After lecturing him for over an hour about how dangerous such an action had been, a majority had agreed that he had no choice but to go to the Hive.

"I can't believe we're bringing Trapper ... Diego ... whoever," Jeffie said. "I can't believe we're bringing him back. He's creepy. Beyond creepy. He's likely to go off at any minute."

"That's why I made Trapper agree to so many conditions."

Jeffie stared past Sammy ponderously. "But why now?"

"He's afraid."

"Of what?"

"I have no idea."

For a while the only sounds were the droning of the engines and the rain spattering the windows as they flew over the tropics of Central America. Each drop reminded Sammy of gunshots. Such a long time passed without speaking that Sammy wondered if Jeffie had fallen asleep.

Then suddenly she asked, "You think we could go back to being normal again? Like ever?"

Though Sammy thought he knew what she meant, he still asked, "Normal? What's normal?"

"No more battle. No more violence. The high that comes from the adrenaline. All of that stuff gone and not missed."

"I don't know."

Jeffie adjusted her co-pilot's chair so it was a few centimeters closer to him. A smile grew on her lips and her eyes danced playfully. "Let me put it this way, Mr. Berhane: could you see yourself as a banker or a sales analyst or a plumber someday?"

"A plumber?"

Jeffie giggled and shrugged. "Well, could you?"

Sammy thought about it, yawning again.

When their eyes met again, Jeffie shook her head and smiled. "Didn't think so. We're in this business for life. It's crazy. I'm crazy. First I was eager for battle when I got to Beta headquarters. Then I got a taste of it in Orlando, and it terrified me. Then the Hive happened, and something in me flipped again. Now I feel so invincible. And that feeling terrifies me. I mean, I want kids. I want marriage." Sammy pretended not to notice how her gaze flickered back in his direction when she said this. "I want to be a part of something incredible and special. And yet I want to be normal too."

"I still don't know what you mean when you say a normal life."

"You know …" Jeffie waved her hand around abstractly. "Normal. Your family was normal. So was my family before …"

"Your mom directs movies. Your brothers are pro athletes. That's not normal."

"Normaler than what we'd have if we ever get—"

"Normaler isn't a word."

Jeffie stuck out her tongue and rolled her eyes.

"Think about it, though, Jeffie. Who do we know that's normal? Who do we know that's had a marriage work? Byron's wife died. Al and Marie are on the rocks. Your parents—"

"Are fine, thank you very much."

"They see each other how often? About a week out of each month?"

"… ish …" Jeffie replied reluctantly. "What are you saying? Marriage is a waste of time?"

"I don't know. Maybe I'm saying nothing." A crack of lightning on the distant horizon drew Sammy's attention.

"I love you," Jeffie said quietly.

Sammy winced. "Last time you said that, you apologized after."

"Well, I retract my apology." Jeffie grabbed Sammy's hand and squeezed it so tight she almost hurt him. "I'm not sorry for loving you. Should I be?"

In a brief break in the clouds, Sammy saw the moon, small but bright in the sky. He yearned to be far away from Jeffie right now, away and alone. "No. I don't think you should be. But when you say it I feel stupid."

"Why?"

A loud beep from the console interrupted him. "*WARNING. YOU ARE ENTERING A NO-FLY ZONE. THIS IS FORBIDDEN AIRSPACE. LETHAL FORCE WILL BE USED IF YOU DO NOT REDIRECT YOUR CRAFT IMMEDIATELY. WARNING.*"

They let go of each other's hands so they could get to work. Sammy punched the communications controls to contact Trapper. "Do not open fire. Friendly aircraft incoming. Carrying a cargo of *emeralds* for delivery. Do not damage the goods."

The warning voice cut off, and Diego's voice came in over the radio. "Sammy, is that you?" The lack of a lisp told Sammy this was not Trapper speaking. "You thought I was going to set out a welcome mat for you?" Harsh laughter filled Sammy's ears. "My systems are locked onto you, kid. Prepare yourself for the boom!"

As soon as Diego's voice cut away, the cruiser's alarms blared. Big red letters flashed from the holo-screen:

INCOMING MISSILES.

Sammy jammed the coms button. He addressed Diego as Trapper even though he knew it was Diego currently speaking to him. "Trapper, abort the attack! This is a friendly aircraft. Abort the missiles!"

"For someone as smart as yourself, I think you may need a dictionary to define the word friendly. Sadly, you have only seconds to look it up."

"Trapper, you invited me here! Don't shoot me down!"

"Invited? Not I. I have no intention of leaving my home. The fact that you survived our last visit is an anomaly that I mean to correct."

Sammy looked at Jeffie in a way that told her to get ready to jump ship. He pushed the button again and said, "Trapper … if you can hear me, please respond. We're going to land this ship, we're walking inside that building, and we're going to help you. Now call off those missiles!"

Diego laughed again, obviously savoring his power. "Who is Trapper?"

Outside the cockpit windshield, the missiles were visible, flares of bright orange light and white plumes of smoke streaked toward their target. The projectiles shot straight into the air, then turned until their noses were pointed at the cruiser.

"This isn't a game. *Call them off, Trapper!*"

No answer came. Sammy didn't waste time readying the hatch for an emergency bailout. Both Jeffie and Sammy shrugged out of their safety harnesses. The missiles shot toward them, closing in fast. "Trapper, don't do this!" Sammy warned. "If you let those missiles hit me, I'm going to find you and kick your—"

The missiles suddenly dropped from the sky and plummeted into the rainforest where they crashed ignominiously into the jungle without so much as a puff of dust. "My apologies, Sammy," a voice with a discernible lisp stated. "Set down on the lawns behind the Hive. Visitors are becoming a common occurrence these days."

In under half an hour, Trapper welcomed Sammy and Jeffie into the upper level of his facility. "Sorry about that," he said as they entered. "Diego still isn't happy with the arrangement we made. I think the missiles were his way of giving you the finger."

"You ready to go?" Sammy asked. "We're on a tight schedule."

"Almost," Trapper answered. "Come in. I need to … tidy up." He returned to his computers as he spoke. "And when I say tidy up, I mean download all our code and delete everything I've done so the fox thinks I've been kidnapped, not defected."

Sammy held up a hand. "Before we take you anywhere, Jeffie and I need to know how far we can trust you. How often is Diego taking control?"

"You just tried to roast us," Jeffie added.

"Why do you think I've agreed to be searched, cuffed, and bound on the ride home?" Trapper told them. "Everything I know, everything I hear and see, I share with him. He gets loose, no telling what he'll do. But I've grown stronger, and he's grown weaker lately. I'll be more help than hindrance. Fortunately, I'm going to give you something that will help even if our agreement doesn't work out."

Jeffie and Sammy exchanged a skeptical glance.

"Fair enough," Sammy said. *Worst case scenario, we put a bullet in him.* He immediately regretted the thought. "Crazy thing is, for the last several days, I've been arguing with our leaders for permission to see you. Then you call me up out of the blue and confirm all my suspicions about the kill code."

"Had you decided to fly here before we spoke over the com, Diego would have killed you. No question."

"Why would he kill me yesterday but not today?"

"We've developed a very tenuous but working relationship."

"Let's get going."

Trapper slid his chair around to his computer console. "Not quite ready, Sammy. Penetrating the resistance's communications network was not easy and left lots of traceable activity on my end. And if I were to get caught doing what I'm doing right now … I can't even imagine the sort of things the Aegis would do to me. Or the Queen."

"How much time do you need?" Jeffie asked.

"Less than thirty minutes."

Sammy cursed silently. This mission was supposed to be a rip and run, grab Trapper and leave. Resigned to waiting, he sat down on the floor and patted on the seat of the free chair for Jeffie to sit.

"Why is Diego willing to let you turn?" Jeffie asked. "Seems he'd be enraged."

"Oh, he wrestled with the decision for days," Trapper explained. "But in the end he knew he had no choice."

"Why?"

A dark look fell over Trapper's face. For a moment he snarled, vicious and feral, then it was gone. "Something's changed. Something big has happened." His empty socket quivered and with trembling fingers, he pointed to a small black device across the room.

Sammy knelt down to examine it. "What is it?"

"She put it here," Trapper spat.

Sammy didn't need to ask who *she* was. "What does it do?"

"She came a few weeks ago. Planted that box to spy on me. Thought I wouldn't notice. But the Hive has been my home for so long ... I knew it moments after she placed it. I neutered the device. It only tells her what I want it to."

"So what exactly is holding us up?" Sammy asked. "You said 'tidying up.'"

"Making sure no one who comes here digging around has any idea what I've been up to," Trapper said, tapping his wrist as though he wore a watch. "And I just need a few more minutes."

"Does this have anything to do with the kill code?" Jeffie asked.

Trapper's eye narrowed on her. "Everything to do with it. Diego is not happy that you know about it, Sammy."

"Our computer techs found traces of it in the data dump we stole from you seven months ago."

Trapper paled. "Diego's furious right now. He doesn't like knowing he made a mistake."

Trapper's expression transformed into one of rage. "I didn't make a mistake!" he said, snarling in a harsh tone. His body tensed and jerked as though he was about to spring. Jeffie and Sammy both scooted back, but Trapper quickly regained his composure.

"You all right?" Sammy asked warily.

Trapper cleared his throat and nodded. "There is no greater secret in the fox's organization than the kill code. Only two people know about it."

"Psssh. Right. I'm sure plenty of Thirteens and Aegis know what happens when they get on the wrong side of the fox. I've seen Thirteens blow up like they had a bomb sitting in their guts. How can the other Thirteens not know about it?"

"They know what the solution does to a degree, yes. But they don't know how it works. To most of them the fox is like Santa Claus or the Easter Bunny. He is a shadow."

Sammy's face twitched as he remembered the shadow from his nightmares, the shadow of himself that could talk and touch and taunt him.

"The fox is a recluse. Very few people ever meet him or know him. Even fewer connect him to his former identity of Diego Newblood. You have no idea how the Thirteen organization works, what goes on in those cells. It has all been carefully constructed by the fox to operate how he needs it to. The Thirteens think they are the embodiment of disorder and anarchy, but in actuality the fox keeps them reigned in using complex behavior psychology.

"Every Thirteen, Hybrid, and Aegis in the employ of N Corporation drinks the *solution*. To them it's a rite of passage that they know can track them, but nothing more. By drinking it they swear allegiance to the Thirteen Brotherhood. The kill switch is a two piece code. What you found in your data theft was the second piece. The first piece identifies a specific target. The second piece terminates him or her. The target can be anyone who has had the solution.

"The kill order always comes from the fox. And always goes through me. Each person who's had the solution also has a number, so I attached the number to the code and ... *boom*. Goodbye. So long. Fare thee well."

"So let's do it right now!" Jeffie said. "Start putting in codes and end this war!"

Trapper aimed his one good eye on Jeffie. "You think there won't be repercussions if I try to execute a kill order without the fox's approval? Wrong. The solution may not be in *me*, but the fox has other ways to quickly cover his tracks. You think the Hive isn't wired? Give it a try. Goodbye. So long. Fare thee well."

"Then what good will the code do us?" Sammy asked.

"There is always another way. The fox is a clean man. You know that, Sammy, you met him. He likes to tidy up after himself. Once his plans for the war are realized and the NWG has fallen, he wants to clean up."

"A mass kill order?" Sammy asked. "All of them at once?"

A shudder passed through Trapper, but he nodded. "Rid the world of Thirteens, Aegis, and Hybrids in one fell swoop. The perfect clean up."

"Minus all the blown up bits," Jeffie added. "The fox will need to hire a few janitors for that."

"You're more talkative this time around, aren't you?"

"My boyfriend's not bleeding to death this time around."

Sammy rubbed his temples, thinking, calculating. "How do we use the kill code without the fox's knowledge?"

"We don't. Eventually he will know. The key is to do it in such a way that by the time he realizes it, it's too late."

"How?"

Trapper checked the time. "The kill rooms. The *white* rooms. There are two of them. One in Rio, one in Orlando. In the very bowels of the earth."

Sammy remembered the N Tower in Rio he'd been taken to. The white button on the elevator panel.

"In case something happens to me, and Diego gets control, I'm giving you this." From Trapper's pocket he produced a cube. His hands shook and for an instant his grip tightened, his face grimaced, and Sammy thought he might not hand it over. But then it was in Sammy's hand, safe.

"A data cube with everything you need to know."

"What's the catch?" Sammy asked. "I could leave right now and break our agreement."

Trapper tapped his skull. "Without the keyword, you can't use the data cube. You need me alive and well through the day of the mission. By then I'll have proven to you that I'm valuable and … somewhat rehabilitated. Hopefully, one day, you'll even be able to excise the *demon* out of me."

"I don't get it," Sammy said. "Why is Diego allowing you to do this? I still remember what you—he—whoever did at the ETC. I still have Byron's memories."

At the mention of Byron's name, Trapper's expression changed to one of fury. He lunged at Sammy, moving so quickly that Sammy didn't have time to get his shields up to blast him away. Trapper's hands went to Sammy's throat and squeezed as he knocked Sammy backward to the floor. Sammy tried to choke out a few choice words, but he couldn't breathe.

Jeffie didn't waste time blasting Trapper off Sammy. Trapper hit the floor hard and skidded until his back slammed into the wall. Then she ran over to the panel where they knew Trapper kept the sleeping gas, the gas he'd used on himself during their last visit. Sammy rolled and scrambled over to Trapper who put his hands up shakily. "It's me. *It's me!* I'm in control."

"How do we know?" Jeffie held the canister ready to spray Trapper.

"Say something," Sammy told him.

"Something," Trapper said with his pronounced lisp.

Sammy relaxed and let Trapper up. "It's him." He leaned against the wall, near the very spot where he'd once sat next to Jeffie while his leg leaked blood onto the floor from fish bites. Jeffie dropped the canister to the floor.

"This is insane," she muttered.

"I'm sorry!" Trapper cried. "Sometimes he just … pounces. You asked me a question about the fox. The answer is I don't know what—" Trapper's face turned into a grinning grimace and his eye and lips twitched violently. "Let me tell them!"

"No!" he roared at himself in Diego's voice.

"*Let me tell them!*" Trapper screamed back. Finally his struggle ended and his face relaxed. "Something's happened to the fox. We think he's been killed or replaced."

"By whom?" Sammy asked.

"How many people do you think are close enough to him to do such a thing?"

An alarm beeped from Trapper's console. He stared at his screens for a long moment, then began to curse and hit himself with brutal swings.

"What?" Sammy asked.

"She's on her way!"

"How does she know we're here?"

"I don't—somehow! It doesn't matter! You have to go!"

"*We* have to go!" Jeffie corrected. "You're coming too."

"The plan has changed. If I don't finish clearing my tracks, she'll figure out what the white room is and what you plan to do with it. Everything you need to know is on the cube. Get out, wait until she lands, then take off as soon as I give the signal."

"Won't she see our cruiser?"

"If she flies straight to the landing pad on the roof, she won't. The building obstructs the view. But if she decides to fly around ..."

Jeffie marched to the door.

"Listen to me for a second!" Trapper shouted. "Without me, you'll need to turn someone who has the solution in their system *and* level six clearance."

"An Aegis or Thirteen?" Sammy asked doubtfully.

"Not an Aegis. And Thirteens won't likely turn. Your best bet is a—a—" Trapper clamped his hands over his mouth and his eye began to water. He muffled protests into the offending hand and finally bit it so hard it bled. When he let go, he grunted in pain. A flash of fury appeared in his eye. Sammy tensed up and prepared to blast, but the moment passed and Trapper's calm returned. "A Dark agent."

"What is a Dark agent?"

"It's what you would have become had your anomaly been discovered in CAG territory instead of South Africa. It's where they send all the anomalies … except the Thirteens. They call it Extraction/Implantation."

Sammy thought of Stripe, and a blowtorch ignited, expanding the darkness inside him like a balloon reacting to heated air. The painful memory of a crocodile bite in his leg caused him to wince until it passed. Jeffie noticed but made no comment, and he was grateful.

"You'll need to infiltrate the Extraction/Implantation site," Trapper continued. "Figure out a way to smuggle a Dark agent out. Without someone who's had the solution … your mission is hopeless."

"Can you give us intel on how to get into the Dark facility?" Jeffie asked, hand on the door.

"It's on the cube." Trapper's fingers raced across a console as his eye watched his myriad screens. A beep came from one of the computer towers. "I still wouldn't pin your hopes on surviving the war."

"Even with Sammy on our side?" Jeffie asked.

For a moment, Trapper smiled. And when he did, he almost looked normal. He almost reminded Sammy of the handsome young man he'd come to know through Commander Byron's memories. Pity surged through Sammy so powerfully that he felt it down his spine and across his shoulders like a ripple of discomfort.

"Go," Trapper said. "Get in your cruiser and take off the moment I give you the signal. Now!"

Jeffie ran out, but before Sammy cleared the room, Trapper yanked him back and slammed the door, locking it.

"What are you—" Sammy started to say.

"We have a few more minutes than I let on before the Queen arrives."

Jeffie pounded on the door and yelled.

Trapper leaned in close and whispered in Sammy's ear. "I saw what you did to my brothers in Detroit."

"I didn't—I just—"

"You can't use it again. If you do, it will weaken your will. The dreams will start soon if they haven't already. The cave."

Sammy's pulse quickened and sweat moistened his brow. *Dreams.* "What cave, Trapper? What are you talking—"

"The anomaly is not something you can compartmentalize. It is not a switch you can flip nor a pill you can take and wait for its effects to wear off. Each time you embrace it, you weaken your—"

"How can you say that? Look at you—"

"Shut up! Just shut up. Are you blind? Yes, look at me. Look at my face."

Sammy stared at the floor, ashamed of himself. "I'm strong enough to resist it."

"LOOK AT ME!" Trapper waited until Sammy obeyed the order. "It can't be done. Let the idea go."

"I can't just let it go. It saves lives."

"And takes them."

"I can control it!"

Trapper's eye stopped quivering and fixed on Sammy. "Play clip 91a020b1."

On the screen nearest to them, Sammy saw himself hitting Brickert in the face while Brickert lay slumped on the floor. Sammy turned away, afraid he might vomit. A burst of laughter escaped Trapper.

"That's what you call control? That feeling of sheer power, so raw and mighty, in your blood, your bones, your sinews. I couldn't deny it. Once I had a taste, it called to me. Beckoned me back for another sample of the rage … the energy. I fought it. Resisted. By the time I found the cave, I didn't stand a chance." Trapper's eye grew wide. "All of us find it. All of us."

"What does that mean? What cave?"

"You'll see. I know what you felt. What you feel. Only because of my disorder am I able to separate the two. Me and the Thirteen. Me and Diego. You …" He looked Sammy up and down with his eye. "You will have no such luck."

"How many times did you use it?" Sammy asked. "Before you couldn't stop?"

"Stop?" Trapper growled a chuckle. "You make it sound like a drug. It's not. It's an essence that infuses itself into you. A state of being. You transform into it. It's been over thirty years, so I don't remember all the specifics. Trapper, me—this person you are talking to—I am the exception. But still those choices have ruined my life. Do not think you can toy with it or use it and walk away unscathed."

Sammy sighed and rubbed his head.

"You love that girl, don't you?"

"I—I don't know."

"You do. You look at her the way I looked at Emerald. If that's the case, never use the anomaly again. You will become a threat to the world. And in the end, they'll have to put you down. But how much damage would you wreak before you die?"

"What if it means the difference between her living and dying?"

"Then let her die."

Familiar words played in Sammy's mind. He didn't know where he'd heard them, but it wasn't the first time this had happened. The voice was one he knew he should recognize, but didn't. It was a feather in the wind, drifting barely out of reach every time he tried to snag it. The voice said, "*You will see more death. Some of them will be people whom you love.*"

Another alarm beeped from the console. Trapper's eye studied it for only a second, then he pushed Sammy away. "Go. She will be here in minutes."

"I can take the Queen."

Trapper shook his head. "She can blast now. Who knows what else she's done to herself."

Sammy's heart beat faster and his neck grew hot. "When? How?"

"I don't have time to explain, but it's true. She is obsessed with you. Now go. I will do what I can, but Diego will try to undo it."

"Trapper ... you're going to die, aren't you?"

"LEAVE!" Trapper tapped the data cube in Sammy's hand. "*Repentance*. Remember that keyword. Now I need all the time I can get to fix this."

* * * * *

The Queen woke to the sound of an alarm. Her clock told her it was an obscene hour of the morning. Her blurry eyes searched the room for the source of the noise. It took several seconds to realize it came from her com. She fumbled for it and put it on. The holo-screen projected the following text:

Intrusion at the Hive. 0351

"Details," she ordered her com.

Two missiles fired. Deactivated before impact. Deactivation order code matches code assigned to <Diego>.

Incoming update … Stand by.

Status update: Unreported test of Hive defense systems.

"Computer, patch through the audio feed from the Hive black box."

"No audio detected," the computer answered.

"Is the box functional?"

"Power supply intact. Other functions offline."

The Queen swore as she scrambled out of bed to dress. The penthouse elevator took her to the rooftop of the Orlando N Tower where a cruiser waited. Minutes later she was in the air and cruising at top speeds for Lake Coari.

What are you up to, Diego?

The flight to Brazil felt like an itch that could not be scratched. A maddening two-hour itch. She sent no advance warning of her arrival, hoping to catch Diego off guard. Something was fishy. *Has Diego turned? Has he figured out what I've done to the fox?*

No. How could he?

Yet Diego had fired rockets at someone … *Who? Who has figured out the location of the Hive? That secret is—*

How many other secrets have the resistance exploited? San Francisco? Detroit? They know the location of our cloning facilities.

What if the resistance is there now? Or Sammy?

As the dense forests of the Amazon appeared beneath the cruiser, her knees started to shake in anticipation. Her imagination blossomed like a summer rose, and she saw herself matching Sammy in combat, and besting him. She raised his body above her head and threw it down to the unforgiving floor, shattering his bones like glass. A small firework of pain went off inside her own body at the thought of it, and she closed her eyes until it passed. *I'm ready.*

Three minutes from the Hive, Diego hailed her via radio. "To what do I owe another unexpected visit?" he asked with a strange lisp she had never before heard. "Shall I roll out the red carpet? Is this a sign we're becoming fast friends?"

"Missiles were launched from the Hive and deactivated. I want to know why."

There was a long pause before Diego's answer came. "A private aircraft flew near the area. At first I suspected it to be the enemy, but they immediately turned around after the missiles were launched. Rather than making a mess in my otherwise pristine jungle, I deactivated the projectiles."

Liar. His newfound lisp threatened to drive her mad.

"Certainly no need to fly down to visit unless you missed me that badly."

"Prepare for my arrival," the Queen said.

"I'm always prepared."

The building was quiet when she entered, certainly no Thirteens were in the building other than Diego. She recalled there had been none the last time she visited, too. Diego had said they were on an assignment.

Something's not right.

The Queen was on edge as she took the stairs up to Diego's lair. The door to the third level was unlocked, but the Queen entered ready to blast should Diego try to ambush her. Instead she found him in his chair typing furiously at his keyboard. One of the screens displayed lines of code, which Diego's one eye was fixed on.

"Always a pleasure to see you, Queen. Please make yourself at home. There's coffee in the kitchen if it suits you." His eye stayed trained on the screen.

"What is this? What are you working on?"

"Rewriting some code," he said very matter-of-factly, the lisp still present. His fingers raced over the keyboard like a demon had possessed him.

"The fox gave you this assignment?"

Diego paused before answering. "No. He asks me to keep the Hive up to date. Should I start asking his permission to relieve myself, too?"

The Queen walked around the room to where she'd planted the box. Diego's eye followed her reflection in the screen. She faced his direction while her hand secretly searched under the console until she found the device exactly where she'd placed it … but the hair was gone, the one she had trapped between the console and the box to inform her if the box was moved.

He found it. Now he is lying, lying, lying.

She took a step toward him. His eye flickered to her reflection, then back to his codes. Her attention shifted toward his work. The

Queen had enough experience with writing and editing computer code that she understood the gist of what Diego was doing. She caught bits and scraps, and started piecing it all together.

He's deleting activity. What activity?

The Queen's eyes raced over the screen. *He made a file transfer, a large one.* Suddenly that bit of activity was gone.

"STOP!" She reached for his chair and yanked hard on it, but Diego stood and let it slide out from underneath him while he continued to type. The Queen blasted him with two powerful hand blasts. Diego's head smashed through the screen. Then she grabbed him by the legs and yanked him out. His face bled from multiple lacerations, but he grinned at her as though he'd won a gold medal.

"You're too late." He jammed a button and several more lines of code disappeared. Then he spat his own blood in her face.

The Queen struck him across the cheek. "What." She smacked him again. "Did." She hit him twice more. "You. Do?"

"Keep swinging, Queenie," he sputtered.

Enraged, the Queen picked Diego up and threw him into his screens. His precious screens that he'd always loved to watch for hours and hours, day and night. Diego hit the floor with a crunching thump that told the Queen some of the screen's glass had embedded itself into him. The sensation of needles deeply piercing her own skin shocked her, but she ignored it and rolled Diego over with her foot so that he faced her. The bleeding was much worse now.

"Queen …" he whispered. "It was him. Not me. It was him." Then he clamped shut and squirmed on the linoleum. "Stop it!"

The Queen kicked him with savage force, feeling his ribs bend and snap beneath the toe of her boot. Her own ribs ached when she drew her next breath. Then she knelt next to his head and put a knife up to the canal of Diego's ear. "Tell me everything I need to know or every centimeter of this blade will worm its way through your brains."

"Trapper," Diego hissed. "He's here."

"Who?" the Queen asked, standing up as fast as a bullet, knife at the ready. "Where?"

"He's in me. The fox knows what I'm talking about. He knows Trapper. Sammy and the girl—they were here … asking questions. He told them things."

"WHAT?" she screamed. "How long ago?"

"Fff—" Diego's teeth bit down on his lower lip until it left oozing bite marks. "He—trrrr … NOTHING! Go to hell!"

The Queen was back on her knees next to him, knife still in hand. The steady amount of pressure of knife-on-ear helped Diego get better control over himself. He groaned loudly with pain as his ear drum burst. "He told them about the ext—*gurrrk*." Choking noises erupted from Diego's throat followed by gagging sounds.

"The extraction site?" the Queen asked.

Diego nodded.

"Is that all?"

There was a pause before Diego nodded again. "It wasn't supposed to be like this. My death was already planned. I had a purpose. The fox … will be … disappointed." Disgusted at the filthy weakling lying before her, the Queen jammed the rest of the knife home and ended his pathetic life. Diego twitched like he was having a minor seizure before a single word escaped his lips in a faint moan.

"Emerald … " And he died.

The Queen stared at him for a long time. Her eyes watered, not from guilt or sadness, but from the sudden sharp, biting pain in her own ear, pulsing and radiating like the ticking of a clock. *What is this?* The pains were happening more frequently and more acutely. So she forced herself to look at Diego as he bled out.

When the pain finally passed, she removed her knife from his head, wiped it on his shirt, and left him on the floor.

* * * * *

Friday, April 25, 2053

Priyanka was right about not getting caught. The cyber investigation task force lasted a week and found no evidence that she had doctored or posted the photos of Katie. Still, the pictures were all the school talked about. Katie tried to ignore it by focusing on her schoolwork, but too many things reminded her of the incident. When she used the toilet in the girls' restroom, she discovered graffiti about her, the mildest of which said that she had her own strain of Chlamydia or that she had memorized the Kama Sutra. Her best friend Courtney demanded that the principal have the graffiti removed immediately, but it took three days for the janitors to get around to it.

Almost a month after the incident, it was time for the second round of voting for Prom Court, where eighteen candidates were whittled down to eight. Katie finished in eighth place while Priyanka finished in first. Only six weeks remained before the final vote. Every time Katie saw Priyanka's smug little smile she wanted to smack it until Pri's nose broke. She imagined herself doing it so many times, it seemed to be all she dreamed about. That and the cave …

Every night she dreamed the same thing. Touching the shadow version of herself, the knife appearing in her hand, and the choice. The house or the cave? She had gone to the brightly lit house, looked through its windows, watched the activity inside for hours. The scene never changed: inside the home her mother and father waited for Katie to come for dinner. A large ham sat on the table, still needing to be carved. The table sat six, but only two chairs were occupied. Katie's dad would get up to look for a knife to slice the ham, but never found it. Her mother called for Katie, her voice growing more urgent each time. The scene was a loop that replayed over and over.

The house did not interest her and the cave terrified her. Just standing at its mouth she could sense its unfathomable depth and vastness. The smell from within was not good, but not foul either; something heavy and thick, foreign and familiar all at once. Katie could not place the scent—not without entering the cave. She'd spent several nights staring into its mouth, her feet right at the edge of the darkness, and she listened, smelled, tried to peer into the black yet discerned nothing.

Days after the vote, Katie's gym class was forced to run a 5K in the pouring rain. Fortunately, Katie had Courtney, Vivian, and Rachel to keep her company as they jogged around with sopping clothes stuck to their bodies and dripping hair plastered to their pale, clammy faces.

"I don't know why I spend an hour doing my makeup in the mornings," Courtney groaned as she glared at their teacher. "And look at her watching us from under her umbrella. She's probably laughing at us."

"Isn't this like illegal or something?" Vivian responded.

Katie was one of the fastest girls in her class, though she hadn't run track this year in order to focus on her studies and avoid shin splints. Through a megaphone, the instructor yelled at them to pick up the pace. Some of the students, Priyanka included, responded by slowing down even more just to spite the teacher. As Katie and her friends gradually caught up to Priyanka and her posse, Katie's eyes bored holes into Priyanka's backside. She wanted to slam Priyanka's head into the pavement until it cracked open like an egg.

Katie stayed on the inside lanes. The outside lanes had hurdles scattered throughout. As Katie and her crew passed Priyanka, Katie gave Priyanka a nudge, pushing her into the hurdles. Priyanka's arm caught on it, and she tripped, landing on the track as the hurdle crashed down on her. Courtney and Vivian snickered as Priyanka growled in frustration behind them.

Not wanting to look guilty, they didn't even look over their shoulders until the sound of shoes slapping onto the wet track caught up to them.

"Think you're all that, Porn Queen?" Priyanka shrieked. "I'm going to—"

Katie grabbed Priyanka and drove her into the soggy grass. When they hit the turf of the football field they slid two meters, tearing up the turf and covering themselves in mud. The instructor was on the far end of the field and didn't notice the ruckus. Katie took advantage of this, jamming her elbow into Priyanka's gut, then rotating her shoulder to bring that same elbow into Pri's chin.

However, it didn't matter, Priyanka had no fight in her. After the blow to her stomach, she tried to curl into a ball, but Katie was all over her. A voice in Katie's head told her, *Hit harder! Harder! HARDER!* She obeyed, raining fists and elbows until the instructor pulled her off.

The gym instructor hauled both girls into the principal's office, caked in mud and grass. Mrs. Simpson, the principal, was in a meeting with another student, but glanced several times out her window with increasingly disapproving expressions. Priyanka wrapped her arms around her stomach, sobbing and shivering, but Katie felt a strange warmth and sense of satisfaction.

And she knew that tonight would be the night she dared to enter the cave.

10 | Promises

Sunday, July 13, 2087

"OUR FOCUS HAS to be on infiltrating Mexico City," Commander Byron argued to the leadership committee after hearing other points of view. Sammy sat next to him, listening half-heartedly. He was still tired from a late Saturday night spent playing blastketball and making out with Jeffie. His lips were still sore and raw in a pleasant sort of way that made him grin whenever he thought about it. "What is the point in planning anything with the kill code unless we have the biggest piece of the puzzle already in our possession?"

"I agree," Anna said. "Let's put all our attention on getting a Dark agent out of the Extraction facility and *then* worry about the rest."

"What can you tell us about the Extraction/Implantation site, Dr. N—Khani?" Lara asked, always reluctant to call on Khani.

All eyes turned to the Tensai whose chest puffed out each time she spoke.

"Sammy's contact at the Hive," Khani began, "has given us all the information we need to access the site under the disguise as an inspection team. The fox uses a quality control firm owned by N Corp through subsidiary companies to ensure secrecy regarding the nature of the facility. Using the protocol on the data cube, we should be able arrange an appointment without alerting anyone in the fox's hierarchy."

"We need to assemble a team of Psions," Sammy said. "People who can pass as inspectors."

"What are the profiles of people used in previous inspections?" Lara asked Khani.

Khani tapped her glasses on her lip while her other hand danced on her tablet. "Psychologists mostly, but a few experts from other fields like mathematics and physical penetration test teams."

"So we need Psions who look old enough to pass as a part of this team?" the commander asked. "How many exactly?"

"Five is the standard inspection team size," Khani answered.

"Count me in," Anna said.

"You and I are the only truly older looking Psions," Commander Byron said. "No offense, Anna."

"None taken. Surviving to being thirty-three is a badge of honor." She gave Sammy a rogue wink.

"Who are the oldest Psions available?" Lorenzo asked.

"More important to me," Commander Byron said, "is who are the most qualified that we can make look old enough. Samuel, certainly, should go."

"He's the most wanted man in the CAG," Thomas said. "His face is all over the news."

"That picture looks nothing like me," Sammy countered. "My hair is longer, I've been growing out my facial hair. Throw a pair of square glasses on me, and no one will connect the dots."

"I agree," Anna stated. "Sammy needs to be on the mission." She looked at Sammy, put a fist to her chest, and bumped her sternum.

Sammy grinned. "I propose a team consisting of myself, the commander, Anna, Al, and Kawai Nujola."

Al stirred at the mention of his name, his eyes puffy as ever. Sammy guessed his friend had gained ten or fifteen kilos in the last three months, most of it in his face and gut. "I'm in."

"I oppose that team," Commander Byron stated in a firm, cold voice. "Li Cheng Zheng should be taken instead of Al."

Al gazed at his dad, then barked out a laugh. "I'm far more qualified for the mission than Li. I'm going."

The atmosphere in the room changed very quickly to one of tense silence. Three days ago, the commander had kicked his son out of a subcommittee meeting for being hung-over. Everyone waited to see what he would say now.

"Albert, you are not fit to go on any mission. You do not take care of yourself. How can you be expected to take care of your teammates?"

"I—" Al sputtered. "You don't have a clue—"

"And while Albert is the topic at hand," Byron stated to the committee, "I motion that he be removed from the leadership committee and any further missions until he gets himself sober and demonstrates some manner of self-control."

"Give me a break, Dad," Al argued. "You can't impose your morals on me. I'm more than qualified for this mission and the committee."

"I made a motion," Byron said to the rest of the room. "Does anyone wish to second it?"

At first no one did. Then Anna raised her hand. Al stared at her as though she'd shot him. Lara and Thomas exchanged a dark look, and Lara presented the motion to the floor with a sigh. "All those in favor of imposing this restriction on Al ..."

One by one, hands went up, even Thomas's. Sammy did not raise his hand, nor did Lara, but still the restriction passed by a two to one margin. Pale, tight-lipped and breathing heavily, Al stood. His hands shook and he seemed determined not to look at Commander Byron.

"This is a mistake," Al announced. "There's no one more qualified or able. So if you idiots want to send our people into a dangerous situation without the best soldiers at your disposal, then the results are on your hands not mine."

Byron reached to put his hand on Al's.

"Don't touch me!" Al shouted, jerking his hand away.

The commander stood as well to help his son, but Al took a swing at his dad with a balled fist. Commander Byron jerked his head back and shoved his son face-first into the table. Al knocked his head into the wood and fell to the floor, nose and lip trickling blood. When Al reached his feet again, he looked worse than ever.

"Clean yourself up, son," he said quietly. "You are not yourself."

"I am—just—" Al's eyes roamed the room, and he seemed to finally realize how he looked in the eyes of the committee. Without another word, he left. Once he was gone, the committee put the five names to a vote. It passed unanimously. Immediately after, the commander excused himself, his face red but frozen in stone.

Sammy did not get home until after 2100, but the smell of booze was so strong in the house that it almost made him gag. Al was slumped over on the couch, his head resting on one propped up hand while his other hand spun an old pistol on top of the coffee table. He did not look up when Sammy entered the room.

Sammy's eyes trained on the gun. For a moment, he considered running for the commander, but somehow he knew that would make things worse. Trying to keep his voice as calm as possible, Sammy said, "Hey Al. You doing okay?"

Al didn't move except to spin the gun again. "You are my best friend, Sam." His slurring was particularly bad tonight. Then his shoulders gave a jerk. "Ha! I called you Sam. I bet I'm the first person to ever call you Sam. Aren't I, Sam?"

One of his teachers in Johannesburg had insisted that Sammy was a girl's name, so he'd called him Sam, and it rankled Sammy every time. "Yep, you're the first."

Al sniggered as Sammy sat down. "I'm tired. I don't know what I'm doing."

"What's the gun for?"

Al glanced at Sammy as if to say, "You know what it's for," but he didn't say a word.

"You mind if I take it?" Sammy asked. He waited for Al to answer, and when he didn't, Sammy reached for it.

Al tightened his grip. "I just … think … maybe I've messed things up. Maybe it's my fault." His shoulders jerked again with another mirthless laugh. "And that's kind of funny, right? Because I've been telling Marie that it's *her* fault. I mean … all she did was get pregnant, right? All she did was give me a beautiful girl."

Sammy sat down next to Al and put his arm over his shoulders. "I know how you feel, Al. I'm still you're friend."

Al began to cry. He picked up the gun and dropped it in Sammy's hands. Sammy used one hand to drop the magazine on the floor. Then he cleared the chamber and another round popped out. When it was done, he let out a deep breath.

"That gun isn't going to solve your problems," Sammy said. "Just make everyone else's worse. You take it a day at a time, and you'll get through this."

Al put his head on Sammy's shoulder and cried until he fell asleep. Sammy stretched him onto the couch and covered him with a blanket. Then he picked up the gun, the magazine, the bullet, and held them all in his hands for a long time. *Was he really going to do it?* Sammy hoped the answer was no, but wondered if he should tell someone. Byron? Marie? Thomas and Lara?

What if it were me holding a gun to my head? What would I want?

Sammy called Commander Byron. Five minutes later, the commander and Sammy carried Al, still deeply asleep, into Byron's car. Sammy did not sleep well that night. And when he woke, he lay in a puddle of his own urine.

The days passed so swiftly that Sammy hardly had time to wonder where they went. The mission date was set for the last Monday in July. Sammy spent most of his time visiting Brickert at the infirmary, preparing for the mission to Mexico City, and convincing Jeffie that she didn't look old enough to go with the team. The only thing that finally appeased her was when he told her she could be the driver who took them from the hotel downtown to the mission location.

The Saturday night before the mission, Sammy and Jeffie went out with Li and Kawai on a long walk following the Milk River. The moon was high and full, the air was cool, and the sounds of the water and wind were a balm on Sammy's mind. It was at these rare moments when Sammy actually felt sixteen. Most other days, he was treated much older and expected to lead. Around his best friends, he could be himself.

"You check in on Al again?" Li asked Sammy.

"Yeah," he said, "he's doing better. Byron knows what to do, and now that Al is letting him ... I think he's going to be okay."

Kawai wrapped her arm around Li's and cuddled into him as they walked. Jeffie and Sammy were content to link fingers. "Should we ask them?" Sammy overheard Kawai whisper to Li.

Sammy and Jeffie glanced at each other, wondering what Kawai was talking about. They walked farther down the banks of the Milk River until they were only a meter from the water. Li and Kawai continued muttering to each other.

"The moon is so full, so pretty," Jeffie said softly to Sammy. "Where's Venus?"

Sammy stared at the stars until he spotted it, then he leaned close to Jeffie and pointed his finger at the bright planet.

"Where's Mars?"

Sammy pointed again.

"Where's Mercury?"

This one was more difficult, but eventually Sammy found it.

"Where's Uranus?"

"It's not visible to the naked—"

Jeffie pinched Sammy's butt cheek and started to giggle. "You fell for it!"

Sammy rolled his eyes. "How lame can you be?" He tickled Jeffie's ribs and she shrieked.

"Stop!"

"Is that Uranus?" He tickled her back and her stomach. "Is that? Is that?"

"I'm going to pee!"

Sammy let up. Jeffie took several deep breaths. Not far away, Kawai and Li were kissing each other as though the world was about to end. Sammy stood up and coughed loudly until they broke up.

"Sorry, Sammy," Li said, "didn't see you there."

"Yeah," Kawai added, "did you guys just get here? We thought we were alone."

Jeffie threw a handful pebbles at the other couple.

"Okay! Okay!" Kawai cried. "Talking about our wedding just … gets me going. What can I say?"

"Is that what you two were whispering about?" Sammy asked.

"Actually, we were wondering," Li said, "if it's time to ask you two to be our best man and maid of honor."

"Us?" Jeffie asked. "Are we old enough?"

"We have no idea," Li asked. They all laughed. "But I don't have any brothers."

"And I don't have any sisters," Kawai said. "You're my best friend, Jeffie. You and Natalia. But I feel better asking you for some reason. I don't think Natalia will take it too hard. By then you'll be seventeen … maybe even eighteen depending on how long the war takes to end."

"So?" Li asked. "You guys cool with that?"

Jeffie looked at Sammy. He shrugged. "Sure."

Kawai grinned widely and kissed Li.

"Take it somewhere else!" Jeffie teased.

The two broke apart again and stood up. "Well, maybe we will," Kawai said with that same huge grin.

Sure enough, the couple left, their feet making soft sounds in the river's bank as they walked away. Jeffie leaned closer to Sammy until her head rested against his chest as they sat on the wet grass. The moonlight rippled in the water, creating a black and yellow gloss.

"You don't get nervous anymore, do you?" Jeffie asked.

"I'm not nervous about tomorrow, if that's what you mean."

"Lucky." She put a hand on his shoulder and kissed his cheek. "I'm nervous, and I'm only the driver."

Sammy stroked her hair. "You're just worried about me."

"It could get bad. And you'll be deep underground. Not a lot of exits if things get crazy. Right?"

"We have contingencies in place. We'll be fine."

"I guess so." She didn't sound satisfied, which made Sammy wonder if there was something else.

"Really, Jeffie. You don't have to worry."

She sat up and hugged her legs. "Okay."

They didn't speak for at least a minute until Sammy said, "Best man at Li's wedding ... What is a best man supposed to do? Doesn't that mean I give a toast and wear a fancier suit than everyone else?"

Jeffie shrugged. "What's a maid of honor supposed to do?"

They snickered together. "I guess they'll tell us."

Jeffie's smile vanished. "I need you to promise me you won't use your Anomaly Thirteen." She said the words so fast that Sammy took a moment to process them.

"No. We talked about this. I can't keep that promise."

"You can. I need you to do it. I need to hear you say the words that you'll never use it again."

"Why?"

"Because I know that if you don't promise, I'm going to lose you. You're going to think you're strong enough to control it, and you won't. Remember what Trapper said to you? I think he's right."

"How do you know what Trapper—"

"I'm not deaf, Sammy. I heard him through the door. I heard it all. I—I think you should listen to him."

Sammy's hands started to shake, and for an instant he wanted to choke Jeffie—to squeeze her neck until it snapped. He closed his eyes and mentally transformed the urge into a leaf on a stream and watched it pass. It was something Croz had advised him to do in their session to help him deal with the Anomaly Thirteen.

"I wish the choice was that simple."

"It is."

"It's not. Would you really prefer to die than I use my anomaly to save you?" He locked eyes with her and waited for her response.

She nodded. He watched to see if her nostrils would flare, the sign that she was lying, but they didn't. Sammy let out a long breath through his nose and shook his head.

"Well, I would rather use it than see you die."

"Do you want to be a Thirteen?"

"What kind of question is that? I can control it."

Jeffie pulled away and kneeled next to him. "You are not special!"

"I'm not saying I am, but I'm strong."

"This is your weakness, not your strength. If you can't recognize that, it will beat you." Jeffie swallowed and ran her fingers through her hair. "I don't need you to be strong, I need you to be a little more humble and see some sense!"

Sammy knew he could not make Jeffie understand. *She would change her mind if it came down to it. She would ask me to break my promise.*

Jeffie frowned when she saw the defiance on Sammy's face. Her tone softened when she spoke again. "Who is your best friend?"

"Besides you? Brickert."

"And you would never hurt him, right?"

"That was one time. One mistake." The urge to strangle her returned. Sammy pictured leaf after leaf to calm himself.

"If it happened once, it can happen again."

"It won't!" His voice sounded more like a growl, and his eyes narrowed on her.

Jeffie jabbed him in the chest. "Tell that to Brickert's swollen face when you punched him how many times?"

Sammy ground his teeth together.

"Didn't matter when you felt his bones break." Her voice was hard and accusing. "Or heard his whimpering. Or saw him bleed all over your fist, did it? You just kept hitting him over and over and over and—"

"SHUT UP!" Sammy bellowed, and his hand flew back, cocked and ready to fly at Jeffie.

She jumped back and covered herself. Then Sammy realized what she had done. His cheeks and neck grew hot. The rage slowly collapsed until it was gone. In its place was emptiness and guilt.

"I'm sorry," Jeffie mumbled. "I wanted you to see."

Sammy hugged her and held her until she started to shake from her tears.

"I don't want to lose you, Sammy."

"You're right. Okay?" He stroked her hair and held her tighter. The thought that he might have hurt her sickened him. It would have been something he could never take back. No apologies or sorrow could undo that. Even if she forgave him, he would never be able to look someone in the eye and say that he'd never hit her. "I promise, Jeffie. I promise I'll never use it again."

11 | Dark

Monday, July 28, 2087

SAMMY STARED OUT the front passenger window of the SUV as it pulled to a stop across the street from the magnificent memorial erected in downtown Mexico City: a bronze statue of men, women, and children reaching to the sky, eyes fixed heavenward. Floating above them and spinning serenely was a golden earth with a black scar where Mexico City was located. Similar edifices stood in Los Angeles, Lima, and other sites where supposed NWG terrorists had committed unthinkable acts over the last several years.

Behind Sammy sat the four members of his team: Commander Byron, Anna Lukic, Li, and Kawai. As Sammy had promised, Jeffie drove the team to the mission site. Sammy absentmindedly played with his closely trimmed mustache as he watched people cross the street around the memorial block. His hair reached his shoulders and gave him a look of distinguished refinement, even for someone posing to be in his mid-twenties. He planned to cut it the moment he got home. The fake glasses he didn't mind so much. As he'd predicted, Sammy looked nothing like the pictures shown all over the news.

With her makeup and hairstyle, Kawai also looked to be in her mid-twenties. Li wore makeup as well, but it had been done very light and fine, with his hair doctored to make him look like a thirty-year-old man suffering from an early receding hairline. Byron, on the other hand, had dyed his hair to a graying brown, and a few anti-aging shots took about five years off his appearance. He looked like a man in his early forties instead of pushing fifty. Anna, meanwhile, did absolutely nothing to change her appearance.

"Good luck," Jeffie said to the team as they climbed out of the vehicle, but mostly addressing Sammy. "Be safe."

Sammy gave her a reassuring smile. "What could go wrong?"

Jeffie grimaced. "Why would you tempt the fates and ask such a thing?"

Byron, Kawai, and Anna closed their doors and crossed the street. Sammy got out, too. Blistering summer air blew his hair, instantly eliciting a sheen of moisture from his brow. He lingered a moment longer at the window with Jeffie. She grabbed his hand and held it, caressing the back of it with her thumb.

"I love you."

Sammy grinned. "Thanks. I'll take care of myself. Don't worry."

Jeffie nodded and let him go. "One more thing," she called to him.

"What?"

She grinned and kissed him. "You look really hot in that suit."

"I feel hot, too. Sweltering, even." Smirking, Sammy joined the others just as they crossed the street, a messenger bag at his side. Li carried a small briefcase, while Anna had an even smaller attaché case. Inside the three cases were compartments of weaponized gas to be used if needed. All wore professional business clothes, retina-altering eye contacts, and nose filters to allow Sammy's team to breathe the gas harmlessly. Sammy hadn't worn a suit since his graduation from Psion Beta, but the dark green material and yellow dress shirt made him feel like a lawyer.

The commander strode stoically as he led the team through the crowds streaming into the memorial: a steel dome supported by over seven hundred flat beams, a name and face of one victim of the bombing engraved on each. A large pool surrounded the dome, its waters ever flowing over the edge into a deep trough. Sammy and his team headed toward the nearby visitor center.

Hundreds of bodies were crammed into the building to escape the relentless heat. The visitor center was half museum and half gift shop. Sammy and Anna pushed through the bodies until they came to the help desk where a man in a red blazer sporting a mustache thinner than a twig stood. "May I offer you my assistance?"

"Actually you can," Byron said, handing the man a business card. "We're here as part of the inspection team. We have business downstairs."

The man in the blazer regarded Sammy's team a second time, now with more interest. "Of course. I trust you have an appointment?"

Trapper's data had warned that this would be the exact question asked according to the system put in place by the fox's organization, and that the response required had to be worded with equal specificity.

"Everything has been arranged according to protocol."

"Good to hear," the man in the blazer answered with a smile. Sammy couldn't tell if it was genuine or not. "Please proceed after me."

He led the group through a door marked EMPLOYEES ONLY, which opened to a short hallway with an employee break room, a stock room, and four offices. At the end of the hall was another door, this one made of metal, and a sign that read ELECTRICAL ROOM, and underneath, the symbol of a hand struck by a lightning bolt.

The room was about the size of a walk-in closet with a concrete floor, electrical panels, and master switches controlling the power flow. Sammy wondered if a secret wall had been installed inside. The man in the blazer entered first, then beckoned the others to follow. Once they were all inside, the man in the blazer flipped three switches and the room began to descend. Sammy tried not to appear curious or impressed. While he recognized the danger the mission presented, Sammy couldn't deny that being back in the field felt good. And infiltrating yet another secret CAG facility was even better.

Then came the sudden urge to kill the man in the blazer. *Grab his ugly coat, pull it over his head, and strangle him with your bare hands. Imagine how good that will feel. The throbbing heartbeat racing ... then slowing ... and* stopping.

Sammy cleared his throat and let the thought drift from his mind. But like a rubber band, it snapped right back with force.

KILL. The force was so powerful it flowed through his body like a physical need.

Sammy closed his eyes, but waiting for him were the images of himself shooting, stabbing, hacking, and ripping. Blood, limbs, and carnage everywhere. It dripped from him, pooling at his feet.

The elevator descended for a full minute into the earth. When it opened, a woman with platinum blonde hair greeted them. "Hello," she said with a nervous smile. Sammy noted the way she gripped her holo-tablet too tightly to her chest, how she glanced momentarily at the man in the blazer, and her overly wide eyes. "I'm Judy. We're so pleased to have you here."

She's nervous.

According to the intel from Trapper's cube, the inspection teams carried great weight with the fox regarding the operation of classified, off-the-books CAG programs. Employees deemed unfit for work in secure areas either received reassignment to remote, barren locations or went missing.

"Let me introduce you to the Project Director," Judy said. Then she thanked the man in the blazer with a curt nod.

The Project Director was a thin, black man with slicked-back gray hair and bulbous eyes. He reminded Sammy of an aged praying mantis. When he smiled and surveyed them all, Sammy got the impression that the man wanted to eat them. His eyes rested the longest on Kawai in a slimy, wanting sort of way.

"A pleasure to welcome you to my facility. I am—"

"Fabian Earl," Anna finished with her hand ready to shake his. "We've heard many things about you and the way you run this facility."

"Only good, I hope," Fabian said, clearing his throat.

"I'm sure you do hope," Anna said in a straight voice.

Fabian didn't seem to know whether to laugh or not. "Well, you'll see for yourself. The work we're doing—the progress we've made—it's remarkable. I'm confident you'll be able to return to our sponsors with your highest commendations."

"We hope so, too," Kawai said.

"Then let's begin!" Fabian clapped his hands together noiselessly.

First he took them through the facility called H.A.M.M.E.R. The tour lasted almost two hours, filled with questions and notes—things inspectors would do. Inside, they observed the mental reconditioning of teenagers ranging in age from twelve to twenty-one. Sammy gripped the handle of his briefcase with both hands to stop them from shaking. He remembered vividly the metal helmet that had spun him around in cognitive circles day after day. When they walked past the cells, and Sammy saw the conditions some of the subjects lived in, he almost went ballistic. One kid was huddled on the floor, wet and bruised, muttering repeatedly to himself, "Happiness is obedience. True happiness is at the next level." His eyes were glazed and dull.

"Why does he keep saying that?" Anna asked.

Fabian itched his ear and cleared his throat. "That's the goal we fixate them on, the H.A.M.M.E.R. subjects. We want them to believe that downstairs is happiness, achievement, a sense of victory and accomplishment. Whenever one of the students graduates H.A.M.M.E.R., we make a very big deal out of it to remind the others that success is attainable."

"How many subjects are currently in each program?" Byron asked.

"One hundred and twelve in H.A.M.M.E.R. We don't consider S.H.I.E.L.D. participants to be subjects. They are agents or agents-in-training."

"Do they have field experience?" Anna asked.

"Limited. Shall we go down and have a look?" Fabian asked eagerly.

As they filed into the elevator, Anna rounded on Fabian. "You never answered the question about S.H.I.E.L.D. How many are there?"

Fabian cleared his throat again. "Isn't all that information available to you?"

"It should be available to you at all times," Byron answered, tapping his head with his tablet stylus. "You are the Program Director."

"We have fifty-two participants in S.H.I.E.L.D."

"What is the breakdown by anomaly?" Sammy asked.

For a moment Sammy thought he saw a hint of insolence on the director's face before he responded. "Eighteen with Anomaly Eleven. Twelve with Anomaly Fourteen. And the rest are Anomaly Fifteen."

"In the reports I read," Kawai stated, "the anomalies call themselves by the NWG nicknames. Why is that?"

"Ah, yes." A deep chuckle came from the director. "I was only a specialist here at the time when the first participants entered the S.H.I.E.L.D. level. The Program Director at the time was a high-ranking military defector from Quebec. He mentioned the names to the students. They came up with the idea for Psion Dark, Tensai Dark, and Ultra Dark. They thought themselves quite clever. We, the directors of the program, refer to them all as just 'agents.'"

When the elevator doors opened, Sammy stepped out into a hallway of black paneling on the ceiling, walls, and floor with white highlights.

"Why such a dearth of color?" Kawai asked.

"Keeps them focused," Fabian said. "This way please. The Dark agents are in the middle of an exercise right now. I think you'll find witnessing it to be far more fascinating than reading about it in my reports."

Fabian led the group to an observation room with a sprawling glass window above what reminded Sammy very much of the Arena back at Psion Beta headquarters, only far more deadly. The shirtless males wore black form-fitting swim trunks that did not reach halfway down their thighs, and the females' shockingly revealing attire made Sammy want to look away in embarrassment. Fabian drank in the sight with his eyes, his eerie, lecherous grin returning as he cleared his throat multiple times.

"Who designed the uniforms?" Anna asked, not bothering to conceal the venom in her voice. "A thirteen-year-old boy?"

Fabian chuckled again. Something in his laugh told Sammy exactly who'd designed the uniforms and why. Worse, Fabian's eyes followed the girls around the room, his lip curling and uncurling, his tongue occasionally flickering out to wet his lips. It made Sammy's stomach roil. "Their bodies are indeed specimens, aren't they?" Then he leaned close to Sammy and said, "If any of them catch your eye, I can arrange a more intimate introduction."

Ignoring the desire to splatter Fabian's brains all over the observation glass, Sammy turned his attention to their activities, mimicking the signs of lust Fabian displayed. In a low voice he asked, "Are the female agents trained in *other* activities as well? Perhaps things more … domestic?"

Fabian raised his eyebrows and leaned in even closer. "Trained quite well. I sample them, even take a personal hand in their education. And I find them all to be, in a word, *exquisite*."

Sammy chuckled in a deep, primal growl. "I bet." Then, in his normal voice, said, "Describe to me what is happening."

"This is what we call the Tri-Skill Challenge. The three teams do not interact, but race to complete Anomaly-specific tasks. The Tensais must manage multiple problems at once, forcing them to delegate, interact socially, and cooperate. Tensais struggle with such social dilemmas. Currently they have to diffuse a bomb, program a device to remotely disable a security system, and design an underwater flotation craft using a select number of resources."

Sammy watched the Tensais work together, or try to, pointing and screaming and one even pulling his own hair. It might have been silly if not under the present circumstances. His leg throbbed again as he thought of his own imprisonment and the things he was forced to experience.

"Most people we bring to the showroom enjoy the Psions," the director stated. "They find their abilities astonishing. It reminds them of comic books … superheroes. The four of you seem unimpressed."

Sammy didn't like the edge in Fabian's voice. He looked at the director, but found Judy staring and smiling at him with that same nervousness as before.

Byron spoke. "We're well briefed. I admit it is fascinating, but nothing outside the realms of science. Now if those Zions start flying—"

"*Psions*," Fabian corrected. "With an *s* sound."

"My mistake," Byron said, even managing to blush a little.

"The Psions' exercises are quite lethal," Judy added in a breathless tone, her smile a little too wide on her face. "Projectile attacks from multiple angles force them to use creativity and elevation to defend themselves. It coerces them to work as a single unit and protect one another. Then we add floor sections that move about randomly, some abstract sound bursts, and things can get tricky very quickly."

Sammy wondered if this type of training worked better than what Byron had done at Beta headquarters. Then he noticed something odd. One of the Psions was bleeding.

"The holograms are harmless, aren't they?" he asked.

"Oh, of course they're not. Without the sense of danger, they don't push themselves. Exercises become too routine. But the agents aren't allowed to participate in these exercises until they're deemed ready. The danger level gradually grows with their experience. The ones you are watching now are our most talented."

Sammy's attention turned to the Ultras. One of them caught his eye. A girl, no older than him, probably younger. Her dark hair and eyes seemed so familiar to him, though he knew he had never met her. "And the Anomaly Fifteens? What about them?"

"The Ultras' challenge is vastly different," Judy continued, her eyes lingering on Sammy in the same creepy way that Fabian watched the female agents. "Appearing and disappearing targets, vanishing floor tiles, and random assaults from deadly holograms. Keeps them on their toes, forces them to multitask, tests their accuracy in action. Ultras are the most vulnerable agents, but also the most deadly. Such a beautiful paradox."

Sammy had seen enough, but he didn't want to leave quite yet. He needed to know what it was about that Ultra drew him to her. As they walked around the S.H.I.E.L.D. area, Sammy waited until he got a chance to speak to Fabian in private, and said, "You mentioned you can arrange … informal visits with the agents."

Fabian's oily grin returned and he cleared his throat. "I can. Of course, if I arrange something I expect a favor in return."

Sammy fixed him with an easy stare. "If it's my evaluation you're worried about, let me set your mind at ease. Do this for me and you'll receive my highest praise in the reports. Each of us gets an itch scratched."

"Good. Good. Which one caught your eye?"

"An Ultra. The younger girl."

Fabian winked and tapped the side of his nose. "You are a devil, aren't you? Not only is she a rising star in their ranks, but she's well trained, I assure you. Are you staying in town tonight? If so, give me the address, and I'll send her to you."

Sammy made the arrangement. He'd never felt more like a steaming heap of filth than in that moment. Hours later, Sammy's team left the underground facility for the day and waited on the curb for Jeffie to retrieve them. While waiting, Sammy informed his team of the deal he had made.

"That is disgusting," Kawai said.

"Yes, but it gets us what we want much sooner than we hoped," Commander Byron said. "Good work, Samuel."

Kawai shook her head, a mask of revulsion on her face. "He kept undressing me with his eyes."

"So what's the plan?" Li asked. "Grab the girl as soon as she appears at the door and take her home?"

Sammy shook his head. "We have to make sure it's not a trap."

"How could it be a trap?" Li asked. "If they knew we were spies, we'd be dead. They had fifty opportunities to kill us."

"Kill five spies, get five dead bodies. Track the spies to their hideout, get hundreds more. There was something off about those people … especially Judy. She was nervous. Beyond nervous. Almost paranoid."

"Maybe the fact that they are all freaking psychos is what tripped your sensors," Kawai suggested. "I can't believe what I saw."

"All the more reason to pull this off tonight," Anna said. "Do this right and we won't need to go back tomorrow and finish our evaluation."

Jeffie pulled up to the curb in the SUV. As Sammy climbed in and removed his nose filters, he said, "Nothing would please me more."

"How did it go?" Jeffie asked.

"Ask Sammy," Li said with a grin.

"Why? What happened, Sammy?"

"Sammy has a hot date tonight."

"Is it a date?" Anna asked. "More like a quick and dirty—"

"Okay, that's enough," Sammy said.

The team made preparations as soon as they reached the hotel. Since they'd planned on staying in Mexico City for two to three days for the evaluation, they had booked decent lodgings downtown. Commander Byron spoke with Sammy as they arranged the room in preparation for the Dark agent's arrival. "She could attack you at any moment. Keep that in the back of your mind."

It's always in the front of my mind, Sammy thought.

"One thing I regret not doing in Beta training is teaching you how to fight against Ultras."

"What do you mean?"

"Psions are excellent against Thirteens and Aegis, but Ultras? They have different strengths and weaknesses than Thirteens. Have you ever fought an Anomaly Fifteen?"

Sammy thought about that and shook his head. "I punched Toad once or twice on the way to Wichita. Does that count?"

"Be careful, Samuel."

Room service had been ordered for two: a veal pasta, bread, mushrooms, asparagus, and wine. Sammy dimmed the lights and put on soft music, things Anna and Byron had instructed him to do. He wore a gray three-piece suit with a dark blue shirt, the collar unbuttoned. Kawai and Jeffie had dressed him, grinning as they did so.

"I'm glad you two think this is so funny," Sammy moaned.

"Your first date." Jeffie giggled. "And it's a blind one."

That was an interesting thought as Sammy reflected on it. He had never spent any money on Jeffie, never taken her out to eat, nor gone to the theater or a concert. He'd never taken anyone out before, despite all the times he'd hung out with Jeffie.

"Some day," he told her, "when this is all over. We're going to go out on a real date. Dinner and dancing. You can dance and I'll dine."

Jeffie kissed his nose. "I like the sound of that."

"You look *really* good," Kawai said. "Does Jeffie tell you every day how good looking you are?"

"I told him how hot he looked this morning," Jeffie stated. "Now, Sammy, you're not exactly the most suave guy in the universe. How do you plan on going about this?"

"What do you mean?"

Anna rolled her eyes. "What's your angle?" she asked. "Judging from Director Pedophile's behavior, these agents are used to being pimped out for favors."

"That's so messed up," Jeffie said.

"We can't worry about that right now," Anna said. "Our top priority is for her to receive the anti-solution so she can't be traced and doesn't blow up when we take her back to Glasgow."

"And me having a ... suave personality will do what?"

"It'll relax her," Jeffie said.

"Get her to trust you," Kawai added.

"All right, ladies," Anna said, "shut up for a second so I can talk to Sammy. We're dealing with a girl who's been brainwashed, hyper-sexualized, and traumatized through her training."

"So I need to remember I'm walking on eggshells," Sammy said.

"No, I'm saying you're walking over eggs that have been trampled, scrambled, fried, and turned into soup. You need to be on your toes, watch for signs of … anything. Improvise and still be delicate. And above all, she needs—"

"To get the anti-solution," Sammy finished, checking to make sure the table was in the right place in relation to the chandelier hanging above him. "I know."

"No," Anna said as she handed him nose filters to put back in. "Well, yes, but she needs to feel safe. You need to talk softly and truthfully. Don't be afraid to show your natural self. And certainly don't try to pretend to be someone you aren't."

At ten minutes before the scheduled time, Anna whisked everyone out of the room. Jeffie gave Sammy a quick kiss. "Be safe. And … you know …"

"Don't worry," Sammy assured her. "I promise that I'll keep my word."

"Any questions?" Anna asked before she left. "Feeling all right?"

Sammy shrugged. "I'll be fine. Just update me as soon as you know if she's bugged or tagged."

Five minutes later, the hotel staff brought the food. Steam rose off the covered dishes, the glasses were chilled, and once Sammy got the music playing, the ambience transformed into something serene and classy. He sat on his bed and clasped his hands, then got up and went onto the balcony. A light breeze brushed his face while the sounds of Mexico City floated up and promenaded around his ears. He stared down to the streets. Not a year ago, Sammy had gazed at the city lights of Orlando and wondered how different his life would be had he not been born with an anomaly. Now he didn't care.

I'm in a hotel room pretending to be a john for a fifteen-year-old girl, which is somehow going to help end a war.

Almost right on cue, a knock came at the door. Sammy closed off the balcony and peered out his peephole. A girl stood outside wearing a single-strapped gold cocktail dress showing off ample thigh and cleavage. In her left hand was a small purse, as gold and sparkling as her dress. Her hair and makeup looked professionally done, and she stared into the peephole as though she could see Sammy through it.

Her eyes were brown with gold flakes, wide and inviting. He had to admit she was extremely pretty. But also somehow familiar.

Where have I seen you before? When he didn't answer right away, she waited patiently rather than knocking again. Finally he unlatched the lock and opened the door.

"Hello," he said, giving her his best smile.

She smiled back, part sweet and part sultry. Her eyes fixed on his in that same welcoming stare he'd seen through the peephole. "Hi, I'm Jane." They shook hands. "It's a pleasure. May I come in?" She spoke with just a touch of an accent. It was slight enough that he couldn't place it, and her voice sounded much older than fifteen. There was a maturity to it that reminded Sammy of himself.

"May I?" he asked, pointing to her handbag.

Jane handed it over as if she'd been expecting the request. From his coat pocket, he produced a scanner, which he used on every item in her bag, including the bag itself. Once he was satisfied everything was clean, he stepped aside and let her pass. She stood several centimeters shorter than he, but walked with a grace and polish that made him think of ballet dancers. He watched her eyes as she entered, how they scanned the entire room at once, noting, thinking, perhaps even planning.

Maybe she's always like this. Maybe they train her to be paranoid.

No. There's something more. She's wary ... on her guard.

Sammy offered her his arm as he walked her across the room. Her skin was soft and her grip firm. "Call me Jared," he told her.

"Jared," she said. "I like that name."

"Are you hungry?"

"I am." Her gaze traveled over the food. "Is all that for us?"

Sammy laughed. "I hope you brought an appetite." He pulled her chair out, waited for her to sit, and then pushed the chair back in for her. It was placed directly underneath the chandelier where another, more powerful, scanner had been concealed. After she placed her napkin on her lap, he served her salad and offered her wine.

"I don't drink," she said. He saw a knowing glint in her eye that told him the choice had nothing to do with her age or morals, and everything to do with trust and wanting to keep her wits about her.

Sammy set the wine back in the ice. "Neither do I."

They ate a few bites of salad in silence before Sammy spoke again, "So ... do you prefer to talk—um—make conversation?"

Jane hid a smile behind her napkin, which she used to dab her lips. Again the thought struck Sammy how maturely she behaved. "Don't be nervous. Tonight will be enjoyable for both of us."

"I hope so." Sammy knew in an instant he'd answered too quickly. "I just didn't want to make you uncom—"

"First time with someone you just met?"

Sammy tried to pretend he was someone else, someone charming and witty. What would such a person say? *No … Anna told you not to do that.*

"First time with someone so beautiful," he finally decided, and found the response surprisingly satisfactory.

Jane's eyes flashed at the compliment. "How old are you?"

"Twenty-three."

"And how are you such a well-placed person at such a young age?"

It intrigued Sammy how quickly she'd taken control over the conversation, or at least thought she had. "I studied hard. Did well on tests."

"And you?" he asked. "Did you join Ultra Dark voluntarily or otherwise?"

For a sliver of a moment, Jane's demeanor slipped. The muscles around her mouth and eyes relaxed, the sultry shine in her eyes dulled, and Sammy saw her plainly: scared and small. But it was gone so quickly, he wondered if she even knew it had happened. It was as though some tiny bit of her had broken through the brainwashing, the hardened exterior, only to be immediately extinguished.

"Voluntarily."

"Why is that? You wanted a life of adventure, not a life of boredom?"

Jane took a sip of her water. "Exactly. And what foolhardy girl wouldn't choose the first?"

"That's what I would choose, too."

"I love my powers."

Sammy chuckled at her comment. "And what exactly are they? I mean, I've read the reports. Watched you practice. But what's it like?"

Jane picked up a knife and held it vertically. Then she balanced it on her finger. Unlike Sammy, who would've had to keep moving his hand to stay under the swaying knife, she held very still and the knife never wavered. "Give me a target."

"What's that?" Sammy asked.

"A target. Something you want to see me hit."

Sammy looked around the room and chose the ugly canvas painting on his wall of two dogs sniffing at a patch of grass. "The Chihuahua. Between its eyes."

Jane bounced her hand, flipping the knife into the air. She caught it, flicked it, and struck the dog exactly where Sammy had told her.

"A well-executed assassination," Sammy declared. "That poor dog."

"You asked me what it's like … " Jane said. "And that's the best I can describe it. As an Ultra you feel powerful. And deadly."

"What does your family think of your abilities? Are they frightened by them?"

Jane glanced at her salad and sniffed. It was a tiny thing, a sound that lasted less than a second. But it was enough. Her eyes. Her voice. Her age. Sammy knew her now. How many times had he heard her name spoken on the way to Wichita while his friend moaned in his sleep? How many times had he heard that sniff?

Jane was Vitoria. Vitoria Prado.

Toad's little sister.

12 | Taken

Monday, July 28, 2087

SAMMY WANTED TO say Jane's real name, but couldn't. Not yet. They planned to capture her, but not until after they knew what secrets might be concealed on or in her body. The scanner in the chandelier would reveal them all. And once they were certain she was safe, they would give her the anti-solution and take her.

Despite the mission, the plan, the set up, all Sammy could think of was Toad. For several weeks Toad had been his best friend and companion. Toad had saved Sammy's life when Katie Carpenter had beaten him in battle. All it had cost Toad was everything. With his perfect memory, Sammy saw Toad's shrapnel-riddled body and the pools of blood that flowed across the floor of the air hangar in Omaha.

"So … your parents?" Sammy repeated.

"Thrilled about my powers," Vitoria answered. "My biggest supporters. I can't imagine them being frightened."

"And—and brothers?" Sammy's voice caught just before he added the *s* on brothers. "Sis—sisters?"

"I am an only child."

Tongue-tied at the memory of his friend, Sammy could only nod.

"Did I say something wrong?" Vitoria asked.

Sammy shook his head and forced a pleasant expression back on his face. "Nothing. In fact, I have to tell you that I find you not only beautiful, but charming."

And I will get you out of this mess if it kills me. I owe Toad at least that much.

He served the pasta to allow another lull in conversation. His thoughts were so occupied with things besides food that he might as well have been chewing rubber. What had been an important mission was now a personal vendetta. He glanced at the chandelier above where a scanner was hiding, taped in such a manner that only Sammy could see it from his angle. Layer by layer, it would scan Vitoria's body for any hidden device—other than the solution—that would allow the CAG to track her back to resistance headquarters in Glasgow.

Conversation continued throughout the meal. Sammy peppered her with questions about the S.H.I.E.L.D. program, and Vitoria answered them as though she was having the time of her life each day. Near the end of dinner a knock came at the door. Sammy feigned surprise at the intrusion, but made a joke out of it. "Not expecting more guests, are we?"

Jeffie was at the door. "Hi … Sorry to trouble you, but I've lost my room key and the thumb plate isn't working. Can you call down to the front desk and have them send someone up to Room 274?"

"Sure. 274."

Sammy shut the door as Jeffie apologized and thanked him again. Giving Vitoria an apologetic smirk of his own because of the interruption, Sammy told his com to call the front desk, which he had programmed as Anna's number. After explaining about Jeffie's predicament, Anna responded in a low, rushed voice, "She's clean except for the earring on her left ear. Proceed to the next phase. We'll get the earring off her before we haul outta here."

"Okay," Sammy said. "Thank you very much." He took the com from his ear and returned to the table with Vitoria. As he did so, he activated the gas canister under the table to release the sleeping gas. "Who forgets their room key? Anyway … what were we talking about?"

Vitoria grabbed Sammy's jacket in two hands and pulled him toward her. "We don't need to talk anymore."

Before Sammy could protest, Vitoria kissed him. She was the second person he had ever kissed, and he immediately noted the differences between Vitoria's lips and Jeffie's. As his heart thundered inside his chest, Sammy pushed Vitoria backward so that she faced him while laying on the bed. The soft hiss of the gas permeating the air was not perceptible above the sound of music pulsing from the stereo next to the hotel room's holo-screen.

Any second now she'll be out and this will be over.

They continued to kiss as Sammy waited for the gas to take effect. After several seconds her lips traveled to his cheek, neck, and ear. The longer they went at it, the more nervous Sammy became that something had gone wrong. A fire lit in her eyes as she reached for the strap of her glittering gold gown.

Screw this. I can't wait any longer.

Sammy's left hand went under a pillow and found the first of two syringes that, when combined, created the anti-solution. As Vitoria's head turned to face him, he grabbed her left hand with his own right and prepared to grab her left earring as soon as he injected her. They kissed again. Vitoria moaned into the kiss as her free hand snaked up Sammy's shirt. At that moment Sammy jammed the needle into her left thigh and emptied its contents into her leg.

Vitoria shrieked and jerked while Sammy snatched at her earring, but missed. She bucked him up into a sitting position and immediately her right foot connected with his temple. Sammy slammed into the headboard, his vision fuzzy. One hand went up as a shield blast, the other slowly crept and searched for the second syringe. According to the instructions from Trapper's data cube, Sammy had thirty minutes to inject Vitoria with the second liquid to render the solution inert.

"What did you stick in me?" Vitoria asked as she touched her earring.

"Don't—" he cried, but too late. "Listen, I'm here to help you!"

Vitoria ripped the bed sheets out from under him with a strength he hadn't anticipated. Then she whipped them up and let them billow in the pulsings of Sammy's blasts.

"Put the sheet down and let me explain," Sammy said, turning up the strength of his blast to ward her away and give himself more space to work. "I won't hurt you."

The sheet fluttered to the carpet, but Vitoria had already moved. She stepped on the bed, bounced toward the wall, and then kicked off the wall at Sammy.

"Vit—" He tried to catch her or shoot her out of the air, but she was fast—faster than a Thirteen. Her knee collided with his skull. As he rolled backward Sammy shot a powerful blast, stronger than he'd intended, and sent Vitoria flying toward the window.

Rather than crashing through the glass, she grabbed the curtain rod and swung herself sideways, then hit the floor. Sammy protected himself with two blast shields, but he had a feeling that Vitoria could get around them with ease. Rather than attacking again, he reached for the second syringe, but it was not under the pillow.

"What did you stick in me?" Vitoria yelled.

Sammy's hands darted around the bed, but the syringe was gone. *It must have dropped under the bed.* "You have to trust me! I know you're really Vitoria Prado. I was a friend of your brother. I'm going to get you out of here!"

He knew it sounded absurd, even creepy, to ask a girl to trust him after he'd arranged to have her come to his hotel room and then stuck her with a needle, but he didn't know what else to say. A fork flew at his head. Sammy blasted it away, gripped the bed with his free hand, and jerked up the mattress. There, on the bed frame, was the syringe.

As Sammy ducked behind the mattress and grabbed the second syringe, the mattress collapsed under Vitoria's weight. The blade of a knife ripped through the material as Vitoria tried to stab him through the bed. Sammy put the syringe in his teeth and blasted the mattress away with both hands. Vitoria and the mattress flew across the room. He heard her hit the wall with a loud *THUMP* and slide to the floor.

She went limp, her right arm and shoulder twitching once, twice, and then she became deathly still. Sammy's breath caught in his lungs. *No. I didn't mean…*

He spat the syringe from his mouth and stuffed it into his pocket. "Vitoria?" he asked, rushing to help her.

When he knelt beside her she swung at his throat with a second knife, one he hadn't even known she had. Vitoria missed by millimeters, but made up for it by kicking him in the back of the head and throwing herself into him. Sammy caught her, wrapped her up with his arms, and blasted backward, flipping them over in the air, and landing on the table with her underneath, wood, glass and metal shattering and screeching.

Someone in the room above stomped on the floor, telling them to keep down the racket. Vitoria stuck her fingers in Sammy's face, trying to gouge his eyes. "What did you inject me with?"

"Nothing …" Sammy grunted as he released her and tried to pull her hands away from his face, "that … will harm you!"

Vitoria punched him viciously seven or eight times in the chest and neck, then kneed him in the face. The amount of time in between each jab was so short that Sammy lost count. Finally he blasted himself off of her, but she was on her feet and tackled him on the bed.

"Who are you?" she asked.

"Someone who wants to help you! I knew Toad! Sapo! Your brother!"

Vitoria threw another fork at him. *Where does she keep getting the utensils?* Raising one arm to shield his eyes, and using his other hand to blast at her, the fork stuck him on the underside of his forearm while Vitoria slammed into the headboard of the bed. Before she could get off him, Sammy uncapped the second syringe and jammed it into her buttock. It sank deep, and he emptied its contents.

Vitoria screamed what he guessed were Portuguese swear words because Toad had shouted similar things when he'd been angry. Rage filled her eyes as she ran at him. Sammy fired blast after blast at her, but she twisted and bent her body to avoid the energy bursts. Sammy backed away the closer she came, but she was too fast. Her foot connected with his face in a burst of pain.

"Stop kicking me in the head!" he shouted, but she countered with an elbow that sent him to the ground, stunned.

In his groggy state he saw three Vitorias, each walking toward him. She grabbed him by the jacket and dragged him toward the painting of the dogs that still bore the knife she'd thrown.

"Vitoria, please," he mumbled as the three Vitorias finally melted back into one. "I was Toad's friend. Your brother. Toad. Rulé Prado."

Vitoria ripped the knife out of the painting and brought it down at Sammy's neck. But before she could connect, she doubled over, clutching her stomach. A deep moan came from her gut as she crumpled to the floor, rolling over onto her back. "What did you do to me?"

"I saved your life—" Sammy started to say when his com beeped. It took him a moment to locate it in all the wreckage of the room. But when he found it, he hurried and stuffed it back in his ear. "I delivered the anti-solu—"

"Dark agents are coming up the stairs and elevators," Anna reported. "We're calling in the stealth cruiser for an air extraction. Keep them busy, and we'll come up behind them."

"Got it."

"Try not to die."

Vitoria rolled on the floor, groaning, face twisted in agony. Sammy stepped over her and scooted the bed frame closer to the window so he could use the headboard as cover. Then he dragged Vitoria between the window and bed, and taped her hands and feet together. About five seconds later, the door crashed to the floor.

"Uh … " Sammy said into his com, "I don't have a gun."

"Why do you think Commander Byron taught you to fight without a gun in Beta headquarters?" was Anna's response.

Sammy blasted the bed at the Dark agents as they came through the door, sending it soaring across the room. A moment later, the bed shot back at him. Sammy dove to his left. The bed crashed through the window and sailed down to the street below.

Glass rained on Sammy. Four Psion Dark agents entered the room: two males, two females, all armed with assault rifles. When he saw them, Sammy swore in Portuguese because he thought it sounded better. They wore armored cloth, similar to what Alphas wore during missions, perhaps a bit heavier.

They opened fire on Sammy who could do nothing but shield and keep moving to present a more difficult target. He also needed to make sure Vitoria stayed out of the line of fire. Bullets ripped the air, peppering the walls and ceiling, spraying debris and glass like confetti. Screams came from the rooms above, followed by heavy footsteps. As Sammy defended himself, he searched the room, the space, and his brain for some way to win—to live. He waited to *see* the answer.

It intrigued him that the Psion Dark agents did not fight like Thirteens. They stayed together as a unit, cohesive and fluid, attacking from positions of safety to prevent any opening for Sammy to retaliate.

Before he came up with a plan, five more people arrived: Jeffie, Li, Kawai, Commander Byron, and Anna. Commander Byron opened fire first. The Dark agents turned quickly. One took a bullet to the back, but her armor absorbed the worst of the shot. She fell down, but quickly recovered. Sammy's team fanned out and took cover around the room. This allowed Sammy to move in and use hand to hand combat. He picked the smallest of the four: a short girl with hair dyed half green and half pink.

The girl shot a dozen rounds at Sammy, but he punched back with a strong blast aimed straight at the gun. The bullets flew away harmlessly, and Sammy's blast pushed the gun slightly to the side, allowing him room to get under her guard. Their blasts met, pushing each other apart. Sammy gently blasted forward with his feet, again shielding her bullets. She tried to blast him away, but he spun to the side, crossed the distance, and hit her under the jaw.

The girl with the colored hair dropped. Sammy grabbed her gun as it clattered to the floor, and the sound of bullets rent the air. A vicious punch hit Sammy high in the back, pushing him to the floor face first. After several missions and injuries, he recognized right away that he'd been shot. The bullet had entered above his shoulder blade and below his collarbone, and exited between his rib and collarbone in the front. Lucky, perhaps, but moving his right arm sent a searing burn through his whole side. As he hit the ground, the darkness inside him roared to life at the pain.

You know what to do ... a voice told him.

No.

Yes. You will die if you don't do it.

I made a promise.

Look around the room. Look at your friends. They will all die unless you use your full potential. Do it!

A flash of light reflected off the glass of the fireplace and caught Sammy's eye. Hovering outside the broken window was a cruiser with several Ultra Dark agents standing on the top of the craft tethered to the hull to prevent them from falling.

"More trouble outside," he told his team. "Six Ultras on top of a cruiser. I'm hit. Clean shot through the back. I don't have any orange goo."

"I've got some," Kawai said, "just hang tight."

Gunshots exploded around Sammy. Blood poured from his wound onto the carpet. He didn't dare move. The Ultras on the cruiser would shoot him down before he could even get a shield up. Screams came from the halls, followed by Byron barking at civilians. "Get back in your rooms!"

Your chances of surviving are slim. DO IT! The pull was strong. It reminded Sammy of his dreams with the shadow, the way it tugged at him and pulsed with power.

Sammy ignored the voice as he pretended to be dead. Resisting the urge to tap into the Anomaly Thirteen wasn't easy. His whole body tingled with the need to unleash it. Playing dead, however, wasn't hard. The pain from the gunshot wound radiated through his whole body, so he didn't want to move. Anna gave orders to the rest of the team, coordinating their efforts to take out the Psion Dark agents. Vitoria, hogtied on the floor, now stared at Sammy murderously.

"The stealth cruiser says it can't move into position unless the other cruiser leaves," Li reported.

"Tell them to shoot down the enemy!" Sammy said.

"They can't risk taking a hit," Anna said. "Structural damage to the hull will allow our stealth cruiser to be tracked."

Sammy listened to the sounds of his friends battling under heavy fire until a body crashed into the bed frame which slammed into his head.

Next thing Sammy knew he was stalking through a black forest, a long key in hand, his feet wet and cold. Gold and silver adorned the key, giving it a heavy, solid feel. To the right was a large, crystal lake. Moonlight sparkled like glittering diamonds off the water's surface. Bobbing on the surface was a raft, chained to a pole jammed deep into the soggy lakeside ground. To the left was the cave.

Sammy walked to the cave's mouth where a dank smell greeted him, carrying a hint of something fouler, more menacing. The blackness in the cave pulsed and pulled even stronger than the shadow-Sammy had, as though the darkness was a magnificent living thing—breathing, heaving, and wanting.

Go inside. The voice was the same as before. The same he'd heard so many times, urging him to unleash the anomaly and become more powerful and invulnerable to pain and fear. *It's the only way.*

A body collapsed next to Sammy. He jerked awake, opened his eyes, and stared into the blank face of a dead Dark agent, a tall black man with a hole in the middle of his forehead. Across the room he saw the green and pink haired girl laying on the floor, still knocked out from the punch he'd delivered her. Only two Psion Dark agents remained. Plus the six Ultras on the cruiser. Two guns lay near him. How fast could he move with his wound? How many could he take out?

You'll be so much faster if you—

SHUT UP, Sammy told the voice.

"Our Elite pilots are detecting incoming cruisers on radar," Kawai reported. "Five minutes before they're on the scene."

More shots were fired. Sammy heard a giant *THUD* as someone crashed into the wall, shaking the floor. He couldn't tell who. Moments later, the rest of his team appeared around him, shielding for him while Kawai applied orange goo, an antibiotic, and anesthesia to Sammy's bullet wounds. Sammy grimaced at the pain until the anesthesia kicked in.

"You okay?" Jeffie asked. Her face was pale and sweaty, but she forced a smile for Sammy, which he appreciated.

"Clock is ticking," Kawai said as the Ultra Darks continued to fire at the team's shields. "Four minutes."

"I have a grenade," Anna said. She removed the device from her pack and showed it to them like it was a show-and-tell surprise. "Class II sticky. It'll take that bird down."

"Those are Ultras," Byron said, "they will shoot your grenade out of the air before it makes it outside the hotel room."

"Not if I personally deliver the package."

"That's suicide," Jeffie said.

Anna breathed deeply and held it in. "No, it's not."

"Let me do it," Byron insisted. "I'm only half a Psion, anyway, Anna. You've got a life ahead of you."

Anna shook her head. For a moment she looked like she was about to cry, but that tough honcho expression returned and her eyes hardened. "Without jump blasts, you wouldn't cross the distance, Commander," she told Byron. "No offense."

She crouched and shielded. Sammy knew there was nothing else to say. No time for other options. "Tell Justice I said, 'See ya.' Now cover me."

The four remaining Psions used one hand to blast while firing their weapons with the other. The Ultra Darks dropped to the cruiser to make themselves as small a target as possible while still firing on Anna. Anna ran to the edge of the building, shielding herself. Jeffie shot one of the Ultras in the head. Byron hit another, leaving four. The cruiser reacted by trying to rise higher in the air, but it was too slow.

Anna barely caught hold of the cruiser's cockpit window with one hand. With the other, she slapped the sticky grenade onto the glass, then showed the pilot her middle finger. The Ultras shot down at her as she clung on, shielding herself with one hand raised above her head. Sammy managed to hit one of the Ultras in the leg, giving Anna a narrow window of opportunity.

She pulled herself up until her feet were flat against the cruiser's hull and blasted herself away. Two seconds later, the sticky detonated. The explosion propelled Anna back in the hotel room, where she rolled end over end into the mattress, her clothes singed, her flesh and hair seared. Jeffie reached her first. "She needs a burn kit."

"I thought you were dead," Kawai told Anna. "That was brilliant."

Despite what must have been certain agony, Anna managed a snort. Sammy detected a trace of disappointment there. "I said tell Justice, 'See ya.' Not *goodbye*."

Sammy laughed. "You're right. Our mistake. Let's call our cruiser and get out of here. We've got about three minutes left."

The Psions worked quickly to help Vitoria and Anna onto the stealth cruiser. Vitoria thrashed and struggled but Sammy had bound her well. With a little over a minute to spare, they jetted away from downtown Mexico City toward Glasgow.

* * * * *

"You told us the plan was foolproof," Julia Navarre, President Newberry's Chief of Staff, said. She looked older than the last time the Council had met. "Why are we seeing mistake after mistake?"

"I never said foolproof," the Queen, disguised as the fox, said.

"The President is concerned."

"The President should never be concerned. It's not his job to be concerned."

"He is the leader of the world."

Holding back a laugh, the Queen responded, "He does not sit on the Council."

"I, too, am concerned," the VP of Comcorp said. "And I *do* sit on the Council. The resistance was supposed to be snuffed out within a week. You told us if we allowed the insurgents to capture a

Dark agent, we could use the agent as a tracking device. What went wrong?"

"Insufficient data," the Queen explained. "We did not know the resistance knew about the solution. The plan was to send in one team when she activated her distress signal, but use this team as an acceptable loss. The ploy was to make the enemy think they had gotten away with something valuable. As soon as the solution was deactivated in the agent, we sent in a second team to prevent their escape. Unfortunately, we underestimated the resistance and our agents were overpowered. The resistance escaped in a stealth cruiser before they could be traced. We must now assume there is nothing they do not know."

"How?" a Council member asked.

"That is not important."

"Many of us disagree—"

"I think what I am sensing here are the early symptoms of panic," the Queen stated firmly. "This bothers me more than any intelligence the resistance might have uncovered."

"Since the attack on the weapons cache near Colorado Springs, we have witnessed problem after problem," Navarre said. "I'm beginning to question your ability to navigate us through this situation."

The Queen saw several heads nod. Almost half of them. "Let me open your eyes. The resistance may have deactivated the solution inside the Dark agent, but it doesn't change the fact that we now have a capable, well-trained, and loyal agent placed in the resistance base. I advise you to watch and wait. The plan will work."

"This report says the Dark agents had the advantage of surprise and greater numbers yet they lost to NWG-trained Psions," the VP of Comcorp said. "What does this say about the S.H.I.E.L.D. and H.A.M.M.E.R. programs?"

"Inexcusable failure," the Queen reported. "Both programs are to be shut down and all participants erased, both staff and subjects. The facility will be converted into a Thirteen cell for acquiring and training new recruits. New Anomalies Eleven, Fourteen, and Fifteen will be interrogated and executed without exception."

14 | Repairs

Friday, August 15, 2087

THE PENTHOUSE WAS a tomb except for the fox's beating heart and soft breathing. Katie was gone and wouldn't return for two or three days, if his guess was correct. This was the fox's moment. He'd toiled for months preparing for today, a day where he had plenty of uninterrupted time. He cleared his throat and spoke to the ceiling.

"Computer, activate in Private Mode."

"Computer activated. Private Mode enabled."

Those words alone sent a surge of bliss through the fox. *Finally.* He had spent countless hours muttering to the computer, using only his voice to build this program while Katie was away. More than once he'd mistaken the quiet for her absence and she'd heard him talking, but she had never figured out what he was doing. If she had, he would be dead. Waiting to be sure she was gone so he could resume his work had been difficult, especially recently as his plan grew close to fruition.

"Computer, enter code 413212 to access secure communications line."

"Code accepted. Communications line now secure."

The fox's joy was real. It fell from his eyes down his face. He wanted to wipe away his tears, but couldn't. So many things he could no longer do. He yearned to have a body restored. The indescribable horror he had experienced at the hand of Katie, watching his own limbs removed crudely—accompanied by such mind-bending pain— had changed him. It had opened his eyes to what he had become from years of removing himself from most of humanity and thinking himself a greater kind of being than his fellow man. It was a lesson for which he had not been prepared, but had changed his perspective in ways he knew he still didn't fully grasp.

"Call Jeffrey Markorian," the fox said.

Less than a minute later a man answered. "Hello?" Markorian answered. "Hello? Who is this?"

The fox had not heard his friend's voice in years, not since the Lark Montgomery incident in Mexico City that Markorian had helped the fox coordinate. Long ago, Markorian had been the fox's go-to guy. He had always looked out for Markorian, even gotten him a well-placed position in the Continental Security Department. But distance had been duly maintained due to Jeffrey's ties to the fox's past.

"It's me," the fox answered.

There was a pause on the line before Markorian spoke again. "Newblood?" The word was a whisper. "Diego, is that you?"

The fox had not been called by his first name in years. "I need help, Markorian. Immediately. Can you help me?"

"Of—of course. Yes, of course." Markorian stuttered as though he still wasn't sure if what he was experiencing was real. "I—I—I swore to always help you. Remember? I swore to always be a friend."

"I know, Markorian. I need a friend now."

"Where are you?"

"Orlando. The N tower penthouse. I need you to listen carefully and act quickly. I do not have an abundance of time."

* * * * *

Saturday, August 16, 2087

"You don't have to come to all her sessions, Sammy," Dr. Rosmir said. Sammy and Croz, the resistance's resident shrink, were preparing to leave the infirmary for their next therapy session with Vitoria. "Croz can handle it. And some people are complaining that you've been missing committee meetings."

Croz was the tallest man Sammy had ever seen. A man in his forties, well over two meters tall, and as gentle as a newborn puppy. Croz also had experience dealing with traumatized children who'd suffered from severe parental abuse, including mental and emotional torture. Once and only once, he'd spoken to Sammy about some of the more disturbing cases he'd worked on. Sammy had listened for about two minutes before telling Croz he'd heard enough.

"I'll take a session with Croz and Vitoria any day over the leadership council," Sammy said. "Nothing actually happens in leadership meetings. The subcommittees are where all the real action takes place. And … it's Saturday, so we have no meetings."

"Oh, is that how it works?" Croz said in his deep voice. "I was invited to attend the leadership council once. Fell asleep. That did it for me. I told 'em no thanks."

"Are we making any progress with Vitoria?" Sammy asked. "It's been over two weeks and—"

"Two weeks is a blink of the eye, Sammy," Croz said, "when you're talking about undoing months or years of brainwashing and conditioning."

"Our mission depends on her compliance. Is it even reasonable to hope she can be an asset? I mean, yeah, okay … I know it takes time. It took me a few weeks to really snap out of it—"

"You're trying to equate your experience in Rio with what Vitoria went through," Rosmir said. "It's not the same."

"Yeah, but I mean—"

"It's not the same," Croz repeated.

Sammy bit back an annoyed response and nodded.

"You ready then?" Croz had a clipboard and a stack of papers all held together with paperclips.

Dr. Rosmir stared at Croz's mess of documents and notes, shaking his head. "Good grief, Croz, why don't you just get a holo-tablet like everyone else?"

Croz looked at his stack and laughed. "It works for me."

Croz and Sammy left the infirmary and took Sammy's car, Lemon, through the underground road system to the small penitentiary on the opposite side of the base. They were almost there when the car stalled. Sammy groaned. "Again? I thought they fixed it."

"Didn't you take it to the mechanic?"

"Yeah," Sammy complained. "It's been behaving well for the last week."

"Speaking of behaving well," Croz said now with a cautious voice, "how are things going with your issues we spoke about?"

"Geez, Croz." Sammy gave a half-hearted laugh. "That was forever ago."

"I know. Just curious."

"Fine. Been doing what you said, and it's been fine."

Croz nodded. "So … it's your car. You get out and push."

It took a minute to get the car running again and another ten to reach the penitentiary. Prior to Vitoria's capture, the building had only been used sparingly as a place for resistance members to get dry after a drinking spell. Most of the resistance affectionately called it "The Pen." Now that Vitoria had taken up occupancy, six resistance members were assigned guard duty, two at a time in eight-hour shifts.

Her "cell" was a comfortable bedroom with bars. It had carpet, a mattress with sheets, and skylights to allow plenty of light. A stack of clothes had been provided for her, and a privacy screen behind which she changed. Sammy, Anna, and Justice had combed over the cell for four hours to ensure there was nothing inside she could use to escape or injure visitors.

According to her guards, Vitoria still requested lots of books. Croz had asked her once if she had always been a voracious reader. Vitoria's nonchalant response was that she had to do something to pass the time. She lay on her stomach, feet in the air, reading a copy of *A Tale of Two Cities.* She glanced at them for only a moment and turned her attention back to her book.

"Hi, Vitoria," Croz said in his usual, friendly tone. "Do you mind if we sit?"

Vitoria wore a pair of denim shorts and a shirt she'd tailored herself by tearing the fabric: the shorts nearly showed off her lower butt, her shirt torn to look more like a loose tube top. It was obvious she was trying to maximize her sex appeal, but Sammy couldn't understand why. She rolled from her stomach onto her backside, sitting in a lewd position. Sammy stirred uncomfortably in his chair and waited for Croz to start the session. Croz didn't seem to notice as he sorted through his stack of papers. She caught Sammy's eye and winked slyly, licking the corner of her lips slowly and meaningfully. Sammy stirred again and cleared his throat.

"How is the book, Vitoria?" Croz finally asked, looking up from his papers.

Vitoria glanced meaningfully over the top of her paperback and kept reading.

"Excuse me ... how is the book, *Jane?*"

When Croz called her Jane, she shrugged. "Have you read it?"

"I have. I've read all of Dickens."

"Then you have your own opinion on it. Why do you want mine?"

Croz chuckled. "I'm trying to be polite ... make conversation."

Vitoria spread her legs a little more. "What do you really want?" Her voice had changed too, transforming from that of a haunted fifteen-year-girl to a sultry Lolita. She sounded thirty, not fifteen.

"I just want to talk," Croz said kindly. "Is that a problem?"

"I bet you'd like to do more than talk, wouldn't you?"

"Just talk."

Vitoria closed her legs. "Nothing I can do about it, is there?"

"If you and I have enough productive chats, I think your circumstances will change and you can do a lot to improve your situation. Is that what you want?"

Vitoria held herself in a ball, face in her knees, eyes on the floor. For an instant she looked scared and small, even trembling slightly. Her dark hair curtained her face so Sammy could only see her golden brown eyes. He had seen this version of her too, but only in the briefest of moments, as though she was not quite able to maintain her façade of strength without occasionally allowing a glimpse into her true state of emotion.

When Croz could see she wasn't going to answer, he changed tactics. Sammy had seen him do this before. "Would you mind if I ask you some questions, Vitoria?"

She didn't answer to her real name, so Croz repeated the question, this time addressing her as *Jane*. In response she gave the slightest of shrugs.

"If you could do anything with your life, what would it be?"

Vitoria's head raised up, and before Sammy saw her eyes behind her hair, he knew what she was going to say. "A stripper," she declared. The scared girl was gone and the sultry vixen he'd met at his hotel room door had returned. The gold flakes in her eyes flashed and her mouth twisted in a smile so warm it gave Sammy chills. "Or maybe a *whore*. I'd love to get paid to lay on my back and just—"

"Thank you for that descriptive answer," Croz finished for her with a fleeting smile. "I know enough about prostitution that you can skip the details."

The rest of the session went much like the last question, Vitoria giving answers so obscene and explicit that Sammy's guts twisted. Each time she spoke, she peppered her responses with small sexual signals, licking a lip, touching or brushing herself, giving Croz and Sammy glimpses of her nearly exposed body. When Croz and Sammy thanked her for her time and left, Sammy wondered if they'd gotten anywhere. Croz sighed when the door shut behind them.

"Is she—does she have a multiple personality disorder?" Sammy asked, thinking of Diego and Trapper. "That's the second time now we've seen glimpses of that—that shell of a person."

"No. She does it deliberately, I think. I've seen multiple personality disorders a few times, and it's very rare. If I had to guess, I'd say she's neither the wanton floozy nor the jumps-at-a-pin-drop basket case that we've seen."

"Then what is she?"

"She's someone who thinks this whole thing is a test."

"What? We saved her. She saw us kill her fellow Dark agents."

Croz wagged a finger. "She was knocked out during most of the battle, if I read your report correctly. Think on that. She wakes up here. People being kind to her, trying to get her to betray the CAG, to open up ... Her seductive manner is her way of thinking the way they taught her to think. Her scared girl act is to get us to let down our guard and sympathize with her." Croz put an arm on Sammy's shoulders as they headed back to Lemon. "My guess is she thinks if she can get one of us in a compromising situation, she can take a hostage and engineer an escape. Then she'll 'win' or 'beat' this test."

"Compromising situation?" Sammy had to think about that before it dawned on him. "Like one of us would do *that* ..."

Croz laughed a deep, booming laugh from his gut. "I find your naïveté refreshing, Sammy. That girl in there is drop-dead beautiful. And if you think many a man wouldn't be tempted to put himself in that room alone with her just for the chance ... Well, you should meet some of the people I graduated from school with, that's all I'll say."

They returned to the infirmary to meet with Rosmir and submit a report on the session. The doctor was in the rehabilitation room with Brickert, testing his agility, blasting, and balance by having him stand on a beam and deflect tennis balls being shot at him at increasing speeds.

Beads of sweat dripped down Brickert's bright red cheeks. He puffed for air and wobbled, but Dr. Rosmir was right there, ready to catch Brickert if necessary.

"I got it," Brickert said. "Just—"

Another ball came at Brickert and nearly caught him in the side of the head, but Brickert jerked back and let it sail past. Unfortunately the motion was too quick for him in his frail state, and he tumbled backward into Rosmir's arms.

"I think that's enough for today," the doctor stated. "Machine off."

Sammy clapped slowly and loudly as he approached. "Looking better every day, bro. How long did you go for?"

"Almost an hour," Brickert answered.

"Well ... more like half an hour," Rosmir said, smiling, "but improvement every day. That's what matters."

"Improvement against tennis balls," Brickert said. "Big deal. Bullets are faster."

"Got a date yet for when you're out of here?" Sammy asked.

"It's not that he can't leave," Rosmir said, "it's easier to keep him here since we're working with him in rehab two to four times a day. Plus the tests, monitoring his bone and tooth repairs ..."

"I get it," Sammy said. He turned to Brickert. "How about food? Can he come out for lunch? I'll bring him right back with not a scratch on him." His tone made it clear to Rosmir how ridiculous Sammy thought it was that he had to ask permission to take Brickert to the cafeteria.

Rosmir waved his hands and tried not to laugh. "Go."

As soon as they were out of earshot of the doctors and nurses, Brickert turned to Sammy. "Thanks. I've been going stir crazy for the last two weeks, I'll tell you."

"No problem. I've been meaning to come by more, but everything's been crazy. Planning missions, doing those therapy sessions with Croz, keeping Jeffie happy. I still feel like I need to be around more." Sammy held his breath as he started up Lemon, but this time the car didn't give him any problems.

"Natalia comes by every day. Keeps me updated. I still can't believe Al and Marie. Splitting up. They still haven't named their daughter."

This surprised Sammy. "You kidding? It's been two months."

"Marie's family has a tradition where the grandparents choose the first baby's name. I guess it goes back about ten generations. She won't consent to anything until the war's over and her parents have met her daughter. Al, of course, is pissed."

"So what do they call her?"

"Baby girl."

"What a mess."

Brickert played with a string hanging off his sleeve. "Everything's a mess right now. Strawberry wishes she'd never joined Psion Beta. Al and Marie hate each other. I can't fight worth a lick. Every time I think about the Thirteens I break out in a sweat."

"Strawberry, huh? I thought she'd get over that. She told me she wants to go into fashion or something."

"She's good at it too. Berry's the only one left in her recruiting class. She thinks she's next—like the group was cursed or something. Scares me a little too. If Berry survives all this, I guarantee you she'll quit and never look back."

"And you?" Sammy asked.

Brickert snorted. "I said I'm having sweats, not peeing myself—" Sammy winced at that comment, "—or designing dresses in my head. I want to get back in the game as soon as I can. Just so long as you don't put me in charge of anything."

"Why's that?"

The look on Brickert's face told Sammy the answer should be obvious. "I've proven I'm not leadership material. I'm lucky Natalia and Strawberry survived." He stared downward and dropped his voice to a murmur. "Hefani … it was me who got him killed, I'll tell you. It was me."

"It wasn't your fault."

Brickert shook his head. "If you had been in charge of a team and someone got killed, you would blame yourself. Don't say otherwise."

Sammy opened his mouth to argue, but Brickert was right. "It's—it's not leadership, Brickert. Things happened. Natalia told us how Hefani kept putting in the code incorrectly. There are some things you can't control."

"I shouldn't have let my team take our eyes off the screens. It only took a few seconds …"

"I've made mistakes, too, Brick."

"Have your mistakes gotten people killed? Or almost killed?"

Sammy stared at Brickert, his best friend, and wondered how he could have ever raised a hand against him. The guilt was still there, it would always be there. "Brickert, I … I have to tell you something."

"What?"

Sammy swallowed and found his throat was filled with sand. "I've made mistakes." His voice almost failed him. The words were right there. *I nearly killed you. That was my worst mistake.* He meant to say them, but instead he muttered, "In Akureyri. I—I thought I was calling the Thirteens' bluff, but they killed a girl without a second thought. I should have known better."

Brickert nodded, but Sammy's words didn't improve his mood.

"It was your first time as a team leader—" He stopped when he saw the tears running down Brickert's face.

For a long while Brickert shook in silence. Finally he sniffed and said in a thick voice, "I froze up. Should have called for help sooner, but I was worried about the gas. Caught off guard. I might have saved Hefani if I'd—a better job."

"Hefani was dead the second he was shot. Your actions saved Natalia and Strawberry. Think about that."

"Berry saved Natalia. I was gone."

"So you can give yourself all the blame and none of the credit? Sounds fair."

Brickert sighed. "I don't know. I wish I was you, Sammy. Wish I had your moxie. Your smarts. People meet you and they immediately want to follow you. I'm just the other guy—"

"Brickert ..."

"And I'm fine with that, I'll tell you. I really am. But I just wish I could have a little bit of what you are."

Sammy couldn't think of anything to say except, "Thanks."

Just as they arrived at the cafeteria, Sammy got a call from Thomas. He wanted Sammy to come down to the air tower for an emergency meeting.

"It can't wait?" Sammy asked, looking at Brickert. "It's Saturday."

"No," Thomas responded. "That's what *emergency* means."

Sammy rolled his eyes. "Be there in five."

Brickert frowned. "Gotta go?"

"Go where?" Jeffie asked behind them. "Another meeting?"

"I can't imagine what it's like to be so important," Kawai teased. "Can you, Jeffie?"

"To be so powerful ..."

Sammy shook his head, grinning. "These emergency meetings are getting old. I gotta go. See you guys tonight."

In the air control tower Thomas and Lara were already present along with a few others. When Sammy saw Dr. Khani Nguyen preparing a presentation he knew he was in for an interesting meeting. She rarely came to the leadership committee meetings, but when she did, it always portended some kind of drama. Her gaze met Sammy's and she gave a curt nod.

Weeks ago, during a particularly long meeting, Sammy had confronted Khani about some of her data. She responded by calling him a *Pretensai*, which he could only assume meant that she questioned his Anomaly Eleven. Justice, who had overheard the exchange, found the remark wildly hilarious, and now called Sammy "Pretensai" every chance he got.

Lara opened the meeting with a few announcements and then gave Khani the floor. Khani took over with her usual smugness. After straightening her glasses, she turned on her holo-projector. "My team has now had ample opportunity to study the data cube which Trapper, a.k.a. Diego, gave Sammy at the Hive. We believe we have mined enough data to help the leadership committee formulate an effective offensive strategy in conjunction with the NWG. Most of what I will discuss revolves around the kill code and two so-called *white rooms*."

Despite how ardently Khani had argued that no such kill code existed, she still managed to convey all this information with a tone that suggested superiority and infinite knowledge. "The kill code can be used to target and eliminate every CAG operative and personnel who has consumed the substance referred to as the *solution*. This substance will cause a chemical reaction inside the body that culminates in a violent explosion. The explosion will be lethal enough to injure, possibly even kill, those within a small enough radius relative to the victim.

"Notes from Trapper, a.k.a. Diego, inform us that the figure known as the fox intended to use the kill code to eliminate all the Thirteens, Hybrids, Aegis, and others deeply involved in the Thirteen organization. To do this, he built two rooms, one in Rio de Janeiro and one in Orlando. Accessing both rooms is necessary to effectively use the kill code on a broad scale. Now, as for gaining access to the said white rooms, that's where things start getting tricky."

Khani brought up a holographic image of two identical towers: the one in Orlando and the one in Rio. "Both white rooms are in the sublevels of the towers below the red and black levels. Only one elevator in each tower descends to the three sublevels."

Her hologram highlighted the special elevators that went down to the sublevels from the main lobby.

"The purpose of these rooms raised several questions in my mind, along with my colleagues. Why not just use the Hive to activate the code? Why build special rooms for it? Our analysis of the data gave us the answers. Control. While individuals can be targeted from the Hive alone, the kill code used en masse can only be achieved from the white rooms. Trapper's notes say that its activation will terminate the lives of over a thousand anomalies and CAG operatives.

"With so much at stake, the fox maintains maximum control over the rooms and the kill code. While these towers are extremely similar, and were built only months apart, there are a few key differences that will, or at least should, impact the way the missions are planned in subcommittees.

"The Rio de Janeiro N Tower was built first, and the fox made some improvements on the Orlando tower. Thus your teams will have a few more options for accessing the white room in Rio than in Orlando. The biggest difference between the two buildings is in the foundations. In downtown Rio, these massive skyscrapers like the N Tower and its surrounding buildings are interconnected via service tunnels. It is possible to use these tunnels to gain access to the elevator shaft connected to the black, red, and white floors. However, getting the white door open is not so easy. It only opens to Trapper, a.k.a. Diego, or the fox. However, it can be recoded to accept anyone with a level 6 clearance."

"Dark agents," Sammy added.

Khani scowled at him as though she didn't appreciate the interruption. "Yes, and most Thirteens. The data cube contains the programming to recode the door. All we need to do is get it into the data slot and provide someone with the clearance.

"The tower in Orlando, unfortunately, is not so simple. The fox took more precautions with this building. The door cannot be recoded, only he can open it."

"We have no chance of getting him to open it," Commander Byron stated. "Are you saying this mission is impossible?"

"Would you people stop interrupting me!" Khani declared. "I wouldn't be wasting your time with all this information if it were impossible. It is possible to breach the door using a plasma blade inserted at one specific point, a built-in weakness as Trapper termed it in his notes. However, the procedure must be very precise or, again, the kill code cannot be activated in the room. If the breach is done correctly, the data cube can override the system and open the door."

"We only got one data cube," one of the Hudec brothers stated; Sammy couldn't tell which.

Khani glared at him as she would a disobedient monkey in a zoo. "Believe it or not, I've made … *duplicates*." Then she rolled her shoulders and continued. "The other difficulty is that the Orlando N

Tower does not share a greater foundation with other buildings. There are no service ways to use to infiltrate the building. The only way to access the elevator that reaches the white floor is getting a Thirteen's fingerprint and using it to activate the panel with the white button."

"Sounds like we have our work cut out for us," Thomas stated. "Thank you, Khani."

"I'm not finished," she said. "The problems go beyond what I've stated. Your coms will be worthless once you get into the sublevels of the towers. This presents a problem because the activation of the kill code needs to be coordinated, happening within one minute of each other. If one tower activates their side without the other, the system will lockdown for an hour."

"Is network penetration out of the question?" Justice asked. "Break into their systems and activate the kill code outside the white room?"

"Both rooms must be activated with the cubes from inside in order to initiate the signal," Khani growled. "Extensive and expensive means were taken to put the two rooms on an isolated and secure network. They cannot be hacked or breached. The job must be done at the terminals inside the rooms. The signal will broadcast out of a dish located at the Hive, so it is imperative that the Hive stay intact until transmission of the signal is complete. Fortunately, Diego has given us access routes to control security and block the communications and weapons systems of the Hive during our attack. This should prevent any internal interference from the Hive during the mission."

"So we've got to access both white rooms," Thomas said, "and prevent the Hive satellite dishes that broadcast the signal from being damaged."

"Yes," Khani took a deep breath, "How you do all that, I leave up to the soldiers to figure out."

"This is our opportunity," Commander Byron stated, planting his finger onto the table. "This is our window to strike. Not only will the blow cripple the CAG, but a large scale, high profile distraction will help provide cover for our teams hitting the Rio and Orlando towers. NWG air strikes will keep valuable CAG resources away from the Hive. This could be *the* decisive battle."

"Teams will be easy to draw up," Anna said. "Send two small teams of Psions into the towers, send the rest of the Psions, the Ultras, Elite, and civilians into the high profile strike. The exception, of course, is the pilots. They need to be in the air."

"Small teams?" Duncan Hudec said. "You must be kidding. Send as many men and women as we can into the towers to make sure the white rooms get activated. That's the most important part of the mission!"

"You send in too many people and you draw all the attention to yourself," Sammy advised. "A small team is more likely to reach the white room if they go unnoticed. A large team may never make it there. Two well-trained Psions can access *and* hold a room with the right equipment."

Lara nodded. "Plans will need to go to subcommittee, but I think those ideas are a great start. Do we have a motion—"

Khani stood up straighter. "I'm *still* not finished."

Frowning, Lara said, "Okay. Continue."

"The Orlando white room and the one in Rio de Janeiro have one more major difference. The Rio room was designed to be the end of Diego's service to the fox. The activation of the kill code in Rio will trigger a failsafe mechanism. Twin blast doors will close, and a bomb will detonate, a bomb powerful enough to ensure that whoever activates the code from this room will not survive the blast."

"Wait," Thomas said. "What are you saying?"

Khani rolled her eyes impatiently. "I'm saying whoever activates the room in Rio will not survive."

Anna stood so suddenly that her chair smacked the wall behind her and tumbled over onto the floor. "And you're just now telling us this?"

Khani didn't blink an eye. "Yes."

"Let's—let's focus on the general picture for now," Thomas said before Anna could unleash her wrath on Khani. "Details will only distract us. This all has to be done on the same day. It's going to require an immense amount of work and planning."

Sammy rubbed his forehead. "Wow. That … logistically—"

"A total freaking nightmare," Justice said. "But what a wild day."

"This is it, folks," Thomas said. "If we do it right, the war may end. To even be able to say that is incredible. We actually have a shot to win it, despite the odds we faced when it started."

"And all we have to do is ask someone to die voluntarily," Lara said. "Or a whole team of people, if that's what it takes to hold the kill room until the signal is sent."

"I will do it." Thomas said, standing. "*I'll* go."

"Sit down, Thomas," Lara barked. "Don't be absurd. What use are you going to be in a room full of anomalies? Target practice? You're pushing seventy and aren't even a sharpshooter."

Sammy wanted to laugh until he saw Thomas' face.

"To not go would be immoral," Thomas told his wife. "It would be passing the sins of the fathers onto the sons. 'Who sleeps soundly through the night whilst boys and girls toil? Bearing our burdens on their back, bleeding on our furrowed soil.'"

Lara's response came fast and sharp, "'My friend, you would not tell with such high zest, to children ardent for some desperate glory, the old lie: Dulce et decorum est pro patria mori.'"

"Are you suggesting I would do this for some kind of glory?" Thomas asked.

"You certainly won't be going to help the cause, so you tell me why."

"I can't stand by while others die for my faults—the mistakes of my generation!"

"We don't need to decide who's doing what today," Justice said. "Let's save that conversation for another time. Preferably one with lots of booze."

A heaviness fell over the room. Tough decisions were coming. Decisions no one wanted to make. Sammy looked at Anna, her jaw set, her eyes fixed on the blueprints of the kill room in Rio. *What are you thinking?*

"I don't agree with this," said Lorenzo Winters. "We can't ask people to walk to their deaths. We have to find another way. Any other way."

Thomas rested his elbows on the tablet and leaned forward. "This is the kind of mentality we have to overcome—that we can accomplish our goals without the loss of some lives. We have spent weeks talking about a so-called endgame. We all know what has to be done, and yet we're not willing to ask someone to do it if it means sacrifice."

"I have no problem with people risking their lives," Lorenzo Winters said, "but suicide? That's what this mission is."

"They aren't the same," Thomas said.

"It has to be Psions," Anna offered. "Anyone else—even Ultras—could be walking into a death box."

"Weren't you listening?" Justice said. "It's a death box no matter who goes in."

"Doesn't matter how many distractions we arrange on that day, though. When … not if … but *when* the fox realizes what's happening, they'll try to intercept the mission."

"It'll be like the Ride of the Valkyries."

"So what?" Sammy asked. "You think our best team of fighters need to go to the kill room?"

"I think two very capable Psions could do the job," Anna said. "It's possible." She looked Sammy in the eye. He knew what the look meant.

Me? he asked her silently.

She nodded. Then she mouthed. "And me."

* * * * *

Friday, April 25, 2053

-247-

"Dad, I have to go to prom," Katie said. She was trying not to shout, but the way her parents looked at her was unbearable. Disappointment. Hurt. Confusion. Prom queen at her school was an incredible honor, not only because of the prestige and the crown, but because the winner earned scholarship money to pay for a year of college. Katie, whose parents were by no means wealthy, had already paid for two years of a four-year school by winning the prize her freshman and sophomore years.

"No," her dad responded, "you really don't."

"I'm ineligible—"

"I'm aware of the rules for prom queen, Katie," her dad finished. He chewed on the end of his glasses. His eyes squinted when he didn't wear them, which made him look sterner. "Your mom and I don't think your actions represent what a prom queen is supposed to stand for, do you?"

"Dad … I have tried to be the kind of person you expect me to be all year! I made a mistake. If I don't go, Bobby John—the other kids … I can't back out. I organized this whole thing for Mrs. Hepworth. Why can't you pick a different punishment?"

"Are you serious, Katie?" her mom nearly yelled. "You beat a girl up." The more emotional her mom grew, the more shrill her voice. It was a sound Katie detested. "There has to be consequences."

Katie sat in her pajamas on the couch, her head bowed. She fidgeted with the fabric of her pants, thinking about how messed up everything was. Mark had dumped her via text after school. Her parents weren't standing by her. Priyanka was winning. Not just winning the crown, but life.

You'll never be good enough for them. Be free from all these cares. Parents, school, peers. Let it all go.

The words both creeped her out and enticed her.

"Katie?" her dad said. "Are you listening to me?"

Katie nodded without looking up. They needed to see her cry, so she contorted her face and held her breath until the tears flowed. Then she looked up.

"You're right. O—okay? You're right. There needs to be consequences. I—I know. But p—please listen. Priyanka posted those ... *horrible* pictures of me. It doesn't matter if they haven't proven it, she taunts me every chance she gets. And I'm just supposed to deal with that. It sucks."

Katie's mom nodded. "Yeah, it does suck. But you know what? The part of life you're in now, no one remembers it once you've graduated."

"Everyone remembers it now. I still have a full year of school left!" Her fist tightened on a pillow. She wanted to hurl it at her mother's stupid face. "It's like you don't even care about what she did to me!"

"You don't think we want to see Priyanka get justice?"

Katie made a rude noise with her lips. "It doesn't seem that way."

"It's more important to us that you don't get dragged down to her level," her father added. "Revenge or retaliation will only get you in trouble."

Oh, she will get justice, Katie silently vowed. The gnawing in Katie's gut told her it absolutely would be the worst thing in the world. But she couldn't say that. She had to convince her parents that she wanted to bury the hatchet between herself and Priyanka.

THAT'S an idea ... bury it right between her eyes!

Katie tried to shake away the thought.

"Katie?" her mom pressed. "I asked you a question."

Katie sighed. Her mom and dad wouldn't understand.

What is the point of having parents if they don't have your back? Free yourself.

"No, Mom," she finally said. "It's not the worst thing. Can we make a deal? If I apologize to Priyanka and make things right, will you let me go to the dance?"

Katie's parents looked at each other before her dad answered, "It's a step in the right direction. Do that and we'll talk it over."

It was the best answer she could hope for. Katie hugged her parents, but imagined herself squeezing them to death. Then she went to bed. Two hours passed before she fell asleep, and during that time she pondered how to regain her status in the eyes of her classmates. It would have to be something subversive yet effective. Something that couldn't be traced back to her.

That night, when the dream began, Katie knew exactly what to do. She ran to her shadow, touched it and got the knife. Ignoring the brightly lit home where her parents waited for her at the table laden with food, she hurried to the cave, plunging into its depths for the first time.

The darkness was so perfect and absolute that it seemed to touch her skin with cold, breath-like fingers. She spread out her hands until she touched the rocky, slick wall, her bare feet skimming along the smooth damp floor. The cave was narrow enough that both hands could touch the walls as she walked forward. After walking almost one hundred meters through pitch cold black, she felt the floor drop.

Katie froze when her foot touched nothing but air. The skin behind her ears grew hot and her breaths shaky. The air was so cold that goose bumps raised up on her legs and her toes curled to stay warm. Something unnatural and ethereal pulled at her, yearning and beckoning her to descend.

Just a little farther. Freedom is near. Everything you want is right down the stairs. Come down. One at a time. Your freedom awaits …

Katie took the first step down the stairs. Then another. And another. And another. And another. Each more deliberate than the last. At first she counted the steps until there were so many that she lost count.

The air cooled as she descended. At first it was pleasant, then a little uncomfortable, and finally so cold that her breaths came in thick puffs and she shivered violently. Katie kept going, determined to find the bottom, but suddenly stopped when she felt a vibration through the air—a sort of pulsing that rippled and tingled her skin.

There's something wrong here. She sniffed from the cold, and caught a hint of something rank and foul. Perhaps even evil.

Come down, Katie. Almost there. Come to your freedom.

The thrumming and pulsing continued steady and strong like the heartbeat of an enormous beast lying in wait for her. She took a step backward the way she came and then another. She turned and tried to run but slipped and hit something hard. When she woke she stood on the floor, her feet cold and clammy.

15 | **Mistakes**

Saturday, August 30, 2087

"TWO MINUTES," Kawai announced. "Get in your places."

Though the lights were off in the gymnasium, the moonlight still shone brightly enough that streamers and other party decorations were visible. The occasion was Brickert's first day out of the infirmary. Natalia and Strawberry had planned the party and invited Psions and several other members of the resistance leadership and their families. Thomas and Lara crouched down near Sammy.

Thomas moaned, "I haven't been to a surprise party since Walter was eight."

"How old are you? Eighty?" Lara teased. "Your joints sound like the Tin Man's."

"So my knees are creaking. Next thing you'll be saying my head's full of straw."

"You old blokes and your obscure jokes," Sammy moaned.

"That was a rhyme," Thomas pointed out. "Are you a poet?"

"Wouldn't you know it," Lara said, giggling like a girl half her age.

Sammy slapped his forehead. "When this is all over, I'm putting you two in a nursing home. And Thomas, you're on my foot."

"Whoops, sorry," Thomas said as he took his boot off Sammy's shoe.

Moments later the gymnasium opened and everyone jumped to their feet as they shouted, "SURPRISE!"

Brickert grinned with red spots growing on his cheeks. "A party? What for?"

"Your birthday," Sammy said as he gave his friend a hug. "Only it's four months and twenty days late."

Brickert snickered and punched Sammy in the arm while Natalia and Strawberry put a party hat on his head, a cape on his shoulders, and a decorated staff in hand which named him king of the event. After Natalia whispered in his ear, Brickert raised the staff high and in a deep voice declared, "Uh … okay … Let the festivities begin!"

As partygoers divided into groups to play games, someone tapped on Sammy's shoulder. He turned to see Anna behind him, fists on her hips and an expression of disappointment on her face. "You've been avoiding me for two weeks."

Sammy took a deep breath and let it out slowly. She wanted to talk about the mission to Rio—the suicide mission. It was the last thing he wanted on his mind, but he couldn't tell Anna that. "I've—uh—I've been thinking about what you said. A lot."

She raised an eyebrow. "And?"

"And ... I don't know."

Anna ran her fingers through her short blonde hair. "You don't need to have an answer today, but the big meeting is coming soon. I will be volunteering myself whether or not you come along. But let me make it clear ... I want you along."

Sammy deflated. "Why? Why me?"

Anna poked him in the chest. "Because you're the best. And if I go on this mission, I don't want my death to be in vain."

Sammy didn't answer for a moment. Then he said, "I—I get that." *You want me to die with you. And I can't—I don't want to.*

"Have you told anyone about it?" she asked.

Sammy shook his head. "I already know what they'll say."

"They won't understand, Sammy. They don't know what you deal with day to day. The demons you face—that you'll have to live with until you die. How could they know what that's like?"

Her words punched Sammy in the gut. His neck grew hot. "I should want to die because of my anomaly?"

Anna's eyes narrowed. "Has it really never crossed your mind?"

"What about you?" Sammy asked, dodging her question. "Why are you so quick to volunteer for death?"

Anna grinned wickedly. "Let me die young, beautiful, and doing something important. I'm talking history books. Immortality. Heroes for centuries. Anna Lukic and Samuel Berhane."

"I'll think about it," Sammy told her. He went to move past her, but she grabbed his arm.

"It has to be a Psion," she said. "If not you, then whom?" Before Sammy could answer, Anna cut him off. "Just think about that. We'll talk more later."

As Anna left, Jeffie and Brickert walked up. Jeffie put her arm around Sammy's waist. "What was that about?"

"Just mission stuff," Sammy answered.

Brickert had wasted no time finding himself a hamburger. A thin line of ketchup even greased his lower lip. When Brickert took a large bite, he winced and held his jaw. "It's still a little tender," he told them, "where the teeth are growing in. Those bastards keep knocking them out."

Not "those bastards." Me.

"Look who's here." Jeffie pointed across the gym to a group of people standing in a circle, talking. Kawai held Al and Marie's baby girl in her arms, cooing at it. Al and Marie stood side by side, looking on.

"Both of them?" Sammy asked.

"They came together. No fighting."

Sammy and his friends went over to where Al and Marie were chatting with Justice, Nikotai, Li, and Kawai. Kawai was rocking the baby now, a fat little thing dressed in a pink jumper and a white bow clipped in her black hair. Sammy smiled at the baby even though it didn't do much but stare back with half-opened eyes.

"Sammy," Marie said, hugging him, "you haven't held Baby Girl yet, have you?"

"Nope. I'm a lame friend, I know. Dr. Rosmir has me on lame-friend meds, but they don't seem to be helping."

Marie laughed. Sammy couldn't remember the last time he'd heard her do that. Al managed a weak smile, but glanced at Sammy as though being around Sammy embarrassed him. They hadn't spoken to each other since Al had put a loaded gun in Sammy's hands and Sammy had taken Al to his father. Since that day Al had been living with the commander.

"Do you want to hold him, Sammy?" Kawai asked.

"Uh …" Sammy looked at the baby again, and before he could answer, Kawai shuffled the tiny thing into Sammy's arms. "Yeah, sure."

The baby was so light and small it surprised him. When was the last time he'd held one? He didn't know if he ever had. She smelled like a light soap or a box being opened for the first time. She grunted for a moment and then sighed. The sound relaxed him and he pressed his cheek against her head, feeling her soft hair and spongy skull.

"So delicate, isn't she?" was all Sammy could think to say.

Marie nodded. Al observed with an unreadable expression, his hands fidgeting. His clothes looked washed and pressed for the first time in weeks. His face had lost most of the red puffiness that Sammy had grown accustomed to seeing, and his eyes had cleared up too. Thomas and Lara had hinted to Sammy a few days ago that Al was slowly getting his act together, sobering up, and trying to give his relationship with Marie a fresh start. He gave Al an awkward smile.

Jeffie squeezed Sammy's arm. "You look good holding one of those."

For a moment a tight warmness spread in Sammy's chest. But it was quickly extinguished and replaced with a cold shuddering at her comment. He handed the baby to Marie. "She's beautiful," he muttered and walked away.

What am I thinking? he asked himself. *I'll never have a baby. What if I pass on my Anomaly Thirteen? What would I say to it?*

Hey, kid, welcome to the Berhane family. Enjoy fighting the darkness I passed onto you … compliments of dear old dad.

Images conjured up in his mind of his children murdering each other, turning on their parents, the way Katie Carpenter had done to her folks thirty-odd years ago. Or like Trapper, creeping out of bed and slitting a throat, painting symbols on the walls in blood. Even worse, Sammy realized, what if *he* snapped and hurt his own children the way he'd beaten Brickert. A chill ran down his spine as his eyes flickered to Marie and Al's baby girl. *No … no kids. Ever.*

Someone tapping on a microphone drew Sammy's attention away from the morbid thoughts clinging to his brain like pocket lint. It was Brickert. Natalia and Strawberry flanked him. In his hand he held a glass of root beer. The spots on his cheeks told Sammy that whatever he was about to do, the girls were making him do it.

"Um … okay, so Natalia tells me I need to give a speech," Brickert began. "And obviously I haven't prepared anything so I'll keep this very brief." He paused, took a sip from his glass, and then wiped his eyes. "I just wanna give my thanks to all of you who helped me. I know how bad things were—how I looked. When the Thir—when the—" Brickert stopped and cleared his throat. "When the enemy took me down, I thought it was over. I didn't know how to process that. And then all I knew was pain and fear, I'll tell you. And then Sammy …"

Brickert drained the rest of his drink in one swallow. But Sammy couldn't bear to listen to another word. He had to leave immediately.

"Sammy you—hey, where are you going?" Brickert asked when he saw Sammy make a beeline for the nearest exit. Everyone turned to watch, so Sammy ran faster, even as Brickert continued to call out, "Hey! Come back!"

Sammy did not go back. Instead he went home and fell on his bed. At some point during the night he heard Brickert arrive. Sammy listened to his footsteps through the house until they stopped in Sammy's doorway.

"You awake?" Brickert asked quietly. "Sammy?"

Sammy did not stir or change his breathing.

"Sammy?" Brickert said a little louder.

Sammy still did not move until Brickert went to his room. An hour later, Sammy finally fell asleep.

The next morning Sammy checked the schedule and saw that Croz had an appointment with Vitoria that he had neglected to mention. *Think you can pull a fast one on me, Croz?*

Sammy quickly dressed and drove Lemon down to the Pen. Croz was just on his way inside when Sammy pulled up. When their eyes met, Sammy saw a hint of disappointment but no traces of surprise on the psychiatrist's face. "If it isn't my therapist-in-training …" Croz called over his shoulder as he walked up the tunnel steps into the penitentiary.

Vitoria was in a ripe mood, behaving more lewdly and obstinate than normal. Sammy thought he could have handled it if she were switching back and forth between the quiet, timid version and the sassy, sensual version, but she wasn't switching. She was stuck today in full on come-and-get-me mode.

She's not improving, Sammy thought, tapping his feet on the floor at a double-time pace. *And Croz has the patience of a glacier. He's not getting the job done.* He remembered Dr. Vogt and how different and more radical his treatment of Sammy had been. Why couldn't Croz do something like that? Sammy had suggested it once, but Croz had shot him down saying, "You can't treat a human being's mind and soul like a one-size-fits-all sweater."

"Did you ever play sports?" Croz asked Vitoria now.

"Pole dancing," she answered, giving him a wink and spreading her legs a little.

Sammy stirred in his seat and folded his arms, still tapping his feet. "Toad said you were really good at football—"

"Sammy," Croz warned him.

"He said you were a great goalkeeper."

"I don't know about that." She grinned mischievously at Sammy. "I'd let *you* score on me." Then she gave a small moan.

"Close your legs," Sammy snapped in a sharper tone than he meant. "You're a lady. And you're definitely not enticing either of us."

"Sammy!" Croz yelled.

"No. Let me talk to Vitoria. Toad called you Vivi most of the time, didn't he?"

"I don't know a Toad," she responded. "Or a Vitoria or Vivi. I've told you a hundred times, my name is Jane."

"Sammy, you need to leave," Croz said.

But Sammy pressed on. "Jane is a common name. When a woman's name is unknown, she's called a Jane Doe. Vitoria means victory. A champion. I think it describes you better."

"That's nice," Vitoria said, but she was anything but flattered.

"You can pretend if you want. If it makes you feel safe. Go ahead. Be Jane. Jane is a nice blanket to wrap yourself in. Jane, the girl who doesn't mind her body being used without her permission. Who endures torment for months without complaint. Who does what she is told to do by her superiors. If you still need protection, use it. I've been there, too, Vitoria. Do you know what my pretend name was when I was tortured? Albert. Albert Choochoo."

Vitoria laughed rudely. "That's the dumbest thing I've ever heard."

"But true. Albert coped with the endless pain that I couldn't when the Aegis got me. He was strong when I was weak. If it wasn't for Albert, I'd have died. Or I'd have become a Psion Dark. And Toad would have been in Ultra Dark with you. Instead, I escaped, Toad came with me, and we became friends—such good friends that he jumped in front of a hand cannon for me."

"Why would my—why would anyone die for *you*?" Vitoria clutched herself, her legs squeezed tightly together and her arms wrapped around her exposed midriff.

"Toad helped me," Sammy admitted quietly. "He was patient with me—as patient as he could be—in some of my darkest hours. I loved him like a brother. That makes you my sister, Vivi."

Vitoria rushed at Sammy. "My name is *JANE!*" Croz tried to stop her, but with her Anomaly Fifteen, she was too fast. She bumped into the doctor, sending his clipboard and carefully paper-clipped stacks flying. Before Vitoria could get any closer to Sammy, he pushed her away with gentle but firm blasts.

She didn't speak after that. Nothing Croz did evoked a response. When he finally ended the session and thanked her for her time, Vitoria spat at Sammy.

"You are no longer welcome in my sessions," Croz told Sammy when the door closed behind them.

"But—"

"Shut your mouth!" Croz shouted so loudly that the two Pen resistance guards jumped. "That was the one rule I had. That you shut your mouth."

"You weren't getting anywhere. She still thinks this is a game. A test."

Croz put a finger on Sammy's sternum. "You wouldn't have even known that if I hadn't told you. How would you know where I'm getting? What do you know about psychology, Sammy? What you read in some books? I've studied it for *years*. It's my job, and I'm good at it as it so happens. But you? You think that because you're smarter than me you can do my job better than me. You are out."

The worst part about their argument was that Sammy still had to drive Croz back to the infirmary to submit his report to Dr. Rosmir. Sammy squirmed in his seat the whole way. When he pulled up to the infirmary, Croz got out, looked at Sammy, sighed, and then walked away. Sammy jammed down the gas pedal and drove back to his house.

Brickert was gone, but Jeffie was on the couch watching the news, waiting. Sammy didn't notice her before he slammed the door.

"Are you intent on destroying all the doors in Glasgow?" Jeffie asked with a small smirk and a careful tone.

"One at a time."

Her eyes lit up even more when she realized he was in a good enough mood to joke around. "You want to talk about it?"

"No."

Jeffie patted the couch cushion next to her until Sammy sat on it. Then she lay down with her head on his lap. She had a barrette in her hair to keep her white-gold locks off her shoulders but it dug into Sammy's thigh. "I love you," she said.

"I know."

"You missed one heckuva party last night. Fireworks even."

Sammy put up his feet so the barrette wouldn't dig so hard into his skin. "Sure I did."

Jeffie sighed. "I was referring to Al and Marie."

"What? They fought?"

"In front of everyone. It was so awkward. You have no idea. One minute a few of us were joking about baby names. Next minute they're shouting until the commander took Marie away. You should have seen his face, Sammy. I thought he was going to punch Al. Maybe he should have punched him."

"Al's cracking, Jeffie. Punching him is not going to help."

"You think he's going crazy?"

"No, not cracking like that. Something broke him. I don't know what. He won't tell anyone." Sammy stroked Jeffie's hair for a while, not saying anything more. Jeffie reached up and touched his cheek.

"Oh crap, I almost forgot. Are you still down for blastketball?"

Sammy's inclination was to say no. "Is Brickert going to be there?"

"I think so. He said he wants to jump right back into the routine. He's working out right now with Natalia and Li. Does this have something to do with—oh wait, you said you don't want to talk about it. Sorry."

"It's fine. Yeah, I'll come." Sammy got up and changed his clothes. Ten minutes later, after giving Lemon yet another boost, they were on their way to the gym.

Blastketball was a game of Miguel and Jeffie's invention. Similar to basketball but with one important change: touching the basketball was not allowed unless the player was within a meter of his or her team's basket. Since the Psions no longer had access to the Arena, it was the way they worked on blasting and kept it fun. Today they played with two teams of five: Sammy, Jeffie, Brickert, Kawai, and Natalia against Li, Ludwig, Rosa, Miguel, and Strawberry.

Often people came to watch and cheer them on as they rocketed off the walls, blasting the ball to one another with speed and accuracy. Today about seventy people watched. Jeffie was by far the best player. Between her stellar basketball skills and her natural accuracy she was a spectacle to watch. Sometimes Sammy even caught himself ogling her while she dunked the ball. He loved the way she fed off the enthusiasm of the crowd, even if it was only a few dozen people.

"Come on, ladies," Jeffie taunted the other team. "You're down by eighteen points. Get your heads in the game!"

Li, who had been dribbling the ball down court using a soft blast instead of his hand, used a powerful foot blast to send the ball arcing through the air. Ludwig used a jump blast from the three point line to catch the ball between two hand blasts. Natalia made a half-hearted attempt at defending the goal, but Ludwig scored on a soft jam, drawing a round of applause.

"Sixteen," Strawberry said, sticking out her tongue at Jeffie.

"Timeout!" Jeffie called.

Sammy's team huddled up around her. "What's the matter?" he asked, "We're killing them."

"My barrette is driving me crazy. Here, Sammy." She tossed the hair clip to him and tied her hair up in a ponytail with a band. "You have pockets."

"You called a timeout for a barrette?" Brickert asked. "You're such a girl."

Jeffie punched him in the arm as the timeout ended. Sammy headed back onto the court and saw Croz standing near the door, hands in his pockets, motioning to Sammy with a jerk of his head that they needed to talk. Sammy told Jeffie he had to go, and ran over to Croz.

"What's up?" Sammy asked coolly.

"I need you at the Pen." Croz said the words with the same tone he might have used if asking for someone to kick him in the shins. "Vitoria tried to kill herself."

"What?"

"When the guards brought her lunch, they found her hanging from a noose made from bed sheets. We've got her on suicide watch, but she's asking to see you. Only you."

"Is it a trick?"

Croz shrugged. "Maybe."

"She wanted to kill me."

"Maybe she still does. I kind of felt like killing you this morning, too." Croz smiled, but Sammy did not return the gesture. "I'd appreciate it if you came down and spoke with her."

"Will you let me go to her sessions again?"

Hands on his hips, Croz rubbed his mouth and considered the request. "Probably not. But if you do this and it goes well … I might be willing to reconsider."

"Let's go."

At the Pen, Sammy found Vitoria on her bed reading *Crime and Punishment*, wearing only panties and a torn, baggy shirt. Sammy stopped when he saw her and looked at Croz. "No," he stated. "I'm not going in there."

"You know," Croz said, "most guys your age wouldn't let the door stop them from getting in there, seeing her like that. How did your wires get so crossed?"

"She's Toad's sister."

"Yes, she's Toad's sister. But in here," Croz tapped his skull, "she's something Toad wouldn't recognize. If you have to, pretend she's wearing granny panties and has a little mustache."

When Vitoria saw Sammy enter she tossed the book aside and hugged him. It was a lingering embrace with her body pressing into his. Sammy quickly released her, noting the sly grin.

"How's it going?" he asked as he pulled up a chair.

Vitoria stuffed her book under her pillow and sat back down. "Fine. I'm happier now you're here."

"Why me?"

Toad's sister smiled and shrugged. "We connect. Don't you think?"

"Is that why you faked an attempt at suicide? So I'd have more motivation to come back and visit you?"

Vitoria sat back in her cut off tee shirt and crossed her smooth, toned legs, stretching them out so her toes almost reached Sammy's knee. The knowing grin on her lips told Sammy his theory was spot on.

"You know what time they bring you lunch. You knew they'd see you and stop you. You knew Croz would take your attempt seriously despite his suspicions. And you thought, what? That I'd have to come back? Well here I am."

"Here you are," she said smiling.

"Now what? You're going to try to kill me?"

For an instant, something on Vitoria's face told Sammy that was exactly what she'd planned to do. Then she burst out in laughter. "No! I don't want to kill you. I *want* you. Croz is nice. The others are okay. It's *you* I look forward to seeing. That night we had dinner together in the hotel, I wanted you in that bed. I still do."

Sammy winced. "Vivi, I would never have done that with you. That's not me."

Vitoria's smile turned sad. "When I was in H.A.M.M.E.R. and then S.H.I.E.L.D. it was the only thing that gave me comfort."

"I'd be a lousy partner. Being … inexperienced and all."

Vitoria raised an eyebrow, her gaze now on Sammy's shorts. Sammy crossed his own legs to stop her from staring at him. He tried to think of a way to change the subject. "Do you feel loyalty to them? To the CAG?"

"I'm a Dark agent. No matter where I am, I'm free." She said the words as though they had been ingrained into her consciousness.

Sammy looked pointedly around the room. "Your surroundings suggest otherwise."

"You give me books, food, a bed. Now if I can just get you in that bed with me, I'd want for nothing."

Blushing furiously, Sammy rubbed his forehead. "Why are you so forward?"

"Why are you so backward?" She stared at Sammy shrewdly, and he stared back.

What's your game? he wanted to ask her. Instead he said, "I watched you in action when we toured the S.H.I.E.L.D. facility. Despite being the youngest of the Ultras, you were already the best. Toad had a natural gift too."

"Toad ... I wish I could say that name meant something to me," Vitoria said in a drawling tone. "But for you ... one mention and you start tearing up. I have an idea. How about instead of all this psycho-nonsense, you just tell me why I was taken and what you want with me."

After a long moment of silence, Sammy spoke again. "We want your help on a mission."

"What mission?"

"I can't tell you that."

"Then I can't help you."

"Well ... you can. You just won't."

Vitoria nodded. "Right."

"You wouldn't even do it for me?"

Covering her mouth, Vitoria laughed. She had pretty eyes, large white teeth, and a full, hearty laugh. "Sure I will. Just for you. Because what we have is so special."

"Haven't you wanted to be part of something bigger than yourself?"

"I am. It's called Ultra Dark." Vitoria threw herself back on her bed, arms spread open. "And it is *amazing!*" She said the last word with such breathlessness that Sammy rolled his eyes.

"Are you always so caustic?"

"Are you always so prudish?"

"I can relate to what you went through, Vivi. Being tortured for weeks screwed up my head. Some days I thought my mind was going to splinter. I have seen horror after horror after horror. And sometimes, even today, I wonder how completely scrambled I am after it all. I don't feel like I should have kids or marry or anything because I am so emotionally and mentally fried."

"Your tragedies don't make me feel better."

"Talking helped me through it. I could show you the things I learned."

"Why don't you show me what's in your shorts? I'm much more interested in that."

"What? No, Vivi—"

"Take off your shorts!" she said, getting up and running over to Sammy. Vitoria was so fast, Sammy barely had time to stop her. She pulled and tugged and shoved her hands into his clothes, kissing his face greedily and wetly. "Take them off, Sammy. No one's here."

"Get off me!" he roared, forcing her away from him with a blast of moderate strength. She landed across the room, bouncing off her bed, and banging into the wall. Sammy cursed at her. "I have a girlfriend, and I—I don't think about you that way."

Vitoria giggled and rolled on her bed, stretching out lewdly, her hands now buried under her pillow. "All guys think about me that way. Girls, too. Maybe you just need a little more time to mull it over. Maybe next time you can bring your girlfriend too."

"No! I don't even know if there will be a next time. And if there is, I hope you'll believe that this is not a test. It's not a game! Can't you see I'm trying to be your friend? That I want you to heal?"

For an instant Vitoria looked like she wanted to kill Sammy, but she threw her book at his face. Sammy jerked his head and let it fly past harmlessly. Disappointed, he opened the door, then turned back to face her. "Geez, Vivi. What did they do to you?"

Vitoria seemed to have some snarky response ready to let loose but she bit it back, and for a moment he saw fear in her eyes, and deep despair. This was different than the other times she'd pretended to be small and vulnerable. Perhaps it was even genuine. *Is that you, there, Vivi? Hiding?*

"What did they do to me?" she repeated. She chewed her lip before finally answering, "Everything."

"I'm sorry." A lump settled in Sammy's chest and his heart ached. "I wish I could take what I know, what I feel, and just … put all of it in your mind and your heart so you could have hope. But I can't. All I can do is sit with you, talk, and try to help you heal."

"Just go." When Sammy didn't move, Vitoria added, "Please."

"Bye." He tapped the door with his fingers. When the door opened, Jeffie was standing outside wearing a blank expression. Croz sat down the hall next to the guards at the desk, watching from the security camera footage.

"Ooh," Vitoria said, instantly reverting back to her dominant sensual attitude, "your girlfriend. She's pretty. Did you see us kiss?"

Jeffie raised an eyebrow. "I saw *something*. Looked more like a puppy trying to lick ice cream off a child's face."

Vitoria laughed snidely. "Jealous?"

"Not really. If he liked it, he'd be blushing right now. I'm seeing more of a green tinge in his skin."

"Take care, Vivi," Sammy said.

When he closed the door, Jeffie took his hand and gave it a squeeze. "You okay?"

"Yeah. I'm fine." He scratched his head. "I don't get her."

Jeffie snorted and linked her arm in his. "I'm glad you don't get her."

"How did you know she faked it, Sammy?" Croz asked when they reached the guard station.

Sammy shrugged. "Instinct."

"I talked to Anna while you were in there. She's going to sit in on the sessions starting tomorrow morning. It'll be better that way. No hard feelings." He patted Sammy on the shoulder as though that made everything better.

Sammy tried to act nonchalant about the decision. "I just want to help her. No one cares about her as much as I do ... or understands as well what she's been through."

"I know," Croz said, "But it's time to try a new face."

Heading toward the doors, Sammy let out a long slow breath and pulled Jeffie closer to him. "All I get with Vitoria is walls. Why do people shut out those who try hardest to help them?"

Jeffie raised an eyebrow at Sammy. "I don't know. Why *do* people put up walls between themselves and the people trying to help them?"

Knowing Jeffie would want to drive, Sammy opened the driver's side door for her and got in on Lemon's passenger side. "I don't put up walls."

Jeffie made an exasperated noise with her lips. "Sammy, you're the King of Wallmakers."

Sammy thought about that while they drove back to his place. When Jeffie parked Lemon, Sammy took her hand in his. "I almost killed Brickert," he whispered. "I attacked him like a savage. I helped put him in that coma. And—and I don't even have the guts to tell him."

Jeffie rubbed his arm and ran her fingers through his hair. "You'll tell him someday, when you're ready. And you know what? It won't change anything. You guys are brothers. He won't even hold a grudge. Just tell him when you're ready."

Sammy pulled away and rubbed his face. "Thanks."

Jeffie smiled. "Don't mention it. Now … we have the rest of the day ahead of us to do whatever we want. Should we call some friends over to hang or would you rather just make out with me on your couch?"

They ended up doing both. That evening, Kawai, Li, Strawberry, Natalia, and Brickert came over to play games. They played late into the night. By the time it ended, Jeffie had fallen asleep on the couch. Sammy covered her with a blanket and went to bed.

Late Monday morning, he woke to the sounds of Jeffie rummaging through his dirty clothes. "What are you doing?" Sammy asked her.

"I can't find my barrette. I gave it to you yesterday and you put it in your shorts. Remember?"

Sammy blinked several times to clear the blurriness from his eyes. "Yeah. Check my pockets."

"I did. I think it fell out."

"Don't you have more?"

"Yes, but I like that one …"

Sammy dumped his dirty clothes basket onto the floor and started throwing socks, shirts, boxers, and other articles onto his bed one by one until he reached the end of the pile.

"I must have lost it. Sorry."

Jeffie gave him an exaggerated pout. "You have to help me find it. We'll retrace all your steps."

"I only went to the Pen—" Sammy paused. In his mind's eye he saw Vitoria staring at his shorts, not his crotch like he'd thought, but at his pocket, tackling him, pulling at him, kissing him. He cursed. "Vivi …"

16 | Volunteers

Monday, September 1, 2087

SAMMY DASHED DOWN to the tunnels. He had no idea if he was freaking out over nothing, but he prayed that Lemon would start up without any problems. Croz and Anna's session was supposed to have started five minutes ago. Normally a drive to the Pen took fifteen minutes. He made the drive in under ten, scolding himself every second of the way.

As he drove, Jeffie sat beside him trying to reach Anna and Croz, but neither answered their coms. Finally she reached the security office and had them patch a call through to the guard station outside the cell, but even they didn't answer. Sammy cursed and punched down on the accelerator. *Don't do anything stupid, Vitoria. Please don't do anything stupid.*

They pulled into the lot, and Sammy jumped out of his seat. As he ran up the steps he could hear a movie playing through the door to the Pen. The guards were always watching movies. Behind him, Jeffie vaulted the steps, but Sammy didn't wait. He banged open the door, ready to act.

The guards weren't in their chairs. Sammy sprinted down the hall to Vitoria's cell. One guard was running toward Sammy yelling into his com, the other was fumbling with her keys to unlock the cell. "Move!" Sammy roared.

The guard hurled himself out of the way as Sammy blasted the door twice before the door burst open. Vitoria lay on the bed, blood trickled from her mouth, her eyes closed. Croz was on his stomach in a pool of blood.

"Sammy …" a voice whispered from behind.

Sammy spun and saw Anna on the ground, Jeffie's barrette jutting out of her neck and between her trembling fingers where she tried to staunch the flow from her carotid artery. "She caught me off guard," she breathed. "So fast."

Sammy knelt next to Anna and held her up, his hands fumbling to staunch the flow from her wounds. He tried to think if there was a med pack nearby he could grab. Then he looked at Jeffie and said, "Check the guard desk for a kit."

As Jeffie ran back down the hall, Anna tried to whisper again, but he shushed her. "You'll be fine, Anna. We have a mission to go on, remember?"

"So now you want to go?" she chuckled, but it was a weak, hoarse thing. "I don't think I'm gonna last that long."

"We'll get you patched up. You'll be fine."

Anna shook her head very slightly. "I'm dead. You have to do it."

"I can't, Anna. I don't think I'm—"

"It has to be … you." She coughed weakly. "I'm your honcho … and I'm ordering you. Promise."

Sammy's face screwed up. "No."

"Promise," Anna growled and coughed up blood. "You are the one to do it. You were … born for it. Pick your teammate. Pick the best. You *can't* fail."

Sammy couldn't breathe, couldn't speak. She looked into his eyes. Blood spattered her pallid face, covered her hands and arms, but her eyes were still so full of spirit and command. He saw need there too. She depended on him. Her lips moved again, but her voice was so faint, so quiet, he had to lean to hear her. "Promise me …"

Sammy still couldn't speak, so Anna continued. "I am a servant of the people. On my own accord I declare my life is not … " Anna's voice trailed away. When Sammy looked into her eyes again, the life had left them. He placed his hand under her head and cradled it.

" … my own. I will give my mind, my strength, and my heart to the service of the government so long as the government serves the interest of the people. With justice as my strength, I will protect the freedoms and liberties to which my people have a right. My life is not my own. I am a servant of the people."

By the time he finished, Anna had breathed her last breath. Jeffie knelt next to him though he hadn't heard her enter. Sammy set her down and whispered in her ear, "I promise, Anna."

Kill Vitoria, a voice from inside commanded him. It was so powerful and urgent that Sammy got up to do just that. He stepped over Croz's body to Vitoria who lay sprawled across her bed. The left side of her face was now a purple, swollen mess, but her chest rose and fell shallowly.

One good blast will do it. Right to the neck.

The urge was strong enough to make his hands quake, but Sammy did not bow to it. Instead he carried Croz and Anna out of the room, closed the door, locked it, and pulled on it to make sure it would still hold. As he did so, several members of the resistance arrived, including Thomas and Lara.

Sammy stayed at the Pen for three hours helping to clean up. Footage from the security cameras made it very clear what had happened. Vitoria had waited until Anna was distracted, and thrown the barrette into her neck. Then she grabbed Croz and tried to force him to open the door. When he didn't, she stabbed him with three expertly placed paperclips that pierced his heart and aorta. Once she had a clear shot, Anna blasted Vitoria into the wall hard enough to knock her out cold. Less than a minute later, Sammy and Jeffie arrived at the Pen.

"I should have known she had the barrette," Sammy told Thomas and Lara. "I shouldn't have even had it on me."

"It was a mistake, Sammy," Lara said. "Croz shouldn't have taken the paperclips in either. We weren't vigilant enough."

"You didn't kill them," Thomas added. "She did."

"I should have known better," Sammy continued, "but my pride, the thrill of the idea that she wanted me ... I should have seen."

Dr. Rosmir was attending to Vitoria's wounds, when Justice arrived.

"Get off me!" the Tensai shouted at one of the guards. In his hand was a gun.

"What are you doing, Justice?" Lara asked.

Justice's glasses were askew, his face twisted in hate. "I'm putting the beast down. I said get off me!"

"You're going to murder her?" Sammy asked.

"Execution is not murder."

"We need her, Justice!" Lara argued.

"No. If Anna hadn't stopped her, she would have had free reign over the compound. She would have exposed us. She's too wild!"

Thomas rushed Justice and shoved him against the wall. "Put that gun down!"

"She's dead." A tear ran down Justice's reddened cheek. "I need to do this."

"She was dead anyway," Sammy said. "She was going to volunteer for the Rio mission. She wanted to die."

Justice pointed the gun at Sammy's face. "Shut up."

"It's true."

Justice's face scrunched up and more tears fell. Thomas grabbed the gun from him and pulled him into a hug. "It'll be okay, son. It'll all be okay."

Justice moaned and sank to the floor.

"We need to hold a special meeting tomorrow," Sammy told Lara. "Everyone invited—the leaders, all the Psions, the Tensais, the Ultras, and the Elite. It's time to move our plan forward, focus the resistance, and tell everyone why Vitoria is here. I'm afraid someone might do something rash if we don't. And if it's all right with you and Thomas, I'd like to lead the meeting."

Lara nodded numbly, her eyes on Justice. Sammy found Jeffie and took her home. He did not sleep that night. It wasn't for lack of trying. In the wee hours of the morning, he rose and jogged through the underground tunnels, hoping to clear his mind, to embrace the death he knew was coming. He wondered who would volunteer to walk with him into the dark valley. Part of him wanted no one to step forward. Another part wanted two others to volunteer and relieve him of his duty. But he'd made a promise and knew he would keep it.

Thomas, Lara, Commander Byron, and Justice met Sammy in the meeting room an hour before it was scheduled to start. Justice looked like he had gotten no more sleep than Sammy. His eyes were dark red and swollen, his clothes and glasses still askew. He glanced at Sammy as he sipped on a mug of coffee. "I'm sorry for the gun, man. I—I never would have—"

"I'm sorry too," Sammy told Justice. "I know you—"

"Yeah," Justice said in a subdued voice. "You were right, though. She wanted it this way, though. Wanted to go out in a blaze. That's why we never … Anyway, she's happier now."

Sammy took a sip from his own mug. "Yes, she is." The weariness went deep in his bones.

Justice touched Sammy on the arm. "Hey, you don't have to be the one. She wanted you to do it, yes, but you don't *have* to."

"I do." Sammy said it so matter-of-factly that Justice took a step back.

"Why?"

"Because I keep my oaths."

An hour later over a hundred people filled the meeting hall. Sammy had been to many leadership meetings for the resistance, the first one being in Wichita, when the resistance members had given him a standing ovation. He received no such praise now. He was no longer the scared kid he'd been. In fact, he felt no fear and that worried him.

Jeffie gave him a sad smile when she entered and took her seat with Brickert, Natalia, and the other Psions. Word had spread among the resistance about what had happened the previous morning, and the somber mood reflected that. Thomas opened the meeting with a prayer and a short speech, explaining in full what happened to Anna and Croz, and reminding everyone of the risk that the resistance's work entailed. Then he turned the time over to Sammy.

"The purpose of today's meeting," Sammy began, "is a call for volunteers. Thanks to the data recovered earlier this year and the hard work of the men and women who've analyzed it, the leadership committee has prepared a plan of action that has a chance to end the war. The move is bold and complex, and will require weeks of further planning and preparation despite what we've already accomplished.

"After planning this mission in subcommittees for the last few weeks, we feel it is time to make a call for volunteers to enlist. Our planned day to strike is November 11. Seventy days. Each one matters. Each one could mean the difference between success and freedom or failure and its consequences. The NWG will join us in our efforts led by Commander Havelbert and Ivan Drovovic.

"The offensive will be executed in four stages. Stage one will take place six days before the main strike. A team of resistance members will commandeer a major news station and broadcast an invitation for CAG citizens to take up arms against the government in Washington D.C."

Sammy paused, remembering the extensive debates they'd had in committees over the ethics and hypocrisy of hijacking a news station to broadcast a message about terrorism. In the end, the committee had ruled in favor of carrying out the mission so long as no deaths occurred in the process.

"Extra care will be taken," Sammy continued, "to ensure that there are no casualties in this stage of the plan. It will severely undermine our efforts if lives are taken while we take the station. During the broadcast, evidence will be presented that the CAG authorized and coordinated acts of terrorism on its own soil in order to implement greater restrictions over travel and communication.

"Stages two through four will all take place on the same day. Stage two will be comprised of a joint strike on D.C., land and air. The attack on the capital will be real, and hopefully massive, but its primary purpose will be to serve as a decoy while other teams execute clandestine operations on specific sites. Successes in all three stages are key to victory.

"Stage three will take place in the territory of Brazil, including a covert op in Rio and an air defense team in the jungle protecting the Hive from a potential CAG aerial strike. Stage four will also be a covert op in Orlando with a select team of operatives."

Sammy paused, trying to decide if he should say the words he had prepared. After a deep breath, he continued. "It goes without saying that these assignments carry with them great risk. Lives will be lost. Families will be separated. I can find no example in history where tyranny has been overthrown and freedom won without the shedding of blood. It will be no different in November.

"We need volunteers, men and women; anyone sixteen and older who will follow commands and be brave in the face of death and bloodshed. We need people who can shoot, who can fly, who have medical training, but most of all, who love liberty. Stage three, at the Hive, will need a team of skilled pilots in the air. Who will lead this team?"

One hand went up immediately. Its owner did not surprise Sammy. It was Kallen Dinsmore. Sammy had served in Charlie Squadron with him. Kallen had saved his life.

"Kallen Dinsmore has volunteered. Will anyone second this?"

"I second it," said Ludwig.

"His proposal is accepted," Sammy announced. "Who will volunteer to go with him?"

Many hands went up, most of them Elite or older Psions, including Al. Notes were taken of the men and women who raised their hands so Dinsmore could choose from among them.

When this was finished, Sammy continued. "Now we need someone to lead the operation against the broadcast station. Who will lead this team?"

Someone cleared a throat behind Sammy. Thomas Byron had his hand raised. Lara hissed at him, "Put your hand down. You're too old."

Thomas responded by standing, his arm still high in the air. "Then I'll ride a horse like Washington, but I'm doing this!" he said obstinately.

No one opposed Thomas. In fact, dozens offered to go with him, the vast majority from the non-Anomaly members of the resistance. Once the matter was settled, Sammy moved on to the next stage. "The strike on the capital will be a vast undertaking. Strategy will be handled by the leadership committee and Commander Byron, our liaison with the NWG military forces, but we still need leadership on the field of battle and in the air. Who will volunteer to command our forces in D.C.?"

Justice Juraschek raised a hand, his face solemn and resolute. Sammy was glad to see him take the responsibility. It was quickly seconded.

"Anyone who wants to join the strike on the capitol will be welcome no matter their training or abilities. Volunteers should enlist with Justice and those he chooses to lead the companies. Now for the last missions … both require two people trained in covert ops to infiltrate the N Towers in Orlando and Rio. There is zero room for failure, therefore we are asking for two Psions. Who will volunteer to lead the team to Orlando?"

Three Psions raised their hands: Ludwig, Li, and Commander Byron. Sammy's chest swelled with pride, and chose among the three. "Commander Byron has volunteered. Will anyone second him?"

At first no one did. And Sammy knew why. Byron could no longer blast from his feet. In that regard, he was only half a Psion.

-282-

"I will second him," Kawai announced. "If anyone will ensure the job gets done, it's the commander."

"Who will volunteer to go with him?"

This time all the Psions offered themselves. Sammy allowed the commander to choose. Byron surveyed them for a full minute before stating, "I choose my son, Albert."

Across the hall, Marie let out a sob and headed toward the door. However, judging by his face, the commander seemed firm in his decision. Now it was time to find the last volunteer.

"The infiltration of the Rio N Tower will be led by myself, which leaves two other spots, one of which is already taken out of necessity by Vitoria Prado. Before I ask for a volunteer for the final spot, I need to say two things: first, only a Psion can go. Second … the nature of the mission is such that—that there will be no returning."

Sammy stared at the floor. He didn't want to look at his friends or Commander Byron. He didn't want them to think he was being brave because he wasn't. Nor was he noble. He was only keeping a promise. And he was tired of it all. No more dead Kadens and Kobes and Toads and Annas and Dr. Vogts and Hefanis and all the others. No more fighting an anomaly he didn't want. No more losing control.

He looked up to see who might have raised a hand—who might have volunteered for death. Brickert, foolhardy as he was, might have. Or Jeffie or Kawai. His friends were brave. Maybe one of them.

But he was wrong.

Every Psion in the room stood. Every Psion raised a hand. Though he had already volunteered to go to Orlando, Commander Byron stood tallest among them to show his support. He was on his feet, wearing an expression of pride, his blue eyes beaming. Al stood too. Walking back from the doors she'd just exited, one arm supporting her baby girl, the other reaching for the ceiling, was Marie. Near her were Rosa and Miguel. Not far were Li and Ludwig. Then Sammy came to his four friends: Kawai Nujola, Natalia Ivanovich, Brickert Plack, and Jeffie Tvedt.

Tears rolled down Jeffie's cheeks as she held her arm high in the air. Sammy remembered their conversation from months ago, before the trek to the Hive. He had quoted to her a verse from the Book of Ruth. *Where thou diest, will I die.*

Is this what she thinks that means? Sammy would not look at her, would not choose her. To choose her was to kill her. But could he do that to Brickert? Or Kawai or Natalia? A gnawing deep in his guts told him he couldn't. He couldn't pick anyone.

Two Psions. The mission requires two.

Another voice spoke to him. *Who do you want to see die, Sammy? Who gets under your skin the most? Maybe Ludwig? Would seeing him die along side you give you some sense of satisfaction?*

Sammy turned the thought into a leaf and shoved it away, berating himself for thinking such a thing. "With so many volunteers, the decision will have to wait until another time. Thank you all for your participation and willingness to serve."

The meeting adjourned, and Sammy watched his friends make their way to the front to speak with him. For a split second, he considered bolting through the back door and blasting down the stairs, but he didn't want to be alone.

Kawai reached him first. "We're going down to the river. You want to come?"

That was not what Sammy had expected to hear, and he was glad. A few minutes later, he and his friends crammed into Lemon and drove through the tunnels lit only by dim strips down its center to separate traffic. Exits had been built into the passageways every three kilometers, ensuring that no one had to walk extreme distances underground in the event of car troubles. He parked the car in the tunnel and they came up near the banks of the Milk River.

No one spoke about the meeting. Instead the conversation revolved around the weather, how summer was rapidly coming to an end in Glasgow, about how this might be one of the last warm days of the year. Determined to enjoy it, they kicked off their shoes and lay on the muddy bank, feet dangling in the cool water. The river wasn't large or deep, and the soft sounds of its sleepy flow soothed Sammy. He wished he could turn off his brain for a few minutes, but all it wanted to do was solve problems. The problem at this moment: which Psion should go with him? Specifically, which person gave him the greatest probability of accomplishing the mission?

Al: highly skilled in combat; mission competent; struggles with staying focused. May also find it difficult to take orders from me. Currently experiencing marital problems and a newborn child. Estimated chance of success: 69%

Though Sammy didn't want to consider Al, his brain still calculated the odds. Al was Commander Byron's only son, and the commander wanted him for the mission to Orlando. Sammy dismissed the thought.

Kawai made a comment to Li about how good the mud felt when she squished it between her toes. Li responded with something about piranhas. Sammy glanced at them. They had been a couple now for months. Both seemed happy.

Kawai: skilled in combat; completed the two-Thirteen sim at Beta headquarters on most difficult level; more mature than most other Psions; showed competence and poise during mission to the Hive; willing to take orders; shows creativity under fire. Estimated chance of success: 77%.

The clouds rolled overhead, an overcast late-summer day, beautiful and balmy. Natalia and Brickert commented on the shapes of some of them, making each other laugh. Sammy joined in watching them blow by. Clouds were transient things, just like people. *We're here and then we're gone.*

Natalia: adequately skilled in combat; showed toughness and maturity during mission to Colorado Springs; seems to perform better around Brickert; follows orders but lacks ability to think on her feet. Recently wounded but on the mend. Should be fully healed by November. Estimated chance of success: 64%.

Brickert chuckled at something Jeffie said, then started to make squelching sounds in the mud by sticking his toes in deep and yanking them out. "Doing this … I almost feel like a normal human being."

"What's normal?" Sammy asked. But as he looked at his friend, the wheels continued to spin. *Brickert: competent in combat; demonstrated extreme toughness and quick thinking during mission to Colorado Springs; shows that he learns from mistakes; follows orders and displays high willingness to excel. Estimated chance of success: 79%.*

Brickert screwed up his face. "I dunno. I think I forgot somewhere between living with other superheroes and getting my face bashed in by sociopaths."

Sammy shook his head. He couldn't ask Brickert. He didn't want to do that to his best friend. Natalia would crumble. He ran through all the names again. Then again. All with their own pros and cons.

Eventually the girls and Li walked down the riverbed, leaving Sammy and Brickert alone. No sooner had they disappeared from sight than Brickert turned to Sammy and said, "I want to go with you."

"No."

"I knew you were going to say that. But listen, we're brothers. There is no way in heaven or hell that I will let you die unless I'm there, I'll tell you. I've accepted death. I did it the day the tower came down in Detroit. I should have been one of the hundreds who bit it then. I'm on borrowed time. Maybe it's for this."

"Are you saying that fate kept you alive so you could die with me in Rio?"

Brickert looked at Sammy. "Maybe."

"Are you becoming religious, Brick?"

"What?" Brickert snickered and sat up. "Like you?"

"I'm not … well, I don't know what I am. I guess I'll find out soon enough, right? The clock is ticking."

"Sammy, please. Please let me do this."

"No."

"It has to be someone!"

"Not you." Sammy said it more firmly each time.

"Why not? Aren't I good enough? Let me make it easy on you. This way you don't have to choose."

"Not you." Sammy dug his hands into the muck, pushing back a sudden surge of rage. "You are not on borrowed time!"

"What do you mean?"

"I mean it's my fault you almost died." Sammy could no longer look at his best friend. "I—I beat the hell out of you after I killed all the Thirteens. I almost killed you myself." His voice broke when he uttered the last words. "I lost control and hit you and hit you until you ... I—I'm so sorry, man."

Covering his face with muddy hands, Sammy fought back tears. Brickert nodded solemnly, his expression unreadable. "I had dreams about that, you know, while I was out. I thought they were nightmares."

"Brick ... I *am* a nightmare."

"I'm sorry, Sammy."

"What are you sorry for?"

"Bearing that burden must've been ... I—I can't even imagine. But look at me. I'm fine."

Sammy put a dirty paw on Brickert's shoulder and pulled his friend into a tight hug. "And you forgive me just like that?"

"Yeah, well, I would have, but now you've gone and ruined my shirt."

A laugh burst out of Sammy. But the laughter broke something inside him and he nearly started to sob. Again he stopped himself. He couldn't cry. Wouldn't. "I don't want to die, Brick."

"I know. You don't have to."

"I do."

"Someone else can do it instead."

Sammy shook his head. "I swore an oath."

"We all swore the same words. The duty rests upon every Psion." Brickert sighed. It carried the weariness of an old man. "So now what?"

"Somehow I have to choose."

"What if we all go with you? All five recruits together."

"That's … overkill … for lack of a better word."

Brickert slapped the mud. "None of us wants to die, and none of us wants to watch you go. You have to do it strategically."

"What does that mean?"

"Who do you think is the best person to take?"

"What do you think's been running through my brain for the last hour? Calculations. Numbers. Data. Projections. All that crap. It's all here." He tapped his temple and got mud in his hair.

"And what does it tell you?"

Ludwig 51%. Rosa 59%. Miguel 69%. Strawberry 54%. Li 81%. Jeffie … "It tells me I need someone who complements my weaknesses, obeys orders unquestioningly, and—and motivates me to use my maximum potential."

Judging by Brickert's face, he knew the answer as well as Sammy.

"But I can't ask her."

"That's your call."

Sammy let out a long breath and sat up, his spine straight. "I am going to do this. It's my choice, so I'm done worrying about it. Jeffie can make her own decisions. If she wants to go then who am I to tell her she can't?"

Gone. *Gone*. *GONE!*

It still did not seem possible that a man with stubs for arms and legs could escape the penthouse. She had torn apart the suite and not found a trace. Despite spending countless hours searching, the Queen was no closer to learning the whereabouts of the fox nor discovering how he had managed to engineer his own disappearance. The notion that he'd grown new appendages and simply walked out was as likely as every other theory. All she had learned for certain was that for over four hours' worth of time the cameras, alarms, and security systems had stopped working.

I had him beaten. Now he is out there gathering strength. What will his next move be? Her retention and consolidation of power depended on guessing correctly. In her mind was a list of names of people she had compiled who were likely to aid the fox. He had no family and few friends; the list wasn't very long. Most of the candidates were from his time at the Elite Training Center. Over the last several days she had observed each of them closely, investigated them, and crossed names off the list one at a time.

Her com rang. It was one of the Tensais working in the N Corp's data analysis department, one of many departments the fox had created to balance the agendas of the Council without government oversight. Using bloated grants and earmarks rather than private funds, he had virtually unlimited resources to move the work forward under a corporate umbrella, answering only to his peers on the Council who helped pull the public opinion and government strings like a puppet master hidden in the shadows.

Before answering, she turned on her voice synthesizer so she would sound like the fox. "Yes?"

"Per your request, we have compiled a new list of sites that are candidates for hosting a large underground movement of rebels. I'm sending it to you now."

A hologram popped up from the Queen's com with a list of five sites. "What makes this list better than the last? All eight sites on your previous list were incorrect. If I find that these ones are a waste of my time as well, you may find yourself looking for a job at a university teaching math."

The Queen ended the call and scanned the names on the list.

```
K.I. Sawyer, Great Lakes Territory
Rome, Territory of Quebec
Blytheville, Southeastern American Territory
Window Rock, Territory of Mexico
Glasgow, Mid-Western American Territory
```

Most of the new proposals were former military bases, closed for decades and turned into smaller communities. All of them had nearby airports and hangars. Three of them—Blytheville, K.I. Sawyer, and Glasgow—had satellite confirmation of people in or around the areas. Investigating the sites would require teams to fly to each location and spend days observing, searching for patterns, and evaluating data.

"The Hive," she told her com. A moment later Chad's image appeared on her holo-screen. Chad was an Aegis flunky who had nearly been killed after failing training, but the Queen had swooped in and saved his life due to his abnormally high ranking on the loyalty scores. She had used her charms to turn him into her own little puppet, her own personal Diego. And as a bonus, his face bore no hideous scars like the old Diego.

"Queen," he said with a hint of breathlessness. "How can I serve?"

"I need five teams to investigate five locations for possible resistance headquarters. How soon can you get me them?"

"How soon do you want them?"

"How soon can you get them?" she repeated.

"Got it."

"Thank you, Chad," she said, smirking.

"You're welcome. Do you ... still plan to stop by this weekend?"

"I think I will have time." She ended the call with a sour taste in her mouth. With one last glance at the list of sites under investigation, she tapped her com and it went away. She missed the days when she was the one out searching and hunting down people. She had been good at that. Now she ran everything. She gave the orders. Perhaps it was for the best, but she wasn't sure.

This had better not be another waste of time.

17 | Trust

Monday, October 13, 2087

JEFFIE AND SAMMY sat outside the Pen, a bag of supplies at Sammy's feet. They sat in silence, something more common since they'd volunteered for the mission to Rio. Jeffie's hand rested on his, but it was cold like the tunnel where they sat. Sammy had learned to appreciate the quiet moments. Most of his days were now spent in training, poring over blueprints and schematics of the Rio de Janeiro N Tower, devising their plot to break in undetected so the kill order could be activated. He didn't want to think about how he was essentially planning his and Jeffie's deaths.

Both were dressed in combat suits, having come straight from another session of fighting holo-cameras recording them from every angle. To prepare for the mission, Thomas and his crew had built a replica of the white floor in Rio, where Jeffie and Sammy sparred with Nikotai, Li, Albert, and a few other Ultras and Psions. Sammy and Jeffie did this for at least an hour every day. But once work was over, they didn't think about it. They didn't talk about it. And no one else mentioned it either. Sammy found it eerie how well everyone skirted the subject. But he preferred it that way.

"You sure you want me to come in with you?" Jeffie finally asked.

"Vivi has to get used to being around you. I don't want to put it off. Just be your normal … charming self."

"I've been told by *certain people* that I'm not charming. I'm energetic."

"Actually, I think the term was 'high strung.'"

Jeffie aimed a half-hearted elbow to Sammy's side, which he dodged. "Will you please just tell me what's in that stupid—"

Sammy scooted the bag closer to him using his foot. "Nope. Secret."

"All right, then." Jeffie stood and stretched. "Let's do this."

Today, rather than reading, Vitoria was exercising. By the sheen of sweat covering her skin and matting her hair, Sammy guessed she'd been at it a while.

"One-seventy-five," she said through clenched teeth as she pulled herself into a tight crunch. "One-seventy-six."

Her stomach, and all her other muscles, were taut and strong. Her hair was a mess, and her eyes blazed a manic fire. "One-seventy-seven."

Despite knowing that Jeffie and Sammy were in the room, she did not stop until she reached two hundred. "What's up, Sammy?"

she asked as she transitioned into a new workout of lunges and twists.

"Can we talk?" he asked.

Vitoria glanced at Jeffie. "Sure. Talk."

"Right," Jeffie said. "Should we pull up a yoga mat?"

Sammy cleared his throat pointedly at her. Then he turned back to Vitoria. "We were thinking more like a chat."

"Not in the mood," Vitoria grunted.

Nor had she been for days. Sammy visited Vivi in the Pen regularly, mostly just sitting with her. After the funerals of Anna and Croz, Sammy had gone to see her. He found her huddled under her blankets stained from snot and tears. It had taken those deaths, he realized, for her to understand that she was free from the S.H.I.E.L.D. program. That she wasn't being tested. For two days she wouldn't eat or drink. Sammy begged her to stop fasting, but nothing he said helped. It wasn't until he convinced Justice Juraschek to come as well that things finally turned.

Justice knelt by the bed, took Vitoria by the hand, and forgave her through his own tears. He pleaded with Vitoria not to kill herself—that if she did so, Anna's work would mean nothing. "Please don't dishonor her memory," Justice told her. "She wanted you to get better, not die."

Finally Vitoria began to take food and drink. Sammy visited almost daily. Occasionally she spoke, always a request for Sammy to talk about Toad. Even after Sammy had exhausted his brain of every memory he had, she asked him to repeat them. Sammy gladly obliged. During the last few weeks her demeanor changed. She no longer dressed or acted provocatively. She slowly stopped glaring at him with wary eyes. And she occasionally even smiled at him.

But Vitoria wasn't smiling now. Her eyes flickered to Jeffie as her scowl deepened. "I brought Jeffie so you could get to know her," Sammy explained. "She'll be accompanying us on the mission."

"You keep mentioning the mission, but you never say what it is." Vitoria raised an eyebrow. "What if I don't want to go?"

Sammy shrugged. "We're pinning our hopes on you not saying that."

"Why me? I killed three of your people." Just like that, the light was gone from Vitoria's eyes, and she was the broken, lonely girl again. "Now you want to give me the combination to the bank vault?"

Sammy shrugged. "That's the situation, Vivi. You've got four weeks to show us we can trust you. If we can't, you're going anyway, but you'll be cuffed, sedated, and a huge drain on our time and resources."

"But you still won't tell me what this mission is," Vivi said as she got back down on the floor to continue exercising.

"In time we will," Jeffie said. "Today I was wondering if I could ask you a few questions to get to know you better."

Vitoria resumed her lunges back and forth across the room. "You can ask."

"What kind of movies do you like?"

"Is this supposed to make us trust each other?"

Jeffie gave Sammy a helpless look. "No. Depending on what movies you watch, I may trust you even less."

The joke caught Vitoria off-guard. Sammy seized on the opportunity. "Toad said you liked pony movies. What does that mean?"

Jeffie chuckled, but quickly covered her nose. "Pony Town? Did you watch that? I loved that show!"

Sammy made a face of disgust. "What?" he asked Jeffie. "You watched a show about *ponies*?"

"Yes! When I was seven and eight, I never missed it."

"Well that's one thing *we* don't have in common."

"Tell me you're joking. You've really never heard of Pony Town?"

"Did you like that show too?" Sammy asked Vitoria.

Vitoria shrugged.

"Every girl in school loved it." Jeffie snapped her fingers and started to sing. She did not have the greatest singing voice, though she wasn't terrible. "*Come on down to ... Pony Town! No one frowns in ... Pony Town!*"

"*We'll have some fun, you'll meet someone,*" Vitoria jumped in.

Then the girls finished together, "*If you come to ... Pony Town!*"

"There's two more verses," Jeffie said, grinning widely. "Do you want to hear them?"

Sammy cleared his throat. "No, thanks. I get the gist of it."

Jeffie turned back to Vitoria. "So what kind of music do you listen to?"

"Tope de mesa," Vitoria answered.

"What's that?"

Vitoria rolled her eyes and stopped her lunges. "In the north they call it tabletop music, but it started in Rio as *tope de mesa.*

Because the beat …" She swayed and gyrated her hips rapidly and provocatively with her arms raised above her head. "It's made for dancing on top of tables."

Jeffie raised an eyebrow at Sammy. "I guess I'll have to look into that."

"My mom used to take me—" Vitoria paled and stopped speaking, her body no longer swaying, her gaze stuck on the carpet. A fat tear rolled down one cheek, but she smacked it off her face with a hard *SLAP*.

Jeffie put a hand on her shoulder.

"It's okay," Sammy said in his gentlest tone. "You can tell us. What do you remember about your mom?"

Vitoria shrugged Jeffie's hand off of her. "What do you remember about *your* parents?" she asked, now using a tough, sullen voice. "Them hugging and kissing you goodbye before sending you off to Psion school?"

"That was my parents," Jeffie said. "Or at least, I wish it'd been. My mom said goodbye to me three weeks before I left because she had a film to shoot. My dad didn't hug me, he gave me a fist bump when he dropped me off at the air rail hub. Told me to stay awesome. Pretty cool, huh?"

"I wasn't asking you," Vitoria sneered.

"My parents …" Sammy said, a lump in his throat, "the last time I saw them they were being wheeled away in body bags."

"Thirteens?" Vitoria asked.

"No."

"Who did it then?"

Sammy shrugged. "I don't know. I don't think about it much anymore."

The haunted, vacant look returned to Vitoria's eyes. "I don't see the point in this. You two should go."

"Vivi …" Sammy sighed, "We just want to get to know you."

"I genuinely want to be your friend," Jeffie said.

Vitoria snorted. "And I genuinely want chlamydia."

"Vivi …" Sammy repeated.

"Give it a rest, Sammy. No one wants to be my friend. You've all seen what I'm capable of."

"We're all capable of horrible things."

"But you haven't done them." Tears welled up in Vitoria's eyes, but she covered her face before they fell.

"I have," Sammy admitted.

"So have I," Jeffie said. "But I haven't been brainwashed. I don't have an excuse for my actions."

Vitoria let out a mirthless, hollow laugh. "Brainwashed. If you believe I was brainwashed, then how can you trust me? I'm a bomb. A bomb that you never know when it's going to blow."

"I'm willing to give you a second chance," Sammy said. "If you can prove that you're worthy of it."

"Should I sign my name in blood?" A faint smile appeared on Vitoria's lips.

Sammy delved into his bag and removed a rope. "Jeffie, tie me to the chair. Tie me well enough that I can't get out."

Jeffie took the items hesitantly. "Okay."

It took her about five minutes to tie him. The ropes bit into his wrists and ankles. Vitoria watched them skeptically.

"You can leave now, Jeffie," he said.

"No. I'm not leaving you like this."

Sammy looked at her. "Please. Trust me."

Jeffie's eyes flashed and he thought she was going to refuse. "Why is it always your way?" He heard the hurt in her voice and wondered if he should have told her his plan after all.

"Trouble in paradise," Vitoria muttered.

Jeffie shot Vitoria a glare. "I'm standing right outside the door."

"It'll be locked."

Jeffie swore at him. "Why—"

"Can we discuss it later?"

Without another word, Jeffie left, shutting the door harder than needed. Vitoria gave a low whistle. "You sure know how to charm the ladies, Sammy. So now what? You and I explore the wonders of bondage together?"

"Take out the last item, please, Vivi."

Smirking sultrily, Vitoria reached into the bag. "Let me guess, it's a giant …" She removed the item, frowning at it. "Knife. Good grief, you couldn't find a bigger one?"

"It's called a bowie knife."

"I know what it's called. My question is *why?*"

"You're a smart girl, Vivi. You figure it out."

Vitoria handled the weapon thoughtfully, hefting it and examining its edge. "Sharp." She ran a finger along the blade and drew blood. "Very."

Before Sammy could even react, she dashed at him and pressed the blade against his throat. Sammy didn't flinch, didn't blink. "I trust you. There's nothing to stop you from killing me except yourself."

Vitoria bared her teeth, her eyes blazed. "You think I won't?"

Sammy kept his face neutral, but when he swallowed hard, he felt the blade sting his neck. "I hope you won't."

"I've killed before. What's to stop me now?"

"I'm your brother."

She gritted her teeth and grabbed his hair, yanking his head back and exposing his neck. It dawned on Sammy that he may have grossly miscalculated. "I had a brother. It wasn't you."

"I know. I wish all this crap had never happened to you. I wish you'd never had to meet me because it'd mean you have a normal life. But I can't do that, Vivi! I can't change the past. Neither can you. But we can change the now. That knife has two uses. It can either cut my throat, or cut my ropes. If you want to cut my throat, go ahead. But I think you'd rather use that knife to cut me free."

Vitoria raised the knife. He steeled himself for the end. *I am an idiot.*

"You're wrong, Sammy." She swung it down with all the speed and strength her Anomaly Fifteen gave her. Sammy heard a crack and fell to the floor, still bound to the chair which now had one less leg. When his head smacked the carpet, his vision blurred.

Vitoria knelt near his head, but he couldn't see her. All he saw was something falling in front of his face like snowflakes and a loud scratching noise. Then it dawned on him that Vitoria was carving the wood.

"What are you making, Vivi?"

She didn't answer, and the shavings continued to float down, some landing on his nose and cheek. They tickled his skin and nearly drove him mad.

"Can you at least sit me back up?" His voice sounded odd because the floor mashed his lips together.

Vitoria jerked him up and put something on his lap. A flower, carved from the wood. Despite its simple design and rough edges, it was lovely. As Sammy stared at it, Vitoria walked behind him and sliced through the ropes, freeing Sammy's wrists. He exhaled in relief.

"You look relieved. Did you trust me or not?"

Sammy rubbed his sore skin. "Trust, but verify." He picked up the flower and examined it. "It's beautiful. You did it so fast."

She touched the side of his head. "I had to know if you really trusted me. I thought when I raised the knife …"

"That I'd stop you? That I had a trick up my sleeve?"

Vitoria looked away. "I'm not sorry."

Sammy pulled the rest of the ropes off his arms and legs, then packed everything back in the bag, including the flower. "Why did you make that for me, Vivi?"

Vitoria looked Sammy square in the eyes. This time her gaze was neither hollow nor lustful, but something different. Something real. "Because I don't love you like a brother."

Sammy had no response.

"So what do you need me for?"

"How do you feel about a trip to Rio?"

* * * * *

Friday, May 30, 2053

Katie used every manipulative tool in her belt in order to get her parents to reverse their decision on attending prom. The one that finally worked was bringing home Bobby John so she could tutor him at the kitchen table. When her parents saw them interacting, and Bobby John's naturally sweet nature, they folded.

The more difficult part for Katie was not getting into more trouble. Her violent urges grew as the days passed. Every time she saw Mark, her ex-boyfriend, she wanted to kick him so hard in the balls that he coughed them up. She also wanted to continue her fight with Priyanka, but Priyanka avoided Katie like she would a nasty pimple outbreak.

Despite Katie's best efforts to control her behavior, little things kept happening that pushed her right to the brink of rage. When she and Courtney argued about restaurants a week before prom night, Katie punched the locker next to Courtney's head and dented it. She drove Rachel to tears by screaming at her for messing up prom decoration purchases. But after every incident, the guilt drove Katie to offer them sincere, tearful apologies.

With all their work with the decorations committee, coordinating the awards ceremony, and the music selection group, the night of the prom came quickly for Katie and her friends. That afternoon, Courtney, Vivian, and Rachel met at Katie's house for pictures. All four girls' dates were kids with special needs. Their mothers cried as they snapped their pictures. Even Katie's father got choked up as he kissed his daughter goodbye.

Two limousines arrived, paid for by the sixteen sets of parents. Four boys and four girls with special needs and their eight dates.

Bobby John's favorite food was steak, so dinner was at a steakhouse. With the help of his mother, Bobby John had bought Katie a corsage. However, he accidentally sat on it in the car on the way to Katie's house, so it was wilted and squashed when he put it on her wrist.

"Bobby John loves you," he exclaimed, tipping the Razorbacks cap that he had insisted on wearing to the dance.

Katie smiled, tears in her eyes. "Katie loves you, too."

Before she left her house, Katie slipped a bottle labeled SUPERLAX into her handbag. As soon as she did so, a faint aching crept into her gut, but she thought of Priyanka, of the pictures she had posted all over the walls of the school, and the pain went away.

Once inside the limo, Courtney leaned over to Katie. "Did you get it?"

Katie patted her handbag and smiled wickedly. Courtney nodded bravely. Then they turned their attention to their dates.

Vivian's beau for the evening, Reblon Mohammed, made everyone laugh. Due to his moderate autism, he behaved a little odd, but he was funny and sincere. Courtney's date, Axel Gardner, didn't say much and always kept one finger up his nose. It didn't matter what he was doing. One finger was always in his nose, the other was usually tightly entangled in Courtney's hand. Courtney smiled at this and even put a finger up her own nose when they did pictures. Axel laughed a deep, booming bark when she did this and put a finger up both nostrils. When Courtney copied him, Axel doubled over laughing. Tim Finlayson, Rachel's date, didn't like being touched or looked at. While riding in the limo, Rachel tried to talk to him and bring him out of his shell. He yelled at her for being too loud, so she crossed her arms and frowned the rest of the drive.

The steakhouse featured several small rooms, each decorated to portray different themes. All of them had a large window overlooking a pool where cliff divers jumped and performed aerial stunts to the view of the crowd. Because they had reserved their room later than most, Katie's group got the caveman theme. Bobby John clapped so hard and so long that Katie thought he might do permanent damage to his hands. In Axel's excitement, he jammed his finger so far up his nose that it started to bleed. Katie, however, struggled to enjoy herself. She kept seeing visions of her dreams—of dark wet caves, eternally long staircases, and a door that pulsed and throbbed with life.

The dream was a regular occurrence, and it never changed. Almost every night she descended the stairs, shivering in the darkness and clutching the knife. When she reached the bottom of the pitch-black cave, she stared blankly into space, weeping and whimpering as some vile, pulsing, stinking unseen thing sent its reverberating waves through her body. Yet as much as her dream terrified her, Katie wanted to know what lurked just out of sight down in the cave's depths. More often than not, she woke with tears on her face and her sheets wet with urine.

After the pre-prom meal, the limo transported them to the hotel where the dance was held. Each couple waited in line to be announced over the microphone. As her group neared the entrance, Katie noticed news cameras, which she thought strange. She had never seen a prom on the news before. But as her group of friends approached, the cameras stayed trained on them.

"Are you Katie Carpenter?" asked one of the reporters, a tall, thin woman wearing too much makeup. "Will you introduce us to your friends and tell us about the program you're involved in today?"

Katie stared at Rachel and Courtney who nodded encouragingly. Apparently being on the news seemed like exactly what they wanted. Courtney and Rachel beamed and batted their eyes, showing off Tim Finlayson and Axel Gardner like they were twin male models. The interview went on for almost twenty minutes during which time Bobby John wet his pants. Fortunately for him, no one caught it until the cameras were off, but none of the kids knew what to do

Taking him by the hand, Katie led him to one of the tables, sat him on a chair, and said, "Stay here, Bobby John. I'm trying to call your mom."

Katie tried three times to reach his mother, but no one answered. After the third attempt, Katie punched and kicked a wall so hard that she dented it. She shrieked and cursed until the rage burned out. *Why was I so stupid to think bringing Bobby John and his ilk to my prom was a good idea?*

When she returned to her friends with the news, Rachel protested, "He'll stink up the dance floor!"

Katie ignored her and turned to Bobby John. "I can't reach your mom, Bobby John. I'm sorry. Do you want to sit here?"

"Bobby John loves you, Katie," he said, grinning. "Bobby John is having the best night."

At that moment, all the rage in her heart vanished and she hugged Bobby John around his thick neck. Bobby John returned her hug with equal ferocity. "Do you want to dance, Bobby John?" she asked.

"Bobby John loves dancing!" He clapped his hands and stomped his feet. Seeing him so excited and joyful made Katie giggle.

Courtney strode up to the table somewhat breathless, two cups in her hands. She looked purposefully at Katie. "I got them. Give me the bottle."

Katie licked her lips and gazed across the room to where Priyanka was dancing in a circle of friends with Mark Newcomer, Katie's old boyfriend.

"Do you still have it?" Courtney asked when Katie didn't move.

Katie nodded, but the pain in her gut returned. The bottle in her bag held the most powerful laxatives on the market. Two drops were enough to make Priyanka soil herself in less than three minutes. And the urge would come so fast and so hard that she couldn't possibly reach the bathroom in time.

"If we're going to do it—"

Katie looked once more at Priyanka, then at Bobby John. "Forget about it, Courtney. Let's just have fun."

The evening passed in a storm of laughter and dancing. Bobby John drew quite a crowd once he really got moving. His dancing consisted of waving his arms in the air wildly and shaking his prodigious gut, but he laughed and sang along with each song. As it turned out, he knew the lyrics better than Katie and her friends put together.

Midway through the night, the deejay quieted the music as the time came to announce the prom court. Katie and her friends shot each other expressions of excitement and anxiety. The president of the student body took the stage and presented the awards.

First was the Class Clown, then the Prince. It was the Princess award that Katie was worried about. If she didn't win Princess, it meant she stood an even slimmer chance of winning Queen since Priyanka had been ahead of Katie at the last vote. "And the winner of Princess is …"

Katie took a deep breath and steeled herself for receiving the runner-up prize.

"Rachel Linn!"

Rachel shrieked. Everyone else gasped at the announcement, and Katie knew why. The vote was supposed to have been between Priyanka and Katie. Rachel taking second in the votes meant that either she or Pri had been a distant third.

The Prom King was announced: Priyanka's old boyfriend, Zach Morris. Katie groaned inwardly, knowing that her chances of winning were now slim.

"And now … the moment you've all been waiting for … the 2053 Papillion High School Prom Queen is …"

Katie's heart stopped beating for that moment. She wanted this. She wanted it more than anything. *Please. Please. Please.*

"Congratulations," the student body president shouted. "Katie Carpenter!"

Thunderous applause erupted around her. Even Bobby John jumped and shouted, "Bobby John loves you! Bobby John loves you! Bobby John loves you!"

As she made her way to the dais, girls mobbed Katie with hugs and teary compliments, pulling her arm and gown in all directions. Even Priyanka hugged her around the waist. A video montage of Katie started to play on a large screen in front of the crowd while she pressed through the throng of bodies. Her eyes were on the film playing above, most of it footage taken by various students and faculty at events or during down time at school. When she was halfway up to the dais, she heard murmurings from behind.

"Oh my—"

"Is she really—"

"*Slut.*"

Katie looked around. *What are they talking about?*

She looked up at the video screen, but it only showed her making goofy faces with Rachel and Vivian during a pep rally. It wasn't until she made it through the crowd to the steps that she noticed the cool air on her thighs, the lack of covering … *My gown.*

She wrenched her head around and tugged at her dress until she saw what had happened. Someone had cut a huge section out of it, exposing her entire backside. The giant video screen went live, her white panties flashing, contrasted by her tanned skin and dark dress. A large red spot like blood decorated her white underwear.

Her hands flew to cover herself, but her thin underwear left so much visible. Several more wolf whistles came from the crowd. Katie froze. Her stomach seized up and tears gathered in her eyes.

"Porn Queen!" one kid near the stage shouted.

"The Red Queen!" another yelled.

Laughter roared from her fellow students, those who had just voted her the queen of the prom.

Some chanted "Red Queen!" Others "Porn Queen!" For a brief instant, everyone around her transformed. They weren't dancing and laughing. They were bleeding, dead, mangled. Blood splattered the walls and the floor. Pools and rivers of it. Then she blinked and the image was gone.

She blinked again, and ran away.

18 | Speeches

Wednesday, November 5, 2087

"FIFTEEN MINUTES UNTIL the evening broadcast," Thomas reported.

Commander Byron and his team took the parking garage elevator up to the lobby of the forty-story Continental Broadcasting Network headquarters in downtown Los Angeles. They wore casual clothes over light body armor with non-lethal neural impulsers concealed in their holsters. Commander Byron smiled as he remembered how Sammy had called them jolts when he'd been picked up in Johannesburg.

Byron liked the men and women on his team. All experienced and battle-tested. All focused on the task at hand. It was a well-planned mission. His father, Thomas, would bring his own team from the north entrance, while Byron's group punched in from the south. Security would be quickly overwhelmed from both sides.

"Teams check in," Thomas announced over the com.

"Strand Team in position," Li said.

"Drake Team in position," Commander Byron said.

"Duck Team in position," Thomas said. "'Remember, remember, the fifth of November. The gunpowder treason and plot.'"

"'I know of no reason,'" Byron finished, "'why the gunpowder treason should ever be forgot.'"

The elevators opened and Byron led his team out. The CBN building was bustling with shoppers and tourists who wanted to be in the building during the primetime evening broadcast. Most of them shuffled around the first floor which boasted a company museum and overpriced food and gift shops. In order to reach the elevators for access to the upper floors one had to pass through the security gate, quarantined off by walls of bulletproof glass three meters tall in the middle of the indoor plaza.

Byron's team approached the south security checkpoints as though they were a group of tourists. From across the lobby, he saw his father's team doing the same. "Drake Team ready to move in."

"Standing by to intercept the signal," said Li from Strand Team.

All at once commotion erupted at the north side of lobby. "Get down! Get down!" voices from Thomas's team shouted. Every security guard on the south side closed their gates and ran to help out at the north end. Byron watched them, waiting.

"Now," he said.

The two Psions on Byron's team jumped the walls using mild blasts to help them, and fired their jolts at the backs of the security guards.

* * * * *

The sun's last rays cast waves of blood red and navy blue against thick white clouds. The Los Angeles weather, despite the overcast conditions, was pleasant, even for November. The wind whipped Brickert's hair as he stood in the open door of the stealth cruiser, Natalia next to him. They stared at the massive city, its skyscrapers stretching on for kilometers in both directions. Some of the buildings boggled Brickert's mind, standing twelve hundred meters high and as round as a small lake. With its buildings of bewildering size, downtown Los Angeles was said to be the pinnacle of human achievement.

Li and the rest of the Psions waited behind Brickert and Natalia. "Thomas's team is moving into position. Let's go in three ... two ... one."

One by one, Li's team dove out of the cruiser toward the roof of the CBN world headquarters. Between their flight suits and their blasts, everyone managed a safe landing. Li injected a tube of blue goo into the lock, waited for it to set, and shattered the lock. Once the door had been forced open, they made their way down a utility staircase until they reached the floor of the control rooms for the broadcast centers.

"Canisters in hand," Li ordered.

Each member of the team held a small gas canister smaller than a deck of cards.

Li gave the signal and simultaneously his team slid their gas canisters under the doors of the control rooms to release their contents. The gasses worked quickly, rendering the men and women in the rooms unconscious before anyone could sound an alarm or disable communication between the building, orbiting satellites, and outside transmission towers. "The guests are sleeping," Li reported to Thomas. "Headed to London now. Standing by to intercept the signal."

"London" was code for the broadcast studio. Li's team split three ways: two teams heading toward the east and west stairwells, while the third group remained, keeping the communications floor secure while hacking into the security channels.

Once Thomas and Commander Byron's teams engaged security on the ground floor, a silent alarm went out to alert local authorities. Li's team hacked and rerouted the signal while several of Thomas's men used com jammers to prevent any outgoing emergency calls from tourists and CBN employees. Pandemonium was breaking out in the lobby, but no one knew about it. When Brickert and Li reached the doors to the main studio, they paused and checked in with the rest of the team.

"At the gates of London," Li reported.

"Do it."

Li nodded to his team. "Now."

* * * * *

After securing the ground floor, Commander Byron and his father left most of their forces in the lobby to maintain order and assure no one left while the rest took the elevators up to meet Strand Team in the studio. By the time they arrived, Strand Team already had control of the floor. The news anchors, technicians, and cameramen had been escorted away to another room and locked inside while the resistance assumed operation of the studio equipment.

"Good work, Li," Commander Byron said, surveying the room. "I like the precision and command you showed."

Li grinned modestly. "I was trained well, sir."

"All right everyone," Thomas called out. "We have ten minutes to prep for the evening news. Just do what we practiced and everything will be fine."

"Are you ready, Pop?" Byron asked his father.

"I feel like I've been preparing for this my whole life."

"Are all systems secure?" Commander Byron asked over his com.

Strand Team confirmed that all systems were go for broadcast. Byron's father took his place behind the news desk, donning a white shirt, a tie, and a suit coat over his combat pants that were hidden behind the desk. With slightly trembling fingers, Thomas placed his tele-prompter contacts in his eyes. After straightening his thick gray-white hair, he gave a thumbs up to the commander, who returned the gesture. "Do I look like a man born to read the news, Walter?"

"Well, you look better than you normally do."

Thomas chuckled heartily. "Good enough."

"One minute to air time," one of the Elite said.

Commander Byron watched his father assume a serious expression as he cleared his throat and sipped water from a bottle. One of the female Elite working a camera counted down on her fingers to tell him only five seconds remained.

At one, Thomas turned to the camera and said, "Good evening. My name is Thomas Byron. I am a citizen of the Continental American Government, and lead a group known simply as *the resistance*. The aim of the resistance is to restore liberty and freedom to the CAG. I come before you with a warning that our government lied to its people regarding the multiple terrorist acts committed by the NWG. Not only that, but the CAG orchestrated and funded these acts against its own people in an effort to restrict our freedoms and liberties with the ultimate goal of achieving absolute control over our lives through an ambitious program called Project Orwell.

"And I have proof."

Now, accompanying his father's face on the screen, were images of evidence the resistance had collected over the years, pictures of purchasing documents, classified reports, and clips of video to entice the viewers to delve deeper.

"You may think I am crazy, dangerous, or perhaps some practical joker, but on the bottom of the screen you will see the addresses of websites you can visit which will show you incontrovertible evidence of our claims. Please take the time to read them, discuss them, and decide for yourself. All I ask is for your uninterrupted attention for the next few minutes while I reveal to you important facts—problems that our great nation faces—and present you with a solution.

"After reading the information provided, I hope you will reach the same conclusion I did: that we are no longer free.

"For the last two decades, our government has manipulated our people through fearmongering, terrorism, and isolation. It has made us think we need its ever-bloating power to survive. But mankind has survived long before governments were given power. We can feed and clothe ourselves. We can build homes over our own heads. We can take care of our own poor, hungry, and sick.

"A government is not a building, a man, or a gun. It is an idea to which we give power. Burn down that building, kill one man, dismantle a gun, and the government will continue if we let it. But once we collectively reject it and tear it down in our minds, we can start to build a new one. It has been done countless times in history.

"In six days we celebrate a holiday, November 11th, Armistice Day. The day tyranny was broken in Europe in 1918, almost one hundred seventy years ago. I invite you to join me on that day. We will march on the capitol in Washington D.C. and overthrow a government which has grown corrupt, insatiable, and blind. A power unrecognizable in character from what it was meant to be. I invite any member of our government who has seen our capital's black heart to speak out and join us.

"I cannot do this alone. You cannot do this alone. But we are not alone. We are many. Thousands, hundreds of thousands, and millions, can do this together. The government can ignore me, it can ignore you, but it cannot ignore us all. If we stand united, bleed united, die united, our freedom is assured. There was once a promise we believed in. That promise was life, liberty, and the pursuit of happiness. Our liberty is vanishing. Without it our happiness will perish. And without happiness, what is life?

"We must fight together, not only for ourselves, but for our children. For our children's children. And so on for generations until complacency sets in once more, and the world calls for a great and new generation to rise up and assume the mantle.

"Some of you may be thinking, 'Yes, that is a nice idea, but if we do not win I will be arrested or killed.' We do not fight because we know we will win. We fight because we know in our hearts we are right. And if we lose, we will die side by side if that is the price to be paid.

"Believe in an America restored. An America rebuilt. An America free. If you share my belief, my vision, and my hope, then join me on November 11. When the sun rises, so will we! This nation, God willing, will be renewed, reborn, restored to its roots: *of* the people, *by* the people, *for* the people, and will not perish from the earth."

* * * * *

"The counter-insurgency team arrived moments after the resistance escaped the CBN station in Los Angeles," the Queen, disguised as the fox, told the Council. She wanted to pluck their disapproving eyes out of their ugly heads.

"What do our analysts say?" one councilwoman asked. "Have the numbers shown what sort of effect we can expect?"

"I haven't sought out an analyst," the Queen answered.

Several Council members frowned. "That's unlike you," another man said. "You always run numbers in situations like this."

"I didn't feel it necessary. I think our chances of success are still quite high. In fact, I believe today was a boon more than a blow."

"Explain."

"A drone tagged the rebel atmo-cruiser, and we traced it back to their base in Glasgow. I've ordered the evacuation of our scouts who were already investigating the site as a possible location for the resistance's operation. As soon as they have vacated the area, we will destroy the rebels. Our victory is assured."

"What is the anticipated time of strike?"

"A matter of hours. We'll have full press coverage of the aftermath. It will be painfully clear that this resistance is quashed and the war is all but over."

* * * * *

A sense of elation permeated the resistance compound. Stage one of the plan, the mission to Los Angeles, had been a success. No casualties were suffered, civilian or resistance, and the website listed during the broadcast now reported huge traffic and downloads. Right now, it felt like winning was inevitable.

Yet there was no time for celebrations or parties; perhaps those things would come later. Brickert didn't know how people celebrated winning a war, but a huge party—or at least a huge hamburger—seemed as good an idea as any.

Ten kilometers out of Saint Marie, he and Natalia lay on the grass wrapped in thick blankets. Li and Kawai were with them. They passed Li's binocoscope around to view the moon, stars, and constellations.

"Where are Sammy and Jeffie?" Li asked.

"They didn't feel like coming," Brickert answered. "We left them back at the airport tower. I had to beg Sammy to let us borrow Lemon."

"They never want to do anything anymore," Natalia added.

"Go easy on them," Kawai said. "Can you imagine what they're going through?"

"I can't," Brickert said.

"But why do they want to be alone all the time?" Natalia wondered.

"I think being around other people," Kawai suggested, "reminds them of … what's coming. I don't even want to try to wrap my head around what it's like, preparing for a mission you know is going to kill you."

"It's not right," Natalia said. "Someone else should have to do it. Someone older."

"Who?" Kawai asked.

Natalia frowned. "Jeffie's sixteen. So is Sammy."

"All we've known is training and now war," Li said. "This is no way to live. Certainly no way to die."

Kawai pulled away from Li, who had his arm around her shoulders. "Didn't you listen to Thomas's speech? It *is* a way to die. And a way to live. It's something noble. It's—it's … *something*. People live and die doing nothing, they look back and wonder what meaning their lives had. If I have a chance to make a difference, I'll die for that. When we swore our oaths, I didn't think hard enough about the meaning. But it's been almost three years since. The words have had time to sink in deep. With Sammy … I think they sunk in right away. He was ready for this from day one. What else did he have at that time? His mind—he grasped it. All of it. And he accepted it."

"And Jeffie?" Brickert asked Kawai.

"Sammy's closer to her than her family has ever been. She doesn't want to live without him."

"That's horrible," Li said.

"It's romantic," Natalia countered.

Brickert could see Li wanted to disagree but chose not to pursue it. Not wanting to dwell on his best friend's death, Brickert turned his attention back to the night sky. Through the binocoscope he saw a tiny flash of orange, perhaps a shooting star. He tried to zoom in, but it moved too fast. When he finally caught it, he realized it was no meteor. His fingertips went numb and he dropped the binocoscope.

"You know what I—" Li started to say until he saw Brickert's face, ashen white and frozen.

"A missile. Headed this way."

"You're not serious," Kawai said, but Brickert was already running back to the tunnel entrance as coms were not allowed to be worn outside the safety of the compound. His friends sprinted after him. Diving down the steps, he reached the car, ripped the door open, and ordered his com to call the resistance switchboard.

"Incoming missile!" Brickert ordered. "Code red-three-red-three. Order an immediate evacuation!"

"Who is this?" the switchboard operator asked.

"DOES IT MATTER? EVACUATE NOW!"

Even though they were too far away to hear them, Brickert knew that sirens filled the compound. Ever since the bio-bomb had struck Wichita, the resistance had practiced evacuation once or twice every three months. *Is that what the missile is?* Brickert wondered. *A biobomb?*

His friends reached the car seconds after he did. Brickert started Lemon up on the first try and flipped it around.

"Where are you going?" Li asked.

"Sammy and Jeffie are back at the tower. They don't have a car."

"Step on it!" Li urged.

They tore through the tunnel, heading back toward Saint Marie. "Can't you go any faster?" Kawai yelled.

Brickert ignored them, gritting his teeth as he smashed the accelerator to the floor. The car's headlights shined bright in the tunnel, bouncing off the glossy walls. Brickert kept his eyes trained for the pull-off. About a kilometer away from the tower where they'd left Sammy and Jeffie, Brickert saw two dark shapes running toward the car. He jerked at the wheel and braked at the same time, but the force caused the bumper to clip the wall, and the car flipped over. Brickert swore just as his head smashed into the windshield and everything went black.

* * * * *

Sammy watched the car flip as though it happened in a blur. His blasts weren't much use against such a large mass, but with Jeffie's help they managed to stop it from colliding into them. The car landed on its side and skidded to a stop only a meter away. Using hand blasts, he and Jeffie righted it again.

Sammy wrenched open the door. Li was still conscious, but groggy. Brickert looked the worst with blood covering his face, but Kawai and Natalia were also out cold.

"We've got about two minutes." Sammy said as he pulled Brickert from the driver's seat. "Help me move him!" Jeffie and Li rushed to help, but as soon as Li got out of the car, he stumbled and fell, his eyes dazed, rolling in their sockets.

Jeffie moved Brickert into the back while Sammy got Li back to his feet. He was much heavier than Brickert, but he dragged him to the back of the car. Once everyone was inside, Sammy tried to start the car, but it wouldn't come to life. He swore and slammed a fist into the steering wheel.

"Not now, Lemon. Please not now." Sammy tried one more time, but the car still wouldn't go.

Sammy and Jeffie knew what that meant. Someone was going to have to get out and push the car with blasts. A rumbling came from somewhere far away, and the ground trembled as through an enormous hammer had smashed it. Sammy's calculation had been off. Just as Sammy opened his door, Li scrambled out of the car shouting, "Stay in! Let me do it!"

There was no time to argue. Sammy closed his door just as Li reached the rear, and felt the car jolt as Li's blasts hit it. Jamming the accelerator, Sammy looked in the rearview mirror to see Li running as hard as he could, a faint wall of white-blue energy approaching from behind. Sammy started to tap on the brakes, but Li waved him on. "No! Get out of here!" he screamed. "GO!"

Sammy floored it again and sped away. In the dimming light, he saw the wall of energy catch up with Li, who ran only a few more steps after it reached him, and his corpse fell to the floor of the tunnel. The crackling light continued to gain on the car even though Sammy drove as fast as Lemon would allow. Eventually the tunnel ramped upward and he swerved onto the highway headed east. Seconds later, the blast of the bomb fizzled out.

Sammy was glad Kawai, Natalia, and Brickert were still out. Jeffie sat in the front passenger seat, her eyes fixed on the mirror, tears dripping down reddened cheeks.

"That could have been us," she said hoarsely. "Should have been us."

Sammy wiped his eyes and kept driving. Several minutes passed in silence until Jeffie spoke again.

"It's like the universe saved us. Like we're fated to do what we plan to do." Jeffie shivered. "Am I crazy for saying that?"

"No," Sammy whispered. They never spoke about what was coming. Not with each other, not with anyone. Sammy didn't want to start now. Fortunately, his com rang.

It was Commander Byron. Relief washed over him at the knowledge that the commander was still alive. "Sir," he said when he answered it.

"Samuel …" the commander sighed. "Thank goodness. Who else is with you?"

Sammy listed the names of those with him. "We—we lost Li, sir." His voice was small and weak when he confessed it. "He saved us. What about your family?"

"We lost many people today, Samuel." The commander's voice sounded strained, almost to the point of breaking. "There will be a time for mourning. Do you remember your instructions for this scenario?"

"Yes sir." Sammy knew better than to repeat them over the com line, but procedures were in place for this type of event. With the eyes of CAG drones, satellites, and search parties looking for any sign of vehicles fleeing, the group had to act quickly. Many people would be caught, hopefully none would give up vital information. It was for reasons like this that Sammy was glad the leadership committee existed, with so much information kept between relatively few people. "And Vivi?"

"Alive. It was a miracle, but she is alive. We will get her to you. Along with the equipment."

"What do I need to—"

"Let us worry about those things. You be safe. My father will be in touch soon."

The line went dead. Sammy drove onward, eyes on the eastern horizon. Grand Forks was the destination. A place he'd never visited. A place he had never wanted to go. Along the way, other resistance members called to confirm Sammy's safety, most of them leaders. All of them said the same thing. "Sit tight. Let us get your equipment to you. Don't pass on any intel over the com."

It was a long time before the sounds of the sirens disappeared. Jeffie crawled into the back of the car to treat her friends' wounds. Kawai awoke first, moaning groggily as Jeffie dabbed her head with clean gauze from the car's first aid kit.

"Where's Li?" she asked.

Jeffie and Sammy exchanged a nervous glance in the rearview mirror. Kawai pushed Jeffie's hands away and turned her head in every direction.

"Where is Li?"

"He died in the bomb," Sammy explained. "He saved us."

Kawai covered her face with her hand. "Stop the car."

"Kawai—"

Her stomach lurched and her hands flew over her mouth.

"Stop the car, Sammy," Jeffie said, "she's going to be sick."

Sammy pulled the car to the side of the road, and Kawai made it two steps before vomiting. She sobbed and retched and sobbed more. Fresh tears rolled down Jeffie's cheeks as she listened to the sounds.

Sammy got out of the car and put an arm around his friend. "It's going to be okay."

"No, it's not!" she cried. "It's never going to be okay. It's never going to end!"

"Kawai, there is a time for this, but not now. We have to get back in that car and drive or else Li's death will mean nothing."

That got her moving a little. Sammy encouraged her into the car, and Jeffie hugged her while Sammy hustled around and jumped back in. They had a long drive ahead of them—nearly eight hundred kilometers. Sammy hoped he could stay awake through the night. The paranoia settling into his bones helped. Every few seconds he checked his mirrors for signs of drones or cruisers following.

Jeffie tried to stay awake by plaguing Sammy with questions that he couldn't answer. All he knew to say was that they had to wait for communication from the rest of the leadership council—or what was left of it.

Jeffie fell asleep after about three hours. Sammy didn't mind. If he ended up needing to switch places with her, it would help that she had gotten some rest. He thought Kawai had gone back to sleep too, but then saw the moonlight reflected in her dark eyes.

"I took him for granted," she finally whispered. "I thought—believed that tragedy was for other people. You … the commander … I don't know why I saw myself as untouchable. It hurts."

"It gets better," Sammy answered softly. "At first you experience it again every day the second you wake up. They die again and again in your heart. But in time the pain is not so fresh and not so horrible.

And then one day you realize you've moved on. That brings its own kind of pain, a guilty kind, but it's easier to deal with. And you find people to fill in the holes in your heart."

Tears fell down Kawai's face, and continued to fall for hours.

The rendezvous point in Grand Forks was a motel called The Bitter Winds. It was owned and operated by a resistance member named Andrew "Red" Benton, a bear of a man in every way: huge, hairy, and gruff. When Sammy and his friends entered a little after 0800, he nodded to them and said, "How many rooms?"

Sammy stopped paying attention to Red, his eyes were glued to the holo-vision where aerial footage showed Glasgow with the footer headline in all caps: "*PRESIDENT TO ADDRESS NATION AFTER TERRORIST COMPOUND DISCOVERED AND DESTROYED.*" And in small letters: "Thomas Byron among deceased."

Liars, Sammy thought. Thomas was alive and well. Sammy had spoken to him only an hour ago. The footage cut away from Glasgow and focused on President Newberry somberly walking up to a podium on the steps of the White House.

"My fellow Americans, we live in perilous times. Yesterday evening in Los Angeles a pro-NWG terrorist organization calling themselves only 'the resistance' seized control of the CBN world headquarters in Los Angeles for the purpose of persuading people to their cause with lies and misinformation. Last night, at 2300 hours, we responded with a statement that terrorists will not soon forget.

"Our forces launched a bio-bomb that detonated on the ghost towns of Glasgow and Saint Marie in Mid-Western American territory. Such a serious measure was held in reserve until our intelligence agencies verified that the sites were the locations of the rebel insurgents. Since then, we've sent in ground forces to secure the area, confirming four hundred and forty-five casualties and no survivors."

That's almost half of the members of the resistance living in the area. Sammy's guts tightened as he thought of all the dead. Next to him, Kawai sniffed wetly and wiped at her red and raw eyes.

"Many of the dead were NWG citizens—transplants and terrorists—sent here to sow discord and fear among us during our war effort. Many of you watched the address from Thomas Byron, father of a confirmed NWG defector, and longtime known suspect. I urge you to inform yourself on the facts. The CAG has provided a website which debunks the claims Thomas Byron made. Several news stories have been and will be released through a conjoined effort between the government and national media to set the story straight. Congressmen and women are traveling to their homes to meet with constituents and answer questions.

"I urge everyone to have patience and the peace of mind that the government will take care of you. We desire and work for nothing more or less than the absolute safety of America. And, as you have seen, your trust in us is not misplaced."

Sammy sighed and looked at Red Benton. "Two rooms please. And a doctor if there's one available." Thomas' speech hadn't worked. The government was already making the resistance look like fools. *No, not fools. Like dangerous, evil people.*

But it didn't matter now. The resistance was in tatters.

19 | Family

Saturday, November 8, 2087

THE STEALTH CRUISER rocketed toward Orlando carrying three passengers: Commander Byron, his son, Albert, and the Elite, Kallen Dinsmore. Dinsmore slept in the back seat. Albert was awake, seated in the co-pilot's chair, his face pointedly turned away from his father.

"Do you remember after Rio," Albert said softly, "when I kept telling you Sammy was alive? And you didn't believe me?"

Byron thought this was a strange question, but didn't say that. His relationship with Albert, though slowly improving, was still tenuous at best. "I do remember." The commander rubbed a little sleep out of his eyes. "The odds were so unlikely. It was not as though I did not want to believe you. My experience simply told me otherwise."

"But I knew I was right. I couldn't explain it."

"You were. And I am still glad you were. Remember, I helped you, gave you access to resources to investigate your hunch."

Albert sniffed and pinched the skin on his forehead above his nose. "I—I don't have that same feeling about Grandma." His voice broke. "Are you okay, Dad? You haven't said anything about her since—since Glasgow."

Byron swiped at a tear forming in his eye. "Now is not the time to grieve, Albert. We have to stay focused. As soon as we start allowing ourselves to think about our pain, we lose our focus. And we really cannot afford that."

Byron rolled his shoulders and every joint popped. His body ached from lack of sleep. After the attack on the resistance, preparation for the mission became ten times more difficult. Each team needed their supplies, and the remnants of the leadership council had only two days to get equipment to where it needed to be. Dozens of the survivors of the bomb and even members of the resistance living outside the compound had stepped up in a big way.

Teams had been mobilized to retrieve essential equipment, personnel, and stored weapons from scattered locations and brought to Sammy, the commander, and Thomas. Sleep had not been a priority. Some teams had driven for almost forty-eight hours straight to make the deliveries on time and keep the planned missions on schedule. Fortunately, Justice Juraschek had worked around the clock with Khani Nguyen to organize the transportation and get everyone and everything to their rightful places.

Hours passed in silence. When Commander Byron wasn't thinking about his son or his mother, his thoughts went to Samuel and Jeffie. The two were headed to Rio in the other stealth cruiser, along with Vitoria. Headed to death if they succeeded. And death if they failed.

Several times during the flight, he considered calling Sammy via his com, but decided against it. Khani Nguyen had cautioned them against using their coms now that the CAG had raided the resistance headquarters. Their coms weren't safe and only to be used when necessary.

It should be me in Rio.

Byron closed his eyes and cursed his legs. *If only they were whole ... it would be me on that mission.*

He landed the cruiser on the banks of the Wekiva River and roused Kallen Dinsmore. After helping to unload their equipment bags and two motorcycles from the cargo, the Elite wished Albert and the commander a safe mission and flew off, back to the north.

"The mission never seems real until drop-off," Commander Byron said. "Does it feel that way to you?"

Albert nodded and looked up at the sky. "We should get going."

They rode down back roads and highways in silence, though they could communicate via their coms should they want. Somewhere up in the sky another stealth cruiser flew toward Rio carrying Sammy, Jeffie, and Vitoria. At times like these, Byron almost wished he hadn't grown so fond of his pupils at Psion Beta.

But that was the life of a soldier. Growing fond of someone and then letting them go. The commander hadn't thought of that all those years ago when he signed up with General (then Commander) Wu. Despite the death Byron had seen even as early as at the Elite Training Center, he hadn't imagined he'd see so much more. He hadn't fathomed that almost everyone he'd recruited would die. He had trained almost a hundred Psions over the years. And while he wasn't certain how many still lived, he guessed the number was somewhere around thirty.

Thirty ... Forty if I am lucky.

Li was the latest. All the other Psions had made it out of Glasgow and Saint Marie before the bio-bomb's blast reached them and ripped their very cells apart. But the impact of Li's death had been swallowed by the loss of Byron's mother. Her group had been in a packed car trying to escape Glasgow, unable to escape the bomb's radius. Byron's father had been speaking to her over the com, urging her on, when her end of the line had gone dead. Bio-bombs had no effect on electronic equipment like coms, only living organisms.

Byron's father refused to discuss his wife's death. Taking his cue from his father, Byron focused on Albert and the mission. The chance that he might not survive was very real. But Albert ... Albert had to survive. His son needed to be there for his granddaughter. Albert had to make things right with Marie.

Almost as though his son had been reading his thoughts, Albert said to his dad over their helmet radios, "Why did you pick me?"

"Lots of reasons."

"Like what?"

Now Byron actually had to think about what those were. "First of all, I trust you. Second, I think you need this."

"What does that mean? Does that have something to do with Marie?"

Commander Byron's silence was enough of an answer for his son.

"I told you I didn't want to discuss her, Dad."

"And I am honoring that agreement. But you asked me to explain—"

"Fine. Never mind."

They rode side by side. Occasionally Byron passed Albert or vice versa, but they stayed about a meter apart. The highway they traveled was long, dark and mostly straight as it headed south toward downtown Orlando.

"Regardless of my reasons for choosing you, I am grateful you accepted. Besides your mother's death, your mission to Rio was the worst thing that has ever happened to me. Martin Trector ... Cala ... Sammy. I thought I had failed you, failed everyone as a trainer and instructor. The idea that my poorly executed leadership had put you in danger ate at me. I offered my resignation to General Wu, but he turned it down and told me to fix the problem."

"You never told me that," Albert said.

"I considered telling you, but I already knew you would not want me to leave Beta headquarters. And I was capable of weighing the pros and cons on my own."

"Are you saying that's what Marie did? Are you condoning her choice?"

Byron swerved his motorcycle around a curve. "No, no. I am not saying anything about that."

"Good, because—"

"I know. Marie is off-limits as a topic of conversation."

They did not speak again until they reached their destination. It was late morning when they parked in the garage of the hotel next to the N Tower in downtown Orlando and checked in with the commander's father. After a long nap and a trip to the store, Byron dyed his hair and new mustache black. Albert's hair became a bleached yellow. He scowled at himself in the mirror when the job was done, fingering his platinum hair with disdain.

Byron chuckled. "Not a bad look."

"Marie's gonna hate it." Immediately after saying those words, Albert squeezed his eyes tightly shut and turned sharply from his reflection. "Let's go down to the street."

They spent the day studying the N building. After the destruction of the Hybrid-producing labs in San Francisco and Detroit, security had tightened: regular patrols around the perimeter, increased numbers of Aegis in the lobby and cloning floors, even the roof had guards. Security protocols at the checkpoints in the garage and lobby were far more rigorous than expected.

No doubt there were many more enemies unseen. The white room they needed to reach was in the depths of the building, almost a kilometer underground. The only way they could access it was via the elevator shaft that went from the lobby all the way down to the sublevels. Elevator 13. But in order to reach the sublevels, they needed an Aegis or Thirteen's eyes and finger.

"We continue our special coverage of recent dramatic events in Los Angeles and Glasgow," a reporter said over the holo-vision in the hotel room. Byron was perched on the windowsill while Albert was downstairs in the lobby taking more notes on the timing of the security guards. "As part of that coverage, we've asked noted poll analyst Samantha Gold to join us. Samantha, welcome to the show. Data is coming from multiple polling agencies regarding public opinion on these events. What is your take on the information we're receiving? Is it accurate?"

"I think the data surprised some and not others," the analyst responded. "Yes, the American public is too smart to believe the statements put forth by terrorists, but one always worries about the fringe population, the conspiracy theorists. So to see numbers from multiple agencies this one-sided … yes, it's a little surprising, but in a good way."

"It certainly caught me off guard," said the show's anchor, "to see that 95% of the population does not sympathize with the resistance nor plans to support their march on D.C."

"But it really shouldn't," the analyst responded. "They're terrorists, and the CAG is in the middle of a war. Yes, solidarity is to be expected, but seeing numbers this high tells me that people are being cautious and educating themselves."

"Excellent points. Government officials are calling on teachers, law enforcement, and employers to educate their fellow citizens on the dangers of participating in this so-called coup. More on this story—"

Byron clicked off the holo-vision and returned to work. The news was a pack of lies. The resistance's website continued to draw well over a million hits a day. The commander's father even took a picture of himself in the CAG capitol in front of a holo-screen displaying the current date, giving the world proof that he was still alive, but the news refused to mention it or retract the earlier claim regarding his death.

That evening, the commander reported their findings to Justice, Khani, and others, feeding them information and discussing tactics.

"I spoke to Sammy an hour ago," Justice said. "He said his team is currently on schedule. One day in and we're looking good."

Commander Byron and Albert took shifts through the night, the commander going first, and Albert second. As Albert slept, Commander Byron remembered the nights when, as a young father, he checked on his baby boy and watched him sleep. He had marveled at the small creation in the crib, tiny Albert's eyes shut, fragile chest rising and falling. A perfect little baby, something he had made. He and Emily had wanted more children, at least two more, but life had other plans. A sigh escaped him as he suddenly and deeply missed her, something that didn't happen often anymore, at least not with such severity.

The next day was more of the same: searching for weaknesses to exploit in conjunction with the plans they had already made. Albert set up cameras and uploaded the feed to Justice and Dr. Nguyen. Ideas came back, but others rebutted them. They had only one more day to decide on a final plan.

During the night shift, Commander Byron sat in a chair watching, thinking, and sipping a mug of hot chocolate—the Byron family drink of choice on a late night. Albert tossed and turned in his bed, trying to sleep but failing. Earlier in the evening Albert had spoken to Marie in the privacy of the bathroom, but the door wasn't soundproof enough to prevent Byron from overhearing their muted argument.

"You want some hot chocolate?" he asked his son.

Albert threw the bed sheets aside and got up. "Sure."

"On the stove." After pouring himself a mug, Albert padded into the room and sat in the chair opposite Byron. "So ... how is my granddaughter doing?"

"Fussy. Marie thinks she might have caught a virus. Doctor Rosmir is going to check on her tomorrow."

Byron nodded. "Is that why you are still up?"

Albert only sipped his hot chocolate and stared out the window. Byron stared out it too. He decided to change the subject.

"Maybe we should just say to heck with our plan and go in guns blazing. What do you think about that?"

Albert gave a dry chortle. "We'd be dead in two minutes."

"Things are never as hopeless as they seem when you can blast."

"If they have Hybrids and Thirteens, it *will* be the case."

"I doubt they have Hybrids here."

"Why?"

"Because they are not producing them as quickly as they were, and any that can be spared are sent overseas to secure strategic points already taken."

"How do you know that?"

"I am the NWG liaison. That is the kind of information they *liaise* ..."

Albert took another long sip. In the nighttime shadows the steam rising from his mug made him look almost menacing. "Why didn't the leadership committee invite me back after I got sober? They never asked me to return."

Byron blew on his drink. What his son said was true. Albert had sobered up quickly after he moved in with Byron, but was never invited back. "Probably because I never recommended it."

"Why not?"

"It seemed you had more important things to focus on."

"You know what sucks the most about being your son?" Albert asked. "You always being in charge of me. Everyone thinks you're perfect. They trust every decision you make. But I know better. I remember how everyone else in Psion Command wanted the Betas armed on their training missions except for you. Your arrogance cost Psions their lives."

"Albert—"

His son slammed down his mug and splashed chocolate on the window. "You can't sit here and tell me that I wasn't good enough to be back on the committee because we both know that isn't true. I'm one of the best."

"Was that ever in question?" Commander Byron tried to mask the anger boiling inside him at his son's accusations, but couldn't do it.

"Sammy has been on the committee since day one. He sits on two of the three subcommittees. His poorly designed plans in Detroit brought down the tower, but that didn't matter. He stayed. I start drinking and I'm out."

"It went beyond your drinking and you know it."

"That's garbage!"

"Go ahead and rage. It will not change anything."

"You're as bad as Marie! You think you can make decisions in my life without my approval! No one cares what I want. No one wants to know what I have to say."

"Marie cares! She made a mistake, Albert. You have your mother's resentment and your grandfather's stubbornness, but you have to find it in yourself to forgive her. Would you ruin your marriage and your life rather than let this go?"

"She had no right to get pregnant without discussing it with me first!"

"Marie was scared. She allowed herself to get pregnant because she thought it would protect you. Is that mistake really worth the hurt you have put her through ever since then?"

"She used a baby to trap me!" Albert stood and yelled.

The commander refused to let his voice rise in response to his son. "And you love your daughter, so why are you so angry?"

"Because Marie had no right—"

"When those sirens went off, you *ran* to Marie and your daughter. Why do you think you did that? Because you are trapped?"

"Marie didn't want me to come on this mission. She doesn't want me to do anything. She doesn't want anything to do with the Psions anymore."

"I know exactly how she feels. What do you think I went through for years after your mother died, not being in contact with my parents? All I had was you. But Marie does not even have that because you refuse to support her."

"See? I knew you'd take her side. I'm always wrong, aren't I, Dad?"

"Always? No. Often? Yes."

Albert snarled, but snickered at the same time. He didn't seem to know whether he wanted to shout or laugh. Then his lips twisted and he fought back tears. Byron saw nothing but a scared twenty-one-year-old boy. "I've lost control of my life. All my attention is supposed to be where? On my daughter? On fixing things with Marie? On the mission? I don't know. It's like everything is saying to me, 'Look here! No, look here!' But the world has become so dark. Ever since Marie told me she was pregnant … it's been nothing but dark."

Commander Byron closed his eyes and exhaled with a lighter heart than he'd had in months. "You finally see, son? You are not mad at Marie. You are terrified for your daughter."

"No, I'm not—" Albert said thickly, his eyes glistening now. "I'm not scared."

"I had the same fear—"

Albert gripped his mug so tightly his fingers blanched, and for an instant the commander feared the mug was going to fly at his head. "I don't know how to be a father! I'm not ready. Every time I look at my daughter I think of the kind of world she has to face … I can't handle it. She's a Psion. And what's the survival rate of Psions, Dad? Huh? How many of us are left?"

"She does not have to be a Psion. Your daughter can be anything she wants." Commander Byron set his mug down and spoke with great care. "Albert, you will be a fine husband and father."

Albert's eyes grew redder. He swallowed hard and shook his head. "I don't know what I'm doing."

"No one does at first. I still learn things from you. I still make mistakes."

A puff of laughter burst from Albert, but there was no mirth in it. "Your mistakes are nothing. Look at me! Look what I've done to my family the last few months. At least your mistakes can be fixed."

"That is only true if you believe it. Marie loves you very deeply. Why do you think she has repeatedly tried to repair your marriage despite your attempts to wreck it?"

Tears now fell down Albert's face. "What do I do, Dad?"

"When you get home, acknowledge it. Own what you have done. Tell her things will be different if she will give you another chance. Let everything you do be motivated by love, and you will not go wrong. Keep your focus on your family and your faith. Everything else is ultimately a distraction."

Albert picked up his mug again, but stopped before it touched his lips. His eyes widened and he set the mug down. "That's it, Dad! A distraction. I have an idea."

"About Marie?"

"No, the mission. But you're right about her too. When—if—I make it home, I'll do what you suggested."

After clearing Albert's new plan with Justice and Thomas, they spent their last day of preparation running through scenario after scenario, plotting minute by minute their plan as best as they could. They worked all through the day and into the evening, stopping only to eat or make a run for supplies. When it was done, they got a few hours of sleep, and then rose late in the night.

Wearing disguises, Commander Byron and Albert left their hotel across the street from the N Tower. Keeping eyes on the patrols around the building, Commander Byron and Albert split up. Albert heading for the alleys while Byron walked up and down the street for twenty minutes before marching into the N Tower lobby. He wore a robe made of sheepskin that they'd found in a rundown second hand store. He hadn't shaved since they arrived, and he smelled like someone who'd been working with pigs quite intimately. In his hands he held a sign which read: *God does not agree with CLONING! CLONES are an ABOMINATION! Exodus 20:4-6.*

To ensure he had their attention, he shouted at the top of his lungs as he rushed forward, brandishing his sign like a banner of war. "Devils! Sons of perdition! Creators of the unnatural! Burn in hell for your sins, you abominations!"

Less than five steps into the lobby and the woman behind the security desk was on her phone. Thirty seconds later, a hoard of Aegis tackled him and dragged him toward the elevators. The tip of a needle stung his neck, and the world went blurry and then dark.

20 | Tunneling

Saturday, November 8, 2087

THE AIR IN the sewers clung to Sammy like hot, foul breath. It permeated his clothes, hair, skin. *I'm going to die smelling like crap. Literally.* Jeffie and Vitoria worked next to him. They all smelled and looked their worst, hair and clothes plastered to skin as they worked the drill which tunneled through the sewer walls and created an angled descent into the foundation of the skyscrapers in downtown Rio.

The city made his flesh crawl. Even the air brought back memories he had never wanted to revisit. The scents of Rio had assaulted him the moment the cruiser touched down in Cemitério São Francisco Xavier on the city's northern outskirts. *I'm back*, he thought as he looked at the city. *My first mission and my last. You tried to kill me once, but I dodged that. I guess I was on borrowed time since then. You win, Rio.*

The sights, the smells, the sounds … they fed the darkness inside him. He could feel it deep in his soul, simmering, roiling, waiting. Sammy, Jeffie, and Vitoria entered the sewers of Rio in the western Centro. It took an hour to make their way to the spot where they would drill.

The team worked around the clock, drilling and pumping their way through ten, then twenty, and finally thirty meters of concrete with many, many more to go to reach the network of tunnels that serviced the major towers in downtown Rio. Sammy and Jeffie operated the drill while Vitoria manned the pump that sent water in and out to remove the slurry residue the drilling process created. The bitter smell of the acid spray from the drills was almost as unbearable as the heat, which blew in steady waves off the machinery, drenching Sammy's masked face and chest in an acrid-smelling sweat. The length of the tunnel they had to dig was almost a hundred meters, its diameter well over a meter. Sammy's skin was raw from the splatter of chemicals and his back ached from crouching inside the tunnel.

"Break!" Jeffie called out over the whining and grinding sounds of the drill.

Sammy nodded and switched off the machine, which gradually whirred and groaned to a halt. "I'm starving," he said.

"Would you like a sandwich?" Jeffie said.

"Whatever." Food no longer interested him. He had to satiate his hunger, but nothing he ate had taste. Jeffie donned her construction worker jacket and left to buy the food. Vitoria turned off the pump and sat down against the sewer wall.

"You should let me go down there with you instead of her," she said once Jeffie was out of earshot.

"We need a Psion, Vivi. That's always been the plan."

"I'm as good as any Psion. You know that."

"It doesn't matter." Sammy sighed. The weariness went everywhere: his muscles, bones, brain, even his soul. It seemed as if the whole world weighed heavy on him.

Vitoria rested her head on Sammy's shoulder. "Please, Sammy. Let me do it. Spare Jeffie and let me."

"I can't change the mission."

Vitoria got up and surveyed the hole, sniffing several times in succession. "Thirty meters, huh? We're ahead of schedule."

"Thirty meters." Sammy's voice was lifeless. He didn't want to look at the hole. The deeper the tunnel, the closer he came to his own grave. He closed his eyes and tried to push those thoughts away, but they had become part of him. Death had become part of him. Barring desertion and fleeing for his life, he was already dead.

When Vitoria sat back down, she slipped her hand into his.

Sammy pulled his away. "Please don't, Vivi."

"Why? Because you love Jeffie?"

"I—I don't—it doesn't matter how I feel."

"You won't hold my hand because of the way you feel about her, *and* you won't let me take her place so she can live. You have a skewed sense of morality, Sammy."

"She chose this. You think I wanted it? It was supposed to be—" He cut himself off before he said something he couldn't take back, but he'd already said too much. *Curse my stupid mouth.*

"Anna," Vitoria finished. "It was supposed to be her, wasn't it?"

Sammy fidgeted with his ventilation mask. "It doesn't matter."

"It does. I killed Jeffie when I killed Anna. I just didn't know it then."

"It wasn't *you*."

Vitoria started to cry. This angered Sammy. What right did she have to shed tears? She wasn't going to die. Sammy wanted to smack her across the face, and the instant the idea crossed his mind, Vitoria scooted away from him.

"What?"

"That look," she said, scooting to her feet. "The look in your eyes! Stay away from me!"

"Vivi—"

She started to run away, but Sammy threw himself at her and snagged her foot before she got away, not an easy task given her Anomaly Fifteen. She scrambled, but he managed to get on top of her and pin her down. With strength that surprised him, she spun and brought her knee up into his thigh, barely missing his groin.

"GET OFF ME!" she screamed.

Sammy clamped a grimy, wet hand over her mouth. Her eyes widened and she pummeled his ribs with the viciousness of a boxer. Rage flared in him again, and the grip on her mouth tightened until he was squeezing her jaw with his larger hands. But the terror in her eyes helped him regain his sanity, and the fury dwindled and shrunk like a deflated balloon. He took the hand off her mouth and wrapped it around her head, hugging her even as she continued struggling.

"I'm sorry, Vivi. I won't hurt you. I'm sorry."

Vitoria cried harder. "You are all I have. Don't you get it? I'll kill myself before I let you die."

"No, you won't," Sammy said emphatically. His breath was hot and his lips were right next to hers. His ribs ached enough that he wondered if she had cracked them. "You won't kill yourself because that would be a piss poor way of repaying me for what I'm trying to do!"

Vitoria shook her head. "When the Aegis came for my family, Dad fought them. They killed him in front of us. They dragged Fabiana, my sister, away while she screamed. I didn't give them any trouble because Mom snapped when she saw Dad die. She went blank and stiff. They carried her out like a mannequin. My mom ..."

Sammy held her tightly. "I'm sorry."

"I had nothing. I tried to kill myself when I was in the Aegis' custody in the tower. When they put me in S.H.I.E.L.D. I had nothing left but hate. They beat me, raped me, humiliated me. Made me ..." Vitoria put her hand over her mouth and stifled a shrill scream. "I'm a monster, Sammy!"

"You're not."

"I am. You don't get it. I killed. I shot a boy in cold blood. Just because they told me to." She sobbed and shook. "I'm a murderer."

"They messed with your brain. You didn't have a choice."

"There's always a choice. I could have let them kill me. I could have stopped myself from killing Anna and Croz and those others."

"People want to survive. They'll do anything. You were terrified, lost, alone, empty. You had to grab onto something to make sense, so you accepted their brainwashing. You have nothing to feel guilty about."

"I don't want to live."

"Don't say that."

"I don't want to live!" Her anguish echoed off the sewer walls, and Sammy pulled her to him to shush her. As he cradled her, he kept up a steady stream of encouragement about how things would get better, how she could go back to Rio, find her extended family, and rebuild her life. He held her until she calmed down. Then she put a hand on his face and turned his head toward her. The gold in her eyes flashed at him, and she drew in closer until her lips were a few centimeters away.

"No," he told her. "Please don't."

She stopped and sighed, then pulled herself away from him. They sat in silence until Jeffie returned with the food. As they ate, the conversation stayed on the drilling. Sammy took little enjoyment in his meal. It had no flavor or smell. It was energy and sustenance. And when it was gone, the work resumed. The day finally ended when they were too tired to continue. Sammy called Justice and checked in via com, then fell asleep with the smell of rot and filth still clinging to his skin.

* * * * *

At 0213 the Queen's com rang. She was staying in her mountain home in the Grand Tetons for the first time in months. Outside of the penthouse in Orlando she could relax and sleep. Being in her own home felt right. Before answering the com, she activated her voice disguiser. Then she saw it was Chad at the Hive. "What?"

"We have something … I apologize for bothering you, but it doesn't make sense."

The Queen cursed Chad silently and turned off the disguiser. "What is *something?*"

"Diego has hundreds of these alerts set up all with different priority assignments. Some of them are instant, and some are daily, weekly … you get the idea. He has so many that it takes time for me to go through them all. I've just come across one for an alert in the sewers in Rio near the N Tower. Some kind of work going on down there and we have no record of work permit requests or prior authorization."

"Who is it?" the Queen growled. *This is not worth my time.* "What kind of work?"

"I have no idea."

"Call the city offices. Tell them you represent the N Corp's security team. You've been alerted that someone is lurking in the sewers around your premises and want them to send someone to check it out. Let me know what you hear."

* * * * *

The drill pushed deeper into the earth through concrete and steel. The second day passed without incident until the late afternoon when, during the hottest hour of the day, a man carrying a flashlight appeared. Vitoria signaled them to stop the drill and climb out of the hole, not an easy task given the tunnel's stretching length and angle of descent. Sammy couldn't get a good look at the newcomer, but he was prepared to blast if need be. The rays of the flashlight hit Sammy's feet, then traveled up his legs until it stopped at his face, blinding him.

"You three working down here?" the man asked in a thick Brazilian accent.

"We are," Sammy said, trying to make his voice as deep as he could without sounding phony. "Structural correction for J and G Construction. How can we help you?"

When the flashlight finally pointed away, Sammy saw the man's face. He had a bushy mustache and eyes that darted between Vitoria and Jeffie. "You're a bunch of kids. What are you doing down here?"

"Kids?" Sammy tried to laugh the comment away, but it ended up sounding small and nervous.

"We told you … we're working," Jeffie said with much more authority than Sammy had been able to muster.

"I'm with the commercial zoning board. I need to see your permits."

Sammy tried to think of a solution that didn't involve incapacitating the man. He looked at Jeffie and Vitoria. "Which one of you has the permits?"

"I do," Vitoria said. And before Sammy could see what she had, Vitoria pulled a gun and shot the man three times in the chest.

"NO!" Sammy shouted.

Jeffie blasted Vitoria backward with her hands, but the damage was done. Sammy picked the man up and examined his wounds, but he was dead in seconds. Vitoria's aim was impeccable. Jeffie jumped on her and pinned her down.

"I'm sorry!" Vitoria cried. "I'm sorry. I'm sorry. I'm sorry. I'm sorry. I'm sorry." She was crying again, hysterical and nearly hyperventilating. "He's not dead, Sammy! He's not dead!"

Sammy had brought restraints in case Vitoria proved uncontrollable. He grabbed them from his pack and slipped them around Vitoria's wrists and ankles. When they locked, Vitoria didn't fight them. She only cried more. Once she was secure, Jeffie pulled Sammy away.

"What are we going to do?" She had an edge to her voice that told Sammy she was barely keeping it together.

"We have to keep working."

"She killed him!" Jeffie hissed.

"And we can't deal with that right now. We have a job. Let's get it done."

"But—"

"I don't know how long we have before someone comes down here looking for that guy. Could be an hour, could be a week. But if that does happen, we have a bigger problem. So let's drill."

Without Vitoria's help, the drilling process slowed. Sammy had to be more careful because Jeffie wasn't able to help him steady the drill, she had to stay back with the pump and its extensions. By the end of the day, they had reached a length of sixty meters. Sammy had hoped to be at seventy-five. The drill blades were slowly dulling, and they didn't have replacements. It had been hard enough to procure just the one machine.

When Sammy went to wake Jeffie early the morning of the next day, he paused before shaking her. Despite the grime and sweat and stench on her, Sammy noted how beautiful she was. He touched her cheek and ran his fingertips along her jawline. Vitoria lay next to Jeffie and watched Sammy with fresh tears running down her face, but closed her eyes when their gazes met. Her arms and legs were still bound.

"I'm sorry we had to do that," Sammy told her. "I'm sorry for everything you've had to go through."

Vitoria didn't move and her eyes stayed closed.

"If I give you some time to stretch your muscles, do you promise not to run?"

Vitoria squirmed and nodded.

Releasing her ankles first, Sammy helped her to her feet, his hand still clasped around her wrist restraints. He walked her away from Jeffie, away from the drilling site, into the darkness of the sewers. "You look tired," he said.

"So do you. I woke up almost screaming every half hour from muscle cramps. What's your excuse?"

"I'm sorry, Vivi," he said, hurrying to release her hands. "I didn't mean to—"

When the bonds around her wrists fell away, her body tensed up as though she wanted to run. Sammy, in turn, tensed up too. "I'm not going to chase you."

She stared at him. "Yes you will." And she took off.

Sammy swore. "Jeffie, get up!"

Jeffie's eyes opened.

"Vitoria ran!"

Sammy sprinted after Vitoria. Despite his larger size, longer legs, and greater strength, he did not have her Anomaly Fifteen. By the time he reached the ladder to the streets of Rio and blasted up through the sewer hole, Vitoria was already thirty meters down the road. Thankfully it was still such an early hour that the streets were nearly bare. Sammy called her name as he ran.

Vitoria peered over her shoulder and kept running. Sammy chased her to a park. When he reached her, she was on a swing, pumping her legs, arcing high into the air and back down. No smile adorned Vitoria's face, but there was something different: a look of freedom or some small measure of peace. Each swing made her hair fan out behind her. Her eyes locked onto his and they watched each other for a while. Sammy felt in his soul that in a different world, a different life, he could have feelings for her like he had for Jeffie. She was beautiful and strong and real, despite being deconstructed and reassembled by the CAG.

Sammy took the swing next to her and swung lightly. He couldn't remember the last time he'd sat on one. It might have been ten years or even a lifetime ago. "We're not going to reach the mark in time without your help," he finally said. "And if we do, it will be from working night and day, wearing ourselves out. We won't have anything left for the last stage …"

"I know." Her eyes had taken on that lifeless, dull quality again. Her face was stone.

"But?"

"If I help you, I lose you."

"You'll be alive. And free. And we'll have all but won the war."

"You love Jeffie, right?" Vitoria asked.

"You're not going down there with us. It's me and Jeffie."

"Because you love her." Vitoria spat the words.

"I—"

"Don't know," she finished for him. "How can you not know?"

"I don't know." He gave her a tight grin. "To love someone is a really huge thing. It means a lot. I can't just say I love someone when I don't know."

Vitoria rolled her eyes. "Whatever. You love her. Still … you'd rather die with her and miss out on growing old together just so you can win? What if the NWG becomes just like the problem you're fighting?"

"Then other people will rise up to do what needs to be done."

"I don't deserve to live. Jeffie does. You both do."

"What makes you say that?" The question hadn't come from Sammy, but Jeffie, who was only a few steps away. Both Sammy and Vitoria turned at the sound of her voice. She took the swing on the opposite side of Vitoria. "I'm no better than you, Vivi."

"Yes you are. The things I've done …"

"You know better," Jeffie said. "We don't have to keep telling you that they aren't your fault."

"Who will I have when you two are gone?" Toad's sister asked meekly.

Jeffie's voice cracked. "You'll have your life. Do with it what you want."

"Vitoria …" Sammy said. "*Please*. We can't do this without you."

Both Sammy and Jeffie watched her, waiting. Vitoria sighed, her eyes on the ground. The sun was just beginning to peek over the horizon, splashing reds and golds into the sky on a palette of stray clouds. A hot breeze blew the girls' hair and made the strands dance around their heads. Jeffie looked over at Sammy, indicating with her eyes that it was time to return to the sewers.

"Vitoria?" Sammy repeated.

She nodded. "All right. I'll go back."

Progress on the hole picked up the third day. They worked from morning to evening, finally within centimeters of breaching the foundation's service tunnels. Sammy and Jeffie stopped the drills and walked the long distance up the tunnel. When Vitoria saw them, she shut off the pump.

"Stopping point?" she asked.

Sammy nodded. They would not drill any deeper until early the next day. Instinctively, Sammy checked the time on his watch, it was nearly evening. "I'm hungry. You pick where we eat, Jeffie."

What he had meant as an act of kindness transformed into a moment of solemnity. Jeffie knew why he had offered her the choice: it would be their last meal. She shook her head. "You decide."

"I don't care. I want you to choose."

Jeffie was not going to budge. So, they both turned to Vitoria. "Is there anything you want?"

Based on Vitoria's recommendation, the three ended up eating at a pizza-tilla, which served hybrid Italian/Mexican food that neither Jeffie nor Sammy particularly cared for, but Vitoria devoured. For dessert, they ordered three bowls of fried ice cream.

Sammy hadn't taken more than five bites of dessert when through the street-side window of the restaurant he saw three men heading down into the sewers. They wore jackets similar to the one the man asking for Sammy's permit had worn, but their cautious behavior—and the large, bulky duffel bag one of them toted—told him these weren't city employees.

"Check it out," he said, directing Jeffie and Vivi's attention to what he saw.

"Aegis," Vitoria said.

"Let's go," Jeffie added.

Vitoria jumped out of her seat, but Sammy grabbed her by the arm. "Are you going to stay in control? Follow orders?"

"I'll do what I was trained to do. Aegis killed my family." Vitoria spun and grabbed his syshée from its concealed holster, but before Sammy could react, she was running for the exit. Sammy got up so fast he toppled the table, spilled ice cream in two directions, and drove the corner of the wood hard into Jeffie's knee. Jeffie limped out the door behind him, running as best as she could.

"Vitoria, stop!" Sammy shouted.

She didn't. Instead, she jumped feet first into the sewer hole. Seconds later, Sammy heard gunfire. Blasts ready, he followed. It was much darker below the street level, and it took time for his eyes to adjust. "Get behind me!" Sammy shouted to Vitoria. But he was too late. She had already killed all three Aegis, each with a shot to the head. Jeffie dropped in behind Sammy, panting, hissing, and grabbing her knee.

Vitoria walked up to one of them and kicked him savagely in the head. "Coward called in for backup," she reported. "They know we're here."

21 | **Broken**

Sunday, June 1, 2053

KATIE HID IN the hotel bathroom, huddled in the corner next to the toilet until her mother came and got her. She didn't speak, she just sobbed in the back seat. Her mother cried too. The drive home lasted an eternity, and when they finally pulled into the driveway, Katie pushed past her parents, stumbled up the steps clutching her stomach, and locked her bedroom door. Sleep finally came hours later. Her dreams were macabre scenes of carnage and mayhem. Gruesome acts of violence filled her mind and played out in visions no one could see or hear but her. They were vivid down to the scent of the blood and the sounds of flesh bending to blades. She woke exhausted.

By mid-afternoon the next day her mother and father were begging her to open the door, but Katie didn't answer until they threatened to break it down. "Leave me alone," Katie finally pleaded.

Perhaps relieved that she was even speaking, her parents stopped bothering her. Katie stayed in her bed all day and stared out the window. The thought of going to school on Monday made her nauseous. And the only thing that made the sickness better were the visions of violence she saw in her mind's eye. The gore and death stirred something in her soul, something exciting and dangerous.

She rolled out of bed and grabbed her yearbook. Flipping through the pages, she studied the pictures, the faces. Then she closed her eyes to remember which ones had mocked her, and circled them in red marker. Katie repeated the process until she had singled out over two dozen students. A sudden wave of revulsion hit her, and she ran over to her trashcan and threw up.

What is wrong with me? Killing people? She threw the yearbook away and crawled back into bed, tears flowing once more. *This isn't normal.*

That night, hungry and a little cabin-feverish, Katie left her room. Her mom was sitting on the floor facing the bedroom door, her back against the wall. Katie's mother lifted her head from her arms when she heard the door open.

"Honey …" she said, standing and pulling Katie into a hug. "I'm sorry, baby. I'm sorry." Her mother had streaks of makeup on her face. Her red eyes and mussed hair told Katie she hadn't slept. "I hurt for you. Your father is meeting with the principal tomorrow. If you don't want to go back, we'll push for your transfer."

"You think word won't spread, Mom? You think kids at other schools won't know? It's probably all over the city!"

"You're the prom queen, sweetie. That means you still have a lot of people who like you."

Again the image of Katie's fellow students flashed in her mind. Dead, decapitated, bleeding, gutted, mashed and bashed … she pushed the vision away and hugged her mother tighter. "I need to think about it." Then she added, "What about Priyanka?"

"She didn't do it," her mom answered. "Mark did. He used a laser knife like the one I bought."

"Priyanka hugged me right before I went up to be crowned."

"Mark admitted to it, sweetie."

A wave of hate hit Katie so hard that she started to imagine various and painful ways to kill Mark. "She had to put him up to saying that," Katie said. "She *had* to."

"Whether or not that's true doesn't matter. Mark confessed and was expelled. But listen, the school wants to know by tomorrow if you're going to transfer so they can get your files from your teachers."

Katie didn't know what to say. She didn't want to go to a new school, and she didn't want to go back to her school either. "Can I please just have some more time?"

Katie's mother regarded her with love and pity. "Sure, honey. I'll talk to them and let them know what you need."

Her parents stuck by her, carefully and patiently boosting her confidence whenever she started to feel depressed again. Courtney and Vivian came by on Tuesday and Wednesday to cheer her up.

"Priyanka did it," Courtney confirmed. "I saw it—"

"We tried to stop you," Vivian added, "but Bobby John was blocking us from getting to you. And everybody was cheering so loud you didn't hear us."

"But why did Mark get the blame?" Katie asked tearfully. "Why wasn't Priyanka expelled?"

"Priyanka." Courtney practically spat the word. "You won't believe what she promised him to get him to cover for her. *She's* the slut. We gave our story to Principal Simpson, she and Mark gave theirs. It was our word against theirs, so Simpson gave Priyanka a one week suspension."

That's not nearly good enough, Katie thought bitterly. *She deserves ... Death.*

Bobby John and his parents stopped by on Thursday. Bobby John hugged Katie so hard she thought she might break in half. "Bobby John loves Katie," he repeated at least twenty times.

Katie smiled for the first time since prom. After Bobby John's family left the house, Katie approached her mother. "Are you feeling better, sweetie?"

"A little."

"I'm so proud of how you've handled this. I know I've said it before, but seeing how great you turned out, I wish we could have had more kids just like you."

Katie tried to hide her grimace by smiling. "Mom, I need to tell you something, but I'm afraid it's going to freak you out."

Katie's mom raised her eyebrows and sat up a little straighter. "Oh?"

"I—" Katie's mouth went dry as she imagined herself telling her mother about the dark dreams, gruesome visions, and bedwetting.

Tell her. She's your mother. She'll love you and want to help you.

She won't understand. Neither will your father. You're the only child. You're supposed to be perfect. They'll send you to a doctor who will put you on medication.

You need help.

They'll think you're a freak for the rest of your life.

Katie made up her mind. "I actually think everything is going to be fine." Even as she said the words, a gnawing sickness in her gut told her she'd made the wrong choice.

Her mother relaxed and smiled with tears in her eyes. "See?" She rubbed Katie's shoulder affectionately. "You just amaze me."

That night Katie returned to the cave. As she descended the steps her body tingled with anticipation, not fear. The dark was an old friend, not a blanket of mystery and dread. Her senses seemed more acute than during previous trips. The cold froze her skin. The smell of something foul and rank now stung her nostrils. Strangely enough, however, none of it bothered her. When she reached the door, she felt it pulsing, a reverberation through her body. Her heartbeat fell in step with its throbs.

A faint light emanated from under the door, giving enough illumination that once her eyes adjusted she could see how the door had a deep red color that reminded her of blackened blood. It twitched and rippled ever so gently with each beat of her heart. When she finally reached out and touched it with her fingertips, the surface quivered, and she jerked her hand away.

It wasn't made of wood. Nor metal. The texture of it reminded her of flesh. She reached for the knob but found nothing. With both hands she searched and pulled and pushed and even heaved her weight into the door, but despite its pliable nature it would not open. She tried the knife in the juncture of the door and its stone frame, but it stubbornly refused to yield. In her frustration she stabbed the door with the blade, and the dagger sank in with ease. Black hot liquid spurted out from the wound, searing her skin with an intensity that made her scream. She jerked the knife down and lengthened the wound, causing more vile fluid to gush out onto her hands and wrists. Then, with one final jerk, she rammed her shoulder into the door and came through on the other side, clean and whole, but knifeless.

The room was sweltering, the scent of death so strong that Katie gagged and heaved, but did not vomit. The smell came from her right where logs burned in a small fireplace, glowing in flames of black and red and white. A perfect and unblemished white pot hung above the flames on a hook, its lid bouncing merrily as thick black steam trickled out from underneath and quickly vanished. The floor shone slick and cold. A moan came from Katie's left, on the other side of the room where stones had been stacked waist high and a giant slab of rock laid on top formed a crude altar. A figure in shadow writhed on it, hands chained in irons of black and silver. When Katie took a step in her direction, the figure stopped moving.

"Hello?" The question was muffled.

The blaze of the fire provided scant illumination, leaving the room in a gray haze. She quietly stepped over to the figure and saw that it was a young woman in a white gown. A black hood covered her head.

"Please," she said. "Don't hurt me."

Something about the scene sent a tingle through Katie's arms, legs, and chest. When she stopped next to the altar, she stared at the hood and licked her lips.

Freedom. Take it from her.

"Who are you?" Katie asked. Her voice croaked from the long trek down the steps and the sudden dryness in her throat.

"Please help me."

Katie knew what she would find when she removed the hood: Priyanka. She held her breath as she yanked the cloth off her head, and almost screamed when she did. It was not Priyanka. It was herself. The two Katies stared at each other, stunned and silent.

Take it from her. Take your freedom!

"How?" Katie asked aloud.

You already know.

Katie glanced around the room for something to use. She tried to pry a rock out from under the altar, but they were cemented in place. Next she tried the fireplace. The logs crackled and glowed. She reached into the blaze and braced herself for the blistering heat, but the flames only tingled her skin like static and sent chills of energy up her arm. Even the logs wouldn't budge. Katie opened the lid to the white pot and a plume of black smoke rose from within. When it cleared away she saw a heart beating on the bottom of the otherwise empty cauldron, huge and swollen, pumping in a steady rhythm.

Katie snatched it from the pot. The huge muscle filled her hand, still beating. But each step she took toward the altar, the pulsing grew wilder until it twitched and thumped so fast that Katie could hardly keep a hand on it.

The copy of herself on the altar stared at the heart in Katie's hand, uncomprehending. "Please. Please, don't."

Katie raised it high above her head, closed her eyes, and brought it down as hard she could on the other girl's face. Over and over and over and over. Black and red fluid splattered the altar, the floor, the walls, Katie's face. When she looked down again at the stone, the girl was gone. Nothing remained but crushed pieces of the fleshy heart.

You are free.

A sense of power filled her body and transformed her soul. She was apart from the world now. She could sense that.

Katie turned to leave the cave, but the door had sealed shut behind her. She put her shoulder against it and pushed with all her strength but it would not yield. No matter how hard she beat on it, clawed at it, even ran at it, it held fast. Finally Katie gave up and fell to her knees laughing as tears ran down her face. Even as her laughter turned to screams, power continued to infuse her.

Back in her bed, Katie woke dry as bone. Dashing out of bed, she examined herself in the mirror. She felt so different, yet nothing had changed.

"Katie!" her mother called from the kitchen. "Get ready for school or you'll miss first period again!"

"Come on, Queen," her father added. "Listen to your mom."

Katie stayed at her mirror, grinning widely.

I'm free.

She glanced at the calendar. *Friday the Thirteenth. Today is going to be a special day.*

* * * * *

Sunday, November 9, 2087

Brickert and Natalia sat in a parked car in downtown D.C. sipping coffee from thermoses at 0400. Brickert rubbed his eyes and put the binoculars back to his face. A team of workers were putting up a fence and pouring concrete to create a barricade of steel and stone. Aegis supervised the workers, directed the foreman, and oversaw the placement of tanks and other armored vehicles. The longer Brickert watched, the more nervous he became.

"What do you see, Brickert?" Justice asked from the back seat.

"Just a second," Brickert answered. "You got anything to report?" he asked Natalia, who scanned the skies with her own pair of scopes. If anyone could spot people in hard to see places, it was Brickert's girlfriend.

She leaned over him to peer out the windows, giving him a good smell of her perfume mingled with the scent of a stale body stuck in a car for almost eight hours. Brickert didn't mind it much, especially since he smelled worse. Her black hair brushed his nose, making him sniff and itch. She'd dyed it black after Li died. It was her way of dealing with the loss. Kawai, on the other hand, hadn't spoken a word since the bombing. No tears. No words. Nothing. She had completely shut down. Brickert wasn't sure if she blamed him or Sammy, or everyone. She wouldn't say.

"Yeah," Natalia said. "I see—I see two sniper nests up on the roofs southwest and northwest of the blockade corners. No one in them, though. Drone gun mounts and cover towers have been set up. I'm tagging the locations for you."

"This blockade looks legit, I tell you," Brickert said into his com. "Concrete molds are three ... four meters high. Rifle towers, I'd

-365-

guess. Armored cars and tanks going thirty to forty meters back. Not necessarily a run and gun situation. It would take a huge offensive on foot to break through it. Swarms of bodies … Normandy style. If we can't dismantle their defenses before the masses reach the blockades, thousands of people will die trying to get to the White House and Capitol Building."

"I'm seeing the same thing over here," said Lorenzo Winters, an older man who'd journeyed with Sammy and Kawai through the Amazon jungles several months ago. "These bastards aren't playing nice at all."

"Any sign of anti-aircraft towers in your area, Brickert?" Thomas asked.

Brickert looked to Natalia, who shook her head. "Not yet."

"So we've got major blockades going up at six points around the government sector and the Mall," Justice said, making marks on the map projected from his holo-tablet. "Armed explosives on the bridges crossing the Potomac. Smaller choke points with drone guns set up around the narrower streets."

"It's a war zone," Thomas muttered over the com. He was back in Hagerstown with the remaining members of the resistance who had survived the bio-bomb. "D.C. has become a battlefield."

"And we need a battle plan," Justice said. "If Sammy and Commander Byron don't come through—if they're delayed even a half hour—it's going to get ugly."

"We can't win with a ragtag team of a few hundred," Thomas said, "but I'll be damned if I don't try."

"People will come," Natalia said. "I believe it."

"So do I," said Thomas, "But how many? Sitting here watching the news … it doesn't look good. They're scaring people away. Warning after warning about lethal responses to any signs of uprising, mayhem, or disorder. Polls and experts showing the movement has no support. Constant reminders that the resistance is decimated."

"They're lies," Justice spat. "Don't believe it."

"What if they aren't?" Thomas asked.

"Then it will be a short battle," Justice said grimly. "What's the final word on our firepower? How much were we able to recover from our stores?"

"Four or five hundred kilos of Class A and B explosives. Enough to level a few city blocks."

"How many cars do we have at our disposal?"

"I'm not sure about that … three or four dozen."

"Any convertibles?" Justice asked.

"I'd have to look," Brickert remarked. "Sounds like you have some ideas."

"That I do. A real wild one if I may say so myself. We use the cars as battering rams. Pack 'em full of explosives and drive them at the barricades. If we do it in a coordinated manner, we can obliterate their defenses. Ultras can take out the snipers while Psions man the hoods of the cars using blast shields to make sure nothing sets off the explosives early. They can use jump-blasts to bail out of the cars before the *boom*."

"NWG's cruisers can provide air support," Thomas suggested.

"They're going to have their hands full," Brickert said. "Less than a hundred cruisers is all they have left. The CAG has five times that."

"Think big, gentlemen," Justice said. "If people turn out, we'll send them over water, through buildings, and any other way we can to get them to the White House and the Capitol Building."

"The CAG will be laid low," Thomas said. "The President, Congress, Supreme Court … all of it."

"You don't honestly think the President and other elected officials are going to be anywhere near D.C., do you?" Justice asked. "They'll be hiding underground or far away. Probably evacuated days ago. Right after your speech."

"Taking the White House will be a symbol," Brickert said. "The Capitol Building, the Supreme Court … all of them will be overrun."

"Why don't we destroy them?" Natalia asked.

"The goal is to incite change, not anarchy," Thomas said. "If we're successful, we'll follow the manifesto posted on the website. Return power to the people. Amend the laws. Repair the damage done from years of apathy through a process to be determined by the people."

"And then we'll ride unicorns into the sunset on a road paved with rainbows," Justice concluded.

"Why do you say that?" Thomas asked.

"Because you're living a dream if you think things change so easily. The people who will determine the manner and depth of change in the CAG are those with money and influence. They'll insert themselves into the process to shape the events in ways that benefit them."

"Then we will maintain a presence to insure that doesn't happen," Thomas said.

Justice merely gave a long, "Mmm hmm," and said no more.

* * * * *

The Queen drove her motorcycle past the neighborhood sign that read "Maple Squares," an appropriate name for a gated community of two and three story homes surrounded by lush maple and oak trees. The trees were especially beautiful in the autumn, explosions of orange, red, and yellow everywhere she looked, and the heavy, earthy scent of fall in the evening was thick and sweet. The Queen couldn't remember the last time she'd pondered on such things or even appreciated the atmosphere around her. Her com told her she was almost at her destination. *This has to be the place. It has to be.*

After weeks of work, the Queen believed she knew who aided the fox in his escape: Jeffrey Markorian. With all her other responsibilities acting as the fox, the narrowing of the list had not been easy. She had studied phone and bank records, emails, private messages, package delivery scans. She had monitored homes with drones and satellites. Now it was time to capitalize on her time and energy spent.

Hunting down Markorian reminded her of the old days, being sent on search and destroy missions by the fox. She was a woman of action—a predator—not meant to be sitting in board meetings and debating matters with hand-wringing council members.

By the time she reached Dogwood Trail, where Markorian lived, the sun was low in its arc while a light breeze made the leaves twirl on the lawns and streets. When the Queen saw Markorian's house, she pulled over and watched it until the sun went down. Using thermal goggles, she checked the home for signs of activity, booby traps, and any other signs of potential danger. Her scanners told her the house was clear and empty, an odd thing considering she had confirmed he was still at home earlier that morning.

He knew. Somehow he knew I was coming.

"Jeffrey Markorian," she told her com. "Trace call."

When he answered, she assumed the voice of the fox and said, "It's me. Where are you?"

"Have you seen the news?" Markorian asked.

The Queen paused. *That question. I've heard it before. Diego.* Diego had asked her the exact same thing when she'd spoken to him pretending to be the fox.

"I haven't seen the—"

Markorian terminated the call. The Queen smirked.

"Location," she told her com.

"Current location of caller is westbound on I-20 in Territory of Texas," answered the robotic voice.

"Trace the GPS signal."

"GPS has been deactivated—"

The Queen swore. Her next call was to Chad. She skipped the pleasantries. "Run face-recognition software on traffic cameras on I-20 westbound for Jeffrey Markorian. Once you have him, track him, and patch his location to my com."

One thing the Queen could not fault the fox for was the width and breadth of his net, capable of closing in on any target in suburban and urban areas with astonishing speed. If Project Orwell was ever completed, the net would be inescapable.

She got back on her bike and headed for her cruiser. Once airborn, she turned her sights west and waited for Chad to call back. He did so less than a half hour later with Markorian's exact position.

"Also," Chad continued, "I have a report on the Rio situation. The man sent down to investigate never responded. I gave him my number to call me directly, but nothing. Nor has he returned any of my messages."

The Queen's mind churned out data like a well-oiled machine. *Something is going on, but what?* "What can be gained in those sewers? Is there some sort of entrance into the Tower? Could this be some remnant of the resistance trying to destroy another clone production site?"

"Nothing that I can see."

The Queen pondered a moment longer. "Dispatch a small Aegis unit. I want to hear their report the instant they have it."

"Consider it done."

Two hours later, she had a visual on Markorian's vehicle heading west on the freeway toward a bridge. Putting her cruiser on autopilot, she dropped the back hatch and drove out on her motorcycle, then cut up the road until she was directly behind him. Slipping one hand to her holster, she removed her gun, aimed, and blew out the rear driver's side tire. Even through her helmet, she heard the sounds of children screaming.

Children ... None of the records she'd read on Markorian said anything about a wife or kids. Revulsion swelled in her gut and tightened her chest with an overwhelming sense of wrongness. Then Markorian's car swerved and screeched to a halt. The Queen got off her bike, gun still in hand. Jeffery Markorian was in the driver's seat yelling to his family to stay calm. His wife unbuckled her seat belt and climbed to the back to cover her children, two little girls and a boy, but the Queen acted quickly, killing one of the girls with a single shot. The old sense of satisfaction and triumph returned, roaring like a dragon inside her chest. But along with it came a terrible pain in her left breast and a dull ache in her head.

After blasting apart the window, she grabbed Markorian and yanked him off his seat. "Where is he?"

"I—I—I—"

The Queen shot his wife next, and more screams came from the car. Several other vehicles came to a stop around them. Other cars weren't prepared for this and slammed into those that had stopped. She pointed her gun at another child, this time the son. "Who dies next, Jeffery?" she yelled at him. "Your boy?"

"He's in Quito! Quito! He has an apartment there. Stop!"

The Queen dropped Jeffery back in his seat. For a moment, she considered just shooting him and leaving the other two children alive. Part of her wanted to do it, wanted to do it desperately. She heard their cries faintly, the sounds drowned out by the Queen's memory of another girl screaming as the Queen had beaten her to death.

Weakness. Pain is weakness.

The Queen shuddered as though snapping out of a dream, tossed a grenade into the car, and jogged back to her motorcycle. The explosion was a pleasant warmth on such a crisp fall day. She used her com to order a clean-up crew for large incidentals, then signaled her cruiser to return and retrieve her.

She flew the cruiser back to Orlando where she spent the rest of the night researching the fox's apartment in Quito. Over the last several weeks, she had checked all of the fox's residences, some as many as three times. All of them had turned up empty. *Why would he go there now? How did he get there? Who is there with him?*

Satellite feeds and drones were no help. Like many of the areas where the fox had residences, scramblers had been placed to cause interference with surveillance. Thermal imaging was blocked and from the available schematics, all she could find was that the structure was heavily reinforced to withstand many different kinds of attacks. She left early the next afternoon to check it out herself.

The cruiser took her to Quito, but dropped her off several kilometers from the fox's residence. She made the rest of the trip on her bike. Knowing that Markorian could not have warned the fox of her knowledge of his whereabouts, the Queen wasted no time approaching the tall apartment building, stacked with balconies jutting out like building blocks in a child's poorly made castle. When she reached a spot with a good view, she waited and observed.

Two hours of surveillance told her nothing. No movement, no heat signatures, but an open window. Her brain whirred more. An open window. It was too good to be true. *He knows I'm coming and wants me to enter.*

Her com rang. *Chad.* "What?"

"The team of Aegis I sent into the sewers called for backup. No response since then. The audio had gunshots in the background. I'm sending a drone in there now to give us a visual."

"Patch it through to my com."

Less than two minutes passed before the holo-screen on her com blinked to life. Through the drone's camera, her view went down into the sewer manhole.

"Go to night vision!" she hissed to Chad.

Immediately the spotlight blinked out and her view changed to night vision. Everything looked normal until the drone flew past three large equipment bags and four dead bodies: three Aegis and one older man wearing a safety vest.

On the left wall she saw a large black spot, a hole. Someone stood just inside the aperture holding a thick pipe that pumped out a liquid. The person's head turned at the sound of the drone. The drone's scanner required less than a second to locate the person's eyes and scan the retina.

    Identification: 13F712072-Jane, Psion Dark agent,
    captured by the resistance.

Behind her, two others appeared to be dragging a massive drill out of a tunnel that went into the wall. As the group discarded the drill and grabbed the large packs on the ground, the drone scanned again.

    Identification: Albert Choochoo, captured Anomaly
    Fourteen, escaped imprisonment.

"Drone!" the girl cried. Then she whipped the flexible piping and slammed it into the drone. The camera feed cut out.

"Get a team into the sewers to find them!" the Queen ordered.

"Who are they?" Chad asked.

"He's in Rio," she told Chad. "Berhane is in Rio."

"Are you going to deal with this personally?"

The Queen didn't answer. *What is he doing in the sewer?* A trap. *They're all laying traps.* The fox, Sammy … she didn't have time for these games. "Send in the rest of my Aegis first. Find out what he's doing. Constant reports *every* step of the way. I'm heading to Rio soon. I just have to do one more thing."

Using her blasts, the Queen jumped from balcony to balcony until she reached the highest one where the window was open. Before she let herself in, she muttered, "You underestimated me once," she said. "I wager you'll do it again."

She expected to find an immaculate, well-organized, and lavish apartment similar to the fox's other penthouses in Orlando, New York City, and Los Angeles. Instead she found a place in disarray. Tools littered the floors and tables. The smell of blood and chemicals hung in the air, thick and fresh. In the main room she saw a cot, heavily used, and a small kitchen in the corner. In the back room was an operating table and used medical and mechanical equipment. The Queen didn't need to spend much time examining the mess to know what had happened.

"Bionics," she told herself. The fox had built himself bionic limbs. "Where are you, you son of a—"

A worn, outdated holo-screen in the corner of the living room blinked on. The fox's face showed on it. His skin had more color, his cheeks and eyes less emaciated than they'd been under her care. "Hello, Katie. I thought you'd find me sooner than this."

She ignored the insult. "The world is a small place. You can't run for long."

"Oh, I'm not running. Do you want to know where I am? Back trace the signal and you'll find me. But we should chat first, I think.

How are you faring in your management of the core CAG objectives? The Council? Do they still expect you to win the war?"

With a whisper, the Queen ordered her com to trace the fox's signal. "We destroyed the resistance base. We're primed to snuff out this offensive coming from the NWG and any CAG insurgents. I expect President Marnyo to surrender soon after."

"And then what? Will you continue to use my identity? I think it's highly unlikely that you'll just disappear."

"I have a plan."

"I once had plans." The fox frowned. "Recruiting you was a mistake, Katie. Perhaps it was my youth. And your beauty. Yes, I think that was it. Those days I believed the end was justified by the means, but now I see that it is never so simple. The means taint the end. I was corrupted. And how can a corrupt man change the world for the better? It took me losing my arms and legs to see that ... and lying in a bed with nothing else to think about but where I'd gone wrong. Now I know. I thought I could shape the world. You say it's small, but that's wrong. The size of the planet doesn't matter, but the diversity of the people. It's richness of culture and thought makes it huge and untamable. To try to homogenize the human race was a mistake."

"Your only mistake was to cross me. And now you have lost your vision. I shouldn't be surprised that you have given up, claiming to have seen some kind of light. You are weaker than ever. And friendless."

"Not friendless. A friend risked his life to carry me out of my prison. He restored me to health. And then he allowed himself to die to protect my secrets."

The Queen laughed. "Protect your secrets? He sang like a bird when I killed his wife and children. You see? You are a fool!"

"Jeffery Markorian doesn't have a wife or children, Katie. Everyone in that car with him were holograms. You only killed him. And only after he told you exactly what I asked him to say. I knew you'd find him. And that you'd come here. This was where I needed you to be."

"Here I am. Yet you talk to me via holo-screen like a coward."

"I think it's because there is one thing that still tickles the back of my mind."

The Queen gritted her teeth, hissed a command into her com, and said, "You're wondering why I didn't kill you?"

"No." The fox's face told her he already knew that answer. "The cave."

A lump formed in the Queen's throat. "What cave?"

"I think it's a fascinating thing, the cave. *Every* Thirteen sees the cave and the shadow. The cave is always there with a second choice. For each person that alternative choice is different, but not the cave. We couldn't explain it no matter how deeply we examined the phenomenon. Our best guess is that on some evolutionary level the cave is embedded into our genetic memory. Each Thirteen chooses the cave over the other option. Don't you find that fascinating, Katie?"

She bristled at the name. "No."

"But what they find in the cave, that's not the same for each person either, I think. Just the cave." He gave a sort of shrug. "Tell me something. Now that you have spliced yourself, have you seen the cave again? Was there a second chance of sorts? I am still not certain that the Anomaly Eleven and Thirteen can permanently coexist."

The Queen did not answer, but what he said gave her pause. Images from her recent nightmares returned: herself, an adult, standing at the bottom of a cave at the fleshy door she had once cut open, now resealed, rotted, and blackened like leather. On the other side of the door she heard a teenage girl screaming to be let out. No matter how hard the Queen and the girl on the other side tried, nothing could reopen the door. Somehow she had become locked on each side of the door.

"I told you before that each person who has Anomaly Eleven—Tensai—whatever you want to call it—each person tends to develop a genius in a specific area, often something they are already good at. For me it was reading and manipulating people. Have you figured out what it is for you?"

"Being you," the Queen growled. She glanced at her holo-screen. *He's on the North American east coast.*

The fox laughed. Several metallic bangs and clangs came from around the room as windows and doors sealed shut. The Queen screamed curses even as she calculated her odds of escape.

"Empathy, Katie. I saw the way you winced in real pain every time you looked at what you did to me. I heard your whimpers as you tried to numb yourself with those creams. You feel other people's pain."

"Let me out of here!" she shrieked.

"And that makes you more dangerous than any other human. The idea that you can feel what you feel, and still do what you do … The new world I will build has no place for Thirteens and Hybrids,

Katie. And certainly no place for the likes of you. I had hoped that when you gained your new intelligence you would regain some measure of your old humanity, but I see that will never happen. Goodbye."

The Queen removed an explosive from her pack and threw it at the fortified window, shielding herself with the strongest blasts she could summon. Fire and heat swirled around her with the fury of a dragon's breath. The Queen sprinted at the window, blasting with all her might. The metal peeled outward like a grinning demon, so she kept at it knowing only seconds remained before—

KCHOOOOOM!

The Queen blasted again just as the concussion of the explosion hit her, hurling her at the window. Energy poured from her hands as she flew. Metallic claws pulled at her skin and clothes and hair, but she found air and space as her body squeezed through the crack. Blackness overtook her, and then she was falling falling falling …

The Queen opened her eyes and blasted just before hitting the ground. A smattering of people had stopped what they were doing to stare, a few screamed. The Queen blasted and blasted, her body bounced off the cushions of energy before smacking her ribs and face on the concrete. Everything was pain: breathing, moving, thinking, but she got up and made it back to her bike all the same.

The cruiser's auto-pilot returned her to Orlando. As the Queen rode the elevator from the rooftop to the penthouse, she collapsed and lay on the elevator floor for several minutes before she found the strength to stagger out of the lift and into the fox's apartment. *Mirror … Where's the mirror?*

The closest was in the bathroom. She nearly tripped twice as she stumbled that way and opened the door with a weak shove. The light brightened at her presence. Crimson red skin was the first thing she saw. Blood everywhere, from her forehead to her chin. A deep cut ran across her nose and cheek, smaller ones on her arms where the metal had eaten at her as she passed through the demon's grin. She had become as hideous as the worst of the Thirteens. *I look just like them.*

The Queen blasted the mirror into shards, bellowing and shrieking in rage. When the anger burned away, she passed out again.

The beeping of her com woke her. The first thing the Queen noticed was that her body didn't hurt nearly as bad as she'd thought it would, especially her face. She was tired and sore, but not in agony as she'd been.

Getting to her feet, she stumbled to her bedroom, passing two mirrors on the way. When the Queen passed the second mirror, she stopped and jerked backward. She gazed at herself as though a stranger stared back at her. *My face ... my beautiful face ...*

It wasn't as bad as she'd thought. The deep cut would take some work, but her surgeons had repaired far worse. Her arms were badly scratched with a few deeper cuts, so was her chest and back. But those would heal in time. *Medicine. I need medicine for my face. Then a surgeon before the scarring sets in. The damage can be repaired.*

The Queen dug through her supplies until she found the ointments she needed. The com rang again. It had fallen out of her ear when she hit the floor. She let it ring while she treated her wounds.

Seconds after she finished patching herself up, it rang a third time.

Chad. The Queen found the com and asked, "Did the Aegis find Berhane?"

"They entered the sewers as you ordered," Chad told her. "Berhane is gone. They've been searching for him in the service tunnels, but there are kilometers and kilometers of walkways. It could take—"

"He's heading for the N Tower. Get the Aegis back there and have them wait until we know exactly where Berhane is. Once we do, attack him. He'll tear through the Aegis like paper, so have a team of Thirteens ready to go down to hit him hard in a second wave."

"No Hybrids?"

The Queen grinned. "Not yet. Let's come at him in waves. We'll wear him down." Her eyes narrowed on her reflection and she grinned at herself.

"I also have a report on the trace you ordered on the fox."

"Where is he?"

"He's in Orlando. Across the city in another safe house."

"He can wait for now. I'm coming to Rio. Once Sammy is exhausted, I will be ready to break him like a porcelain doll."

22 | Elevators

Tuesday, November 11, 2087

THE AIR IN the forest was so hot Sammy could taste it, bitter and metallic like the large key in his hand. His shadow had given it to him as he did every time Sammy had the dream. To the right, a vast lake called to him with its usual promise of a cool and refreshing eternity. A raft bobbed and splashed in the choppy waters, silently inviting him to use the key, unlock the padlock, and float away into infinite peace. But to the left was the cave … it beckoned to Sammy in a whisper so faint he couldn't actually hear it, yet in a voice so sweet he craved more.

His feet took him toward the cave, seemingly of their own accord. Into the blackness. It was cooler here, especially on his wet brow, and the further in he walked, the cooler it grew. Had he not been in abject darkness, Sammy would have seen his breath. Yet he continued to sweat.

Finally he reached the steps. Countless times before, he had stood on the precipice, his wet, cold toes dangling over the edge of the first stone stair. Though he'd thought about it numerous times, he had never gone down.

You're going to die. Don't you want to know what's down there?

That one suggestion was all it took. Step after step Sammy descended, still dripping sweat that fell in small *plops* onto the stone. He could tell when he was nearing the end because the scent changed, gradually growing so fetid and rank that breathing became painful. At the bottom Sammy bumped into what could only be an iron door. He ran his fingers along the paneling and touched the bracings until he found the large keyhole on the left side. Its shape perfectly matched the head of the key in his other hand.

"Sammy," a weak female voice called to him from inside. "Save me."

Jeffie.

It was her voice. He knew that. And yet he also knew that it wasn't her. Something in his gut told him to get away, get out, RUN.

"Sammy ... she's hurting me. She's killing me!" Jeffie pleaded with more urgency. The pain in her voice put his nerves on edge.

He held up the key and tried to decide.

Something jostled him. The darkness, the cave, the smell, the key, and the door ... all of it faded away. He was huddled in a small nook with Jeffie and Vitoria cramped in with him, the girls still asleep.

Sammy swore under his breath. He had told Jeffie and Vitoria he would keep watch. A glance at his watch told him he'd been out for over four hours. *Stupid. Careless.* Yet he'd needed the rest. *And I didn't wet myself for a change.* Even a few hours of cramped, fitful sleep was better than nothing.

After a drone had spotted Vitoria in the sewer, the three teammates had dashed to grab their equipment packs and head down the tunnel they had carved into the city block's foundations. Once inside the foundation's service corridors deep in the earth, they ran for over two hours carrying their heavy packs. The service tunnels were a vast and byzantine maze that connected not only to the N Tower, but multiple skyscrapers in the vicinity. Sammy had committed the whole of it to memory, down to the small nooks and crannies like the one they slept in now.

He sat up, dizzy and fatigued. The air around them was thick with the scent of drilling chemicals and body odor. *We need water,* Sammy thought. He knew which pipes carried it, but also knew that bursting a pipe would be the same as flashing a sign at the Aegis saying, "Here we are!"

Sammy activated his com to check in with Justice and Thomas, but he was too far underground to get any reception. He checked the time. 0542.

He nudged Jeffie first. "Hey," he whispered, "wake up."

Jeffie's eyes opened, one completely blood shot, the other only half so.

"Hiya," she muttered, her voice hoarse and dry. "How do I look?"

"Hotter than ever."

She laughed weakly. "What time is it?"

"Four hours left. And some change." They had coordinated with Commander Byron to activate the kill code at 1000 Rio time and 0800 Orlando time because Rio was two hours ahead of Orlando. The march on Washington D.C. would begin at sunrise, which would occur at 0645. By the time the marchers actually reached downtown D.C. the CAG agents would be dead.

Jeffie watched Vitoria for a long time. "Is she going to make it out of here alive? Will she even go when she's done her part?"

Sammy sighed and tried to rub the sleep from his face. "Can we make her do anything she doesn't want to do?"

"We don't have a suit for her," Jeffie added.

"If it comes to that, it comes to that."

"I can hear you," Vitoria muttered.

"Oh good," Jeffie responded. "Because it's time to get up."

Toad's sister cursed in Portuguese. "Am I in hell? Because it's blazing hot and I'm stuck with the two of you." Sarcasm laced her weary voice.

"What now?" Jeffie asked. "We still have a lot of time to kill before we need to be in the white room."

"We have four hours." Sammy kicked his large equipment pack. "It's going to take us a while to get back to the N Tower. I led us far away to lose the Aegis. But I bet they're still looking for us. Maybe Thirteens too. We need to drink as much water as we can stomach and make our way to the elevator without them finding us."

Sammy pulled his gun and fired a round to burst open the pipe. Cold water sprayed out in a wild gush from above, splashing onto Sammy's face, in his mouth, and running down his neck into his clothes. It was the greatest thing he could remember. He drank and drank, letting the water cool his body and refresh his spirit. The pleasure of it reminded him of his dream—the cave and the lake—and he wondered why the cave had ever enticed him. After he, Jeffie, and Vitoria drank their fill, they picked up their packs and hurried away.

It took Sammy well over an hour to lead them to the right elevator. The moment the lift doors opened, Jeffie destroyed the video camera inside it with a single shot. Sammy popped the top hatch of the box and jammed the elevator's rails so it couldn't move while Jeffie helped Vitoria climb up through the top. Once they were all on top of the elevator Jeffie lit a flare.

"How far up is it?" she asked.

"Is what?" Vitoria asked.

"The crawlspace," Sammy answered. "This elevator won't take us to the white floor. It's not even part of the N Tower. It's one of many that service all the levels of these utility tunnels. But this one in particular runs up to the ground level of a building across the street from N Tower. And," Sammy nodded his head toward the empty space above them, "up there is a crawlspace that connects this elevator shaft to the shaft of elevator number 13 of the N Tower. Elevator 13 *does* reach the white, black, and red floors. But those floors are much deeper than where we are now."

"So we go up, over, and down," Vitoria said.

"Up, over, and down." *To our deaths.*

The air in the elevator shaft was much cooler compared to the furnace-like heat in the utility tunnels. As they climbed the elevator's thick cables, the sweat and water soaking their clothes chilled them.

By the time they reached the connecting crawlspace, Sammy's arms and legs were cramped and his fingers raw.

They rested in the crawlspace for as long as they dared, but getting caught or trapped inside the small passageway would mean being turned into Swiss cheese by enemy guns. Sammy had no idea if Elevator 13 was above or below them, but he guessed it was above. When it was time to enter the second elevator shaft, Jeffie dropped a flare. They watched it tumble down out of sight. Then, warily, they started the descent. According to Sammy's com it was 0715. Almost three hours to kill. *Or be killed.*

Halfway down, the second elevator shaft grew lighter, the illumination coming from beneath them. Sammy cursed; he'd been wrong. The elevator was below and moving upward rapidly.

"Jump on it," Sammy said as the box approached. "Try not to make any noise."

The elevator reached them in moments. The car was silent save for the rushing of air around them. The three managed soft landings, the Ultra with help from the Psions. Vitoria knelt and pressed her ear against the top hatch of the elevator, then signaled to Sammy that she wanted to make a move. He signaled back to do no such thing. She repeated her request more adamantly.

With a curt nod, Sammy gave her his gun. Vitoria stayed on her knees for a moment longer, muttering to herself. Then she stood, aimed her gun in five places, and fired five times in rapid succession. Sammy and Jeffie pulled open the top hatch and found four dead Thirteens inside, each with a bullet to the head. Jeffie dropped down and whirled to destroy the camera, but didn't fire. Vitoria had already taken that out too.

Jeffie glowered at her. "Showoff."

Vitoria smirked as she pushed the emergency stop button. However, the elevator did not stop. Vitoria's smile vanished and she pushed it again.

"They've overridden the controls," Sammy said. "We have to get out!"

They worked furiously to cut through the floor as the car rose rapidly. Once Vitoria and Jeffie had the floor partially cut, Sammy blasted the rest away. "Take the packs and go, Jeffie!"

After Jeffie jumped down feet first, Sammy followed. Vitoria went last. As he fell, he used wall blasts to slow his descent. When Vitoria caught up to him, he caught her in his arms with an "*oof.*"

"I swear ... you don't ... look this heavy," he groaned. Despite the joke, getting them down the shaft in one piece was not easy. It took well-timed blast after blast off the walls with only his feet to safely descend. When he needed a rest, Sammy grabbed the cables and hung on with his limbs coiled around the cords, Vitoria hanging beside him.

"Are you going to make it?" she asked.

His arms were done, he hadn't eaten in hours, and Vitoria felt like a boulder. "Oh yeah," he said. "I'm fine."

When they reached the bottom, she fell out of Sammy's arms onto the ground. Sammy sat down amidst the hydraulics and machinery that powered the lift. His arms hung limply at his side.

"Destroy the elevator?" Jeffie asked.

"No. That's Vitoria's only way out."

"Sammy—" Vitoria began, but he cut her off.

"It's not up for discussion." He pointed up at the doors to the white floor a few meters above them. "As soon as you open those doors, you get yourself to safety. *Then* we'll destroy the elevator."

They fell silent. Sammy wiped the sweat off his brow, took a deep breath, and let it out as slowly as he could. His arms still ached; the rest of his body was no better. He climbed to his feet, slinging one of the packs over his shoulder.

"We're here way too early," Jeffie said. "There's too much time to kill before Byron and Al—"

"Things haven't gone as planned," Sammy answered. "What do you want to do? We can't risk getting caught in the utility tunnels and not reaching the white floor. And we can't hide in the elevator shaft."

He dug through his pack and took out three packs of energy paste and distributed them to the team. Vitoria shook her head. "You only brought four."

"And you need one as much as we do." Sammy held it out to her until she took it. The paste was bitter and tangy, but gave him a much-needed boost. Yet it couldn't fix the weariness deep in his bones that came from the knowledge that his time was rapidly running out.

"Okay," Jeffie said with a deep breath. "Let's do this."

* * * * *

Byron sat in a cell in the depths of the Orlando N Tower, waiting for the interrogation he knew would come. His face and arms were bruised from the Aegis tackling and subduing him in the lobby of the building hours ago. He'd hoped they would believe what they wanted to see: a deranged homeless man raving about things he did not understand. Fortunately, he'd gotten his wish.

After sedating him, roughing him up, and searching him, the Aegis found no weapons or contraband, so they chucked him in a cell without performing a more thorough examination. But soon they would return. Once they realized he had two rather expensive bionic legs, they'd draw blood and run a DNA test. Being an operative in the NWG before the Schism meant his DNA was still on file in CAG records. In minutes, they would know exactly who he was.

Still a little groggy, the commander lay on the floor wondering how many other people had been trapped in the same four walls surrounding him. Sammy had spent weeks on the black floor in Rio. How many other terrified children, broken parents, and lost souls who ran afoul of the Aegis and Thirteens had been imprisoned here? He ran his fingers on the smooth surface of the white wall, and stopped when he felt a series of scratches.

He peered at them in the dim light. It took almost a minute of squinting and running his fingers over them before he made out the words: *We are alone*. Each letter was fainter than the one preceding it. Some poor kid had gouged the words into the wall. Had Sammy carved something similar almost two years ago? Byron touched them again and nearly lost his composure.

"God ... what have I done with my life?" he asked in a whisper. "I have led children ... even my own son ... to the slaughter. Is this what you wanted from me?"

Not two years ago Commander Byron had possessed such vigor and enthusiasm for his work. All the way up until he was removed as the head of Beta headquarters. He had trained all the Betas, the best fighters and the worst. He thought of Victor. Could Wrobel's betrayal of the NWG and subsequent madness have been prevented with a little more attention and care from a friend? It both amazed and terrified Byron to think that in the great and vast river of life, he'd had enough influence and power to shape the course of events large and small. It was a burden so few men and women ever experienced.

What if I could have prevented this war? What if one decision somewhere along the way made the difference?

Before Commander Byron could ponder on these questions further, the door opened and two Aegis grabbed him under the arms and led him out of the room. To keep up appearances, Byron mumbled incoherently to himself in Amos's voice. "This ain't no bread house. Where's Marjorie? She said they got the best bread at the bread house, don'tcha know?"

"Shut up, old man," one of the Aegis said, twisting Byron's arm so hard he nearly broke it.

Byron groaned and complained in character, though his arm pulsed painfully each time he moved it. He hoped he hadn't torn a muscle.

They led him down a hall to a room with a black door. Inside was a chair, which they thrust him into and slammed the door shut. Then they stripped off his clothes leaving him naked and cold. As he'd suspected, they quickly noticed his bionic limbs. The Aegis who first spotted them drew his weapon and pointed it between Byron's eyes.

"Move and you're dead." Then, using the jerking and shrieking language of the Thirteens, he told his fellow Aegis to secure Byron and call in back up. Minutes later, seven more Aegis and a Thirteen arrived. One of the Aegis, under the Thirteen's orders, removed the commander's bionic legs while another drew his blood. His method for extracting the blood was crude. He cut Byron with a knife and caught some in a vial.

The bionic legs that Dr. Rosmir had fashioned for Commander Byron after the battle on Capitol Island were beautiful and well-designed with an implant attachment surgically integrated into the commander's bone so the limbs themselves could be removed easily for updates and reparations. Had they not been so easy to disconnect, the Aegis might have simply hacked them off with a butcher's knife.

It wasn't ten minutes before the DNA test identified him as Walter Tennyson Byron, former Elite-turned-NWG government agent. They even had access to his pre-Schism classified medical files, which revealed that he was a Psion.

The atmosphere in the room changed. The Aegis drew their guns and pointed them at the commander's chest. The sole Thirteen in the room fixed his blood red eyes on Byron's. He had burned a ring of triangles onto his face, all pointed inward, making his face look smaller and more menacing. His teeth were ground into sharp points as well. The scars on his throat and the deep, raspy voice told Byron that the Thirteen had badly damaged vocal cords.

"Why are you here, poet?" Triangle-Face asked. "Another bomb? Planning to take down our towers one by one?" He shoved a knife up into the commander's nostril, but didn't put enough pressure on it to open the skin. "Your D.C. diversion won't work. Every tower is guarded. We already have a team sent to detain the infiltrators at the Rio Tower."

The pressure from the blade increased until the commander felt a stream of blood tumble down onto his lip. Commander Byron blew it onto the face of the Thirteen, who grinned and licked at it. Then he pulled the knife through the commander's skin, creating a flare of pain. "Remember those creams we used to use on our more stubborn prisoners?" Triangle-Face asked one of the Aegis. "Why don't you go find some so we can use them on this one? This poet will tell us everything he knows rather quickly."

"Wait!" Byron said, now through thick blood covering his lips. "I will tell you! I am a decoy."

"From what?"

"The white floor. They wanted access to the white floor. Needed a high profile target to draw your attention."

"No one can get to the white floor, poet," the Thirteen growled. "Not without our knowledge."

Byron said nothing. Instead he met the Thirteen's gaze and waited for him to make the next move.

"If what you say is the truth," the Thirteen growled, "you'll get a quick death. If you're lying, the creams ... and a death as slow as I can make it."

"The team is already there. Check for yourself." Byron's voice carried a mixture of distress and pride, hoping to convince the Thirteen that what he said was true.

Triangle-Face growled, frustration in his red eyes. The white rooms had no cameras, no surveillance systems. A team would have to go down and check the doors for signs of forced entry. Commander Byron watched him closely.

Following a series of jerks and shrieks, the Thirteen left the room. If Byron had to guess, he'd say Triangle-Face's orders had been to kill the prisoner if he moved. All the Aegis kept their guns trained on him. The bloodlust shone in their eyes. *They may not wait for an order to kill me*, Byron thought as he counted methodically in silence.

When he reached one hundred, he smiled at the Aegis around him. "I thank you all for being so hospitable. I feared my interaction with you would leave me much more injured than a simple nose piercing job gone bad."

A couple of their fingers twitched.

"But as I simply cannot sit here all day, I leave you with one parting word … *Emeralds*."

A soft click came from one of his bionic legs resting two meters away from him. Byron doubted anyone else heard the sound. He took a deep breath through his nose and then counted upward from one, praying that the Aegis didn't stab him before he reached ten. At eight, everyone in the room except himself dropped to the floor. He took another deep breath through his nose, clogged with deeply implanted nasal filters, and waited until the gas dissipated enough that he could safely speak.

"Albert," he ordered the com built into his bionic leg. He waited half a minute, but no answer. A brief flare of worry rose in his chest. He quickly extinguished it by reminding himself of his son's skill and capability. "Albert."

Still no response.

"Albert."

Byron pulled at his restraints while his stubbed legs dangled over the end of the chair, the metallic attachments gleaming whenever they caught the light. Each second that passed without an answer felt like an hour.

"Albert."

He tried to tug himself free again but lost his balance and fell to the floor, his face smacked hard on the tile. Stars burst in his vision and pain blossomed in his skull. He lay on the ground unable to move, his cheek mashed against the floor. He could do nothing but hope the Aegis did not wake. Byron had never felt so helpless or pathetic. *It can't end this way. Sammy and Jeffie are counting on me. Their deaths will not be in vain.*

The door swung open. He strained his muscles to get free, but it couldn't be done.

"Dad?"

"Hurry!" the commander hissed.

Several rounds were fired as Albert gave a bullet to each of the Aegis in the room. Then he uncuffed his father.

Byron rubbed his wrists where the skin had peeled away from his attempts to wrench himself free. "What kept you?"

"It's only been a few minutes, Dad. I gassed the Thirteen, cut off his thumb, and shoved him up out of the elevator hatch. Then I got here as fast as I could. I thought I worked pretty efficiently, thank you very much."

"Is everything in place?" the commander asked as he reattached his legs to their mechanic joints and donned the uniform of a dead Aegis.

"Yep."

Albert had been atop Elevator 13 for hours. While Byron had entered the lobby dressed as a belligerent homeless man, Albert had killed an Aegis patrolling outside the building, taken his clothes, and entered the tower in the Aegis' uniform. Once inside the elevator, Albert had covered the surveillance camera with a tiny screen that showed a twelve-hour recording of people getting on and off an elevator from the same angle as the existing camera. Then he slipped through the top elevator hatch and waited for the signal. *Emeralds* not only triggered the gas from the bionic leg, but told Albert to come immediately to the black floor and retrieve the commander.

Byron checked the time. "Two hours until launch."

They left the room with the black door and checked the rest of the cells on the floor for prisoners. They found none. Albert had propped open the elevator with the body of Triangle-Face. Using the dead man's finger and eye, they ordered the elevator to take them to the white floor. Just before the elevator passed the red floor on its way down, the lift abruptly came to a halt.

"What's going on?" Albert asked.

"I think our plan has failed."

Albert grabbed his pack still atop the elevator, next to the dead Thirteen, and retrieved from it the plasma blade. He fired it up and jammed the blade into the floor where it slowly began to cut through the thick plate of tempered steel. The commander's son was nearly halfway done cutting a hole when the elevator began to move again.

"Hurry," Byron muttered.

Albert looked up. "What's happening now?"

"They have taken control over the elevator."

-396-

The lift finished the descent to the red floor. Byron jammed the DOOR CLOSE button, but it didn't stay closed. As the commander crouched low and took cover behind the right door side panel, his son did the same on the left. A grenade flew toward them just as the doors opened, but Byron blasted it back the way it came. The shrieks of Thirteens followed.

BOOM!

Debris and smoke filled the air accompanied by a heat wave that dampened Byron's face with sweat. Using a flexiscope from Albert's pack, he peered around the corner. Through the smoke and ash he saw figures moving about. Some Thirteens were dressed in their red-melting-to-black uniforms, jagged 13 symbols blazoned over the breast, others had fully mutilated bodies in wanton displays of undress.

"Finish cutting the hole," the commander ordered. "I'll keep them back."

They were a swarm of bees, angry, humming, and constantly moving. Each time the commander thought he had one in his sights, he fired his syshée, but missed. With his other hand he blasted a shield wide enough to protect himself and Albert, who crouched behind him. Not for the first time, he wished he had his real legs, and the ability to jump-blast. He was an old man now, slow, and needed every advantage he could get.

Albert resumed cutting with the plasma blade. Meanwhile, the nearest Thirteens worked their way in closer. Byron finally clipped one of them in the leg, but she hardly reacted. Two more Thirteens launched into the air trying to jump over his shield. Commander Byron shot at one, but the Thirteen twisted around before the gun even fired. The other he blasted back with a strong hand blast, leaving Byron momentarily defenseless. In that instant, a bullet punched through the tricep of his left arm.

"Albert!" the commander cried as the nearest Thirteen kicked him in the face, breaking his already badly cut nose and sending an explosion of sparks through his vision.

Before the commander could recover, a gun was in his face. Without hesitation, the Thirteen holding it began to pull the trigger when his head jerked and blood spattered in the commander's bleary eyes. The Thirteen fell on top of Byron. If not for the gore pouring from the Thirteen's head, Byron might have left the body there for cover.

Albert had their attention now. The commander's wounded arm burned and ached, but he used both hands to blast the Thirteen off him. Albert had already managed to kill two enemies, but more remained.

"You finish cutting, Dad!" Albert said. "I'll handle them."

Byron tried to use the plasma saw in his injured condition, but between his hurt arm and his need to keep an eye on Albert, he did a poor job. *I should not have come. I am too old, too slow. My pride may end up getting both of us killed.*

Using their bizarre, animal-like communication, the Thirteens cautiously advanced on the elevator. They could not all attack at once for fear of being bottle-necked and picked off, one by one. Two more grenades flew at the elevator, immediately followed by two more. Albert blasted all four back with reflexes that would have impressed an Ultra. A bullet ricocheted off Byron's bionic leg in the process.

"Watch those shields!" he told his son.

The explosion from the grenades was tremendous. Black smoke filled the air, and the last thing Byron saw before the cloud filled his vision was two Thirteens torn apart from the detonation. Albert was shoved to the back of the elevator where his head slammed into the wall. A female Thirteen attacked through the haze. She had a shock of red hair styled in a Mohawk and a face tattooed to look like it was covered in rivulets of wet blood. Byron dropped the saw and drew his gun, emptying his magazine, but missing every shot. His left arm was weak and unable to keep the gun steady. Rather than trying to reload, he abandoned the gun and focused on blasting her. She attacked between his blasts, weaving in, out, and around to get in close for hand to hand combat. Just as she got near, Byron used one hand to blast himself off the ground and slammed his weight into her.

His momentum drove the Mohawk Thirteen out of the elevator and into the wall, cracking ribs and plasterboard alike. She tried to sink her teeth into his neck but bit down on his shoulder when he jerked backward. Commander Byron brought up a hand to blast her head at point-blank range, but she spun away only to attack again, knocking Byron to the ground. His shoulder, arm, and face roared in pain.

Struggling to beat just one Thirteen, the commander lamented. *What good am I?*

He jammed his hands up under her ribs and blasted her up into the ceiling where she hit the remnants of the plaster and crossbeams. As she fell she reloaded her gun, fast as anything Byron had seen. He raised his hands to shield, but the bullet cracked his collarbone and exited through his back, like a torch blowing through his body. He blasted again, blindly, and forced her back, her head smacking wetly into the stone wall.

Commander Byron lay on the ground, fire spreading through his shoulder and back. *Failure.* He had volunteered for this mission to prove something: to show himself and the other Psions that despite his age, despite his mistakes, despite his injuries he was still useful. But all he had done so far was prove the opposite.

No. I am not useless.

He tried to pick himself up as the smoke choked his lungs. Around him he heard more gunshots. *Firing at Albert!* Between the bullet hole in his left arm and his right clavicle, Commander Byron could not get up. He gritted his teeth and tried again. At least four Thirteens remained. Albert could not handle them all by himself. The harder he pushed the more agony he created until something popped in his shoulder, and he blacked out.

"Dad! Dad!"

When Byron opened his eyes, Albert was dragging him back into the elevator. He looked much messier than the last time the commander had seen him. "How long was I out?"

"About fifteen minutes. Don't move."

Albert removed an orange goo dispenser from the med kit and a syringe full of antibiotic. As Albert jammed the orange goo into his father's wounds, Byron tried not to react but the pain was unbearable. His son's wide eyes, pale face, and pinched expression told him the damage wasn't insignificant.

"Maybe give me the anesthetic first next time …" the commander muttered.

Albert grimaced as he retrieved the second syringe from the kit. "Sorry."

The anesthesia brought a wave of relief. The commander sighed. "Patch me up. We need to go."

"You're a mess, old man."

"You should find a mirror, kiddo. Is your head all right?"

"Tender, but in one piece," Albert answered. His face was covered in a reddish pink mess which had once belonged in some Thirteen's skull. Commander Byron winced and grimaced as his son worked quickly to stem the flow of blood and get his father in stable condition. When Albert finished, he helped the commander to his feet.

"Thanks," Byron said. The anesthesia was kicking in, leaving his body stiff but pain-free. "How much time do we have?"

Albert checked his com. "An hour and a half. Almost on the dot."

Byron took a step which immediately transformed into a limp. He hadn't even noticed the pain in his uppermost thigh until now, his shoulder and arm had hurt so badly. But when he looked down at his leg, he saw the slice through the fabric of his pants and a line of blood seeping through his torn skin, just above the joint where his bionic leg met his own flesh. *A graze*. Byron had never taken three bullet wounds in one battle until today. Seeing his own blood in such quantities starkly reminded him of his own mortality, and he yearned for the days when he thought himself invincible.

"Elevator's still not responding," Albert said, punching the DOOR CLOSE button repeatedly. "They disabled it."

"You took on four Thirteens by yourself," Byron said as he counted the bodies on the ground.

Albert sighed and nodded. "Yeah. Remember I did it in the sims before I graduated. Sammy worked with me."

"I remember … I just—I am impressed. You are better than I ever was."

"The circle is now complete. When I left you, I was but the learner. Now I am the master."

Commander Byron looked at his son. "Is that a quote?"

"Dad … Star Wars. Come on."

"Star Wars?"

"That movie you showed me when I was little. I watched it about ten times. Don't you remember?"

"We need to finish cutting the hole."

"I'm on it," Albert said. As his son resumed working with the plasma blade, Byron kept a lookout for any surviving Thirteens who might try to surprise them. The biggest surprise, however, came when the elevator gave a sudden lurch. Albert's head jerked up. "What was—"

The elevator plummeted.

"Out! Out!"

"You first!" Albert said. "I'll boost you."

The commander stumbled on his wounded leg and caught himself on Albert's shoulders. Lifting his injured leg was not easy. He put that leg down and tried to stand on it instead, but that was worse. Gritting his teeth, he shoved himself up and let his son's blasts force him through the hatch and out of the elevator. Right before Albert jumped, the elevator crashed into the bottom of the

-402-

shaft. Albert's head hit the ceiling, the skin split open, and he fell back to the floor. Blood snaked down over his face.

"Albert?" Commander Byron asked weakly. "Son?"

23 | Drones

Tuesday, November 11, 2087

THE WHITE ROOM was white. For some reason, Sammy hadn't expected that. The black floor in Rio hadn't been all black. Nor had the red floor in Detroit been all red. But this one had white floors, white walls, white ceiling. The elevator doors opened to a small anteroom, which he could tell would seal off the main room from the elevator when the kill code was triggered. The room itself was large but not huge. About eight meters by ten meters according to his estimates.

"I—I thought you needed me to get in here," Vitoria said.

"Not in here," Sammy responded. "In there." He pointed to where a small door occupied the center of the back wall of the white room.

On the right of the door was a thumb and retina scanner. Following Trapper's instructions on how to recode the door, Sammy found a tiny switch on the underside of the scanner panel and flipped it. This revealed a port into which he slid the data cube prepared by Trapper to recode the door with Vitoria's retina, thumb print, and voice.

As the data cube did its work, Sammy checked his com and saw that they still had over two hours before it was time to send the signal. He walked around the room, his fingers brushing the flat smooth walls. Then he stopped and pointed to two spots close to the center of the room. "There and there. Company may be coming." He nodded to Jeffie and Vitoria. "Set up the projectors."

"This data cube has passcode protection," the panel next to the door informed Sammy. "Please state the passcode to activate your cube."

"Repentance," Sammy muttered.

"Passcode accepted. Please submit retina for scanning."

Sammy looked back where Jeffie and Vitoria were assembling two holo-projectors in the middle of the room, one nearer to the left wall, the other to the right. "Vitoria. It's time."

For an instant, Sammy saw some of that old rebellion in her eyes. "And then you're going to send me away?"

Sammy nodded. "Just like we agreed."

Vitoria locked eyes with Sammy, her expression stoically blank. Jeffie stopped what she was doing to watch. As Vitoria stepped closer to Sammy, her lip began to tremble and a tear leaked from her eye. "Sammy …" she whispered. "Please don't make me go."

"Vivi—"

"Let me die with you. I don't want to be alone. I can't—can't live that way."

Sammy's voice broke as he asked, "Will you open the door?"

More tears streamed down her face as she put her thumb on the scanner. A green light showed that her thumb print was accepted. Then she put her eye over the retina scanner. A second green light appeared. Finally she said her name, "Vitoria Prado." A third green light blinked on and the door in the back of the white room opened.

Behind the door was a small alcove less than a meter wide and two meters deep. Inside was one screen and one keyboard on a desk. The cursor on the screen blinked next to two magical words:

```
<INPUT COMMAND:\>
```

Sammy hugged Vivi. "Thank you." He held her out at arms length. "Now listen. Today is not your day to die. I want you to take a gun—"

"No—"

"*Take a gun.* Get out of here. And don't look back. Go to the safehouse and call the resistance operator. They will take care of you."

Her face screwed up in pain. "I want to stay!"

He hugged her again, and this time she hugged him back. Then he pressed a gun into her hand. "Go. Live a good life for my sake."

She backed away, hurt and confused and scared. Sammy wanted to weep with her as he watched her climb through the elevator hatch just as the doors began to close. He waved weakly, but she didn't wave back.

"I'm ready, Sammy," Jeffie said, steadying one of the two projectors. A red line, called the danger line, ran across the projector bases. While Jeffie steadied them, Sammy bolted the machines to the floor, making sure the danger line on one base lined up with the other. Once this was done, they quickly donned their zero suits. This would allow them to move about the room without interacting with the holograms emitted by the two projectors.

Seconds after they finished changing clothes, the elevator returned to the white floor with a soft *ding*. Jeffie blasted two shields. Sammy turned on the projectors.

"Battery levels at one hundred percent," a robotic voice stated from one of the two projectors.

"Enter Mode One," Sammy ordered.

The machines projected the images of twin drone guns around themselves so the projectors were no longer visible.

"Safety measures off," he ordered the machines. "Destroy all targets in front of the danger line."

A sudden *BOOM* came from the elevator as the doors blew outward. The smoke cleared and Sammy saw shields large enough for the Aegis to crouch behind, fully covered. Almost a dozen men and women in muddied brown-green uniforms poured out of the broken lift. Behind them, the elevator dropped the rest of the way down the shaft like a stone, crashing just out of Sammy's sight. The drone guns whirred to life and spat bullets at the Aegis as they poured inside. Their shields had small bases for the Aegis to steady and support them with their feet, which allowed them to use both hands to shoot.

The bullets of the drone guns scratched and dented the Aegis shields, but did little else to harm the enemy. They made their way around the room, sticking to the walls, as Sammy knew they would. *So predictable, yet so effective.*

He and Jeffie stood apart. The angle of their shoulders formed a wedge. Their blasts shielded them from all angles except the rear. The drone guns' rapid fire was deafening and shells littered the floor from all the guns both friendly and foe. Sammy couldn't keep track of all the rounds from all the guns as he was accustomed to doing during battle. He watched the Aegis, analyzed their movements, and noted the minute communications they sent one another to adjust their form and position as they reacted to Sammy and Jeffie's defenses.

"There could be more on the way," he told Jeffie. "Take out as many of them as possible before they surround us."

"What do we do?"

"Blast their shields. The drone guns will do the rest."

Together they made a coordinated effort of moving about and blasting shields. High and low attacks, side to side shots, and occasionally powerful direct attacks knocked the Aegis off balance. The drones made the Aegis pay for each exposed bit of head or shoulder. It wasn't long before the white walls were sprayed with red and pink and gray, and the bodies of the fallen hampered the Aegis' movement around the perimeter of the room.

More Aegis arrived, this time by way of rappelling down the elevator cables. Sammy and Jeffie had already killed nine of the original twelve with a tenth injured. They carried their shield and hopped out, stepping around and over the bodies of their brothers.

Sammy took advantage of their cautiousness and attacked furiously before they could launch a coordinated counterattack.

Using the walls and the heads of the Aegis, he stayed airborne for almost ten minutes, punishing them from above while Jeffie and the drone guns tore them apart. In the eyes of each Aegis, he saw Stripe, his tormentor in Rio. The Anomaly Thirteen and its poisoned darkness swelled inside him, yearning to be free. The growing carnage around him didn't help, either. The scent of blood and bowels and body parts clotted his nostrils. Smatterings of it flew everywhere. It sickened and exhilarated him. He danced on the edge of danger and loved it. Yet the closest Sammy came to receiving a wound was when a bullet whizzed past his left ear as he flipped through the air with a jump blast while shielding himself with his hands.

When it was all over, thirty bodies and shields scattered the room, even blocking the elevator door from closing. Sammy ordered the projector to enter stand by mode to save battery power.

"Levels at seventy-one percent," the battery reported.

"Let's move the bodies," he told Jeffie, "get them into the elevator shaft."

Stacking the bodies was hard work. Sammy's arms and legs protested at each Aegis he picked up or dragged across the white floor. He noted the way Jeffie's body sagged when she tried to stand up straight, the heaviness around her eyes, and how her breaths were long and drawn, almost like sighs. He wanted to say something to comfort her, but couldn't. *No time for rest.*

"How's your ammo?" he asked Jeffie.

She gave him a thumbs up.

"You okay?"

Jeffie nodded. "Are *you*?" Her tone told him she wasn't only asking about his physical state.

"Fine."

"Are they sending more?"

The answer was yes, but instead Sammy said, "We'll find out soon."

They split the last of the energy pastes, but Sammy wasn't sure it did anything to help. Ten minutes later, the rappelling equipment the Aegis had used shot up the cables with a high-pitched whirring sound. Sammy and Jeffie exchanged a dark look.

A few minutes later, the noise returned accompanied by animal-like shrieks echoing down the tunnel, growing louder each second. Thirteens. They exploded from the elevator shaft just as Sammy gave the command to reactivate the projectors. He counted thirteen newcomers. The Thirteens lack of protection meant they should be mowed down like weeds, but some of them picked up the shields of the fallen Aegis. Others used nothing but their constant motion and rapid reflexes to confuse the drones.

Unleash me and win.

Sammy ignored the voice and shot blasts at the Thirteens. The drones' bullets passed through him as harmlessly as wind, but caught one Thirteen in the thigh, piercing him. If the Thirteen felt any pain, he didn't show it. Instead he whipped his gun around and shot at Sammy, but Sammy had already moved, dodging four other Thirteens' fire with a rapid blast to the upper right wall and then another off it.

He and Jeffie had to be careful with their zero suits. The technology allowed holograms to pass through them, but the electric current in the zero suit had to remain unbroken or else rather than passing through their bodies harmlessly, the holograms would treat them as any other space in the room. With the projectors' safety controls turned off, a bullet could mean instant death.

Sammy and Jeffie changed their focus from offense to defense. They had to keep the Thirteens in front of the red line on the projectors' bases to keep them in targeting range and because the projectors were vulnerable from behind the line. Half of the Thirteens shot at Sammy and Jeffie while the other half targeted the drones. The more they attacked the drones, the heavier the drain on the holo-projectors' batteries, which had to consume more energy to deflect the bullets. Already the batteries were down to sixty percent charge, and not a single Thirteen had died.

"Coordinated attack!" he ordered the drones. "One target at a time. Jeffie, pick the same target as the drones until it's dead. Then switch to another."

This new strategy worked better. Sammy worried about keeping the Thirteens behind the line while Jeffie picked them off one by one. Yet three times the Thirteens managed to get past the blasts and the drones to attack Sammy and Jeffie in close range. Sammy made the first one pay by catching her off-guard and blasting her into the wall hard enough that she blacked out. Then the drones and Jeffie put enough bullets in her to turn her into a pencil.

The second Thirteen who made it past the red line fired both guns at Sammy from less than a meter away. Sammy protected his exposed flank from other Thirteens with his left hand and blasted away the bullets with his right. The Thirteen shrieked. Sammy wanted to use his burn blasts to melt the Thirteen's eyes out of his skull. The rage inside him bubbled and spat, urging him to release his full potential. But Sammy forced himself to focus. He shielded with one hand and shot strong blasts at the Thirteen until he caught him on the leg and made him lose his balance. Still shielding, Sammy blast-jumped off the floor, flipped over, and put his shoes on the ceiling. Then he blasted again and flipped once, shooting down and landing on the Thirteen with a bone-crunching smash.

During this, the third Thirteen made it past the red line. Jeffie pushed the rest back with blasts and bullets. The Thirteen whipped his pistol at Sammy, but Sammy arched back and lost his balance, landing on the fallen and broken Thirteen beneath him. As Sammy fell, he shot at the Thirteen with foot blasts, missing with the first blast, but spinning her around with the second. The Thirteen shot at him as she spun, but her shot went wide to Sammy's left. He could tell instantly it had no chance of hitting him, so he didn't shield. Instead he blasted at her with hands and feet, pinning her against the wall so Jeffie could kill her.

"Take her out, Jeffie!"

But Jeffie didn't fire. Sammy glanced back and saw her on the ground, scooting back and grabbing her knee with one hand and shielding herself with the other. Blood seeped from her wound as she tried to staunch the flow.

"Jeffie! Take the shot!"

Jeffie let go of her knee and picked up her gun. Sammy dropped his blasts just as Jeffie fired several bullets into the Thirteen's chest and abdomen. Not her cleanest work but adequate. Sammy got back to his feet and blasted back the other Thirteens.

"Stay down," he told Jeffie as he moved in to provide her better cover. "Shoot from the floor."

Sammy worked even harder on the remaining Thirteens, picking them off one at a time with the drones' help. Although they were less than half in number as the Aegis, it took Sammy more than twice as long to finish the Thirteens off. The last one was a tricky bugger. He stood less than a meter and a half tall but was as spry as any Thirteen Sammy had faced. Implanted pearls in the skin of his face and green-black tattoos gave him a reptilian appearance. His forked tongue snapped each time Sammy attacked. Jeffie was low on bullets, saving them in case more enemies came, so Sammy did all the work. He finally caught the Thirteen with a blast that stunned him enough that the drone guns could do their job, and the Thirteen ended up just like the others: a bloody mess.

Pools of blood now replaced the once pristine whiteness of the room; the stink of it made the air hot and thick. Sammy's zero suit was more red than blue now as was Jeffie's. The screen of the zero suit covering his face was splattered with blood as well, making it difficult to see in some areas.

He knelt next to Jeffie and rolled up her pant leg to examine the wound. She hissed in pain when he moved it. The tears in her eyes reminded Sammy that despite all her experience and training, she was still just a sixteen-year-old girl.

"We don't have a lot of med supplies," she protested. "Save them for yourself."

Sammy ignored her and treated the wound. Then he took out one of their two zero suit patches, unrolled her pant leg, and placed it over the hole in the special fabric. The charge in the suit activated the patch, and the patch wove its metallic fibers into the suit, restoring the electrical current.

"You okay?" he asked her.

"Been better," she answered.

They cleared the room of the bodies. Sammy wanted to destroy the Thirteens' rappelling descenders clamped to the cables, but the gear had already disappeared.

"More Thirteens?" she asked, grimacing each time she put weight on her injured leg.

Sammy sighed and sat down to preserve what little strength he had. "I hope not." He checked the time. "Still an hour and a half before time to activate the code."

"Ugh," was Jeffie's reply.

"She's trying to tire us. She knows I'm here."

"Who is *she*?" Jeffie asked.

"The Queen."

"How do you know?"

Sammy shrugged. "Maybe I'm wrong. Maybe we just need to wait ninety minutes." But he knew she would come as well as he knew his own name. Blood soaked his hair and clothes and made his skin sticky. "Battery report."

"Forty-nine percent," the battery replied.

"I am exhausted," Jeffie admitted. "And starving. Do you have a cheeseburger in your pack? I could really go for a cheeseburger. Extra ketchup."

Unleash me. I can help you destroy her. It is the only way you can win.

I've beaten her before. I'll beat her again.

She can blast now. Remember what Trapper told you? You can't hope to win without unleashing me!

Sammy closed his eyes and almost fell asleep, but high-pitched whirring noises forced them open again. *More coming.* He wanted to cry. Jeffie looked like she wanted to as well. As the sound grew louder, he and Jeffie stood, arms hanging to their sides, waiting. Blood and sweat dripped down their faces, but they couldn't wipe it off through the zero suit screens. Enemies dropped silently onto the pile of dozens of bodies at the bottom of the elevator, sliding down them into the white room. Their faces mirrored Sammy's. *Hybrids.* His own clones. Ready to attack the original.

* * * * *

On the 94th floor of the Rio N Tower the Queen hovered over the shoulder of a technician working in the Computer Sciences division. Constant communication passed between the Orlando and Rio towers.

"They've checked the black and red floors in Orlando," a new report came. "No sign of the intruders. The main elevator plummeted down the shaft. Now disabled."

"If Sammy is on the white floor in Rio, then Walter Byron must have gone to the white floor in Orlando," the Queen stated, not for the first time. She rounded on her techs, eyes ablaze. "Find out what is down there!"

"We're trying!" said one tech in an insubordinate tone. The Queen stared and memorized the tech's face. *Later. Something long and painful. Perhaps I'll flay you.* The thought excited the Queen, but her enthusiasm quickly turned into a deep itching in her skin followed by bolts of pain and revulsion as she envisioned peeling back someone's skin piece by piece.

Get control.

"How can no one know what's down there?" she asked. The notion was absurd. Not one tech had any idea about what was on the white floor. It couldn't be a coincidence that the only two towers with white floors were hit simultaneously. *But why?*

Techs had searched through databanks, schematics, and code but uncovered no helpful information. How had something hiding in plain sight been kept such a secret? The Queen had known about the floor. She'd been in the undergrounds of both towers, but she'd never given the white button on the elevator panel a second thought.

"Chad, give me a report!" the Queen said into her com.

But there was still no answer from him. She glanced at her clock. *Almost an hour now with not a word from that little—*

Either Diego had wiped all information regarding the white floor out of the Hive's servers or it had never been there at all. And the fox had so many cursed firewalls around his most precious pieces of information that it would be a wonder if they ever broke through them. Regardless, Chad had proven himself worthless. The Queen would kill and replace him at her next opportunity. Another jolt of pain shot up to her torso, making her queasy.

"Here's something," one of the techs said. "A memo from the CEO of N Corp marked urgent … sent to the architect of the towers. Apparently the two towers were built simultaneously."

"Give me the memo!" the Queen snapped at the worker. When the girl sent it to the Queen's com, the Queen scanned it quickly. "This tells me nothing except that he wanted the white floor done in white. Why are you wasting my time?"

"I'm sorry, ma'am."

The Queen wanted to kill this one too. Instead, she left. "Call me when you have something that isn't completely useless."

She read the note again:

```
The tactile esthetics of the room are unimportant. White
represents a classic symbolism that I find important.
```

A memory popped into the Queen's mind. As a young girl, she'd been invited to her friend's baptism. Her friend wore a white dress as she descended into a font filled with water. The dress had billowed out in the water, then clung to her friend's skin. Someone at the ceremony had said the white represented purity and cleansing.

Cleansing. Diego's word. What had he said to her before she killed him? That the fox had a purpose for him, a planned way to die. Somehow the two were tied together. She knew it. Cleansing of what?

The Queen *saw* the answer. Cleansing. White. Simultaneous. The solution.

"No," she muttered to herself. "No, no, no." More words came to her mind, this time they belonged to the fox: *The new world I will build has no place for Thirteens and Hybrids.*

The fox was ashamed that he had to use the Thirteens, the Aegis, and these even newer Hybrids to achieve his ends. He viewed it as a problem, and to counter it, he'd created the *solution.* He planned to snuff out the Aegis, the Hybrids, and any remaining Anomaly Thirteens in an instant.

You bastard. You bastard! She ran back into the room with the technicians. "Are there any terminals on the white floors?"

One of the technicians typed furiously on her keyboard. "Yes. One on each."

"And are they connected to a mainframe within our master system?"

"I don't know."

"If they are, you find a way to block those terminals."

The Queen watched them work for five minutes, their frowns growing deeper by the second. They all seemed reluctant to be the one to give her bad news. Finally one of them spoke up, a girl no older than twenty-five. "The terminals are unreachable. They are each hardwired to satellite dishes. At the Hive."

"Can't we just shut down power to the two white floors?" the Queen asked. "Isn't that something we can do from here?"

"The white floors aren't powered through the—"

The Queen got in the girl's face and screamed, "What *can* you do?"

"I—I—I don't know!"

"What options do I have right now?"

"If—if they've already gained access to the room ... security will have to remove them."

The Queen called Chad again. "How quickly can we get major explosives sent up to Orlando and Rio?"

Still no answer.

"CHAD!" The Queen swore and threw her com across the room. "Will someone tell me what is going on at the Hive?"

One tech was brave enough to speak. "Everything is offline. Possibly shut down by an external network breach."

"Get a team of cruisers and have them destroy the satellite dish on the Hive."

"What?" one of the techs asked. "We can't—"

"DO IT!"

She would not let Sammy succeed. The Hybrids were going down to fight him now. They would not prevail. They were too green, and Sammy's prowess in combat was all but unmatched. The Hybrids had their Achilles' heel. It took years for a Thirteen or an Aegis to prepare for combat with a Psion. With only a two-year lifespan, the Hybrids simply didn't have enough time to train.

But Sammy was near her. Only a hundred floors below. Wearing down with each body she made him kill. *Soon … where they have failed, I will succeed. I nearly beat Sammy in hand-to-hand combat without Anomalies Eleven and Fourteen. Now, with them, I will destroy him.*

* * * * *

With Jeffie's knee hobbled, the Hybrids posed a more difficult challenge than the Thirteens. They were not as skilled at attacking, but much better at defending due to their blasts. Sammy forced himself to play a purely defensive game. The battle wasn't the only thing on his mind. The batteries on the projectors were down to little more than twenty-five percent, and he had less than an hour remaining before it was time to launch the signal. Of the nine Hybrids, only one was dead.

Between fatigue, Jeffie's injury, and the Hybrid's ability to shield the bullets from the drone guns, Sammy wasn't certain he and Jeffie could clear the room in time to send out the code signal at 1000.

There is a way, Sammy. I can help you. You are going to die anyway. What does it matter if you let me help you get there?

I want control.

You want to release your rage.

The voice was right. The emotion—the anomaly—was right there beneath the surface. And it grew each time Sammy looked into his own eyes—his cloned eyes. All Sammy had to do was let it rise a little more and it would erupt. The fatigue would disappear, and Sammy could destroy these sick clones, these unnatural copies of himself made without his permission. He could tear their hair out, rip out their eyes ...

Ignoring the voice, Sammy drew closer to Jeffie. Three of the Hybrids had hand cannons. Two had jiggers. The other three had automatic rifles. They were picky with their shots, shooting only when they saw an opportunity, which Sammy and Jeffie had to close quickly.

"Enter Mode Two," Sammy told the drones. Mode Two was a purely defensive holographic projection designed to protect the holograms from attack.

"Why did you do that?" Jeffie asked.

"To save battery."

"And what about saving our lives?" she yelled.

"Do you trust me or not?" he yelled back over the sound of two hand cannons firing simultaneously.

"Do you really have to ask?" Jeffie crouched low to shield herself while pushing the Hybrids back with blasts. They grew closer now that the drone guns were off. Sammy blasted back two Hybrids and shielded the fire from two more. Shrapnel from one hand cannon whizzed over his head.

The Hybrids pressed and pressed, pushing Sammy and Jeffie back. Sammy's plan was to get the enemy used to having the drones off. Then he and Jeffie would blast over them and get near the elevator doors. Once the Hybrids had turned their backs to the drones, Sammy would reactivate the drones and obliterate the Hybrids from both sides. However, Sammy wasn't sure he could get to the opposite side of the room.

Each time he tried to elevate himself with blasts, the Hybrids shot him backward with blasts of their own. Jeffie stood even less of a chance with her bad leg.

There is still a way.

Sammy ignored the voice and checked his com. Less than forty minutes remained until the time to activate the signal.

You're not going to make it in time. All those people are counting on you to send out the code.

Sammy gritted his teeth and blasted back two more Hybrids. His mind searched for options, desperate to *see* the way to win this battle quickly. The Hybrids continued to use their blasts effectively, shielding themselves well and taking regular shots at Sammy and Jeffie.

For one instant, Sammy saw an opening and took advantage of it, blasting himself off the wall to his left and then up against the ceiling, firing down bullets and blasts. As he did so, he drew his feet up to use his foot blasts as shields. The Hybrids closest to him shot their blasts back to knock him down. Jeffie caught one of them in the ribs, but he continued to fire at Sammy, grazing his leg and tearing a hole in his zero suit. Sammy cursed and dropped into a defensive stance when he landed. Jeffie saw what happened and shook her head.

Minutes ticked away. The Hybrids pressed them back until Sammy and Jeffie's backs were almost to the wall. The voice in Sammy's head screamed at him to unleash the rage, the Anomaly Thirteen, and win the battle once and for all.

What if it's for the best? I can't finish the mission if I'm dead. He looked at Jeffie. *I won't hurt her. I can control it that much.*

He took a deep breath.

Yes, that's it. Do it! the voice urged.

Sweat cascaded down Sammy's temple. He licked his dry lips with a dry tongue as he made up his mind. But before he could do anything else, two Hybrids fell dead. Then two more. All died from expert headshots to the back of the skull.

Vitoria!

The other four turned to her and returned fire. As soon as they gave Sammy and Jeffie their backs, the duo went to work. Another Hybrid fell before the other three gave up shooting and started shielding on both sides. By then it was too late. Jeffie continued firing while Sammy used several blasts to get above the Hybrids and force them to adjust their shields. As soon as they did so, Vitoria or Jeffie capitalized on the error. Within five minutes of Vitoria's arrival, the Hybrids were dead.

The same time the last Hybrid hit the ground, so did Vitoria. Sammy and Jeffie ran to her. When Sammy saw Vitoria's white face and the blossoming circles of red in her chest and stomach, a vision of Toad flashed in Sammy's mind.

"You're not dying," he told her. "You're not dying. Jeffie, get the med pack." He clutched Vitoria's hand. "Just give me a second to fix this."

"No." Vitoria gazed up at him with bloodshot eyes, face wrinkled with pain. Her voice was unnaturally wheezy and wet. "Don't try to save me."

"Why?" Sammy asked. Jeffie returned with the med kit and dumped it in his lap. "Why can't you live? Isn't it enough that Toad died?"

"I miss him. I miss my mommy and daddy. I miss them all. There's no place for me here. I'm too—I'm too ... old."

Sammy shook his head at such nonsense. "You're just a kid. You have to live your life!" He let go of her hand and fumbled with the kit, but Vitoria's hand slid over his, her grip weak.

"You gave me something better than what I had. Thank—" Vitoria coughed up blood. Sammy lifted her head onto his lap and stroked her hair as she struggled to breathe. As the blood and fluid filled her lungs, drowning her, Sammy watched, numb and stunned. Her eyes closed softly, but he continued to stare.

Finally Jeffie shook him. "We need to patch up your suit and get the bodies out for the last part. You said she's coming. Remember? The plan, Sammy ..."

A desire to strangle Jeffie energized Sammy's limbs. But instead, he hugged her.

24 | Leadership

Tuesday, November 11, 2087

ALBERT WASN'T LIGHT, and Commander Byron wasn't young. The fight with the Thirteens had taken a lot out of him. Years, perhaps. The commander had reassured his son that everything was going to be fine. That he was going to take care of everything. The words were identical to what he'd told Albert as a baby when rocking him the day after Emily died. He'd baptized his son's face with his tears that night.

A little over an hour left. He had no time for tears. The clock was ticking; he and Albert had to move.

The first time Byron tried lifting his right arm above his head, he almost retched. The arm moved fine despite the break, but the sensation of the pieces of his shattered clavicle bone rubbing against each other turned his stomach.

"Not to worry," he told Albert even though Albert was still unconscious, "I will be fine."

It took him three tries and ten minutes to lift Albert up through the elevator hatch using careful, steady blasts, but he finally did it. Once Albert was atop the elevator, Byron joined him and worked at the doors to the white floor. Prying open the elevator doors took some work and muscle, but once he cracked them a few centimeters, Byron used his blasts to shove them apart.

Everything was so white it was hard to tell where one wall ended and another began. Byron rubbed his eyes. The only thing not white were the smears of dried blood left wherever he touched. He dragged Albert to the back of the room to the small door in the center of the wall. Both he and Albert had practiced this part—cutting the door in such a way that they triggered the failsafe mechanism that opened the door. But Albert was better at it than Byron, his hands steadier.

The commander propped his son up against the wall next to the door and pulled the plasma blade back out of the bag. Then he removed a tape measure and found the spot on the door ninety centimeters from the bottom and forty centimeters from the left side. Byron marked this spot with a blue pencil. The bone in his shoulder bulged his skin every time he raised his arm too high.

Once he was ready, Commander Byron pressed the tip of the plasma blade against the marked spot on the door. His right arm trembled. He switched hands, but the left arm was worse from the tear in his muscle.

I can do this. I am not useless.

The cut into the door had to be shallow enough to avoid destroying the failsafe mechanism but deep enough to reach it. Byron closed his eyes and said a short prayer before igniting the plasma blade. Then he made the cut into the door, pressing the blade deeper into the metal as it softened from the heat. He stopped abruptly, suddenly afraid that he had gone too far into the door. His throat went dry as he removed the plasma blade from the cut. Shining a light into the door, he saw the failsafe switch, slightly melted, but still intact. Sighing with relief, he flipped the switch. When the datacube port next to the door slid open, Byron inserted the cube and waited for it to do its work. Once it was done, the white door opened to reveal a small workstation with a desk, chair, and an older model computer and holo-screen.

"Looks just like my first office." Byron smiled at his son, then frowned. He knelt beside his boy and checked his pulse for the fourth time. It was there. And he was breathing. Byron opened Albert's eyes and checked the dilation of his pupils. Taking Albert's hand in his, the commander held it up to his chest. "Everything is going to be okay, son. I think you have a serious concussion. Possibly a cracked skull. But I promise you will make it out of here. Okay? I promise."

He propped Albert up behind the desk and sat in the chair. The screen flashed.

<INPUT COMMAND:\>

All right, Samuel. The ball is in your court. We believe in you. Byron checked the time. They had exactly one hour. *Sixty minutes. This could have been a lot worse.*

As soon as the thought passed through his mind, a Hybrid dropped down the elevator shaft.

* * * * *

An hour and a half before sunrise, Brickert and Natalia sat outside on the balcony of the small studio motel room crammed with a dozen people sleeping on the floor, couches, and beds. The pair held hands and cuddled, partly because the November air in D.C. had a bite to it, but mostly because they wanted to be close. Natalia's head rested on his shoulder, and Brickert's head on her crown. Her smell was light like honey, something he savored. He pulled her a little tighter to him.

"You like my new hair color?" she asked, examining the now chestnut colored strands closely.

"Yeah. It looks … normal. I can't remember the last time it was like that."

"It's been a while. I just—just wanted to blend in."

Brickert gave her a small hug and nodded. In a crowd of people, blue or purple or even deep black hair would stick out to snipers and gunmen. Natalia played with Brickert's fingers, occasionally kissing them. Every minute or so, she would tremble against him, though not from the chill. Brickert nuzzled the top of her head and whispered, "I love you."

Natalia sighed. "Thanks. I love you, too."

As they held each other and listened to the sounds of the city, Brickert wondered how many people would arrive to help march on the capitol. Were they on their way right now? Or was the resistance alone? If so, the resistance would be nothing more than the wind. Here one instant and gone the next.

"You think they will come?" he asked Natalia. "You think the speech worked?"

"Yeah, I think so."

"How many are going to show up?"

"A million!" Natalia said, laughing. "Honestly, I don't know. A lot, I hope."

"What if it's only hundreds? Or dozens? And they're all crazy homeless people."

"Then we might lose," Natalia said. The mirth was gone.

"People are too scared or skeptical to show up. You've seen the news."

A long silence passed between them before Natalia spoke again. "People believe what they want to believe. Not what they learn or see."

"What do you believe?" Brickert asked.

Natalia turned to him so she could look him in the face. Her eyes were red, and her nose dripped. She'd been crying.

"What's wrong?"

"I think I'm going to die today." Her voice squeaked when she admitted this. "I don't know why, but I have this awful feeling about it. I'm not even sure if it means we're going to lose the battle, it's just—it's just me."

Brickert tightened his embrace. "No, no, everything's going to be fine. You have to stay focused and positive."

"I am focused! I want this to be over. I want to go home and see my family again. That's another thing we never talk about. What's going to happen to us when this is over? There's no Beta headquarters. There's no Alpha. There's hardly any Psions left!"

"Commander Byron will figure it out," Brickert said.

"He's practically on a suicide mission! I don't think he's coming back either."

"Why are you suddenly so scared?"

Natalia shook her head. "It's just this feeling in my gut." She sat up and faced him. "Promise me something, okay?"

"What?"

"Just promise me, then I'll tell you."

Brickert chuckled, but no smile played across his lips. "That's never a good idea."

Natalia flashed a vanishing smile. "No, it never is. But do it anyway."

After rolling his eyes, Brickert said, "All right. I promise. What?"

"The mission comes first."

Brickert understood what she meant. "What makes you think I'd do otherwise?"

"Because you risked your neck for me on the mission in Colorado Springs, remember? That stunt you pulled almost got you and everyone else killed."

"Hey, I saved your life!" he said.

"No. I'm not saying that. I'm grateful." Natalia put a hand on his face. "I'm so grateful. When I first became a Psion, I thought it was just silliness. We had neat powers, we played cool games … and it was like a dream. A dream that I was in a select school. You woke me up, opened my eyes."

"By saving your life?"

"I'm talking about before that. You took training so seriously. Especially after we thought Sammy had died in Rio, I didn't get it. You did. When we started dating, I began to understand your passion. I started trying harder, and it saved my life in Orlando when we were in the garage. Now I need to know that you're going to let me die if—if the mission requires it."

Brickert understood that she was referring to the opposite scenario as well. If Brickert got into trouble, Natalia would not come to his rescue if doing so endangered the mission. So he nuzzled her forehead and said, "Okay. I promise."

Natalia smiled sadly. Then she kissed him. Brickert kissed her back hungrily knowing that it might be the last time. Minutes later they were interrupted by Justice. "Rise and shine, folks," he said without his usual gusto, his mouth set in a hard line. "Time to grab a quick bite and go over the plans one more time. Operation Old MacDonald starts in less than ninety minutes."

The operation name was Thomas Byron's idea in memory of his wife who grew up on a farm in Iowa. All resistance teams were named after farm animals. Friendly snipers were called geese, friendly cruisers were eagles, and enemy cruisers were hawks. Brickert was in charge of Sheep Team.

A half an hour before sunrise, the resistance headed to their starting points. For Brickert that meant the rundown shopping mall at Prince Georges. Brickert had been given a flashy white convertible to drive with as much explosive and ordnance as the demolition crew could pack under the hood. Justice Juraschek would start from the mall, too, with Strawberry as his Psion.

"Snipers are already getting into position to provide cover," Justice said. "Once they see us speeding toward the barricades, they will start firing. Be alert. Let's go over the routes again."

Brickert knew his route as well as he knew how to make a perfect hamburger. Justice would take Horse Team south on 16th Street into D.C. while Brickert and the rest of Sheep Team made their way to Highway 50, and Natalia (Pig Team) took Highway 29. Once each car had destroyed its blockade, the teams would move in and help clear out enemies for the masses to march into the city.

"Any reports of marchers?" Brickert asked Justice.

"Some. A few hundred gathering at College Park. About a thousand at Army Navy Country Club. Might be some people up at Glover Archbold, but I don't know. Thomas is sending organizers to each place."

The news was a bitter disappointment, but Brickert would not let it deter him. He shook hands with the rest of Sheep Team and wished them well. His team comprised of one Elite and ten other resistance members with varying amounts of combat training. Despite Brickert's protests, Justice put him in charge, and named the Elite, Erin Malm, second in command of the team. Brickert went solo in the first car while the rest of Sheep Team rode a van thirty meters back. The doors to the van had been removed to give its occupants an immediate exit in the event of an attack. After reviewing the plans one last time, Justice ordered everyone into their cars. Brickert gave Natalia one last hug, and started up his convertible.

Driving down the highway with over twenty kilos of class B explosives near the engine made his palms sweat. He checked his mirrors every ten seconds and never got closer than five meters to the car in front of him. Flashing signs on both sides of the road warned drivers to stay away from barricades, and that any signs of civil unrest would be met with lethal force. Brickert's destination was the intersection of 7th and K Street on the northeastern side of the city. The barricade filled Mount Vernon Square. As Brickert drove down, he flipped his com onto the broadcast channel.

"Marchers approaching the Potomac bridges," Lorenzo said. "CAG agents are ordering them to halt or they will open fire. Permission to direct them to proceed?"

"Negative," Thomas returned. "We have no snipers in position to provide cover on the bridges. If you cross the bridge, you will sustain heavy casualties."

"Wait until we have people in position to aid the crossing," a third voice said.

Brickert switched his com back to the private line between him and his direct commander. "Justice, I'm less than three minutes from the blockade. Do I still have a green light?"

"You getting bricky, Brickert?" Justice asked.

"What does that even mean?"

"Dunno. I just made it up. You're still green-lit. All teams are in sync. The rest of Sheep Team with you?"

Brickert checked his rearview mirror. "Roger that. I see them."

"Blow them all to hell, Bricky."

"Aye bloody aye." Brickert took a deep breath and held it. Far ahead he saw the blockade. The sun was just beginning to peek above the horizon, but cast no glares yet to blind his vision.

"Enemy snipers have spotted you, Sheep Leader," one of the resistance snipers reported from the goose nest. "We've got scopes on him, but put a shield up just in case."

Three seconds after Brickert followed the sniper's advice, his windshield shattered. It startled Brickert enough that he jerked the steering wheel and cursed.

"You okay, Sheep Leader?" asked Erin Malm, his second in command.

"Fine, just lost my windshield is all," he reported as he blew the rest of the windshield out using three strong hand blasts.

"Sorry about that," the same sniper said. "We took him out."

"Sixty seconds until impact," Justice told them. "Maintain your speeds and we'll do this thing right. Things are gonna get real wild on the farm."

Brickert counted down in his head as he turned on the car's auto-nav system, locked in his speed, and climbed onto the car's hood to protect it from enemy bullets. "Lay down suppressing fire!" he shouted when CAG agents fired on him.

Behind him, the van pulled to a halt and his team poured out, firing on targets at the blockade. The convertible sped toward its end destination while Brickert rode it like some mad surfer.

Six … five … four. A Thirteen aimed a rocket launcher at him, but took a sniper round that tore apart most of his skull. *Three … Two … one …*

Brickert launched himself high into the air as the car sped on until it smashed into the blockade and exploded with a thunderous *BOOM* that ripped the air.

"Sheep Blockade destroyed," he reported as the concussion from the detonation shoved him backward toward the parked van. "Sheep Team moving in."

* * * * *

After clearing the white floor of the Hybrid's bodies, Jeffie checked the time on Sammy's watch. *Twenty-six minutes*, she realized. *I have twenty-six minutes to live.*

Twenty-six minutes was the length of a cartoon. It took her that much time to eat lunch. A perfect shower lasted about that long. Was that really all the time she had left? Because it wasn't enough.

Keep it together, she told herself. *Keep it together for Sammy.*

The stench in the white room was so thick and noxious that she didn't want to breathe. They had piled the bodies in the elevator shaft. The dead filled the entire pit space and halfway up the area the elevator would normally occupy. Vitoria's body went in last. Jeffie could tell by Sammy's face that he was going to lose it again if she didn't do something, so she hugged him and whispered that Vitoria was okay, that she wasn't hurting anymore. In the back of her mind were four other words that she didn't want to say or think, but they stuck in her brain: *You'll see her soon.*

Sammy sat on the floor in the back of the room. It was the only clean place left because so few Thirteens and Hybrids had died in that area.

"How much battery is left?" she asked him.

Sammy glanced at the holo-projectors wearily. "Twenty percent."

"Do you still think she's com—"

"Yes."

"How do you know?"

"I just do." Sammy turned his eyes on her. "She'll come, Jeffie. She's probably on her way now."

Jeffie could tell he wasn't going to say more, so she put her hand on the top of his head and turned it until their foreheads touched. "What do you think our lives would have been like if there hadn't been a war?"

Sammy sniffed and with a heavy voice said, "I have no idea."

Jeffie closed her eyes and tried to pretend. She wanted to see something beautiful before she died, not blood and guts staining the walls and floor. "I would have had kids. Three. How many children did you want?"

"I—I—Jeffie, why are you—"

She gripped his wrist. "Please, Sammy. Just for a minute."

"I—I guess about four. Or five."

"Okay, so we'd have four." Him playing along helped her more than she could ever say. It let her soul fly away with her imagination. For a moment, she was gone from Rio, from the underground, and from the blood. "I'd have one more child … for you."

Sammy snorted, and it made her giggle. "For me? Why?"

"Because I love you."

Sammy looked at her and then looked away, lifting the screen of his zero suit off his face so he could wipe the sweat and blood from his eyes and nose. *Please say it, Sammy. Please. I just want to hear it once.*

"I always wanted to live near the water," he said. "Maybe on an island. I don't know. At least on the beach."

"That sounds lovely."

"Lovely …" Sammy repeated. "That's a word old women say."

Jeffie tried to smile but her muscles wouldn't work. "You could be a professor. Put on a sweater every day. Have one of those pipes." The thought of that made her giggle. "And teach at a college—a college on the coast."

"What would I teach?"

She stroked his cheek. "Whatever you want. And at night we'd put the kids in bed and play a game or read a book. I'd put my feet on your lap and read until I couldn't stand it anymore. Until I'd have to kiss you. And then we'd make love whenever … wherever we wanted."

Sammy looked like he was about to cry, but instead he laughed. Jeffie didn't know how he did it. "I'm gonna die a virgin. When I was in therapy in Wichita, I told Dr. Vogt that I didn't want to die without—you know."

"I'm sorry, Sammy." Jeffie found herself again on the verge of tears, but refused to do it. She couldn't cry.

"Don't apologize. I wasn't ready. I'm still not."

She grinned grimly. "How about now? Here?"

They both laughed. Then Jeffie heard a moan come from the elevator shaft. A Hybrid. Before Sammy could move, she hopped up, winced at the pain from her bad knee, and put a bullet in the Hybrid's head. Satisfied he was dead, she hobbled back to Sammy and sat down.

"What do you think is happening up there? I hope it's working. I don't—don't want it to be for nothing."

Jeffie rested her head on Sammy's shoulder. "Are you ready?" he asked her.

Jeffie only sighed. "No, not really. But I can't say that, can I?"

Sammy stroked her hair and kissed her forehead.

"I'm sorry," she said. "I'm fine ... I promise."

"I know you are."

"I'm ready—really, I'm ready." Something wet tricked down her face, a tear or someone's blood. She wiped it away. "How much time do we have?"

"Twenty minutes."

"How are you so calm?"

He leaned in and whispered in her ear. "I'm terrified."

Jeffie hugged him fiercely. "I don't want to die."

"Shh," Sammy said. He took her hands and locked eyes with her.

"Jeffie, it's okay. You can go. You don't have to do this."

"I do."

"I can do it by myself. If I just use it—"

"We can't risk failure!" Jeffie shouted. She didn't know why she was so opposed to it. In a way, it didn't even matter if Sammy used his Anomaly Thirteen. But at the same time, it seemed to matter more than anything. "Two of us increases the odds by—"

Sammy let her go. "I know all that. I'm just saying ..."

"Then stop *saying*. I'm all right."

"Okay."

"Are you, though? Remember your promise, Sammy."

One of the rappelling descenders made a whirring noise as it shot back up the elevator cable. Jeffie jerk her head toward the elevator. *Someone's coming.*

"This is it." Sammy said.

Jeffie's hands started to tremble, so she squeezed them tightly to make it stop. "You promise you won't use it?"

Her question irritated him. "Yes, I still promise."

Sammy helped Jeffie to her feet. Tears welled up in her eyes but she pretended they weren't there. She checked the time on Sammy's com as he inspected the holo-projectors. *Eighteen minutes …*

Sammy's face paled as he looked at her shoulder.

"What?" she asked.

"Your zero suit has another hole."

Jeffie's feet went numb. "And you've already used the last patch."

25 | Triumph

Tuesday, November 11, 2087

EVEN AS THE blockade shattered in a flurry of fire and stone, other explosions echoed in the distance. The nearest blockades were only two or three kilometers away. Atmo-cruisers arrived overhead, NWG and CAG, battling it out in the sky. The CAG intended to provide air coverage for the blockades and drop missiles on crowds, so the NWG's job was to keep them occupied. Brickert's team used the van for cover as the CAG agents in the ruins of the blockade tried to prevent them from crossing deeper into the battle zone.

Geese—friendly snipers on the rooftops—gave regular reports of where Brickert needed to direct his team's attack while they picked off soldiers. Their efforts allowed Brickert's team to slowly advance into the rubble his car had caused. The smell of melted slag and concrete stung Brickert's nose along with the scent of charred flesh. Brickert directed his team to break into four groups of three and fan out using the snipers' intel to press the enemy from advantageous angles.

"Tanks are closing in on Horse Team's location," one of the geese reported. "Horse Team still hasn't breached the blockade."

"Pig Team taking heavy fire," a second goose said. "Multiple casualties."

Brickert's breath caught. Pig Team was Natalia's, located about a half kilometer to the southeast. Horse Team was Justice's, located a similar distance away, but in the opposite direction. Justice's blockade was one of the most important to remove because it gave marchers a direct path south to the White House. *Natalia or Justice?* Helping one might mean the death of the other.

"Sheep Team," he called out, "secure the area, eliminate all targets, and proceed to Horse Team's location at double speed."

All buildings in the area were locked and barred on government orders, forcing Brickert's team to use the streets and alleys to sniff out the most clear paths to get behind the blockade that Justice's team had failed to break.

A group of Aegis fired at Sheep Team as they made their way down K Street to 16th. Brickert reported them to the geese. "We've got our hands full with our own problems," one sniper responded.

Think, Brickert, he told himself. *What would Sammy do?*

Sammy's a leader. I'm not.

Brickert shoved those thoughts away and looked around for some way to get a jump on the Aegis. That was what Sammy liked to do: confuse the enemy with a barrage of movement and attacks until their frustrations overcame their defense. *But I'm not Sammy. I can't do the things he does.*

Brickert scouted the block ahead for a spot that provided cover. He saw a large pile of cars in the middle of what was left of Franklin Square. The trees in the square had been leveled, the area filled with debris, vehicles, and turrets for gunmen, but there didn't seem to be any guns in their vicinity. Most of the drones had been planted on the blockades facing north.

"Squad D," he said, "move ahead up to that car pile. Squad A, B, and C will provide cover. All four squads will leapfrog across the square until we reach 16th. Keep eyes out for enemy soldiers."

As instructed, Squad D went first, while Malm's B Squad and Brickert's A Squad provided suppressing fire at the Aegis. When the Aegis saw D Squad moving, one of them lobbed a grenade. Brickert shot several rapid blasts at the grenade until one connected and sent it back at them. Several shouts came from the Aegis' vicinity as the grenade went off, scattering them like roaches. Brickert and Malm's squad picked off as many as they could.

Above Brickert's team, two CAG cruisers chased and fired on an NWG cruiser. The roar of their engines rang Brickert's head like a bell. The heavy machine guns of one of the CAG's ships sprayed bullets at Brickert's team as it passed.

"Take cover!" Brickert shouted, though he doubted he could be heard over the booming engines. Debris and dirt splashed like water with each bullet's impact, as his team dove for protection. Malm got caught in the path of the gunfire. The bullets tore into her and threw her into the side of a car.

Brickert led his squad to her position as he reported their situation to the geese. When he reached Malm, he knew at once she wasn't going to make it. Her hands quaked as she reached into her pocket and removed a slip of paper from above her breast. Blood smeared across it as she handed it to Brickert. It was a picture of herself, her husband, and two boys. "Make sure I … get home. And finish this."

Brickert nodded and put the picture in his own pocket. "I will."

Malm closed her eyes. Brickert tagged her location on GPS and requested a medic and evacuation as soon as possible.

A goose spoke over the com. "Sheep Leader, we still need you at Horse's location ASAP. How far are you from his signal?"

"On our way." Brickert barked orders to his squads and led them further west past Franklin Square to McPherson Square.

McPherson was about half the size of Franklin and had almost no debris to be found. Gun turrets had been erected on the north side facing K Street, and another line of defenses had been built along H Street to the south, but in between very little stood in Brickert's way. He sent Squad C across first, ordering them to move with caution to draw out enemy positions. The three other squads followed behind, eyes open for signs of movement or fire.

Two seconds later an explosion filled the square with smoke and dirt as half of Squad C was obliterated. "Fall back!" he ordered Squad C. "Proximity mines! Fall back!"

Only one of the three members of C made it. Brickert called in more casualties. "Stay behind me," he told his team. "We've got to punch through whether we like it or not. I'll sprint across with my blasts on the ground to set off any more bombs. Give me cover on both sides and the rear, but don't stray far from where I walk!"

Brickert led his team across the square with hand blasts directed at the grass. Three more mines went off before they reached the opposite block. Once they'd reached the blockade, Brickert asked the geese where he was needed. "You're going to have to hit the blockade from the east. They've got a tank directly south firing rockets and artillery over the blockade. Take out the tank, if you can."

"Any report on Pig Team?" Brickert asked.

"Haven't heard a word from them in about ten minutes."

Brickert wished he hadn't asked. Cruisers soared overhead, chasing one another back and forth through the air. Their engines roared like dragons and spat bullets of fire. One of the CAG ships took a bad hit and plummeted into the buildings west of the blockade on 16th Street. Dust and debris flew through the air, pelting Brickert's team and sending them for cover.

"Goose Nest, this is Sheep Leader," Brickert shouted into his com. "Can we get air support for that tank? It's hell down here!"

"The eagles have their hands full," the bird reported. "Hawks are all over the place, outnumbering our birds at least three to one."

"We can't even spare one?"

"Do your job, Sheep Leader."

I am not a leader! Brickert almost screamed back. For one brief instant, he wanted to chuck his com as far as possible and then just run—run from the battlefield and never look back. But he fought down the insanity and forced himself to focus for his team's sake. He couldn't help Natalia until he got Justice's squad out of its jam. After taking the briefest of moments to collect his cool, Brickert checked the time.

0724.

Sammy would activate the kill code in thirty-six minutes. Then the nightmare would end. *But in the meantime, how am I supposed to take out a tank?*

* * * * *

Gunfire. Commander Byron was so tired of gunfire. He'd heard enough for three lifetimes. *Twenty minutes*, he told himself, *assuming Sammy sends the signal out on time.* Twenty minutes. He could stay alive for that long.

The Hybrids sent waves of revulsion through his gut. At some point in the last couple of years, he had started to think of Samuel as a second son. He guessed it probably began when he had ventured to Rio and found the tiny bunker Samuel had lived in for weeks, hiding from the CAG. Seeing Samuel's face on these Hybrids filled him with a sense of rage such as he had rarely known.

All Commander Byron could do was send out wide hand blasts to keep the Hybrids in the elevator shaft, filling the space between him and them with an invisible wall. The ten Hybrids blasted, shot, and beat at his blasts with all their Anomaly Thirteen-filled fury, searching for cracks in Byron's defense so they could push forward, blast up, attack their way out.

It didn't take long for them to learn that when a few of them blasted together, they could push him backward. First they would jump blast, then hand blast, timing their jumps and blasts in unison. From there they quickly shoved him far enough back that they had room to climb out of the shaft. Byron waited until the Hybrids were grouped together, then he raised his left leg, aimed his heel at the group, and said, "Fire left rocket."

His bionic foot erupted in flame and flew into the shaft, detonating in fire and smoke around the Hybrids. Some of them saved themselves with blasts, others died. Byron counted four among the dead. The clamps that had attached to his bionic foot now flared outward to form a stubby sort of paw but left him with a significant limp.

The remaining Hybrids forced him back again and gained footing on the white floor. The commander crouched and blasted at them high and low, retreating and keeping his blasts up to offer protection and offense at the same time. The Hybrids shielded and shot at him. His right hand itched for his syshée, but he didn't dare—not with five guns pointing back at him.

I am not useless. I am not worthless. People are depending on me.

"System report," he ordered the computer.

"All systems activated," the computer responded. "Awaiting command."

"Status of network report," the commander said next.

"Network connected but inactive."

This did not surprise Commander Byron. The network would not be active until Samuel or Jeffie stood next to the computer and held the standby button down. The standby button alerted the other station via a green light that the user had entered the kill code into the terminal and was ready to activate it. If the light was green, the network became active. If the light stayed red, the network was only connected.

Two Hybrids tried to flank him, one on each side. Byron gave up more ground, but was running out of room. His arms were stiff and his injured leg protested at each step. *Come on, you old man. This is what you were born to do.*

The anesthesia was starting to wear off, and he had no time to give himself more. *Grin and bear it.*

In his mind's eye he saw a smiling, chubby face, sickly green-brown hair, back and arms covered in tattoos. *Emily.*

Byron couldn't think of her right now. *Need to focus. Too much on the line.*

Bullets and shrapnel bounced off his shields, but the Hybrids were getting more and more creative in their efforts to work around them. Commander Byron struggled to keep up. Sweat poured down his face, and a stitch in his side was slowly turning into yet another ache.

One Hybrid moved too quickly on Byron's left. The commander tried to turn but nearly stumbled on his stump of a foot. The Hybrid fired a jigger at Byron's head, narrowly missing. A second Hybrid slipped around his right and shot Byron in the hip. Byron grunted and fell.

More shots came, this time from behind. One Hybrid took a bullet to the neck, the other in the shoulder. Byron got his shields up just in time to block two hand cannons. He raised his right foot. "Fire right rocket."

The Hybrids scattered so fast that the rocket killed only one of them. Another, however, took a bullet in the stomach during the confusion. Next thing Byron knew, Albert was kneeling next to him.

They blasted together, their shields forming an all but impenetrable wall of energy.

"You don't look so good, Dad." Black crusty blood covered Albert's pale face and his left eye drooped.

"Worry about them, not me. How much time?"

"Five minutes."

Byron winced from the sharp pain in his hip. Three hundred seconds. *I can make it that long.*

* * * * *

He's weak. Bleeding. Tired.

The Queen saw the pile of dead bodies as she rode the elevator cable from the penthouse to the underground. Her body tingled as she flew through the air, her hair whipping her face. Sammy hadn't activated the solution yet. She still had time to prevent disaster. Her weapon of choice was a new mini-blitzer, better than the prototype she'd used in her first encounter with Sammy at Baikonur. It used smaller superheated discs, which allowed her to carry more rounds per cartridge and heated up the discs at a faster rate. Her goal was to put one disc in both of Sammy's eyes. First the left, then the right.

I will beat him. I will win. I will prove once and for all that I am the supreme being. I proved it to myself. I proved it to the fox. Now I will prove it to Samuel Berhane.

Once Sammy was dead, no one would dare rise up against her. Once he was dead and she saw the discs from the blitzer open up his skull, only then would it all be over. Down there was her destiny. Her power. Her freedom.

She had set herself on this path long ago. It had taken her to the school. To the prison. To the fox. And now to an elevator in the bowels of the earth.

To face Samuel Berhane.

* * * * *

It took Sheep Team over twenty minutes to reach the tank. Enemy sniper fire sent them running for cover until the geese could locate the snipers and take them out. Sneaking behind a low wall, Brickert's team flanked the massive tank's left side.

"We need to watch this beast and see if we can figure out any weaknesses," Brickert said.

"Sir," said one of his team. Brickert flinched at the word. "It's almost 0800. If we wait just a few minutes …"

Sammy and Commander Byron will activate the kill code and take out most of the CAG forces.

"Copy that," Brickert said. "Hold tight and wait, Sheep Team. Eyes out for enemy fire. Let's see what happens at 0800."

The tank continued to launch shells over the blockade at Horse Team. Brickert flinched each time, hoping that Justice's team would be all right. *Come on, Sammy. Come through for us.*

He checked the time again. 0758. Ten seconds later a deep boom echoed from the west. It sounded like thunder but the sky was clear. It was immediately followed by a second boom and a third.

"What's happening?" Brickert asked.

"The charges on the bridges just blew. All bridges leading into the city are down. Hawks are targeting the swimmers and boats in the Potomac. All eagles are heading to the river to protect the marchers."

Brickert kept one eye on the clock. 0759.

Any second now ...

The rest of his team sensed his anxiety. They were quiet and tense, waiting, hoping. The tank fired off two rapid rounds.

"Sheep Team!" one of the geese called over the com. "Horse Team is taking more casualties. *Get that tank!*"

0800.

Brickert breathed a sigh of relief and waited for signs of the kill code taking effect. The tank fired again, shouts came from the other side of the wall, more gunfire filled the air. In the distance Brickert heard the roaring of cruisers. A drop of sweat ran down his cheek.

"Sir," one of Sheep Team said, "I don't think—"

Brickert nodded. According to mission planning, if Sammy and Byron missed the 0800 kill code time, the next one wouldn't be until 0815, then 0830, and so on every fifteen minutes. But for all Brickert knew, Sammy or Commander Byron's team was dead or captured. No matter the case, one fact was apparent: it was up to Brickert and Sheep Team to save Horse Team and help the marchers get past the blockades.

* * * * *

The Queen landed on the body of 13F712072-Jane. *Traitor.* The Queen spat on her pale face. Beneath the dead girl were dozens more corpses. Blood and bits of Thirteen spattered the white walls, ceiling, and floor of what was otherwise a very boring white room. Two tall white columns stood erect in the room's center, and along the junction of the back wall and floor was a long, coffin shaped rectangular projection, the only area in the room that bore no traces of the battle. Between them stood Sammy and his blonde whore. The Queen noted the sag in their stances, their labored breathing, the uncertainty in their eyes. A low laugh erupted from her gut.

"I respect you, Sammy," she admitted. "Your performance against the parade I sent you has earned it, regardless of our previous meetings. You are a true warrior."

The Queen saw how his muscles tensed. He was ready despite his fatigue. The girl … it was hard to tell. The Queen had never met this one before, she couldn't read her quite as well. "I respect you so much that I will let you choose who dies first. You can watch her go, or I will spare you the horror and kill you first."

Sammy did not answer. Perhaps he did not have the energy to spare. It made no difference. The Queen's mini-blitzer stayed at her side in its holster. She didn't want to reveal her blasting capabilities to Sammy. Not yet. She relished the moment when he realized what she had gained—that she had become his equal.

"If you won't pick, then I'll do it for you. I don't care if you hurt while it happens, Sammy. I don't care if it's fast or slow. I just want you to die. You're the last person in the world who has beaten me at anything. Once you are gone, I will transcend the world itself. Like the phoenix I've always known I am."

The Queen moved first, a quick lateral step. She wanted to see how they would respond, how they coordinated their defense and attack. Her body vibrated with energy, her earlier injuries forgotten. This was reality. This was freedom and purpose. This was life in its most pure and refined state.

Sammy attacked first, charging at her only to use a jump blast over her while the girl shot three rounds at the Queen's chest. Using her superior speed and perception, the Queen noted the specific angle of the gun, and threw herself to the right, giving herself plenty of distance before the gun was even fired. Any blasts Sammy might have fired at her back went wide. The Queen responded by ripping her mini-blitzer from its holster and firing.

The blonde girl tried to blast shield, but the disc went through the blast and took off two of her fingers. Gasping silently in shock, she clutched her cauterized hand. Sammy barreled into the Queen from behind, but she let the momentum flip her over and landed on her feet.

"If that's the best you got," she taunted, ignoring the dull sympathy pain pulsing in her own fingers, "it's going to be a short fight." Then she smirked at the girl. "Are you okay? Since I don't know your name, I'll call you Stubby. Is eight your new favorite number, Stubby?"

The girl attacked again, and the Queen imbibed her rage as though it were cool water. Sammy tried to blindside her, but the Queen dodged and fired at the blonde girl again. This time she missed, or thought she did until she saw a nasty cut along the girl's cheek. This seemed to infuriate Sammy even more.

"Not so pretty now, is she?" the Queen asked. "Not like me."

Sammy narrowed his eyes, but did not attack. *Good, Sammy, get angry. The madder you are, the more I'm winning.*

Unfortunately, she was wrong. Sammy and the girl seemed to draw strength from each other's pain, and communicated more coherently without words, silent or otherwise. The Queen held off as long as she could without using her blasts until the two Fourteens worked her into a corner. At that point it became blast or die.

She wished that she could witness the shocked expressions on their faces as she flipped over them with a powerful jump blast. It would have been a feast for her spirit. But by the time she landed and faced them, they were already reacting, adjusting, maneuvering.

"Really, Sammy?" she called out. "You have nothing to say? I know I just shocked the hell out of you."

Still he favored her with no words. She pushed them back with blasts, using her speed, skill, and intellect to keep her distance. But the Psions would have little of it. They pressed back, never letting her rest. So she changed her tactic to one of patience.

The Queen was fresh and they were not. Twice more she caught the girl with the blitzer discs, first across the left forearm, then deep in the right thigh. The girl could hardly walk after that, let alone fight. When Sammy's friend became a liability, he could not move fast enough to protect her.

Seeing them struggle filled the Queen with glee, and she savagely beat Sammy across the room, deflecting his blasts aside like the weak, pathetic things they were. "I thought you'd be better than this! You have no one left to dive in front of you and save you. Remember the boy, Sammy? I do! I can still smell his guts splattering the inside of that cruiser like gelatin."

Sammy's face filled with rage.

"I'm going to do the same thing to your slut!" the Queen crowed. The girl was limping along, groaning and trying to get behind her. "Isn't that right, Stubby?"

Without so much as a glance, the Queen whipped the gun behind her and shot the girl through the throat. The disc nearly took off Stubby's head, but instead blood spurted through her windpipe as she grasped and clutched at it in a vain attempt to staunch the bleeding. The Queen laughed as she jump-blasted backwards, soaring over the scene like a hawk.

Enraged, Sammy shot after her like a bullet, hands outstretched, blast after blast after blast flying past her or bouncing so weakly off her own shields that she couldn't even feel them. When he finally drew close enough, she feinted right and then sent a powerful blast into his right knee with her left foot. His joint buckled backward, and then the great Samuel Berhane fell. Seeing it was like watching a mighty redwood fall to the earth. Before he could recover, the Queen pulled the trigger on her blitzer and sent a disc through his stomach.

"NOW DO YOU SEE?" she screamed. Her chest heaved from the effort. She hadn't realized how much energy twenty minutes of pure fighting could cost.

Sammy's eyes darted left and right, searching for help, desperately looking for something to save him in the very last hour.

"Now do you realize, you stupid, worthless … *nothing?* Do you see just how insignificant you are compared to me? You were nothing but a product. An aberration! I am *the Queen!*"

Sammy stared at her, barely breathing. Now his eyes locked on hers. The Queen's stomach lurched. Her airway was tight and restricted. *Empathy*, the fox had said. Her gift was empathy. *Not a gift. A curse.* She would beat it as she had beaten everything else.

"Say something, Sammy," she said, choking back a sob of pity as she looked at his dying form. "SAY SOMETHING!"

But he said nothing.

The Queen swore and cursed at him, taunted him, but he remained silent as he lay on the ground, beaten, red pooling around him, tears dripping down his face. Queasy, emotionally and physically drained, and ready to be done with it all, she pointed the gun at his left eye as she had promised herself she would. "You weren't worthy after all."

And she fired.

13 | **Freedom**

Tuesday, November 11, 2087

THE BATTLE WAS not winnable. All bridges crossing the Potomac and Anacostia Rivers had been wiped out, leaving only the north and east as viable routes to reach downtown D.C. However, the northern and eastern blockades remained intact, and most resistance teams had suffered heavy casualties trying to destroy them. Help would not come from NWG air support. The battle in the skies had rapidly turned in favor of the CAG due to their overwhelming number of cruisers. If Sammy or Byron had failed their mission, the resistance and NWG would need as many marchers as they could get to swarm the blockades. But the longer the CAG delayed the crowds, the longer the CAG could hold the city with their superior air support.

Brickert's attention was on the tank. He and his team had come up with a plan. Squad C drew the tank's attention by lobbing grenades while Brickert used several blasts to get on top of it. As he expected, the tank had an electrified hull, but Brickert used a hover blast to avoid electrocution. While hovering, he jammed his hand against the commander's machine gun as it rotated toward him. When the machine gun fired, Brickert's blasts jammed the barrel and sparks exploded from the sides. Thick black smoke erupted from the gun.

Using a canister of blue goo, Brickert made a ring of blue around the top hatch. After the goo set, he used two strong foot blasts to separate the entire hatch from the tank. The pops and sizzles told him that the damage to the hatch had short-circuited the electric current. Gunshots rang out when the hatch fell, but Brickert had his shields ready.

"All squads to me!"

The rest of his team climbed onto the hull and assisted him in clearing out the tank's occupants. Once they were in control, Brickert called the geese on his com, "We have the tank. Where do you want us?"

"You—you *have* the tank?" one of the snipers asked.

"And it's fairly functional."

"Excellent work, Sheep Leader. Destroy the blockade."

One of Brickert's team had a basic knowledge of how to operate the controls, so she drove while Brickert and his team worked out how to fire the main gun. Once they had that down, Brickert left three operators inside and bailed with the rest of his team. At first the agents behind the blockade thought nothing of the tank's presence, but when Brickert ordered his team to fire their mindset changed.

The blockade's defenses quickly fell apart under the assault. "Tell Horse Team to pull back from the blockade," Brickert told the geese. "We're going to ram it."

When Justice's team saw the tank mowing through the barricades and towers, they attacked from the north. Within minutes the two teams had obliterated the blockade and its defenders. Justice had lost both coms and half his team, but had two men who were well-equipped to operate the tank. "You want it," Brickert told Justice, handing him a spare com, "you can have it. Where are we needed?"

"Pig Team is in shambles on the east side," Justice said. "We need you over there to open the blockade while we clean up the north."

It was exactly where Brickert wanted to be. "Is Natalia ...?"

"I don't know much. Take Sheep Team down there and find out."

"Yes, sir."

* * * * *

"These clones are as stubborn as the real Sammy," Albert complained. And for good reason. The last three Hybrids wouldn't die. They were too sharp. Too fast.

One more minute, the commander told himself. *One minute, and I can see Emily.*

He saw her face clearer now. It wasn't the face of a teenager, but a woman. Long, healthy brown hair, bright eyes both fierce and kind, and lips that always had a grin hidden in the corner. He remembered that beaming grin the first time she held Albert after his birth. She looked up at Byron and laughed.

"He's got your chin already!" she exclaimed. "See it?"

Soon.

Albert bled from his hand, a fleshy hole right through his palm from getting a blast off a moment too late and catching a jigger. Blood still covered his face from the elevator accident. It covered him so badly that Byron wondered how his son could see.

Do not worry about Albert, Emily. I will make sure he gets out of here alive.

Byron had taken another wound too—a glancing blow to the left shoulder. Unlike Albert, he had no body armor. His whole left arm was on fire. He kept the arm raised for fear that if he lowered it, he would never raise it again. He kept it raised for Albert. For Samuel. For his granddaughter. He had accepted that he was deep in death's clutches, but he would not allow it to get his boy.

At 0759, Byron asked the computer to check the status of the network again. The computer responded that the network was still inactive. *Something is wrong. Something has gone horribly wrong.*

As blood dripped from their wounds, the Byrons stood and fought their tireless foes. Shielding, pushing, blasting them back. Always on defense.

"A Psion's bread and butter is his shields," he used to say back in the old days to his Psion Corps.

"*Her* shields," Emily would correct him.

"We are going to need to hang on for fifteen more minutes," the commander told Albert, shaking himself back to the present. "Network is still down."

"Come on, Sammy," Albert said. "You can do it."

The three remaining Hybrids made a strong offensive as though they could sense their time was running short. Hand cannons fired as they jump-blasted up and around, but not quite over. Albert met them in the air and blasted them down while Commander Byron protected his son from below.

His left arm nearly dropped, but he clenched his jaw and fought through the pain and exhaustion. Albert kicked his legs up and pushed one of the Hybrids back far enough that it gave the commander an opening. He drew his syshée with his right hand and fired four times, hitting the Hybrid twice in the ribs.

The remaining two Hybrids redoubled their efforts, guns and bodies flying at Commander Byron. The commander took a deep breath. *You can do this. If Samuel can fight five, you and Albert can take two.* He stopped thinking and let instinct dictate his movement. This was what he'd trained for, what he'd been born for.

A shot from one of the Hybrids found his leg, but the limb was bionic. A Hybrid tried to dive under him, under his blasts, so Commander Byron broke his face on the metal limb. Before the Hybrid could recover, Byron aimed and pulled the trigger, but all he heard was a click.

Reload.

Back in the day, Byron could reload as fast as anyone. Less than a second sometimes. Today he was a second too long. Albert jumped blasted again to push the last two Hybrids back again, but took a shot to his unprotected leg, up near his waistline. The commander jammed his magazine up into the grip, pulled back the slide, and fired in one smooth motion.

One left.

"Come on, you bastard!" Byron bellowed at him, partly in anger, and partly to get his own blood pumping. "You think I am going to die alone?"

He glanced back at Albert, who had too much blood flowing from his leg. *The femoral artery.* "Use the goo!" the commander ordered his son.

"I'll be fine," Albert hissed through his teeth.

"*Use the goo!*"

Drops of blood fell from the commander's own body, mostly from his left arm, but also his leg. The Hybrid standing across from him was whole. Byron's arms sagged, begging to fall by his side. The stubs of his legs were sore and weary. Each hot breath he took stung all the way down to his lungs.

"Computer," he called out at 0813, even as he stared down the last Hybrid, "network status."

"Network connected but inactive."

Come on, Samuel. You have to come through for us. You have to.

"I told you to come and get me," he growled at the Hybrid. "Are you deaf?"

The Hybrid roared and pounced. Byron ran at him. Their shields pressed against each other. Byron tensed up and summoned everything he had left and pushed harder. The Hybrid slid back and let out an unintelligible scream. As he pushed back, Byron almost lost his footing.

"You are a waste of good DNA." Byron leaned in more and continued to blast as powerfully as he could with his hands.

The Hybrid kicked out a foot and tried to blast the commander's foot out from under him. As the Hybrid did so, the commander jerked his body aside. The sudden loss of pushback caused the Hybrid to fall over. He pulled his gun out as he fell. The commander did likewise. Each pointed the gun at the other and fired. The commander's syshée connected with the Hybrid's face, leaving behind a nasty mess. But the Hybrid's bullet found the commander's soft unprotected belly.

* * * * *

Brickert's team raced eastward on foot. As they ran, they received intel from the eagles and geese where to go. "... last spotted at the intersection of 7th and Pennsylvania," one goose reported. "Pig Blockade is still standing."

"Marchers are going to come through the Monument Mall," another one informed. "Leaders are trying to reroute them. That area is a kill zone."

The CAG cruisers launched missiles in the distance. Very few NWG cruisers remained. This worried Brickert. They ran almost two kilometers through the streets until they reached an old Navy Memorial plaza with a huge globe etched into the concrete walk. The blockade here was lines and lines of razor wire supported by concrete crowd control barricades and gun towers. Almost a dozen drone guns had been mounted near the front and CAG agents with rocket launchers sat on nearby rooftops.

"Do we have any air support available to help with this blockade?" Brickert asked the goose nest.

"You keep asking for air support, man. We've lost almost all our eagles. You gotta make do. I can lend you two snipers."

"Fine," Brickert responded, "tell them to take out the rocket launchers first." Then to his team he said, "We've got to get through this maze. Use the concrete barricades as cover. Our top priority is the drone guns. Once they're down, we'll move forward over the blockade to find Pig Team. How many grenades do we have?"

"I've got two," a woman from Squad D reported.

"I've got one," a man from the same squad said.

"If anything happens to those two, make sure we recover their grenades," Brickert told his eight remaining team members. "We'll use them on the drones as soon as we're close enough. Squads A and C form Squad A, Squads B and D are now Squad B. I'll go with Squad A since it's smaller. Squad B, head north to the fountains for cover. We'll go right and draw their fire. Signal when you're in position to hit the drones."

Brickert led his team in the opposite direction. "How are we doing on those rocket launchers?" he asked the goose nest.

"Sorry, we've got a new target. Can't help you at the moment. Word is that the marchers are headed down Pennsylvania Ave toward the blockade. You need to clear the path for them."

"How many marchers?"

"I don't got a number. Just clear the path."

"They're going to get mowed down by the drones!" Brickert protested. "Send them in from the north. The northern blockades are clear!"

"It'd take hours—" An explosion came from above, one of the rooftops of the towers overlooking the battlefield. Brickert swore under his breath. The goose nest had just been destroyed. No response would come now, nor would any help come to take out the rocket launchers.

His squad had moved in thirty meters when they were spotted. The first rocket flew toward them in a curling pattern, hissing like a viper and trailing hot white smoke. Brickert shot blast after blast at it with one hand while shielding their exposed flank with the other. "Come on," he muttered. "COME ON!"

Finally he hit the rocket and it exploded less than fifteen meters away. The force of the explosion was strong enough that it almost knocked him over. The Aegis holding the rocket launcher prepared to fire again.

"Move! Move!" Brickert told his squad.

* * * * *

Duncan Hudec sat on the goose nest, watching the battle through the scope of his sniper rifle. Up high, through the scope, it was an entirely different battle. It reminded him vividly of his days in the Elite Black Ops when they had stormed terrorist strongholds in the desert mountains. From such a vantage point, the entire battle became nothing more than ants scurrying around from hole to hole. And with the sniper rifle in his grip, Duncan assumed the role of the boot.

Hudec was one of three men stationed at his location. All in all there were four nests and fourteen snipers. Between CAG snipers and cruiser missiles, they'd already lost two nests and half the gunners. And he was pretty sure that one of the cruisers wheeling around in the air had just spotted his location.

Duncan radioed the NWG cruisers and told them the situation, but of the four remaining cruisers, one was badly damaged, and two were locked in dogfights. The fourth was kilometers away trying to protect the marchers in the water and surveying the area for hazards. So Duncan had only one option: try to take down the hawk with his sniper rifle. "Hawk has eyes," he told his fellow gunners.

All three snipers in the nest shot at the CAG cruiser, but it was like throwing pebbles at a rhino. The ship moved too fast to get an accurate shot, which meant they needed a miracle to get a hit on the pilot through the windshield.

"How are we doing on those rocket launchers?" the Sheep Leader asked.

"Sorry," Duncan responded, "we've got a new target. Can't help you at the moment. Word is that the marchers are headed down Pennsylvania Ave toward the blockade. You need to clear the path for them."

The cruiser was now headed straight toward the tower where Duncan's nest was located. *Maybe he don't see us. Maybe he's just turning around.* Even still he aimed his scope at the windshield and pulled the trigger. A miracle indeed. The brains of the Aegis pilot blew out the back of his head.

"Nice shot, Dunk!" one of the other snipers hollered.

"How many marchers?"

"I don't got a number," Duncan answered as he fired at another CAG cruiser. "Just clear the path."

"They're going to get mowed down by the drones!" Sheep Team Leader protested. "Send them in from the north. The northern blockades are clear!"

"It'd take hours—"

A sharp, ear-splitting whistle cut him off, and a missile from a second cruiser slammed into the building underneath the goose nest. Duncan was thrown over the platform railing, saved by the harness he wore which connected him to the building. Rifle still in hand, he dangled over the edge. Behind him, his two nest mates hung unconscious or dead, he couldn't tell which. The platform groaned as it slid, and the top part of the building slowly started to collapse. Duncan had time to fire one more shot.

Our Father who art in Heaven. He hefted his rifle up to his eye, waited for the rocking to lessen, and found a target in his scope: an Aegis wielding a rocket launcher, aimed at Sheep Team's location. The rocket flew in a burst of smoke straight at the team.

Hallowed be Thy name. A loud groan came from the building accompanied by the squeal of metal scraping over metal. The rocket exploded moments before hitting Sheep Team. Another miracle.

Thy kingdom come. Duncan put the Aegis in his crosshairs just as the enemy reloaded his launcher and put Sheep Team in his sights once more.

Thy will be done. A deep groan came from the building. Duncan fired first, killing the Aegis with a single shot.

On earth—The building crumbled with a loud lurch, and Duncan Hudec fell.

* * * * *

Janna Scoble flew her cruiser in a loop to get a better angle on the CAG cruiser. The attack on the Hive had started hours ago when, in the early pre-dawn hours, resistance fighters breached the Hive, captured a man named Chad, the Hive's caretaker, and shut down all of its systems except the parabolic antennae needed to transmit a code. She didn't know what the code would do, and didn't want to know. Her mission, along with twelve other cruisers, was to protect the Hive for as long as possible.

Six months ago, Janna Scoble joined the resistance. She had spent three months before that trying to convince her husband about her passionate beliefs, but couldn't sway him. After his third refusal, she stopped asking. Her decision to go without him was not easy, and one she was sure many people would not make, but something deep inside her told her to go. So she went.

A month after her arrival to Glasgow she learned she was pregnant. After a week of sleepless nights, debating whether or not she should return home, she met with Lara and Thomas. They assured they would support whatever decision she made. Janna ultimately chose to stay. The tipping point was meeting two young men named Brickert and Sammy. As a nurse in the infirmary, she learned about their actions in Detroit, how one had risked all to save the other from a collapsing building. She realized that she, too, could risk all for her cause.

Now, twenty-seven years old and seven months pregnant, she flew a cruiser because she was one of the few resistance members who'd survived the bio-bomb *and* had flying experience. Her father had been one of the last commercial pilots before the air rails effectively ended the commercial airline industry. She couldn't count how many times he'd said to her, "Everyone is born with wings, Janna. We just have to learn to fly with them."

The CAG cruisers launched their missiles at the Hive, only to be foiled again and again by the resistance pilots. From what she could tell, the resistance had neither superior training nor the advantage of numbers, just sheer willpower and determination to win. They destroyed the CAG ships at a rate of two for every one resistance ship lost. Janna had managed to destroy one and damage another, which another resistance pilot picked off. Her cruiser had taken some stray bullets, but nothing too substantial.

"We've got four CAGs coming in a diamond formation," the Elite air captain, Kallen Dinsmore, announced. "I need all cruisers in my quadrant to come to my coordinates."

"Roger that," one pilot said.

"Roger," Janna said as well.

In moments, the three cruisers joined together to stop the four CAG ships making a run at the Hive. The front three fired missiles, which were all matched and eliminated by the resistance's own missiles. "Fire at will," Dinsmore ordered, "More ships to my mark."

Two of the CAG cruisers took gunfire and veered away. The third tried to get a second missile off, but a new resistance ship entered the fray and intercepted the missile with his own. The fourth CAG ship, however, careened straight at the Hive.

"Get that bogey out of the air!" Dinsmore said. "Someone nearby who has missiles, take it out."

Janna was nearest but she was out of missiles. She looped around to improve her angle of attack, her guns firing on the ship, but she was unable to take it out. A nearby resistance cruiser launched a missile, but a CAG cruiser nulled the missile with one of its own. Janna's console told her the fourth CAG cruiser was preparing to launch its missile. Janna had no way of stopping it.

Except one.

"Thank you for my wings, Daddy." She patted her bulging stomach. "We got this one, don't we?"

Janna jerked her controls and directed her cruiser directly into the CAG ship's path. She collided with the CAG cruiser just as its missile released. She jammed on the eject button, but knew she would not make it in time. Fire and heat filled the cockpit as the missile detonated, followed immediately by the explosion of the CAG ship.

* * * * *

The air reeked of sulfur. It was November in D.C. but felt like July. The heat came from the molten pavement, the smoldering stumps of trees, and the fires in the buildings lining Washington Circle Park at 23rd and K Street. But Kawai had been in hell long before the battle began. It had started when she woke up and Li was gone, killed by the bio-bomb.

There hadn't been many boys to fall for in the village where she grew up. Some she knew so well they were more like brothers. Many had no ambition, a few had far too much. Her discovery by Commander Byron due to an incident during a gymnastics competition had been a welcome blessing. She had never once missed her village.

Over the course of two years as a member of Psion Beta, Kawai had developed strong feelings for three people: Martin Trector,

Sammy Berhane, and Li Cheng Zheng. Martin died in Rio, Sammy couldn't tell one female from another unless her name was Jeffie, and Li ...

Kawai didn't want to think about him anymore, but he was all she could think about.

"Kawai, where are you?" Nikotai, Cow Team's leader, shouted.

"Squad Bravo is down," Kawai reported back. It took every last bit of self-control she had not to cry. The haze and smoke was so thick from the rockets, she couldn't see. "Rockets. I—I tried to blast them, but I could only save myself."

The blockade her team had been charged with destroying had only been partially demolished from the car she'd driven into it. Most of the southern half had crumbled, but the explosives hadn't all discharged, leaving too much of the blockade intact. The Aegis and other agents had made them pay for the damage with drone and rocket fire.

"We have to get behind those rocket towers," Nikotai pressed. "I need you to provide cover."

Two rows of cement crowd barriers stood between the nearest rocket towers forty meters away. Six drone guns had been mounted on the barriers before Cow Team's car had collided into the blockade. The drones acted as sentinels that riddled holes in anything that looked dangerous or moved too fast on the western side of the blockade. So far Cow Team had taken out four of them, but a pair still remained.

"Can you make your way back to my location in two minutes?"

Kawai reached Nikotai in ninety seconds. Of his original fourteen team members, eight remained. Nikotai pointed north.

"They're coming. I don't know how many, but the marchers are coming. And if we can't take out this blockade, they're going to get cut down. And that's on us."

Dave Hudec, second in command of Cow Team, nodded.

"Kawai, you need to get us through using your shields. All seven of us are going behind you. Can you do that?"

"I can try," she said meekly.

"I can't count on a try. Can you do it?"

"I can do it."

Nikotai seemed satisfied with her answer. "Dave has grenades. So do Ilima and Dustin. I've got plenty of ammo. We just need to get into position to take out the towers and drones."

Kawai led the team to new cover behind two cars stacked one on top of the other, the top car upside down. Both were smoking hulls. The rounds of the two remaining drone guns clanked off their frames like hail on a window during a storm. Nikotai had to shout to be heard over the noise. "Keep an eye on that rocket tower, Kawai! And there's a second tower behind him, two Aegis with rifles."

"What now?" Hudec yelled to Nikotai.

"Take Kawai, Matthews, and Todd. Knock out those drones. We'll stay here and draw the attention of the rocket tower."

The task Nikotai had given Hudec was not an easy one. One drone was twenty meters to the right, the other a little farther to the left. Kawai could not easily shield everything and everyone. She needed another Psion.

I need Li.

"We'll take the closest one first," Dave Hudec said.

Shielding for Matthews and Todd was easier than Hudec. He was a bear of a man, while Ilima Todd and Dustin Matthews were both much shorter than Kawai. But Hudec had more combat experience from his days with his brother, Duncan, in the Elite Black Ops. Todd and Matthews were volunteers—survivors of the bio-bomb attack on Glasgow—and it amazed Kawai they had managed to avoid catching a bullet this long.

Nikotai's superb aim prevented the Aegis in the rocket tower from getting off another round of missiles, but both drones and the rifles took aim at Hudec's group.

"Get us to that barrier!" Hudec ordered, pointing to a molten cement barrier just tall enough for them to crouch behind.

The drone gun was only seven or eight meters away. Kawai concentrated on shielding the group from it as they ran across the park. Ilima tripped and hit the pavement. The drone gun picked up on her movement and ripped into her.

"Get away from her!" Hudec roared. Seconds later, one of the drone's rounds caught the grenade on Ilima's person and detonated it. The rest of the group ran for cover. "Give me your grenade, Matthews!"

"Why?"

"Because I need it."

"What? You think I'm gonna die?"

"Just give it to him," Kawai said. "We're not going to let you die."

Dustin Matthews handed it over. Hudec pulled the pin and waited a beat before tossing the grenade into the blockade. Two seconds later, the boom came and the drone stopped firing.

"Let's go."

Other than passing what was left of Ilima Todd and marking her GPS location, the crossing to the second drone was uneventful. The Aegis fired another rocket at Nikotai's group, obliterating much of what remained of the damaged vehicles, but Nikotai made the Aegis pay for it with his life. Now he and his two companions hunkered down behind a heap of park benches.

"In position to take out the second drone," Hudec said.

"Rocket tower is down," Nikotai said. "Do it."

Hudec pulled the pin, waited, and threw, but the drone gun shot the grenade midair where it detonated harmlessly. Kawai had her shields up, but somehow Matthews wasn't covered. Bullets or shrapnel or both hit him in the eye, throat, and chest. He was dead before he hit the ground.

Dave Hudec cursed.

"I shielded—I thought you were—" Kawai tried to explain to Dustin, but his glossy eyes and blood-speckled face left her frozen.

"Todd and Matthews are down," Hudec reported. "What are our orders?"

Another rocket erupted from the tower—the same tower Nikotai had reported as clear. It flew toward Kawai and Hudec.

"Incoming bogey!" Nikotai shouted.

Kawai fired concentrated blasts at it while more shots rang out across the park. The rocket exploded next to the drone gun, disabling it. Kawai scanned the area for signs of more incoming fire. "Are we clear?" she asked.

No one answered.

Kawai chanced a glance behind her but saw no one. "Hudec?"

Crackling sounds came from her com. Nikotai's voice. She couldn't make out the words. Kawai dropped down and almost sat on Hudec. Most of the top of his head was gone and a pool of blood spread out underneath what was left. She gazed across the park at the tower where the Aegis stood with their rifles, sights trained in her direction.

Tears leaked from Kawai's eyes. She couldn't breathe. Couldn't think. Couldn't fight. Not anymore. No more deaths.

One. One more death.

Kawai jumped the barrier and ran at the tower. Her eyes fixed on the Aegis, willing them to shoot her. Another Aegis from the rocket tower stood and pointed his launcher at her path, but three holes plugged his chest before he could fire. Something hot and fast whizzed past the left side of her head. Another brushed her right arm. A third. A fourth. More. All barely missed. Still Kawai ran at the tower, arms and legs pumping wildly, her ears filled with the sound of white noise.

She was more than halfway there when one of the rifle-bearing Aegis took two bullets: one to the shoulder, spinning him, and one to the back. The other Aegis ducked for cover.

No!

And before Kawai knew it she was off her feet and crashing into the grass, blindsided by someone bigger and faster than she. It was Nikotai on top of her. For a moment she thought he was dead, but then he looked at her.

"What are you doing!"

She had no answer. Only sobs.

He grabbed her and pulled her under his chin. "You're going to live. You're going to survive this."

"I was supposed to die!" she shrieked. "Why did you save me?"

"I didn't save you. I tackled you. They must have fired thirty rounds before I could reach you. All at you. All missed."

"Why?" It wasn't a question from her lips but a demand.

"Fate. Luck. I don't know." Nikotai let her go. "That part's up to you."

* * * * *

Sammy was back in the forest. One minute he'd been laying on his back, exhausted, looking up at pure white, the next he was here. Scattered rays of moonlight filtered through the trees. Everything was wet with an autumn smell of molding leaves and wet earth. *You can still win, Sammy,* a familiar voice said. *You can still save her. But there is only one way. It has to be my way.*

"You again." Sammy knew the voice. He'd heard it so many times. "Why do you keep bugging me?"

Sammy walked faster until he came face to face with the shadow. They mirrored each other in height, but the shadow had no features to distinguish it—a being of pure black. Sammy could see eyes moving in sockets, but no iris, no pupils, no sclera, just black. He saw lips and teeth, all black. No blemishes or wrinkles or scars.

Only black.

When Sammy held up a hand, the shadow mirrored him, but Sammy did not touch it. He only looked. The closer his hand came to the shadow hand, the more he felt the energy of it pulsing and pulling. "Are you going to give me the key or what?"

You think this is a game?

Sammy connected their palms and fingers. The shadow brightened and shrunk until it disappeared, leaving Sammy with the key. The beautiful key. The head of the key was rounded in gold and silver. The polished metal gleamed brightly in the moonlight, its shaft and cuts perfectly tapered and tuned.

Choose.

To Sammy's left, the cave. He had descended its depths but never unlocked the metal door he stood at and contemplated more than once. To his right, a lake, massive and serene. It extended out as far as he could see. At the edge of the lake was the raft. The raft was a pathetic thing, held together by twine, its log boards raggedy and uneven. Yet somehow he knew it would stay afloat with his weight on it.

"I've already chosen."

You have not. Listen to the sounds in the cave.

Sammy walked closer to the cave's black mouth and heard voices coming from below. Quiet laughter, kisses, soft whispers. *Jeffie's voice.* They were the unmistakable sounds of love. The sounds transformed into her pleas for help—pleas he had heard many times in the dream. He knew they came from behind the iron door at the bottom of the cave's steps.

Only the cave will give you the power you need to save her, the voice told him. Sammy sensed the raw power down there, the promise it held. A rush of cool air from within blew over his face, filling him with an energy that made his skin tingle.

"What source of power is so great that it hides in a cave?" Sammy wondered aloud.

The power is in you. But down there is the way to unlock it.

At those words, Sammy understood perfectly what he should do and what sort of power such a place would unlock. He took a step backward, then another, and then he ran to the raft.

Loneliness. That's where this raft takes you. Jeffie's death. And yours. You will die wondering what could have been … if you'd only descended into the lair of power.

Sammy laughed. "You don't know the future." He used his key on the padlock that secured the chain connecting the raft and the pole. Then he stepped gingerly onto the raft, threw the chain off, and sat. "I made a promise."

When he pushed off from the shore, a sense of calm filled him. He tucked his knees up to his chest, rested his chin on his knees, and listened to the waters as they splashed around the edges and through the cracks between the logs.

The voice in his head grew dim, faint, and eventually silent. But the water whispered his name. "Sammy … Sammy … Sammy."

He dipped a hand in the water and savored the coolness of it. The pale blue moon was big and full on the horizon. It seemed to Sammy that if he floated long enough, he'd crash into the sky. Then a black spot appeared in the middle of the moon and grew larger as Sammy drifted onward.

An island.

The strip of land wasn't much longer or wider than two or three cruisers put together. A small grove of trees stood in the center of it, their trunks straight and proud. In the midst of the trees, something reflected the moonlight, glinting white or gold. When the raft bumped into the shore, Sammy climbed out and headed toward it.

Vines hung down from trees like a veil, their tendrils swinging softly in the breeze. From within he caught a scent of something like apples or nectar. He pushed aside the vines and walked through the veil. White flowers clung to the vines on the other side. In the center of the petals were seeds of gold, silver, and topaz. The flowers captured every ray of moonlight and reflected them so perfectly that the inner sanctum of the island was as bright as day. Sammy's eyes widened as he turned in a circle, examining all of it with wonder and awe.

In the center of the island was an elegant altar of stones almost twice as tall as himself. Each stone was cut and shaped, smoothed and polished so the altar looked more like a miniature Mayan temple, larger at the base and slightly tapered so that each successive row was smaller than the one underneath. The lowest layer of stones was jet black. But each successive level grew lighter until the perfectly square slab at the top was whiter than even the flowers.

Seeing nothing but the altar, Sammy considered going back to the raft, but he did not want to leave. Then it occurred to him what he should do. He climbed the rocks, and with every rock he ascended, he felt something leave him—something he didn't mind parting with. Finally, at the top, he pulled himself onto the altar. It was more comfortable than he would have believed, so he laid down, stretching himself out. Energy rushed into his body, filling him with light and joy, so much that he glowed with it. Every fear, worry, doubt, and regret vanished from his mind.

A smile grew on his face. He couldn't contain it. He didn't want to. And when the energy and joy became so great that he could hardly bear it, Sammy closed his eyes and woke.

26 | Liberty

Tuesday, November 11, 2087

BRICKERT'S SQUAD WORKED their way to the front of the blockade as quickly as possible, motivated now by incoming rockets from the rooftops. Their noted presence allowed Sheep Team's other squad to reach the drones virtually undetected. The grenades did their job, taking out three of the four drone guns stationed at the wall of the barricade.

"Incoming rocket!" one of his squad members shouted.

Brickert whirled and blasted while shouting into his com, "Can someone get a hit on that guy?"

Moments later a NWG cruiser slammed into the building where the launcher-toting Aegis had been, exploding and spraying glass and metal like rainfall. *I didn't mean like that.* The image sobered him. How many good men and women would die today? *Sammy, Jeffie ... who else? Is Natalia already dead?*

"Do we have any air support left?" he asked into his com.

"All the eagles are down!" Justice responded. "All the goose nests have been taken out. Do what you can to disable the block—" The voice cut off abruptly.

Justice too?

Brickert ran for the last drone gun as three CAG cruisers flew overhead. As they passed, they split their ranks, one veering off left, another right, and the third going straight up. Squad B provided cover for Squad A as Brickert led A to the front of the blockade. It took several blasts to disable the last drone gun, and when he finally did, the enemy cruisers fired their missiles at his team.

"Take cover!" he yelled.

All nine soldiers on Sheep Team dove for the dirt as two missiles roared in and rocked the ground, spraying earth and smoke like blankets over everything in sight. Brickert's ears rang from the concussion, hot blood trickled down the side of his head where debris had cut him. "Sheep Team report!"

Only four answered. Brickert called for medics to his location.

"No medics left," another voice said. Brickert believed it was Lorenzo Winters, but couldn't be sure. "Tag the bodies and move on."

We can't win, Brickert realized. *All our cruisers are gone. They're mopping us up.* He checked the time. 0841. Sammy was almost an hour late activating the kill code, if he was alive at all.

Brickert got up on unsteady legs. The first thing he saw when he climbed the blockade with the remaining four members of the team was Natalia's smoldering car. The explosives in the car had detonated well short of the first barricades, but Sheep Team found no corpses in or near the vehicle. Knowing medics would not be coming, Brickert split his four soldiers in twos to search for what remained of Pig Team.

Brickert gave Lorenzo an update of his team's situation while he searched. "We've breached the northwest blockade. No sign of Pig Team, but we've got a small squad of cruisers circling overhead. They're prepping to attack again." Brickert stared up into the sky to spot the cruisers, and saw an odd shape in one tree's branches.

A well-executed jump-blast got him into the tree. It was Natalia, her body cradled by three branches, her face and arms cut and bleeding, burns traveled up her right leg and ribs. Brickert said her name softly and felt for a pulse. It was weak, so was her breathing. He said her name a second time, but she did not stir.

Taking her in his arms, he jumped down from the tree and carried her onto the nearest patch of grass that wasn't exposed to overhead cruisers. "I'm sorry," he told her under his breath so the com couldn't pick up his voice. "I should have disobeyed orders and come after you. I don't think we're going to win, Natalia. I don't think—"

At least a dozen cruisers flew overhead, streaking and roaring through the sky at something in the distance—a long black shape. Brickert moved in front of Natalia to cover her. "What is this? What's happening?"

He stood up straight to see, but still couldn't see through all the wreckage. A dozen missiles launched at once, their sounds followed by a strange roar. Brickert jumped back into the tree, climbing as high as he dared. His eyes widened and his breath left his lungs in one great rush.

"They're coming," he shouted down to Natalia, his team, whoever could hear. "I can't believe it. There's so many ... The people are coming. Not hundreds, not thousands. Hundreds of thousands, Natalia! Hundreds of thousands. And those cruisers—" His face whitened and his jaw slackened. "The marchers are going to be massacred."

Tears filled his eyes. Thousands upon thousands would be turned back or slaughtered. *Where are Sammy and Byron?*

* * * * *

"Sammy ..." Jeffie's voice came through his com, whispering so softly he barely heard it. His eyes fluttered open, dry and sore. When he realized he'd fallen asleep, he gasped and jerked.

"*Sammy.*"

"Sorry. I'm awake."

"Oh, great. You're awake. What is the deal with you and falling asleep during really important, really stressful situations? I'm covered in dead people and having a panic attack over here."

"I didn't know I was asleep," he whispered back.

"The batteries are almost dead. She's killed me, and you're about done. How was your nap?"

"Short, but I actually feel a little better. Not so tired." Sammy peered through the coffin-shaped holographic projection that hid him from view where he lay on the floor near the back of the white room. Near the elevator stood the Queen pointing what looked like a miniaturized blitzer at Sammy's holographic image. Disappointment etched her face as she fired one into his left eye. Then she adjusted her aim slightly to the right eye and fired again.

"How much time is left on the battery?" he asked Jeffie.

"Less than a minute. Five minutes until kill code activation."

"What to do with your body?" the Queen asked Sammy's hologram that now lay motionless on the floor. "Maybe I'll preserve it. Start my own personal museum."

"I don't think it'll keep," Sammy said as he rolled over the floor, out of the holographic box he'd been hiding in. No sooner had he stepped out then all the holograms in the room flickered away, the batteries finally drained. The white pillars in the room flickered and disappeared, revealing the twin holo-projectors underneath. "See?" Sammy gestured to where his fake body had lain. "Meat nowadays. You never know what it *really* is."

The Queen's eyes looked like they might pop. She took a step back, her blitzer pointed at Sammy's chest. "No ..." She closed her eyes and shook her head. "No ... I killed you. I just killed you. You're dead."

"It's 1025, Sammy," Jeffie said as she climbed out of the elevator covered in the gore of the Hybrids and Thirteens. "Less than five minutes until the next—"

The Queen jerked her head to look at Jeffie. "And you! I KILLED YOU BOTH!"

"Too many crazy pills for this one," Jeffie told Sammy.

"You know what they say about women and the hot-to-crazy scale."

"Are you saying *I'm* crazy?" Jeffie asked.

"Shut up!" the Queen fired a blitzer at Jeffie, but Jeffie jumped away. "This isn't real! This is a lie! The fox … someone … I killed you!"

"Yep." Sammy tried to stay light on his feet, but his body was slow and worn. "I'm just an illusion. So if you'll go on upstairs back to your therapist—"

"I had the element of surprise!" She fired another round, this time at Sammy, but he ducked it and shot a blast back at her.

"Not really a surprise, Katie," Sammy said. "Diego told us about your new skills. Why do you think I brought these?" He pointed a thumb at the holo-projectors. "We spent weeks recording ourselves fighting other Psions and Ultras. For you. I knew you'd figure it out. Knew you'd show up." He sniffed and wiped an eye mockingly. "This was my going away present for you."

She attacked him with blasts. He dodged and fired a blast back at her. The little nap had re-energized his arms, but his legs still felt stiff as boards and his head was full of fog.

"You look like you've been through the ringer," Jeffie said to the Queen. "Did our holograms wear you out?"

"Cowards!" she snarled, diving at Sammy.

The Queen was faster than him, stronger, more tireless. Her Anomaly Thirteen gave her those abilities; Sammy had passed on them. But he had to believe he was *better*. He hopped over her while firing blasts back at her, but she nulled them with blasts of her own.

"You couldn't beat me so you used tricks!"

"Yeah," Sammy said, circling her, "I guess I did. But you sent your army of undead ahead of you, so I think we're even." He signaled to Jeffie to reopen the back door and prepare the terminal for the command.

"One minute!" Jeffie called.

The Queen saw this and laughed. "That signal will never go out." She fired three blitzers at the computer but the discs did not penetrate the reinforced metal.

She fired again, this time at Sammy. He barely avoided the blitzer, and used her missed attack as an opportunity to draw in closer. The Queen tried to blast him away, but he jumped and shot himself back down at her from the ceiling. His knee connected with her nose, making a distinct crunching sound.

When Sammy saw the blood run down her face, he laughed. "Seriously, how many times have I broken your nose? I think your plastic surgeon owes me a gift basket."

The Queen cursed at him and sent a blitzer disc at Jeffie.

"Look out!" he shouted.

The blitzer disc caught Jeffie in the lower torso, slicing a thin line clean through her abdomen and passing through just where her kidney would be. Jeffie cried out as she grabbed at the wound and fell.

Sammy blasted himself at the Queen, wrapped his arms around her, and drove them both to the ground. He roared every curse he knew while pummeling her head with his left hand and slamming the blitzer in her hand into the floor with his right. The Queen propelled both of them upward with blasts from her free hand and feet, nearly forcing Sammy's skull into the ceiling, but he narrowly avoided it with blasts of his own.

"Sammy ... the code," Jeffie said. "Ten seconds."

"Can you fight?" he asked her.

"I can hold her off!"

"You're not going anywhere!" the Queen screamed and grabbed at Sammy. She drove him to the floor so fast it stunned him. Before he regained his wits she swung the blitzer at his head. Sammy raised his hand to block her, but Jeffie rammed the Queen in the left flank, knocking her off Sammy. He shot across the room to the alcove with the desk and screen. His fingers flew over the keyboard, entering the code that Diego had guarded for years. All for this moment. But by the time he finished typing and jammed down the standby button, the clock read 1031.

* * * * *

Pain deeper and hotter than anything Jeffie had known radiated through her side as she bowled into the Queen. *Ignore it. Protect Sammy. You're dead anyway.* The Queen grunted as she and Jeffie tumbled to the floor. She blasted Jeffie away, glaring as though Jeffie were lower than animal droppings.

"Don't touch me!" the Queen snapped as she wiped a trickle of blood from her lip. "This doesn't concern you. Leave if you want. I don't care."

"Afraid to face me, Katie?" Jeffie asked, sounding braver than she felt.

Using the Queen's first name had the effect Jeffie wanted. She blasted and ran at Jeffie, who stood in place, absorbed the blasts, and let the Queen tackle her. When they collided, Jeffie wrapped her up tight, then bit the Queen in the neck. She bit as hard as she could and tasted blood. The Queen shrieked and blasted Jeffie away again, sending her skidding across the floor on her back. The collision created waves of agony up and down Jeffie's side, but she ignored it, struggled back to her feet, and spat the Queen's blood from her mouth.

"You taste like chicken."

The Queen turned her attention to Sammy, filthy names spewing from her mouth. But before she could reach him, Jeffie blasted the Queen away and scrambled to block her path. The Queen shot her blitzer, sending disc after burning disc at Jeffie until her trigger brought nothing but an empty clicking sound. Jeffie tried to dodge them all, but couldn't. The Queen was as fast and clever as Sammy. One disc hit Jeffie's leg as she flipped, searing the inside of her thigh; another sliced through her ribs on the right side. A third narrowly missed her face, but left a thin burn on the bridge of her nose and cut strands of her hair as she whipped her head around.

Between her injured knee and punctured abdomen, landing on the floor was pure torture. And the Queen was waiting, blitzer at the ready, hitting Jeffie so hard in the face with the butt of her weapon that the bones in Jeffie's face crunched. Blood choked Jeffie's airway and she coughed up spatters of red phlegm. She grabbed the Queen blindly and blasted with her feet, carrying both of them near the elevator shaft. She meant to land on the Queen, but the Thirteen twisted around in the air. When Jeffie hit the ground, she thought she would never move again.

"Sammy …" she said. "I can't breathe—"

"Get back to the computer!" he said as he charged the Queen. "I'll take care of her. Just tell me when it's 1044!"

The Queen tried to stop Jeffie, but Sammy blasted the Queen back against the wreckage of the elevator door. Jeffie spat out more blood and phlegm, then began to crawl, pulling herself by her arms while her legs dragged. The force of the floor against her body burned her insides. Jeffie could hardly breathe, hardly talk, hardly move. She didn't know how to tell Sammy that she didn't think she could make it across the room, let alone live another fifteen minutes.

* * * * *

The Queen swung the blitzer at the blonde girl's head as though the gun was a baseball bat and the girl's head was a ball sitting on its tee, but Sammy stopped it with a blast. It flew from her hands and landed in the elevator amongst the bodies.

Grunting, the girl continued to crawl at a snail's pace. *She can't reach the computer. She can't.* But Sammy now blocked the Queen from getting to her.

The Queen blasted, dove, charged and spun, but Sammy would not let her pass. He blasted at the Queen again, but she met him with her own blasts, angled to push his aside. Sammy tried to adjust, but she was faster, her blasts stronger. Her elbow met his chin; her fist rammed his gut. Air rushed from his lungs. The Queen tried to bowl past him, but he snagged her foot and pulled her down on top of him.

"Let go!" she shrieked.

When the Queen tried to blast Sammy's head and snap his neck, he gripped her hands in his, locking their fingers together. She yanked and pulled but couldn't loosen his grip. Then he blasted them both into the air, and their heads connected with the ceiling. A tremendous pain filled the Queen's skull.

Sammy's eyes rolled back as he fell to the ground. The Queen's thoughts turned hazy. *This is my chance ... to kill ...* She crawled toward him even as her vision blurred and darkened. *Must ... now.* She put a hand on his head. One blast, it was all she needed to finish it. Then the girl would die so easily.

Do it! Before you black out!

The pain growing in her head debilitated her. It was not only from the collision with the ceiling, but from what she knew Sammy would feel if she were to finish it. Sammy was no longer visible in all the blurriness. The Queen tried to ignore the pain, fought to remain conscious, yet the darkness won.

When her body collapsed on the floor, she was no longer in the white room, but the cave. Whereas before the cave had always been black as pitch, now it was light and filled with glass windows. Each glass window was a stained and muraled face. She recognized the first ones: her parents. Her first victims. Seeing them made her stomach roil uncomfortably. The condensation on the glass made their eyes weep even as they followed her, their expressions frozen just the way they'd been when she killed them. She turned her eyes away from their faces and walked down the steps faster.

Next were the Queen's victims at school, the girls and boys she'd found who had laughed at her at the prom. She began to jog down the steps, taking them two at a time.

Following her classmates were guards and officers and others she'd killed in prison. Then came other inmates, then civilians—people the fox had sent her after. Face after face after face, each in horror, agony, or disbelief at the notion of their own deaths. All dead by the Queen's hand. The last faces at the bottom she knew well. They belonged to Sammy and the pretty blonde girl. Even though she hadn't killed them yet, they were as good as dead when she woke.

When the Queen finally reached the black door of flesh at the end of the cave, she found it still locked. The girl's voice, the Queen's own teenage voice, still pleaded from the other side to be let out.

"What do I have to do?" the Queen screamed in frustration as she beat at the door. "Where is the knife?"

No one answered. The Queen slammed her fist into Sammy's glass face, sending shards of blue, black, and white onto the cave floor. She picked up the largest of them, one of Sammy's eyes still visible, and stabbed it at the door. Unlike last time, when the knife's blade had sunk easily into the flesh, the glass shattered against the door. The Queen found another shard and tried again, but this attempt also failed.

She remembered the last time she had entered the cave, and what she had found inside: the altar, the fire, and the pot. Within the pot had been a heart.

"No."

Even as she said the word, she realized what the cave demanded. From among the glass shards, she found the longest. Her quaking hands held it up high until the light from other windows made the glass glow, and then she plunged it deep into her own chest. And after minutes of work, she finally removed her own beating heart.

Holding it up to the door, the blackened flesh began to turn brown, then pinkish. It gave a quiver and started to pulse. And when she touched the heart to it, it fell away like a curtain that had been ripped from its hanging rod. Swallowing hard, the Queen re-entered the room for the first time in almost thirty-five years.

Young Katie sat on the floor, her hair covering her face. Her skin was a pale yellow and tight like a mummy's. When the Queen entered, the girl looked up at her, and the Queen recoiled. Katie's eyes were sunken in, her face sallow with hollow cheeks, and her lips dry to the point of cracking.

"Are you here to save me?" she asked when their eyes met. "I— I made a mistake."

"No," the Queen answered, still clutching the beating heart in her hand. "*I* made the mistake. I tried to have it all."

"Please …" the girl moaned, struggling to her feet only to have the Queen push her back down. "I want to go."

A clanging sound came from the far end of the room, drawing the Queen's attention. It was the white pot. She dragged the girl over to have a look at it. As expected she found it empty. That was when it all clicked.

"I can turn it off," she muttered to herself. "One or the other."

Two Anomalies. Set at odds against each other. The empathy of the Anomaly Eleven. Or the cold power and fearlessness of the Anomaly Thirteen.

She looked at the heart. At the pot. At Katie. And at the altar.

The choice was easy. She yanked Katie by the arm and threw her atop the altar. Katie screamed. "What are you going to do?"

The Queen tightened her grip on her own heart. "I'm going to finish the job."

* * * * *

Sammy blinked awake just as the Queen pounced. His head throbbed, but he was cognizant enough to roll away and get back to his feet. A glance at his com told him it was 1039. He and the Queen had only been out for a minute or two. He shook his head to chase away the thick cobwebs.

Across the room Jeffie was still trying to drag herself to the computer. Her pace had grinded to a halt. She couldn't seem to pull herself any further. Fresh blood trailed behind her, and she sobbed as she tried to crawl.

"Hurry, Jeffie," he said. "Get to the computer! Five minutes!"

"I can't make it," Jeffie cried from behind. "You do it. I can't."

"You have to do it, Jeffie!"

The Queen rushed and blasted at him. Sammy tried to blast jump, but was too slow. She caught him by the legs and flipped him over. Sammy barely prevented himself from slamming his head into the floor by using hand blasts to steady himself.

The Queen used the opportunity to attack Jeffie, but Sammy blasted himself off the floor at the Queen, driving into her less than a second before she reached Jeffie, who was only halfway to the computer. The Queen and Sammy tumbled to the ground over each other. The Queen rammed her elbow into Sammy's face and tried to blast the side of his head, but Sammy rolled over and kicked.

The Queen caught his foot and twisted, trying to break his ankle, but Sammy let his body turn. As his other foot crossed in front of her face, he blasted and shoved her backward. He hadn't expected to catch her off guard with that move, but it gave him an opening to tackle the Queen and buy Jeffie more time.

As he did so, he climbed onto the Queen's back and wrapped his arms under hers, taking away her hand blasts. She tried to roll and shake him off, but Sammy held strong. She fired her foot blasts, but without a surface to push off, the blasts only made Sammy and the Queen rock up and down.

Sammy angled his palms at the Queen's neck. One good blast would kill her. But when he did it, nothing happened. He tried to blast again. Nothing came.

I'm too tired, he realized. *Gonna have to do this the old fashioned way.*

"Keep going, Jeffie!" he shouted. "Four minutes!"

"She can't!" the Queen cried out with exultation. "She's weak. You're both weak."

"Go, Jeffie!" he urged while the Queen tried to slam her head into his. "Go!"

He had never felt so much emotion for anyone as he did then, seeing Jeffie squirm on the ground like a worm, agony wracking her body. Many would have given up. But not Jeffie. She loved him. She had told him so more than once, but he had never returned the words.

Why? Why didn't I?

The Queen raged and jerked and spasmed in attempt to throw Sammy off her. Sammy felt the energy leaving his limbs.

"What if I can't?" Jeffie was in tears as she looked back at Sammy.

"DIE!" the Queen screamed. Blood dripped from her face, and she sucked down air. "Both of you ... die."

A deep burn crept up Sammy's arms to his wrists and fingers as he tried to contain the Queen's struggling. He wouldn't be able to hold on much longer. He was too exhausted to blast. Too drained to fight. Too spent of energy to do anything but hold on. "You can, Jeffie," he breathed. "Because …"

He'd wanted to be sure of it before he said the words. He'd wanted some kind of sign. Something meaningful. But this was it. This was meaningful, that they were willing to die together. Living together would be better, but that wasn't an option.

"Because I love you," he croaked, voice still hoarse from being choked. "Because I know you can."

Jeffie turned back and continued to crawl. The Queen's eyes filled with horror. Her face paled. She screamed and grabbed at Sammy's hair, threw herself from side to side. Finally Sammy's arms gave out and the Queen squirmed from his grip. She tried to get her footing to blast at Jeffie, but Sammy darted forward and slammed her into the wall.

The Queen blasted, but he hung on to her until they fell to the floor. Sammy struck the ground first but rolled on top of her. As she raised her hands to blast his face, Sammy jerked his head aside and drove his fist into her face. The skin split in her cheek. Her eyes rolled back only to refocus on his face. She brought her hands up again, but Sammy seized her wrists, butted her head with his own, and punched her twice more.

She yanked her wrists from his grasp, but he locked his fingers with hers in both hands. The Queen blasted with her feet, trying to flip them over, but he anticipated it and twisted around so she landed on her back once more with a heavy thud. Her hand came loose and she jammed it into his face. Bones cracked and new pain exploded as his left eye went dark. Then Sammy returned the favor by pummeling her again.

The Queen's face swelled grotesquely, but he knew his was no better. Sammy turned his good eye on Jeffie, who was now three-quarters of the way across the room, lines of blood tracing her movements like red ink.

Taking advantage of this moment of distraction, the Queen blasted Sammy up, and he slammed into the white surface of the ceiling and fell back down in a shower of dust. He tried to break his fall with blasts, but still couldn't summon them. Instead he crashed into the floor and felt his ribs crack.

Kneeling on the floor, the Queen panted from the effort. Sammy didn't want to move but necessity compelled him. He pushed himself up and walked toward her. She fired blasts at him again and again, driving him back. Still he kept coming. As he did, her own blasts began to weaken. The Queen gritted her broken white teeth and curled her bruised, swollen lips but couldn't summon the energy to stop him.

When Sammy reached her, he grabbed her hands and shoved her against the wall. Looking in her eyes, he saw something he'd never seen before.

Defeat.

"You cheated." She muttered the words like a curse.

He let his fist fly into her gut. "You forgot, didn't you?"

The Queen doubled over and groaned. "Cheater."

Sammy hit her again. "Pain." His knuckles ached, but he did it again. "Suffering."

The Queen fell to the floor, and her mouth moved soundlessly.

Sammy knelt over her and struck her again. "Pain gives us strength. Stripe taught me that. Here. In Rio."

He was in control, but she couldn't hurt anyone again. So he hit her more. "You thought your Anomaly Thirteen would give you freedom. Endless strength."

And more. "But you followed a lie, Katie. And that is why you lost."

The Queen stopped moving. Her right eye was not quite swollen shut. It fixed on his, and for a moment Sammy saw only a girl. Her lips quivered. "I wish ..." She spoke softly, and he had to lean to hear her. "I wish ..."

"What?" he asked.

The Queen's eye widened enough that Sammy could see her brown iris surrounded by so much blood that she looked like every other Thirteen. Her hands shot out, wrapped around Sammy's throat, and squeezed. "That you would die with me."

Her grip on Sammy's throat was stronger than any vise. Sammy gagged trying to breathe. He tugged at her hands but they were locked. His eyes searched for Jeffie, for help.

Across the room, Jeffie pulled herself up to the terminal. Her face had no color. She'd left all her color on the floor of the white room. Their eyes met. Jeffie raised a finger, but Sammy's mind had kept count of the time. It was 1044. One minute. Even as his face reddened and the vision in his good eye started to blur, he nodded to her to activate the code at 1045. Then, step by step, he dragged the Queen toward the elevator, even as she continued to choke the life out of him.

As the moment approached, Jeffie held up five fingers and ticked them down.

Four.

Three.

Two.

One.

She pushed the ENTER button. Immediately two white blast doors began to close, separating the white room from its antechamber in front of the elevator. Sammy held the Queen in place until the twin doors clamped down on her body, squeezing her to death.

"Blast to me!" Sammy gasped to Jeffie in his broken voice.

She flew toward him. He grabbed her, wrapped his arms around her for support, and said, "Again!"

She blasted them through the space between the doors. As they flew through the air, Sammy let go of Jeffie as she flipped over and blasted the Queen from behind with everything she had left in her. The Queen flew inward and the blast doors slammed closed just as a tremendous explosion roared through the white room. The last thing Sammy saw before everything went white was the fire blossoming toward him like a brilliant red rose.

* * * * *

As Commander Byron staggered back to Albert, he realized his son had still not used the orange goo to close his leg wound. Albert's face was terribly pale, his eyes only half opened.

"I told you to use it!" Byron cried.

"No," Albert said. "Dad, you. Please. It has to be you. I don't want to go back. I've messed things up. I've blown it."

Commander Byron fumbled through the med pack until he got out the last bit inside the tube. He hoped it was enough to save his son.

"Dad, your stomach," Albert said, pointing vaguely. "You can raise her for me. You'll do a better job than I ever will."

Byron ignored Albert and prepped the tube. Albert grabbed the commander's hands, stopping him from using it.

"I don't want you to die, Dad."

The commander almost lost control. "And I will not survive losing you. You wait and see when your girl gets a little older. You will understand."

Albert tried to scoot away. "No."

The commander took him by the ankle, and pain shot up his wounded arm. "Do you love Marie? Do you really love her, Albert?" He was almost shouting now.

Albert's face turned a pale pink, and his eyes welled up. "Yeah."

"Then you have hope. Make it count."

Finally Albert relented. The commander put the orange goo in his son's leg, tore a strip from his pants, and tied it tightly near the hip. His limbs grew weak the longer he worked. When he finished, Albert was already so drowsy he could hardly move. The commander found a syringe of epinephrine and injected it into his son's leg. Then he ripped his own shirt and bandaged up the wound in his stomach as best as he could. But he knew it would not be enough.

With the last of his strength, he hobbled to the computer and looked at the screen. The time read 0839. Byron winced. *I missed the 0830 launch time.* The network was still inactive. *Come on, Sammy.*

Commander Byron checked on Albert, shook him gently. Albert's eyes fluttered open. "What?" he mumbled.

"Everything is going to be okay," he reassured his son. "I am going to take care of everything."

His bandage was soaked with blood. His right arm wouldn't move now, and his left ached so badly it made the commander want to pass out.

Commander Byron leaned over and kissed Albert on the cheek. "I love you, my boy. Emily and I will be waiting for you."

Albert stirred. "... love you, Dad."

When Byron tried to stand up straight, the pain gnawed at his gut where the last slug had torn into his insides. Everything was cold. Even his legs, which shouldn't feel anything, were cold. He fell down onto his hands and bionic knees.

"Hold on," he groaned. "I just need five more minutes."

He crawled to the computer and watched the seconds tick by, forcing his eyes to stay open and his heart to keep beating.

0841.

0842.

0843.

Byron's eyes closed and his chin hit the table where the computer sat. A green light brightened next to the standby button. A buzzing sound jarred him awake. "Network connected and active."

0844.

The seconds ticked. He said them aloud to give himself something to hold on for. *Stay alive, Walter*, he thought to himself as he counted. *Stay alive for your dad, your son, and your granddaughter.*

At 0845, he pushed the button.

`Kill code activated.`

Byron sighed and fell to the floor. Just before he closed his eyes again, he saw his son. He reached out for his face, but it was too far. "Emily ... Albert has to stay. Help him. Send someone."

Byron scooted over the ground until his head rested on his son's lap. A soft, high-pitched sound came from across the room. Byron opened an eye, all he could open, to find the source. It was a man rappelling down the elevator shaft. His footsteps approached cautiously, probably trying to step through all the mess. It wasn't until the feet were centimeters away, that Byron caught a glimpse of the leg, a bionic leg like his.

"Help ..." he whimpered. "My son."

A face appeared in view that the commander did not recognize. But the eyes he did. He hadn't seen them in many years. "You."

The man did not smile. His eyes fixed on Byron's wounds. "You don't have much time. Neither of you do, Walter."

"Take Albert. Come back when he is safe."

The man nodded. Strong arms—bionic arms—lifted Albert from under his father. As the man cradled Byron's son, he turned back to the commander. He nodded to Byron with eyes filled with respect. "You were always better than me. In every way, I think. Say hello to Emerald for me."

Commander Byron smiled, closed his eyes, and exhaled.

-499-

* * * * *

At 0847 the CAG cruisers fell from the sky like giant meteors crashing down from space. As far as Brickert could tell, not many were injured. When the crowds saw them fall, they pressed forward. The Aegis, the Thirteens, the Hybrids … all gone. Obliterated by the solution. Brickert didn't really believe it at first. His joy was quickly replaced by the knowledge that the victory had cost him his best friend.

Even as they stormed the White House, Brickert didn't grasp what was happening. They were a sea of people, a giant wave washing inside the halls and carrying out the filth on their backs. As many had predicted, President Newberry was gone, hidden away somewhere safe. That didn't stop the crowds from removing the staff members inside who hadn't been evacuated. So far as Brickert could tell, no one was killed.

Thomas and Justice led the charge through the buildings and communicated with the remaining team leaders to keep the masses orderly. After the White House was cleared they directed the crowds to the Capitol Building, where another sort of cleansing took place, along with more arrests. News choppers and cruisers hovered over the scene while reporters on foot followed the crowds inside with cameras. Local law enforcement and government service agents set up new barricades, assisted with crowd control, and arrested looters who descended on the nearby buildings. The crowd continued to swell, but there was no way of getting any kind of count. Ambulatory services arrived to care for the injured and cart away the dead. With all the shouting and chanting, Brickert could hardly think. He carried

Natalia to one of the medics and explained what had happened to her. They loaded her into a vehicle with four others, gave Brickert information on where to locate her, and drove away.

In the early afternoon, a makeshift podium was set up on the steps of the Capitol Building with two speakers. Thomas prepared to give a speech. But before he could begin, a dozen trucks and vans pulled through the crowd. Workers emerged from the vehicles and began assembling proper conference armamentarium. The crews were directed by a man who Brickert had never seen. Judging by Thomas's face, he didn't know the man either. They spoke for a several minutes, the man and Thomas. When they shook hands, Brickert noticed that the man's hand was bionic.

When their conversation ended, Thomas took the podium and addressed the crowd. He gave a long and passionate speech, similar to the one he had given in Los Angeles. The crowd interrupted him at least a dozen times with chanting and applause. When Thomas finished, the man with the bionic hand came forward. Before speaking, he showed a film.

It was a cobbling of recordings and videos that showed President Newberry and other government officials colluding with media organizations and terrorist groups to sway public opinion. It showed a man named Jeffrey Markorian giving testimony and evidence that he had worked with the CEO of N Corporation to orchestrate several attacks on CAG soil and frame the NWG for their actions. The video went on for almost two hours, playing to a stunned, silent crowd as news cameras continued to gather at the perimeter.

When the video ended, the man continued to speak. He introduced himself as Daniel Newsome. His speech lasted only ten or fifteen minutes, but it was one of the greatest things Brickert had ever heard. It was eloquent, simple, powerful, and memorable.

The speaking and cheering rang out past sundown. Local grocers and restaurants brought food and water. People slept on the ground, in the wreckage. All through the night people gave speeches. But none of them stuck with Brickert as much as Daniel Newsome's did.

The following week was chaos. Brickert, Justice, Nikotai, and other members of the resistance were most often in hospitals and morgues visiting the injured, identifying bodies, and meeting with civic leaders.

President Newberry hastily announced from a secure, classified location that the evidence presented against him and his administration was fraudulent, but documents surfaced the same day that implicated him, his Chief of Staff, and dozens of members of Congress. Seven days after the Battle of Washington D.C., President Newberry resigned along with over half of the CAG Senate and House of Representatives.

President Marnyo held a summit with several CAG territorial governors appointed by the Supreme Court to act as a Wartime Executive Council. Barbara Gillespie, Governor of the Northeastern American Territory, was appointed Interim CAG President of the council. Regional legislatures chose delegates from among territorial congresses to serve as Wartime Legislative Officers until special elections could be held, first for both houses of Congress, then for a new President of the Continental American Government.

Special funeral services were held at the Hallgrímskirkja in Reykjavik for Honorary NWG General Walter Tennyson Byron, and several other resistance leaders including Lara Byron, Li Cheng Zheng, Duncan and David Hudec, Samuel Harris Berhane, Jr., Gefjon Tvedt, and others. Brickert attended with hundreds more. Thousands lined the streets of the city for the procession. Among the distinguished guests were NWG President William Marnyo, Interim CAG President Barbara Gillespie, and her interim Vice President Daniel Newsome, a veteran of the Elite, multiple limb amputee, respected businessman, and philanthropist.

Talks between the NWG and CAG lasted for almost a month before Marnyo was promised the reparations he requested. As evidence mounted against the CAG and its collaboration with N Corp, documents were revealed regarding Project Orwell, the existence of secretly trained and executed anomalies, and the Extraction/Implantation Program's connection to the Safety Laws. The more information leaked, the smoother the talks went. When all was said and done, Texas, followed by several other territories, ceded membership in the CAG and either declared independence or petitioned for inclusion in the NWG.

Two years later, in January of 2089, Daniel Newsome, endorsed by President Marnyo, Thomas Byron, and Interim President Gillespie, was sworn in as the President of the Continental American Government, campaigning on a platform to end corruption, restore freedoms to the people through the limitation and reduction of centralized government, and advancing quality of life through greater strides in cloning and scientific research. Brickert was invited to attend the inauguration ceremony as a guest of honor, but he declined in order to attend a friend's wedding.

Epilogue

Thursday, November 18, 2100

COMMANDER BRICKERT PLACK strode across the courtyard at Alpha headquarters on Capitol Island. Snow covered the brick walkway and benches surrounding it. The evergreens were heavy and white, but the air smelled clean. He checked the time and winced. A moment later his com rang.

"Hey," the commander said. "Sorry. I just noticed how late it is."

"Yeah, Mr. I'll-Be-Home-Early," his wife chided him.

"I knew this would happen, I tell you," Commander Plack said. "Every time I say I'm coming home early—"

"The universe is out to get you. Get your butt home. People are already here and waiting."

"Okay. Love you."

After the call ended, the commander picked up his pace. It was the android's fault. Every time he met with the Tensais regarding the android, the meetings ran late. Congress wanted stricter guidelines installed before the robots were allowed to go fully active. Androids were the hottest debate in science. Politicians, philosophers, academics, and military leaders all had given their input on what was now referred to as the *Skynet Rules*, or the laws on the limitations of androids. The news covered the topic daily.

General Juraschek had asked Commander Plack to be the liaison between the NWG Senate Committee on Appropriations and the Tensai Alpha teams working in NWG R&D centers in Montreal. Meetings often lasted all day. Afterward, Juraschek requested a briefing from his commanders.

Despite the hour and the setting sun, the commander stopped in the middle of the courtyard to admire the statue in place. He did it every day without fail. It was bronze and beautiful, two men and two women, each staring off to the east, to the rising sun, an expression of bravery and optimism adorning their faces. The commander knew each face well. The plaque underneath said:

"It is easier to fight to preserve the freedoms we already enjoy than to pay their cost in blood."

—Thomas Byron (September 7, 2019 - November 5, 2091)

Then it had four names listed:

Honorary General and NWG Commander Walter Tennyson Byron (August 19, 2039 - November 11, 2087)

Ultra Dark Agent Vitoria Prado (July 1, 2072 - November 11, 2087)

Psion Alpha Agent Samuel Harris Berhane Jr. (November 18, 2070 - November 11, 2087)

Psion Beta Agent Gefjon Tvedt (January 30, 2071 – November 11, 2087)

Each time Commander Plack looked at it, he remembered the training, the battles, the sacrifices. It reminded him of those he had lost and what he had gained since then. He found it hard not to go home with a smile after putting things in perspective.

Fifteen minutes later, he arrived at his house. Natalia flitted around the kitchen tailed by their two boys: Harris and Patrick. When the commander saw her, he gave her a wink. "Now I know why you wanted me home early." He took a strand of her hair in his hand. "You wanted to show off your new hairdo, right? It looks fantastic, I'll tell you."

"I haven't been this blonde in years," she said, blushing. "How was work?"

"Boring," he said, grabbing a knife to help her cut vegetables. "The kids?"

"Oh just great …" his wife said, passing him cucumbers. "Guess the new word Patrick learned today."

"Um … Psion?"

"*No.* He learned the word *no.* And he's been saying it all day." Natalia kissed the commander on the lips. She tasted like sweetened cream. "Harris thinks it's hilarious so he asks Patrick questions all day just to hear him say it."

"Patrick, do you like breathing?" Harris asked his little brother.

"No," Patrick answered emphatically.

Harris's giggle was infectious. Even Commander Plack and his wife started to laugh. Commander Plack looked around the living room.

"So you were lying when you said people were here …"

"Yep."

"What time are they coming over?"

"Whenever you call them."

Dinner was grilled chicken salad. Commander Plack complained that they hadn't had burgers in a month, but when Natalia gave him the stink eye, he stopped. Harris tried to help Patrick eat his food, but ended up spilling most of it onto his lap or the floor. Both of them needed baths before bed, which the commander did while his wife tidied the kitchen. Patrick refused to let the commander bathe him, and ended up soaking the bathroom floor and the commander's clothes. No sooner did he have them dressed than his wife shouted his name from the living room. "You have a call."

"Who is it?"

"Who do you think? Your co-conspirator."

"Patch it through to me." When the commander's com beeped, he answered the call. "Yo, Rachel. How's it going?"

"He's suspicious."

"Of course he is. You do this almost every year. It's his thirtieth birthday."

"Yeah, but I've been telling him for a month that the party is set up for Saturday. I thought I had him fooled."

"He's also the smartest man in the world."

Commander Plack heard another voice in the background. "Is that Brick? Let me talk to him."

"No!" Rachel said. "You can't—" Her voice grew more faint. "Hey! Give me back my com!"

"Brick ..." Jared's voice was now much clearer. "You don't really think I'm going to fall for this, do you?"

"I have no idea what you're talking about, I'll tell you."

Jared laughed.

"Jared ..." Despite thirteen years of practice, the commander still had a hard time calling Jared by that name. "Just play along with Rachel. *Pretend.* You know you'll be glad you did later."

"Are Al and Marie coming?"

"Yeah. Hope is coming too. She wants to play games with you. You know she's got a crush on you, right? I'm talking a crush the size of that new Arena you put into Beta headquarters."

Jared snorted a laugh. "Yeah, Marie told me."

"Don't embarrass her. She's twelve. Thirteen. Crap, I forgot how old she is. Anyway, come over in about thirty minutes. I have to put my stinkers in bed first."

"It takes you thirty minutes to do that?"

The commander checked the time. "I promised Harris a story tonight."

"Oh yeah? Which one?"

"He calls it 'The Uncle Story.'"

"What's that about?"

"You. He just doesn't know that particular detail."

"You tell Harris stories about me?"

"Yep," the commander said. "In great detail. He loves them."

"Whatever. Thirty minutes. See you then."

"Yep. See you."

The call ended with a beep. The commander shouted to Natalia, "They're coming over in thirty. Is that okay?"

"Fine," she yelled back.

The commander hustled his kids to bed. Patrick went down quickly, but Harris's way of winding down was talking. The commander listened patiently in the dark room, holding his son's small hand while rubbing the back of it with his palm. Finally, when Harris seemed to have gotten everything out of his system, he took a deep breath and said, "Okay. I'm ready for the story."

The commander nodded. "It'll have to be a shortened version since we have company coming over."

"Who?"

"Some friends. It's a not-so-surprise birthday party for Jared."

"Can I stay up? Please?" Harris started to pout until the commander tickled him. Then he pulled Harris' covers up to his chin.

"All right, where should I start?"

"The beginning."

"Okay, here we go. 'The street lights of downtown Johannesburg cast long shadows through the dirty front windows of an abandoned grocery store …'"

THE END OF THE
PSION SERIES

AFTERWORD

*

Fellow bookworms,

I can't believe it's over. I really can't. I've been working on the Psion series for almost ten years, and now it's over. Of course, the Psion *universe* isn't over. I plan to revisit it. Not necessarily these characters, but the fallout. The way things changed. Specifically what happened in the first century or three following the events of the Silent War. For now I'm calling it the Clone Saga, a name inspired by that convoluted mess of a story arc in the Spider-man comics. Stay tuned for more information.

For now, though, I need to say thank you. After Psion Beta, I wrote that if you wanted to read more books, I needed your help and support. And you gave it to me. My dreams have started to come true because you bought my book and told others about it. You got me to this point, Fellow Bookworm. *You* did. And I am so grateful.

Many people have said to me over the years that they wish Psion Beta was picked up by a publisher or was turned into a movie. Those are my dreams too. If you want to help me make it happen, please share the books. Please tell everyone how awesome you think they are! Please review each of them on Amazon. Please get them in your library. Word of mouth is still the greatest marketing tool.

I also want to mention a few people, the same who I've mentioned in every book. My Beta readers: Britta Peterson, John

Wilson, Dan Hill, Jana Jensen, Natasha Watson, and Benjamin Van Tassell. These friends have proofread almost every book I've written, and always given me solid feedback. I am incredibly grateful for them. Also my proof readers, Caity Jones, Shannon Wilkinson, and Laura Gray for helping me dot my T's and cross my I's. And, of course, Brandon Dorman and Britta Peterson for their help with the cover and internal art.

My good friend, Adam Morris, aka Maad Rosmir, has been my consultant whenever I needed some advice. Kill Sammy or don't? Kill Jeffie or don't? Kill Byron or don't? I teetered so many times between these three characters, and he helped me to envision exactly how I wanted it to end. No, not every character survived, but in the end I decided that some of them had suffered enough.

Will there be more about the main cast? Maybe someday. For now I don't have any ideas left in the tank to take me back into the Psion series. If something comes along, will I write it? You bet I will. I hope I've earned your trust and support so that when my next series comes along, you'll buy and share it.

Last of all, I have to tell my wife how much she has helped me to finish the series. Late nights, long days at libraries, irritability from stress, frustration at different steps along the way. She's put up with it all, and I couldn't have done it without her. I am so thankful she has been my partner in this endeavor. Thank you, Kat.

Until next time …
Long live Sammy!

— Jacob Gowans

www.jacobgowans.com

CPSIA information can be obtained
at www.ICGtesting.com
Printed in the USA
LVHW08s1352200718
584440LV00002B/99/P

9 781517 505052